BEAUTIFUL NIGHTMARES
VOLUME TWO

AMY PENNZA
ANNA FURY

COPYRIGHT

Beautiful Nightmares Volume Two

© Amy Pennza & Anna Fury 2025

All rights reserved. No part of this publication may be reproduced, stored or transmitted in any form or by any means, electronic, mechanical, photocopying, recording, scanning, or otherwise without written permission from the publisher. It is illegal to copy this book, post it to a website, or distribute it by any other means without permission.

This novel is entirely a work of fiction. The names, characters and incidents portrayed in it are the work of the authors' imagination. Any resemblance to actual persons, living or dead, events or localities is entirely coincidental.

Cover design by Maldo Designs

Temper the Flame art by Rym Oleksa

Kiss the Slipper art by Rym Oleksa

CONTENT NOTICE

Beautiful Nightmares contains adult themes. While these fairy tale retellings may feel dark at times, the deep love between our characters is a beautiful light at the end of the tunnel. Each book ends with a happily ever after. You can find content notes on our author websites.

amypennza.com
annafury.com

Take care of yourself, and email us with any questions.

amy@amypennza.com
author@annafury.com

TEMPER THE FLAME
AN MM BEAUTY AND THE BEAST RETELLING

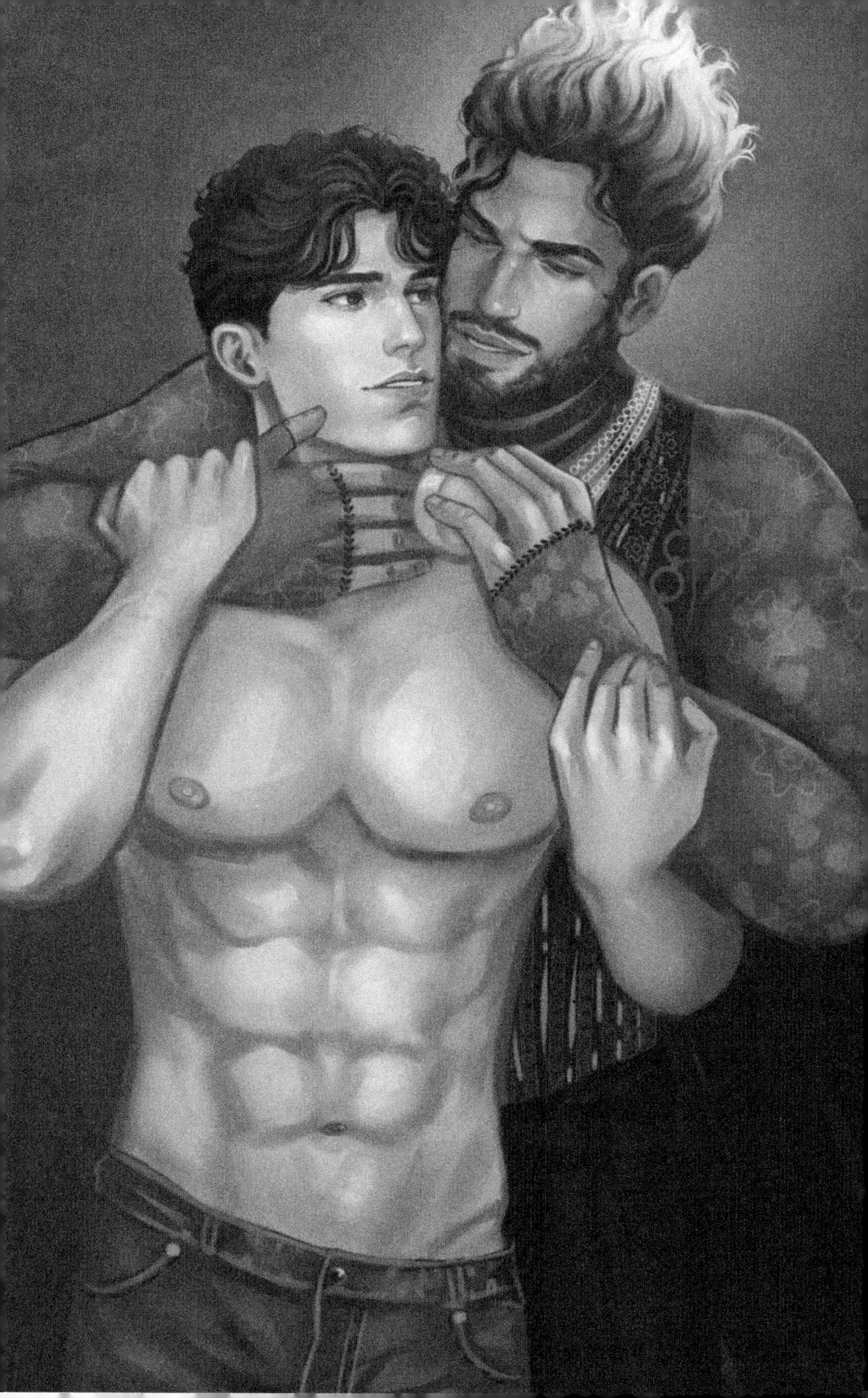

CHAPTER 1
FUOCO

I sit in the vaulted Great Hall thrumming bejeweled fingers against the glossy black armrest of my chair. The cavernous space rings with music and laughter as my court gathers for the evening meal. Dragons and other creatures of the Myth line the tables, each courtier garbed in dazzling colors and dripping with jewels.

Servants wend their way through the crowd carrying trays of food and mead, stopping occasionally to fill a goblet or replenish a plate. A siren harpist plucks sweet melodies from the corner. A fire blazes in the hearth, its crackling flames sending sparks up to the ceiling to mingle with the smoke of incense that burns in braziers along the walls.

My court is a marvel of grandeur and revelry—and it never, ever changes. Day after day, week after week, month after month, it's the same. The same conversations circle round and round like a never-ending carousel. The same music plays in my ears. The same people laugh at the same jokes and drink the same drinks.

"Are you enjoying yourself, my lord?"

I turn to find my enforcer, Varden, watching me with curiosity in his amethyst eyes. He lifts his wineglass and gestures toward the crowd, saluting the merriment. "It's an exciting evening."

Exciting isn't the word I'd use, but I nod. "A night like no other."

Varden sips his wine. On my other side, my second enforcer, Nazzar, digs into a dessert stacked with so many layers of chocolate and cream it threatens to topple over.

Lirem, my third enforcer, is absent.

As I study his empty chair, I return to drumming my fingers. It's not like him to skip dinner. He's usually back from his rounds well before the evening festivities begin.

An elderly servant appears at my side and places a tray of raw venison steaks before me. When I turn to thank her, she ducks her head, obscuring her face and leaving me staring at her white cap. I swallow the sigh that rises in my chest. My human servants never willingly meet my gaze. Most of the time, they avoid looking at me altogether. It's been this way since I accepted the role as leader of the Fire Syndicate. Even in human form, I terrify the humans who dwell in my territory.

It could be my sheer size. I tower over every one of them. It could also be the demi-form I take when my temper rises. When emerald-green scales slide down my arms and my hair turns the same shade, my servants scatter.

I try to keep my temper at bay. But dragons are passionate creatures. Our fire always simmers just beneath our skin.

"Your meal, sir," the woman says, backing up a step. She keeps her gaze down and folds trembling hands in front of her. "Freshly hunted and uncooked just the way you like it, sir."

I shove down the irritation that bubbles whenever the servants act petrified in my presence. I've done everything I can to make them comfortable. They're handsomely paid. They enjoy plush living quarters. I even provide magical healthcare right here in the castle.

Still, they're afraid. Always afraid.

Even in my current humanoid form, the sour stench of the woman's fear burns my nostrils. Her heart gallops in her feeble chest. It's on the tip of my tongue to remind her how much I've done to maintain peace on this plane—how much effort I invest in making sure humans can live in harmony with various creatures of the Myth.

But I swallow my explanations along with my sigh. Reminding your subjects why you lead them doesn't inspire loyalty—or love.

Actions speak louder than words. It's a distinctly human phrase. In the Myth, words work just fine, especially if you can imbue your words with magic. But I've adopted the human saying. I've tried to fit in.

"Thank you, Ellen," I say, arranging my features in what I hope is a reassuring smile. Rheumy eyes dart to mine and drop quickly to the ground. Before I can say anything else, she turns and scurries away.

I release my sigh.

Varden snorts, drawing my gaze to him. He gives me an exasperated look as he lowers his wine. "When will you learn, Fuoco? The help will never see us for anything other than the monsters we are. They're not going to be your friends."

"I don't want them to be my friends," I say tightly. *I'd settle for them not wetting themselves when I glance in their direction.*

My enforcer shrugs. "Humans are narrow-minded, clannish creatures. It's hardly surprising they blew up their civilization."

I grab my glass of wine and swirl it, inhaling the musky tannins that were once popular in the California region of the United States. That whole area was reclaimed by the sea after the humans' nuclear wars "blew up their civilization" as Varden calls it. In truth, they destroyed the planet. The explosions were so powerful, they ripped the Veil between the human plane and the Myth realm. Magic poured into the human world, devouring technology and wreaking havoc. Even with all of our powers combined, the creatures of the Myth only possessed enough magic to mend one plane. We had a choice: repair our world and let the humans die out, or fix their plane and abandon the Veil to the mists of history. We chose to save the humans.

And now we're all one big, happy family.

Suppressing a snort of my own, I bury my nose deeper in my glass. The cabernet's rich, herbal bouquet releases the knot of tension between my shoulder blades. Wine is one of the pleasures of this plane. The humans got that much right, at least.

Maybe I could start a winery here in the North, in what was once known as "upstate New York." The Fire syndicate covers nearly a hundred thousand square miles. The weather is temperamental, especially in the winter, but I'm a dragon. Surely I can think of a way to keep grapes warm.

The castle has a greenhouse. That might work...

"I've angered you, my lord," Varden says in a low tone.

I set my wineglass down and turn to him. Rings glitter on his fingers. A stack of priceless bracelets adorns his wrists. His linen shirt is bespoke, sewn by my court tailor. Like all dragons, Varden loves fine things. And like most of my people, he finds it difficult to relate to humans.

"I'm not angry," I say. "Merely frustrated. The Veil between this world and ours fell nearly two hundred years ago. Humans should be accustomed to seeing dragons by now. I'd like to be able to walk among the people. Maybe talk to them."

Varden frowns. "But...why? What could they possibly have to say that's important?"

Irritation sparks in my chest. "They're unlikely to speak to me if I approach them with that attitude. We are not the dragon houses of old, lording our rule over beings we deem lesser." I lean toward him as I warm up to a topic near and dear to my heart. "The humans may appear weak to you, but I have found them to be—"

"They will never be *us*, Fuoco." Varden's purple eyes glint in the candlelight. "They will never shift into great beasts and take to the skies. I would not call them lesser, but we are certainly not the same."

My sigh returns. Varden and I have had this discussion so often I sometimes feel like I'm cursed to forever repeat it. We're unlikely to see eye to eye. But he's actually more liberal in his views than the majority of dragons. Unlike most of the Myth, my kind rarely ventured through the Veil before it fell. Not even the strongest glamour can conceal a dragon in flight. So we mostly kept to the magical plane—until the humans destroyed the Veil and sent the two worlds crashing into each other.

But Varden was born after that cataclysm. This plane is all he's ever known, and he's more at ease around humans. Still, his insistence on *othering* them hinders my goal of a truly integrated society.

"You don't shift, either," I remind him. "And if you don't find your *selsara*, you'll *never* shift." As his mouth tightens, I let a hint of my beast seep into my tone. "We're not so different from the humans, Varden. As my enforcer, you work closely with all of my people, including the humans who live in this syndicate. It will benefit everyone if you at least attempt to understand them."

And I *need* him to understand them. I need him to serve as an intermediary between me and the people. Like the rest of the dragons in my court, Varden hails from one of the lower houses, which means he won't take beast form until he finds his fated mate. All dragons are tall and powerfully built, but those from the lower houses blend more easily with humans than I ever could. Varden is several inches shorter than my own seven feet. No one could ever mistake me for anything other than a dragon. My enforcers don't suffer the same impediment.

For a moment, Varden seems like he wants to argue. Then he sits back in his chair and runs a beringed hand through his short, dark hair. He falls silent for a moment before saying, "You're right, of course. It's difficult to undo generations of ingrained thinking."

"If I didn't think you capable of change, I wouldn't have chosen you to serve as an enforcer." Varden has been by my side for six decades. I couldn't run the syndicate without his steady presence. I put a hand on his shoulder. "You bring honor to my house and yours, Varden of House Forza."

He opens his mouth, but whatever he might have said is interrupted by the Great Hall's double doors flying open. The glossy panels crash into the stone, making every head in the Hall turn toward the entrance. I rise and prepare to shift.

An elderly human male falls through the opening and onto both knees. Lirem appears behind him, his face twisted into a sneer. My enforcer's pale blond hair tangles around his broad shoulders. His eyes glitter red as he stares down at the human. One of Lirem's sleeves is torn at the elbow, revealing the shimmering red scales of his dragon. He lifts his head and locks gazes with me. The look in his eyes tells me everything I need to know.

This human is a thief or a killer. Maybe both.

I round the high table with Varden and Nazzar on my heels. Except for the sound of our boots on the flagstones, the Hall is silent as we approach Lirem and his prisoner.

The human is filthy. He remains in a crouch at Lirem's feet, his white hair streaked with more than a month's worth of dirt. His clothing is full of holes, his shoes falling apart.

A highwayman, perhaps. The Fire Syndicate is isolated in the North. The road between my territory and the rest of the syndicates is long and often treacherous. My enforcers and I do our best to provide protection, but we can't be everywhere at once. My syndicate is a haven for monsters and humans alike. All are welcome. But not everyone wants to live peacefully. Thieves prey on the humans who travel the road from the Fire Syndicate to the other three territories. This man is likely one of them—a degenerate who would rather steal than do an honest day's work.

Lirem kicks the man in the side, making him grunt. "Stand before Lord Fuoco."

The man gets to his feet. He lifts his chin and meets my gaze with a brazen stare. Eyes the color of the sea pierce me. My nape prickles as an odd awareness settles over me. If I didn't know better, I'd think he was unafraid. He's either too stupid to be intimidated, or he's lost his mind.

I look at Lirem behind him. "His crime?"

"I caught him stealing from the apple orchard." Lirem crosses thick arms over his broad chest. Red scales peek from under his collar. When he finally meets his selsara and shifts, his dragon will take the same brilliant shade. Until then, his inability to shift makes him more approachable to the humans in my territory.

Although, the man in front of me probably wishes he'd never crossed paths with Lirem.

He continues to stare me down, his sea-colored eyes unflinching. His hands are balled in fists at his sides. His muscles tremble.

Definitely insane. I'm nearly three hundred pounds of muscle. I could flatten him with one blow.

If only it were that simple.

I let my beast rise. The human's pupils reflect the green flames that dance in my eyes. "You know the punishment for stealing," I tell him. "Do you wish to say anything?"

At last, the man begins to sweat. It trickles down his dirt-streaked forehead and pools in the purple hollows beneath his eyes. His chest rattles as he draws quick, shallow breaths. Death is a shadow just behind him. Regardless of tonight's outcome, he's not long for this world.

I give him a minute, then two, allowing silence to stretch. Behind me, the Great Hall stays quiet. My court watches. And waits.

Lirem gives me a meaningful look. "Let's take this outside, shall we, my lord?"

I nod and gesture toward the door.

He grips the human by the scruff of the neck and steers him out of the hall. As Varden and Nazzar follow, I face the court. A range of expressions greets me. Irritation. Boredom. Impatience. The last is the most prominent. My court is comprised of Myth creatures. The execution of a human thief is hardly compelling entertainment. If an activity doesn't involve wine or fucking—or some combination of the two—my courtiers generally want nothing to do with it.

I raise my voice. "Everyone, please return to your dinners."

Almost immediately, chatter resumes. Knives and forks clink against plates. Laughter rises from one of the tables. I turn to head outside, but a flash of white stops me.

Ellen stands in the shadows in the far corner of the Hall hugging an empty serving platter flat against her chest. Her face is a mask of horror, her eyes sheened with tears. Suddenly, her eyes flick to me. With a startled gasp, she turns and flees.

I don't sigh this time. Instead, something else rises in my chest. Disappointment?

Or is it shame?

Laughter rings out again. Pushing the feeling aside, I stride out the doors and into the courtyard. I've ruled the Fire Syndicate for almost two hundred years. My subjects know what to expect. My rules are simple.

No theft. No murder. No assault.

And no exceptions.

That's the way it is. The way it *has* to be. When monsters and humans mingle, the rules must be crystal clear. It's the only way to maintain peace. I can't allow the emotions of one human servant to cloud my judgment.

The courtyard is vast—large enough to accommodate my dragon form and the fire I spew when I mete out justice. Lirem drags the thief to a thick metal post and fastens chains around his waist. Then he yanks the man's arms above his head and locks them in metal cuffs.

"Not iron, eh?" the man says, his raspy voice almost shocking after his previous silence.

His words are a taunt. Everyone knows creatures of the Myth despise iron. The metal hurts us and weakens our magic. An iron spear, crafted by an early human I encountered, is responsible for the tiny scar that runs down my stomach.

I step close to the human. "I don't tolerate thieves. If you have any last words or family I should care for, now is the time to say so."

The old man sneers, sea-colored eyes darting over my shoulder to where Lirem stands behind me. "Don't tolerate thieves, huh? What about those under your own roof?"

My enforcer snarls and moves past me. He raises a hand, but I grab his arm before he can land a blow.

"Hold, Lirem," I say quietly, meeting his red gaze. "There's no honor in venting your frustration on a dead man."

There's a tense moment of silence. Then my chief enforcer gives a curt nod. "Yes, my lord. My apologies."

I release him and turn back to the human. "Dragons didn't steal from you, *thief*. None among the Myth have taken from your kind. On the contrary, we've given you everything, including your world. We didn't ask for the Veil to fall, and we certainly didn't ask to be pulled into this plane. Believe me, ours was far nicer."

As he did in the Hall, the man holds my stare. Vitriol burns in his eyes. Dirty lips press tightly together.

Which is why I don't anticipate the glob of saliva he launches at me. It lands on my cheek with a disgusting splat.

"You dragons with your fancy clothes and shiny jewels can fuck off!" he shouts. "Treasure-hoarding thieves, the lot of you. Burn in hell!" His blue eyes are wild as he jerks against the cuffs securing him to the post.

"Only one thing will be burning tonight, old man," Lirem snarls as

I wipe the saliva from my face. My enforcer's fangs appear between his lips as his red eyes glow more brightly.

"Enough," I growl, hearing the anger in my voice. Lirem hears it, too, because he shuts up and turns to me with a chastened look.

I loosen my mirrored tie, remove it, and place it in his waiting palm. When I turn, Nazzar is behind me, his quick fingers unlacing my black corset. I shrug out of it, and he catches it before it can fall.

My shirt goes next, then my pants, and then I stand nude in the courtyard with moonlight streaming down on me. But I'm not unadorned. My jewelry remains, the metal enchanted to shift with me when I take beast form.

Lirem and Nazzar jog toward the safety of the castle. The human thief casts a dismissive gaze down my body.

I know what he sees—and I know his dismissiveness is an act. Even in human form, I'm not easily dismissed. Seven feet tall and packed with muscle, green scales glitter like emeralds from my shoulders to the tops of my thighs. More emeralds decorate my jewelry, from the stud in my ear to the rows of bracelets around my wrists. The Prince Albert piercing through the tip of my cock glitters with tiny diamonds. The barbells in my nipples are plain silver tonight, as is the barbell that nestles under the base of my dick. The guiche piercing behind my sack includes a rare blood emerald from the Old Country.

The man says nothing, but he licks his cracked lips as he yanks on the cuffs.

He's nervous now. I'll make sure he's not nervous for long.

Stepping back, I let the fire overtake me. It spreads through my mind like a trail of embers igniting. The blaze explodes in my chest, and then I'm standing in dragon form in the courtyard staring down at the tiny, chained man.

He cries out, his bravado evaporating.

I take no pleasure in it, nor do I relish this task. But I can't allow the lawless to ruin the syndicate for everyone else. Opening my mouth, I call my fire, feeling it mix with gas from the sacks just inside my cheeks. It sizzles hot in my throat as I drag in a breath to give it oxygen.

"Wait!" the man calls out. "I've got a wife, a fam—"

A stream of fire silences him, his skin bubbling and cracking. He shrieks as his flesh melts from his bones. Within seconds, bone disintegrates into dust. Fire flows from my mouth as sorrow spreads through me. Taking a life is the worst thing I have to do for my syndicate. Each death is a stain on my soul, and some days I wonder just how black it can get before it's as dry and worthless as the remains before me.

Now-empty cuffs clink and jangle against the post as I call my fire back and let it die in my throat. The stones around the post glow bright orange. But they'll cool quickly. I built my castle with my duty in mind, choosing granite strong enough to withstand hot temperatures.

Lirem jogs back to me as I shift. He offers clothing, but I wave it away. "You're getting slow, old friend," I say, pointing to his torn sleeve. "Did the human have a weapon?"

"A knife," Lirem says, his voice gruff. "He surprised me. Popped up from some bushes on the side of the road. He was obviously lying in wait for one of us." Lirem scowls. "These fools never change. You'd think the humans would greet us with gratitude. Instead, we get knives."

"It will come with time. Most of us lost everything when the Veil fell. But we've built something good here. Perhaps one day, the humans will see it as we do."

Lirem looks unconvinced, but his scowl fades as he glances toward the castle. "Tell me there's fresh venison for dinner so I can forget this entire sordid night."

"I left a platter on the table. It's yours."

"You dined already?"

I shake my head. "I'm not hungry." I look at the stars just beginning to emerge in the night sky. "I think I'll go flying."

His scowl returns. "Don't tell me you're upset over killing a thief."

I look to where the dead man's dust now swirls in the early evening air. The breeze picks up, spreading it over the cooling stones. In an hour or so, no trace of him will remain.

"Fuoco—"

"I'll return by morning," I say, striding away from my enforcer before he can accuse me of being sentimental. Or weak.

An hour later, I streak down the coastline of Old New York City—now known as the Hallows. Electricity is scarce in my territory, but there's enough of it here to illuminate the syndicates below.

The Statue of Liberty slumbers on her side in the bay, the wounds she gained during the humans' war hidden by the seabed. Her head rests in the Sea Syndicate, which is ruled by Triton. He and his mermen are unlikely to be near the surface, so I wheel and glide down in a lazy spiral. Flapping my wings once, I alight on one of the spikes of the statue's crown.

The ocean is choppy, its waves frigid and restless in winter. Water crashes against the statue's face and drips down her cheeks like tears. I watch the tide as I catch my breath from the long flight. The waves are murky and black, the crests tipped with foam. A thick wave builds, smashes against the statue's shoulder, and sends an icy spray across my leg.

I shake the moisture away, then look at the ocean and raise a brow. *Settle down, would you?*

At once, the water retreats.

That's better, I say in my mind, my communication limited in this form. *No need to be rude.*

The waves crest more slowly, the sea's cadence less violent. After a moment, I twist around and face the statue's feet. One sandal rises above the waves, its toes pointed toward the shiny towers of the Air Syndicate. Ruled by the gargoyle Gothel, the Air Syndicate is the only part of the Hallows that resembles what used to be New York City. Like all gargoyles, Gothel loves buildings. Over the years, he's purchased properties and raised new skyscrapers, restoring Old Manhattan to its former glory.

But I'm not here to admire the buildings. I want to talk to their master.

Lifting my snout to the sky, I let out a roar. Then I settle more comfortably on the crown and wait.

Half an hour later, a winged figure appears at the edge of the tallest tower. He lingers for a moment, then disappears. Amusement curves my lips. *Admission granted.*

Shoving off the crown, I swoop across the bay and flap my wings. Currents buffet me as I approach Gothel's tower. Light flashes, guiding me to the spinning glass window at the top of his library. Dozens of panes retract, creating an opening large enough for me to sail through.

Snapping my wings close to my body, I streak toward it. Wind screams in my ears as the opening looms larger. I dive through it, pull up fast, and shift as I drop four stories to the ground.

It rears up and meets me far sooner than I'm ready for it. I land with a heavy grunt and wince at the sting that reverberates up my legs.

Gothel leans against his desk in human form, his powerful body wrapped in an expensive three-piece suit.

Another power play. He shifted and dressed. I know without asking he won't offer me clothes. Not that I'd deign to wear anything he offers. Gothel's wardrobe is pricey, but his taste is woefully uninspiring. Aside from a pocket watch, he doesn't even wear any jewelry.

"Rough landing," he murmurs, smiling as he puffs at a cigar. Big, dark horns swoop up and away from his head. Whiskey-colored eyes glint in the electric light.

"Smoother than most of yours," I say easily.

"It's been a while since you visited, Fuoco. What do you want?"

Straightforward and to the point. This is why I prefer Gothel over the other syndicate lords. Triton is too dramatic and self-righteous. Wotan is a brooding asshole. Gothel is reasonable. Most of the time.

I stalk naked across his office and grab a cigar from the box on his desk. When I turn, he stands at the ready with a lighter. Sucking in a deep hit, I sigh when pleasure spreads warm and tingly through my gut.

"Your girl gets better with every batch," I say, raising my cigar in salute.

Gothel smiles. "True. She outdoes herself."

We smoke in companionable silence. When he doesn't push me to state my business, I take a moment to study him. He looks different. Sated and happy. Peaceful. I've heard rumblings as to why that might be, but I'm curious to confirm it.

"You haven't answered my letter," I say as I exhale.

Golden eyes narrow. "I can't take a student, Fuoco. I'm a mated male now. My teaching days are behind me."

So the rumors are true. I suppress a growl at that less-than-fortunate news. "Tell me more, my friend."

A smile touches his lips. "I took him as a student and he wormed his way into my heart. He hasn't left."

I raise my brows. "I wasn't aware you had a heart." But now that I listen for it, I hear the slow, steady beat. The sound is irrefutable evidence that Gothel speaks the truth. He's heart-bound, as the gargoyles call it. Mated for life. "Congratulations," I add. "I'm happy for you."

"I can recommend other teachers," he offers.

Sighing, I examine the tip of my cigar. "I'll take you up on that. I'm being hounded daily by a dragon who believes his daughter would make the perfect consort for me."

"You don't want a bedmate?"

"Not at the moment." This is hardly the first time some enterprising father has pushed a daughter—or son—at me. I've taken consorts in the past. Under the right circumstances, it can be a beneficial arrangement for both parties. But lately, I long for something more than a warm body in my bed. I long for my fated one. *The* one.

I look at Gothel. "I was hoping to dump her into your capable hands and get her father off my back in the process."

"Noble of you," he says. "What's wrong with her power?"

"We're not sure. It manifests so sporadically, we can't tell if she possesses foresight or compulsion. But the latter is so rare among my kind, I suspect it's foresight and she simply doesn't want to see the future."

Gothel smiles. "Maybe it's something else altogether." He flicks ash into a cut-glass ashtray on the edge of his desk. "Something a bit stronger, perhaps?"

Now he's just fucking with me. Like all gargoyles, his power is that he understands power. He undoubtedly understands mine—and my reluctance to discuss it.

"I feel confident it's foresight." I offer him a lazy smile of my own. "I highly doubt it's anything more than that."

Golden eyes glint with something that might be amusement. "I'll send a letter of introduction to two others who might be able to help."

"Many thanks." Remembering her father's latest visit—and the *three-hour* dinner I sat through—I shudder. "The sooner the better."

Gothel's smile gleams in his eyes. "You heard Wotan is recently mated as well?"

"Yes." News travels slowly to my syndicate, but that particular bit of gossip spread like wildfire. "I can't imagine any male taming him. I think I'd like to meet this enigma."

"Maybe you will," Gothel says, puffing at his cigar.

Unlikely. At least not any time soon. Winter is always a tense time in the Fire Syndicate. More than any other season, it seems to produce crime and disruption. And after tonight, I'll have to keep a close eye on the road and the villages around it. Where there's one thief, there are inevitably more.

"Thanks for this," I say, waggling my cigar. "And for the help with the female."

Gothel inclines his dark head. "Any time."

After a few more pleasantries, I thank him again and head for home. As I fly north, my thoughts drift back to the courtyard and the ashes I left behind. The thief is gone, but his accusations ring in my head.

Treasure-hoarding thieves, the lot of you.

I snort, sending smoke rolling from my nostrils. He dared to call *me* a thief after Lirem caught him red-handed in the orchard. To an outsider, death for stealing apples might seem overly harsh. But rules are rules, and mine exist for a reason. I planted the orchard with seeds from the Myth. The fruit there grows wild and uninhibited. The magic it contains can wreak havoc in the wrong hands.

My subjects know my laws. No theft. No murder. No assault. *No exceptions.* Opening that door invites disaster. The Fire Syndicate is the most peaceful and prosperous of all the syndicates. In the two centuries that I've ruled the North, I've worked hard to build a community where everyone feels safe. It's a refuge. I'm determined to keep it that way.

But as the spires of my castle appear in the moonlight, my head fills with visions of sea-colored eyes and a woman's white cap.

CHAPTER 2
BEAU

I leave my sack of bread against the wall of my father's workshop.

Whirring sounds greet me as I open the door and step inside. No surprise, Dad is hunched over his worktable, his shoulders rounded as he tinkers with his latest contraption. My greeting dies on my lips as I let my gaze wander over his shoulders.

He's lost weight. And he can't afford to lose more. A lump forms in my throat as memories of last winter wash over me. The electricity in our cottage hasn't worked in five years. Firewood is great and all, but only if you have access to it. The dragons ration it the same way they do bread. Dad wept when I chopped up the machine he invented to feed the birds that sometimes frequent the patch of grass behind his workshop. But it was either that or watch him shiver under a mound of threadbare blankets. I watched my mother die when I was ten years old. I might be pushing thirty now, but I'm not ready to lose my father.

Suddenly, Dad lifts his head and looks over his shoulder. Brown eyes framed by gold wire spectacles fill with worry. "Beau? Has something happened?"

Forcing cheerfulness into my voice, I smile and cross the short distance to his worktable. "Nothing at all. I'm getting ready to make deliveries, and I thought I'd check on you before I go."

Instantly, my father frowns. He casts a fearful look at the open door behind me and lowers his voice. "You won't take any bread to Robert, will you?"

The sack of bread outside the door weighs on my conscience like an anchor. "I won't take any to Robert," I say carefully. It's *technically* true. Robert doesn't keep the bread.

Dad's gaze sharpens. "Beau—" His words cut off as he lapses into a coughing fit. His once-broad shoulders shake violently as he curls forward and wheezes. The pencil tucked behind his ear threatens to tumble to the scuffed floorboards. His hip bumps the table, setting his tools and instruments shivering and clinking together.

"Here," I gasp, shoving his chair away so I can grasp his arms and guide him away from catastrophe. Or at least a really big mess. Tools of every shape and size litter the table. Glass beakers hold a colorful assortment of liquids of questionable origin. Dad loves working with magic, but magic doesn't always return the favor. The last time his worktable got upended, it cost three hundred dollars to repair the hole his "experiment" blew in the workshop's wall. I worked fourteen-hour days and slept in my apron to avoid paying interest on the money I borrowed from the village blacksmith.

Dad's cheeks turn red as he continues coughing. His arms under his ratty, patched sweater feel like twigs ready to snap. Alarm beats a loud drum in my head. "Let's go inside—"

"No." Dad pulls from my grip as he speaks between rattling coughs. "I'm...almost...finished"—he sucks in a breath—"here."

Exasperation rises. "Can't it wait until tomorrow?" I fight the urge to reach for him again as he leans heavily against the table. White hair wreaths his head, the wispy strands defying gravity as they stretch toward the beamed ceiling. The cough subsides, and the brilliant red in his cheeks fades to a dull pink. Weak sunlight streams through the shop's window and slants over the beakers, making the liquid inside sparkle like gems. As my father's gaze falls on a bright green beaker, a smile touches his lips. He points at it and turns to me with excitement dancing in his eyes.

"You see that, son? It's a new type of fuel I've been working on." He holds his forefinger and thumb an inch apart. "I'm *this* close to perfecting it. A few more tweaks and I could heat the whole village for the winter!"

My exasperation rounds a familiar corner. For as long as I can remember, Dad has been "this close" to some kind of breakthrough that will transform our lives. When I was a kid, I got excited right along with him. As a teen, I endured my peers' taunts about my "batshit crazy" father. Now that I'm an adult, I do my best to shield him. It took me a long time to understand my father—and to accept his quirks with the same grace my mother wielded so effortlessly. Maurice Bidbury is never going to heat the whole village. But Mom couldn't tell him that, and neither can I. His inventions fuel his soul. Snuffing that flame would stomp out *his* fire, and I'd rather pretend than ever see the light in my father's eyes wither to ash.

"Sounds great, Dad," I say softly. "I can't wait to see it."

His smile turns wry. "I know you don't believe me." He waves a hand as he faces the table. "Old Man Bidbury up to no good again. Crazy as a fox." He turns his head and shoots me a knowing look over the tops of his thick lenses. "Isn't that what they say in the village?"

I fold my arms over my chest. "I think it was crazy as a loon."

He gives a bark of laughter as he begins tinkering again. "Not one soul in the village knows what a *loon* is. They've been extinct for a hundred years." His spectacles slide down his nose. Rather than stopping his work to adjust them, he wriggles his nose to force them back up.

Shaking my head, I step close and gently nudge his glasses into place. Then I pull a bundle wrapped in wax paper from inside my jacket and set it on the corner of his table. "Promise me you'll eat, okay?"

He pauses his work. Slowly, he places a hand on the wrapped bread. He rests it there for a moment before lifting his gaze to mine. "Only if you promise to be careful when you venture out."

"I always am."

Dad's expression turns skeptical. Anxiety floats in his gaze, and I can see him shuffling through replies in his head. Finally, he sighs. "You're twenty-eight years old. I can't stop you from doing what you're going to do. I just..." He glances at the window. "If they catch you..."

I cover his hand with mine. "They won't." When he opens his mouth, I move my hand to his shoulder. "Eat, Dad. I'll be back within an hour." The green liquid begins to bubble. As Dad and I look at it, sparkles shimmer above the surface. I squeeze Dad's shoulder. "Looks like something is happening."

"It is." He fumbles at his scattered instruments, clearly seeking his notepad. "I have to record the levels," he says as he searches, knocking over an empty beaker in the process.

I reach across him, snag the notepad, and settle it at his elbow.

"Ah! There it is." As he begins rummaging for a pencil, I pull it from behind his ear and slip it between his fingers. "Thanks, son," he murmurs, scribbling furiously. He darts a look at the bubbling liquid as his hand flies across the notepad. "Fifty-nine! That's more promising than I expected!"

I rescue the toppled beaker and set it out of the path of danger. As I go to the door, the whirring starts up again. "Sixty!" Dad exclaims. When I turn in the doorway, he pumps a fist in the air. "We're nearly there, Evangeline! Nearly there, indeed."

My heart squeezes. Sometimes when I squint, I can almost see Mom standing at his shoulder like she used to, her lovely face beaming with pride. Maybe I'm wrong. Maybe Mom believed Dad would heat the whole village one day.

"I hope it works, Dad," I say.

He waves a hand without turning around. "It will, Beau. Just you wait."

I slip out the door and close it behind me. Then I grab the sack of bread and prepare to break the law.

∼

TEN MINUTES LATER, my heart pounds as I press my back against the exterior wall of Robert the bookseller's shop.

Sweat trickles down my spine and soaks into my waistband. In this part of the village, the buildings are so close together it's difficult to see the sky. My vision is limited to a narrow strip of washed-out blue.

But the sky is the least of my concerns. The only dragons I'm likely to see today are the kind stuck on solid ground. Lord Fuoco's enforcers can't take beast form. Dragons adhere to a rigid social order, with those capable of shifting sitting at the top of the pecking order. So-called "lesser" dragons—the non-shifters—take orders from their more powerful counterparts.

That doesn't mean the lower-ranking dragons aren't dangerous. The enforcers who patrol the village are tall, hulking males who move faster than the eye can follow. A few months ago, the one with red eyes followed me home.

Lirem. He accused me of cheating on my taxes. When I showed him my records with his signature at the bottom, he broke the front window in my shop. Lesson learned: next time, just pay the extra taxes. It would have been cheaper than replacing the window.

Wind gusts down the alley, sending icy fingers burrowing under my coat. With a quick look left and right, I gather my courage and dart around the edge of the shop. A dozen breathless steps later, I wrench open Robert's door. Bells tinkle as I duck inside and pull the door shut behind me. The scent of old books fills my nose. Tension drains from my shoulders.

"Beau Bidbury," a feminine voice drawls.

The tension snaps back into place. I squeeze the knob as my heart pounds harder. For a second, I consider opening the door and walking into the street, dragons be damned.

The heady scent of rosewater replaces the smell of books. A second later, the voice sounds at my shoulder. "Aren't you going to say hello?"

Steeling myself, I face Gastonia Legum, the blacksmith's daughter. Wide blue eyes fringed with thick, dark lashes take my measure. Gastonia's plump lips curve in a sensual smile. "You look even more handsome than the last time I saw you."

"Thanks." I lower my gaze and find myself staring at her breasts. Heat enters my cheeks as I jerk my eyes back up. "Um, you look…nice. Also."

She touches a glossy, dark ringlet that drapes over her shoulder. "Me? Please, I look *dreadful* today."

Confusion drifts through me. Gastonia looks the same as always. Black hair. Nice clothes. Pretty face. The unmarried men who enter my shop wax poetic about her curves. Some of the married men do too.

"I'm a total mess," she adds, a glint in her eyes.

That glint lifts the hair on my nape. At the same time, my confusion grows. Does she want me to…agree?

A shuffling sound makes me look past her, and my confusion turns to relief as Robert bustles from behind a curtain in the back of the shop.

"Beau!" The bookseller beams and rounds the counter that holds a cash register and stacks of books. His gaze drops to the sack in my hand as he nears. His smile fades, replaced with caution. In a lower voice, he asks, "Extra delivery today?"

"Yes." I hand him the sack and speak in the coded language we use for this particular transaction. "I baked too much. I thought maybe you could use the bread."

Robert nods. "It won't go to waste."

"Glad to hear it."

He looks at Gastonia, who watches our exchange with a shrewd expression. "I'll just take this to the back." He gestures at the shelves. "Help yourself to whatever you want, Beau."

Joy leaps in my chest. "You sure?"

Robert tosses a grin over his shoulder as he moves to the rear of the shop. "Of course. But good luck finding something you haven't already read."

I chuckle as I walk to the shelves. Unfortunately, he's right. I've probably read every book in the store. Robert doesn't get new shipments very often. Paper is expensive, and books are difficult to come by in the Fire Syndicate. When I was a kid, the dragons burned most of the village's books as a punishment for a bad harvest. Back then, Robert's father ran the shop. The dragons threatened to burn him, too, but Robert threw himself in front of his dad. Robert still bears scars from the knife the dragon slashed across his forearm during the scuffle. That was years ago, but the dragons haven't aged. No matter how much time passes, they remain strong and unstoppable. And merciless.

Shoving the bad memories aside, I trail a finger over a row of worn spines.

"Why do you like books so much?" Gastonia demands at my shoulder.

Startled, I turn and find her frowning at the stacks. "You don't like to read?"

"No." She flicks her blue eyes to mine. Her smile reappears as she dips her gaze to my chest. She snags her bottom lip between white teeth, then slowly releases it. "I have other interests."

My stomach knots. I know where her interests lie. She's made it abundantly clear. Six months ago, she cornered me in the bakery and pressed her body against mine. When I disentangled myself from her arms and pushed her away, she looked like she wanted to slap me. Instead, she drew herself up and gave me a scathing look. *"Really, Beau, it's like you're not even trying."*

The thing is, I *have* tried. For as long as I can remember, I've tried to be like other men. I'm not sure when I realized I was different. It was early on, though. Before Mom died.

I never told her. What would I have said? *Mom, my stomach felt sick when Winifred Matherby tried to kiss me behind the school. Also, I can't stop thinking about her brother's chest when he changes his shirt after gym class.*

"Do you have any other interests?" Gastonia asks now. She drifts closer, her shoulder brushing mine. Her eyes glint again. "Besides baking and"—she glances out the shop's window and lowers her voice to a purr—"risking death by giving food away?"

I suck in a breath. "Gastonia—"

"The dragons will kill you if they find out." Her eyes drop to my mouth. "You're a very bad boy, Beau Bidbury."

My heart clatters against my ribs. "I'm n-not trying to be. I just want to help." As she steps into me, I take a hasty step back. "Little kids are going hungry." Gods, would she *tell* on me?

She stops her advance. Rosewater thickens in the air as she tilts her head, sending more glossy ringlets spilling over her shoulder. "You're a good man. I admire that. Any woman would be proud to stand at your side."

The knots pull tighter. "I should go." I look at the door, which suddenly seems like a portal to happiness instead of a gateway to danger. "I, um, have a lot of work to do."

"No, you don't." She moves forward again, her breasts in serious danger of brushing my chest. "You bake first thing in the morning and sell all of your bread by noon." Rosewater clogs my lungs and makes my eyes sting. "It's three o'clock. This is the time of day when you sit in the window of your shop and read."

My jaw drops. "You watch me?" My ass bumps into something hard and solid, halting my retreat. She's backed me all the way to the counter.

A teasing note enters her voice. "If you put yourself in the window, Beau, don't be surprised when customers ask how much you cost."

Heat sears my nape. Discomfort crawls through me as I grip the edge of the counter and grope for a response. My parents raised me to treat women with respect. But Gastonia never fails to render me tongue-tied.

"Everything okay?"

I turn and find a frowning Robert in the curtained doorway. His brows pull more tightly together as he looks from me to Gastonia.

She flashes a winsome smile. "Beau and I were just chatting about the price of goods. Everything is more expensive these days."

Robert nods but his frown stays put. "That's true." He moves around the counter, and Gastonia backs away as he steps close and offers me a book. "I forgot I had this. It's new from an author in the Hallows. Epic fantasy. I thought you might like it."

Gratitude wells as I accept the book and flip through the first few pages. "No dragons, though, right?"

Robert laughs softly. "No dragons."

I smile as I tuck the book inside my jacket. "Thanks. I'll return it as soon as I can." Robert has always been kind to lend me books. He does the same thing for the poorest families in the village. Tomorrow, he'll fill a cart with books and my bread and make his rounds, delivering food and knowledge to kids who can't leave the fields to attend school. If the village produces a substandard harvest, the farming families will suffer the most. Dad thinks I take too great of a risk baking extra bread for hungry kids. But Robert is the real risk-taker. Without him, the farmers' children would starve body and mind.

"I should get back," I say. "Dad is waiting for me."

"No problem, Beau. Thanks for stopping by." Robert turns to Gastonia. "If you wait here a moment, I'll grab the books you ordered."

"Another time," Gastonia says. "I need to get home, too."

Several new knots form in my stomach. She's going to tag along, and there's no easy way out of it. Her father's blacksmith shop is one street over from the bakery. On the bright side, she can't accost me in public. Gastonia is bold, but even she draws the line at groping men in front of an audience.

At least I think so.

I mumble my goodbyes to Robert and head for the door. The bell tinkles merrily as I gesture for Gastonia to precede me. We step into the street, and I grit my teeth as she falls into step beside me. The village shines under the winter sunlight. That's nothing new. From the outside, everything looks clean and well-maintained.

But as every villager knows, the *inside* tells a different story. For every fresh coat of paint and sparkling clean window, there's a bare pantry and cold hearth. The dragons only care about the village's exterior. Dad says Lord Fuoco doesn't want interference from the other syndicate lords, so he takes care to keep up appearances. Personally, I think the dragons simply don't give a crap about anyone other than themselves.

"Afternoon, Beau!" someone calls, and I turn my head and make eye contact with Mrs. Pepperdine as she's pulled down the street by several of her children. They flap around her legs like goslings, each one towheaded and dressed in patched clothing. Just before they round the corner, she cranes her neck and shouts, "Can you have six loaves for me in the morning?"

I'm running low on wheat—and everything else—but I raise my voice. "Not a problem, Mrs. Pepperdine."

A smile blossoms over her frazzled features. "Thank you!"

Gastonia gives me a look as we continue down the street. "You don't have enough wheat for six loaves, do you?" It's a question, but her tone tells me she knows the answer.

"I'll make do."

"With what?" Gastonia links her arm with mine and gives a dainty laugh. "Air?"

The urge to shake her off is so overpowering I almost stumble. But I cling to my composure as we move toward the bakery. When I don't answer, she leans more heavily on my arm. Wind whips across the town square, stirring dead leaves.

"Someone should pick those up," Gastonia mutters. "Those thugs will blame us if the streets aren't spotless."

Nerves prickle over my skin as I dart a look around. "You shouldn't call them that."

She makes an angry sound. "Why not? It's the truth. The dragons are nothing but bullies."

I can't argue with that. But it's dangerous to say such things out loud. Lord Fuoco's enforcers have eyes and ears everywhere. Insults don't go unpunished.

"He burned John Robinson last night," Gastonia says in a low voice.

A gasp lodges in my throat. I pull her to a stop and search her face. "You're certain?"

Gastonia nods, her expression grim. "Fuoco summoned my father to the castle this morning to replace the manacles on the post."

Pain stabs my heart. Resignation follows in its wake. It was only a matter of time before John got caught. After one particularly brutal winter, he took to robbing travelers on the road that connects the North to the other syndicates. He distributed the food he stole to the villagers.

Gastonia's mouth tightens. "My father says Robinson was a fool."

No. He was brave. Far braver than I could ever be. Without John, children would have died last winter. Dad will be devastated when I tell him.

Gastonia takes my arm again. "Come on. We shouldn't stand in the street."

She's right, so I let her pull me forward, and I keep silent as she launches into gossip about various people in the village. The weight of John's death—and all the other executions—is so heavy, I don't pay much attention to her chatter until she says, "My father will lend you the funds to restock your supplies."

"Thank you, but no." I'd rather work around the clock than owe Gastonia's father again. The blacksmith is almost as bad as the dragons when it comes to collecting payment. Tall and strapping with a chest like the horses he shods, Gastonia's father carries his hammer when he knocks on doors for money. According to the history books, blacksmithing wasn't an affluent profession before the Veil fell. But factories are a thing of the past. Magic won't tolerate the technology required to keep something that big running. Someone has to make everything from nails to door hinges. Gastonia's father is busy—and rich.

Gastonia strokes her free hand down my forearm. "Of course, if we were engaged, it wouldn't be a loan. Daddy would just give you the money."

I stop in front of the grocer's shop. Through the window, a fruit display holds a shriveled apple and two blackened bananas. I barely notice as I fix my gaze on Gastonia. My heart pounds, but it's not from nerves this time. Now, anger kindles in my veins. I've been polite. I won't be polite to a fault. "Gastonia, we're not getting married."

She lifts her chin. "Every man in the village wants me. Why should you be any different?"

You have no idea. I draw an even breath. "It's not you. I don't want to marry anyone."

Irritation flashes in her eyes. "So you're going to sit alone in your bakery for the rest of your life?" She sweeps a dismissive gaze over the shops around us. "Don't you want more for yourself than this backwards village?" She's tall for a woman, and our faces are nearly even as she steps closer and tips her head toward the window of the grocer's shop. "Look at us." When I turn toward our reflections, her expression in the glass becomes triumphant. *My* face looks shell-shocked, my brown eyes wide and my cheeks flushed under the dark stubble I didn't have time to scrap away this morning. A chilly breeze ruffles my brown waves that never cooperate. As if to prove a point, an errant lock flicks over my forehead.

Gastonia's blue eyes track it as she takes my hand and lowers her voice to the silky purr the men in the village rave about. "We're the two best-looking people in this provincial town. Imagine the children we'd create."

Everything within me recoils. Facing her, I tug at my hand. "I don't think that's a good reason to have children."

"You're right," she drawls, her grip surprisingly strong as she refuses to release me. "There are much better ones."

Gods. I tug harder. "Gastonia—"

"I could change you, Beau." She licks her pink lips. "You don't know what you're missing."

Panic bolts through me. "I d-don't know what you mean."

Her eyes glint. "Oh, I think you do." She tightens her grip and jerks me forward so our hips collide. When I draw back, she does it again.

"Gastonia..."

Just as our tug-of-war becomes a true battle, a teenage boy stumbles around the corner. "Beau!" He doubles over, his hands on his knees as he speaks through choked breaths. "Dragon...in the...bakery!"

My insides turn to ice. One thought replaces all the others in my head.

Dad.

I don't think. I just run. Wind whips through my hair as I race to the bakery, my feet flying over the pavers. Villagers leap out of my path, their faces a blur and their exclamations following me. I ignore them as the ice spreads to my limbs and numbs my senses. When I reach the bakery, I grapple with the latch a few times before I manage to seize it. I fling the door open, making the hinges squawk in protest.

Lirem turns from the counter with a bun in his hand. As his red, glittering gaze falls on me in the doorway, he rips a bite from the bread. Chewing, he advances toward me, his long, embroidered coat flaring around his polished boots.

Dimly, I'm aware of Gastonia behind me. *Go*, I tell her silently, but of course she doesn't. The bakery is empty, thank the gods, but that doesn't mean Dad is safe. Images flash in my head in rapid succession. Dad lying in the workshop in a pool of blood. Dad slumped over his table with a knife in his back. Dad burnt to a crisp, nothing but ashes left for me to bury next to Mom's lonely grave in the village cemetery.

"Stop it," I whisper.

Lirem lifts a blond brow. His shadow falls over me as he halts a few paces away. Still chewing, he runs a deliberate gaze down my body. He swallows, and his deep, raspy voice fills my tiny bakery. "Who will stop me?" His lips curl in a slow grin, exposing sharp-looking fangs. "Not you, surely." Red eyes flick to Gastonia over my shoulder before returning to me. "Courting, baker? It's not very responsible of you to leave your store unattended." He lifts the bun, his long fingers sinking deep into the butter-glazed bread. "Someone might rob you while you're away."

My throat is so dry, I have to swallow a few times before I can speak. "Can I help you with something? Sir," I tack on hastily. The title sets my teeth on edge, but humiliation is better than death. I'll call Lirem whatever he wants as long as Dad is okay.

The dragon looks around my shop, his shoulder-length blond hair brushing the high, stiff neck of his collar. Jewels the same ruby-red as his eyes glitter among the silver embroidery. His coat probably costs more than everything I own—or ever will. *"Don't you want more for yourself than this backwards village?"* Gastonia asked. Yes, but not like she meant it. I don't want things. I just want to live without fear.

I want that for my father. I want him to have a warm bed and medicine that will cure his cough.

I keep one hand on the latch. My other dangles at my side, my fingers curling into a fist as I wait for the giant of a male to make his next move. When my father was young, Lord Fuoco didn't have enforcers. Before he grew tired of dealing with humans, he ruled alone. A handful of older villagers remember seeing him. They say he's even bigger than Lirem and the others. One farmer's voice shook as he described the syndicate lord as "taller than a tree with hair like green fire."

But I'm not sure I believe it. Lirem is several inches taller than my own five-foot-ten. His shoulders are so broad they could take out my shop's doorway. His clothing obscures his red scales, but I've seen them in the past. If Lord Fuoco is bigger, I don't ever want to meet him.

Lirem settles his gaze on me. "You're short on your taxes this month."

Outrage burns my chest. I should have expected this. He's had it out for me since the broken window incident. "I believe there's some mistake. I'm current on my taxes, sir. You collected them yourself, remember?"

In a blink, the dragon's fist grips my sweater. Red eyes burn less than an inch from mine, and the scent of my bread wafts over my face as he hisses, "Insolent human." He hauls me onto my toes, his knuckles lodged against my throat. "If I say you're late, you're late. And you'll pay the fine."

My heart gallops in my chest, each beat pumping fear through my veins. But there's misery, too. The fine is fifty coins. That's my entire profit for this month. Without that money, I can't buy wheat or fruit or any of the other supplies I need to stock my shelves.

"Sir—" My plea cuts off as bread fills my mouth. He moved so quickly, I couldn't track it. I gag on the half-eaten bun as he shoves me into the door and stalks to the cash register. Rosewater hits my nose, and Gastonia is at my side, her fingers gentle as she pulls the bun from my mouth. Her blue eyes meet mine briefly, a warning in the sapphire depths.

A sharp crack splits the air. I bite my tongue as Lirem smashes the register open and scoops coins from the drawer. He drops my profits into a velvet bag and cinches it tight. In another blurred move, he sweeps an arm across the counter, knocking stacked plates and a glass cake dome to the wooden floor. Gastonia backs us against the door as he rounds the counter, his boots crunching over broken glass.

He pauses in the middle of the shop. With a fang-tipped grin, he scoops the base of the cake dome from the floor and hurls it through the window I replaced.

Gastonia screams as glass shatters, shards scattering over the floor and skidding to a stop at the tips of our boots. More heavy footsteps, and then Lirem's broad chest fills my vision. He grips my jaw and forces my head up.

"I don't like liars, baker. Remember this lesson, hmm?"

I hold his stare as fury simmers under my skin.

His fingers dig into my jaw. His lips curve in a smile that doesn't reach his red eyes. "You and I will meet again soon." With a final hiss, he shoves me hard and leaves the shop.

For a long moment, silence reigns. Then the distant sound of whirring drifts through the ruined bakery. I sag against the door as relief swamps me. If Dad's working in his shop, he's okay. Lirem didn't touch him. That's all that matters.

Gastonia flings herself against my chest and twines her arms around my neck. "Oh you poor thing," she breathes in my ear. "Don't worry about the money. I'll talk to Daddy." She strokes my nape. "I'll take care of everything."

I stand woodenly, my arms limp at my sides. I don't need to look at the cash register to know Lirem took everything. How am I going to tell Dad? Forget supplies for the shop. Now I don't have enough coin to buy groceries for the cottage.

Weariness settles over me as Gastonia continues murmuring in my ear. Her breasts press against my chest. In a minute, I'll gather the energy to push her away so I can check on Dad. But right now, the only thing I can do is stand still as my head fills with a single, burning thought.

I hate dragons. And that will never change.

CHAPTER 3
FUOCO

It's late as I sit before the fire in my bedchamber with a glass of wine at my elbow.

Outside my window, a bright moon hangs in a pitch-black sky. This plane is so much darker than the Myth. Those lands are long gone, but they're vivid in my memories. Even at night, the sky there sparkled gold and pink. The human world is plainer. It certainly doesn't sparkle.

Behind the Veil, the dragon realm was dotted with volcanoes wreathed in mist. The lords of the great houses built their castles from cooled lava flows, and the obsidian spires glittered opalescent in the sun. My father's castle was the grandest. House Drakoni thrived, our influence stretching from the elven lands all the way to the Lathendriel Sea.

Homesickness sours my gut.

Or maybe it's the bite of jealousy. Gothel's relaxed, happy face swims before my eyes. He looked so pleased with himself—a newly mated male eager to return to his beloved.

With a grunt, I pluck my wineglass from the table at my side. Before the rim touches my lips, the curdled stench of fear burns my nose. The scent signature is elderly and female.

Ellen. The servant from last night. She must have brought wine to my bedchamber before she finished her duties this evening.

Sighing, I set the glass on the table and stretch my legs before me. Flames snap and blaze in the hearth, their sinuous dance beckoning me like a lover. But I long for another kind of companion—one made of flesh and blood. Someone who doesn't tremble at my countenance or quake when I glance in their direction.

If a male as forbidding and ancient as Gothel can snare a mate, surely Fate won't keep me waiting much longer. Even Wotan managed to find a male willing to tolerate his cantankerous disposition. And just an hour ago, news arrived from the Sea Syndicate. Not to be outdone by the other lords, Triton recently took two mates: his long-time lover, Ari Razorfin, and a young sea witch.

"Show off," I mutter, drumming my fingers on the plush velvet arm of my chair.

Why not me? I've dreamed of my selsara—my fated one—for hundreds of years. I've been preparing for him even longer, filling my mountain lair with a hoard of jewels, costly furs, and priceless treasures. I've spared no expense readying the place where I'll woo and spoil my mate. Marble veins the walls. The ceilings drip with crystal. Elven craftsmen constructed a sumptuous sunken lounge area big enough to fit my frame and accommodate hours of bedsport.

I built my lair a day's flight from syndicate headquarters. The castle is always bustling with activity, and privacy is difficult to come by. By contrast, my lair is a peaceful retreat where I can pamper and seduce my fated one. Just as soon as I find him.

And he is a *him*. Dragon mates can be either sex. In some cases, Fate matches a dragon with two or more selsaras. But polyamory isn't my destiny.

No, Fate has paired me with a male. Like all dragons, I've dreamed of him since I was a fledgling. Until recently, those dreams have been so hazy, I couldn't tell if my mate was male or female. But the past few years have brought clarity. Not only is my mate male, he's *here*, somewhere in the North. Out there in the darkness beyond my window, my mate's heart beats in his chest. When I meet him, I'll press my claiming jewel into his flesh and bind him to me forever.

My cock tightens as I rest my head against the back of my chair and let my mind wander into the flames. *Dragon dreams.* Shadowy snippets of my future dance in the fire. As the flames leap higher, my mate appears.

His frame is muscular but smaller than mine. Wavy chocolate-brown hair dances on a breeze as he turns to me with a throaty laugh. His face is unfocused, his features too blurry to make out. I let my gaze roam the rest of him, searching for exposed skin. I find it on his forearm, where his sleeve is rolled to his elbow. *No scales.* But that doesn't matter. Whoever—and whatever—he is, he's perfect for me.

But his shirt is worn, the fabric thin and patched. Even as blood pumps to my cock, a growl rises in my chest. No mate of mine will wear rags. The first thing I'll do when I find him is take him to the court tailor. My beloved will wear the finest silks and velvets. I'll drape him in jewels befitting his station.

In the fire, he walks ahead of me, his lean hips and firm ass turning my growl into a moan. "Show yourself," I murmur, palming my cock through my trousers. I grip my length and squeeze. Pleasure rolls up my dick in a warm wave and settles hard in my stomach. "Come to me."

Lately, I speak that command aloud. In the morning before the castle wakes, I stand on my balcony and send my entreaty into the wind. My father would dismiss it as whimsy. My mother, who has always been loving but practical, would tell me I'm wasting my time. Dragons believe things happen when they're meant to and not a moment before. I can no sooner summon my mate than I can snap my fingers and make him appear. If I could, I would have done it long ago.

My cock pushes painfully against my trousers, so I yank them open and free my shaft. My hot length fills my palm, my Prince Albert winking in the firelight. Pearlescent moisture pools at my slit and drips over the curved ring. The flames roar higher as I swipe the bead and bring it to my lips.

I'll feed him my cum one day. When I find my selsara, I'll train him to crave my taste. He'll beg for it on his knees, his beautiful mouth watering. Breath hitching, I lift my shaft and toy with the curved bar that pierces the base of my cock. My beloved will know every hard, throbbing inch of me. And I'll return the favor.

"Fuck," I gasp, fire spreading under my skin. Arching my back, I stroke my dick and stare into the crackling flames. My dream fades, but I don't need it. My imagination supplies me with a parade of possibilities. The nameless, faceless male crawls nude across a beautiful carpet. He nuzzles my thigh, then turns and lifts his ass. His hole winks at me, calling for my cock. Heavy balls swing between his thighs. He's pierced in that soft spot behind his sack, the jewel in the silver ring the same green as my scales.

"*Selsara*," I moan, entranced by the vision.

My chair creaks as I jerk my cock faster, my hand flying up and down my pulsing length.

In the vision, I kneel behind my mate. Bending forward, I lick at his sack, then suck one soft globe into my mouth. I tug gently, swirling my tongue over the smooth skin. A groan floats back to me, letting me know my beautiful mate likes my attention. I release his tender flesh with a *pop* and run my tongue up his taint, swirling over the piercing that marks him as mine.

A ragged moan joins the crackle of the flames. I don't know if it's real or part of the daydream I'm conjuring. And I don't care. My balls draw tight as I stroke faster, slicking moisture from my tip to my base. My hips jerk, and I grunt as my mind returns to my selsara. We're fucking now, pleasure threatening to boil over as I watch my dick plunge between his firm, round cheeks.

Orgasm overtakes me, blackness blotting out the vision as I clench my teeth and spurt into my hand. Pleasure batters me and then recedes. I bring it back with a few quick tugs, my head spinning with visions of chocolate-brown hair and a tight ass.

"Selsara!" I cry hoarsely as waves of ecstasy crash against me a second time. When I come down, I sprawl in my chair with my spent dick in my hand. The soft chirp of insects drifts from outside. Moonlight spills over the carpet, reminding me that duty will come far too early in the morning. I should go to bed.

The problem is, I'm tired of sleeping alone. The fireplace crackles on, the flames indifferent to my longing. Absently, I lift my hand and let fire build under my skin. In a flash, the cum burns away from my fingers, leaving clean, whole flesh behind.

I'd much rather watch my mate lick it off. Propping my chin on my hand, I stare into the flames.

Where are you?

～

AFTER A RESTLESS NIGHT, I stalk through the castle's greenhouse. Winter sunlight streams through the glass, the pale rays falling on rows of pumpkins, corn, and tomatoes. The syndicate's villages don't always produce plentiful harvests. When the humans' crops fall short, Lirem and my other enforcers distribute food from my own stores. The only part of my lands off-limits to the humans are the enchanted orchards.

But the humans are welcome to everything else. If I add some grapevines, I could start making wine. It'll take a few years to create the first vintage, but it would be nice to bring the process in-house instead of purchasing wine from the Hallows. And if anything is likely to endear me to the villagers, it's free alcohol.

Winemaking plans dominate my thoughts as I leave the greenhouse and approach the East Tower. Its pale stones reflect the sun, which is unseasonably warm for December. An arched door framed by scrolling masonry marks the entrance to the castle's underbelly. I enter and descend the spiral staircase, my knee-length coat flaring around my legs.

Heat rises, caressing my skin and making my beast stir in my chest. I take the stairs two at a time, excitement swirling as the temperature soars. At last, the staircase opens into a cavern supported by broad pillars that stretch twenty feet overhead. Massive fireplaces line the walls, each one housing a roaring fire.

But it's the workstations that draw my gaze. Dragons sit at each one, their skilled fingers molding jewels and metal into precious works of art. Gems of every size and color twinkle as the metalsmiths and jewelers labor at their craft.

I wander down the line, returning nods and greetings. The male I came to see stands at a large table at the very last station, the muscles in his broad back rippling as he bends over his task. He straightens and turns at my approach, his handsome face spreading in a smile.

"Good morning, my lord."

"Zayek," I say, clasping his shoulder. He's shirtless, his black scales reflecting the fire. "Any progress?"

Garnet-colored eyes crinkle at the corners as my head jeweler turns and plucks something from his table. When he faces me again, he holds a golden, jeweled vambrace. "You have good timing, Fuoco." He taps a pair of long metal tweezers against a small hole in the metal. "I was just about to place the last gemstone."

Anticipation flutters in my chest. "May I see it?"

He hands the vambrace over, his smile in place as he watches me examine the jewel-studded armor, which starts in a golden cuff and grows broader to accommodate a male's forearm. In ages past, a piece like this would serve as protection rather than adornment. Any serious knight would have skipped flashy gems, which would have inevitably been knocked from their settings by a sword or lance.

But this vambrace isn't meant for protection. No, this beauty is for pure pleasure. *Mine.* Because I have every intention of seeing it on my mate. Ideally, he'll wear this piece and nothing else.

The vambrace is gorgeous, its golden surface engraved with my house crest depicting two dragons. Their tails intertwine. Jaws stretch wide as they spew fire into the sky. Small, round emeralds wink in their eyes. More green gems scatter over their bodies, forming tiny scales that must have taken hours to set. Zayek is a master of his craft, which is probably why my father was so furious when I swiped the jeweler from under my sire's noble nose.

"It's breathtaking," I murmur, turning the piece in reverent hands.

Zayek points to the spot where the cuff begins to flare. "I thought about adding a row of chocolate diamonds here. Something a little different. What do you think?"

Visions of soft brown hair flit through my mind. "Perfect." I meet Zayek's gaze. "This is your best work yet, old friend."

Satisfaction gleams in the jeweler's eyes. "I hope your selsara will love it as much as you do, my lord."

My heart sinks. "Yes." *When I find him.* I chat with Zayek a moment longer before taking my leave. As I head down the line of dragons, my gaze snags on a necklace spread over one of the tables. Thick, square-cut rubies march down the silver chain. The dragon working on the piece shifts his elbow, revealing a medallion bearing the crest of House Lastri.

Lirem's house. The dragon in the center of the medallion clutches arrows in its claws. A ruby dots the beast's eye.

Treasure-hoarding thieves, the lot of you.

The dragon at the table lifts his head. His bright eyes fill with polite curiosity as he meets my gaze. "Is there something you need, my lord?"

"No. No, thank you." I turn to go, only to swing back. "How many pieces have you made for Lirem this month?"

"I believe this is the tenth, sir." The jeweler hesitates. "Is that…all right, my lord?"

"Yes," I say at once. "Yes, of course." With a wave and a smile, I go to the stairs. An odd apprehension prickles over my skin as I recall the man I burned two nights ago. *Treasure-hoarding thieves.* He meant it as an insult, but there was truth in his words. From our first flight, my people build hoards. Every dragon creates a lair—and then fills it with treasure.

But we don't accumulate these riches for ourselves. As much as we enjoy the finer things in life, our hoards are strictly for our mates. To a human, I suppose it looks like greed. But instinct drives us. Dragons long to please our mates. When I find the male from my dreams, I'll carry him to my lair and lay him in a bed of coins. I'll pledge my body and soul to him. Promise to see to his every need for all time. I'll surround him with gold so he'll know I can deliver on my promises.

Lirem and my other enforcers do the same. I don't draw lines of distinction between the upper and lower houses. My enforcers are free to avail themselves of my jewelers' services. When the jeweler finishes Lirem's necklace, my enforcer will add it to his hoard. His treasure.

The thief's words shouldn't bother me. And yet they continue to ring in my head as I reach the top of the stairs and exit the tower. I pause, my gaze on the greenhouse shimmering in the sun. The humans harvested their crops two months ago. According to Lirem, the yield was plentiful. He and Varden have yet to tap into the castle's stores.

But the post-harvest season is just as important. If the humans don't prep their fields for planting, next year could be a lean one. Lirem and the others check the fields, but they can't see things as I do. It's one thing to walk rows of dirt. It's quite another to view it from fifty feet in the air.

Turning on my heel, I head for the courtyard. It's still early. I can strip, shift, and take to the sky without anyone noticing. It's been too long since I patrolled my territory. I'll view the fields and check on the villages. At the very least, I'll be able to identify any roofs in need of repair.

And maybe I'll sense my mate.

As soon as the thought enters my head, I push it away. After so much time, I can't get my hopes up. My dream man is out there, but I'm unlikely to find him today. Everything happens in its own time.

I simply have to be patient.

CHAPTER 4

BEAU

I'm running low on patience. Scratch that, I'm running low on *everything*.

Heat blasts my face as I thrust a wooden paddle into the brick oven built into the bakery wall. My stomach sinks as I withdraw the first—and only—loaf of bread I baked this morning. Although, "loaf" isn't the right word. More like "lump."

Biting back a growl, I deposit the doughy, misshapen mess onto a cooling rack and lean against the battered counter behind me. The heel of the lump slides lower as it cools, making the unfortunate-looking bread look like it's frowning.

Yeah, well, join the club. I used the last of the fruit and wheat for Dad's supper last night. I'm out of milk and sugar, and I scraped flour from the bottom of the bin to make this loaf. It wasn't enough. I can't sell this to anyone. I certainly can't fulfill Mrs. Pepperdine's order. And after Lirem's visit, I don't have coin to buy even the most basic supplies. I'm out of options.

That is, unless I swallow my pride and go to Gastonia's father.

Instantly, my stomach knots. It wouldn't be a loan this time. It would be a betrothal. My chest tightens as the lump begins to spread over the cooling rack, half-cooked dough dripping through the gaps in the wire mesh. Can I really sell myself that way? Because that's what it would be—a coldblooded transaction.

It would also be unfair to Gastonia. After a lifetime of trying not to be different, I know I can't grin and bear my way through a wedding night—or any of the nights that would follow. Mom told me I'll recognize true love when I see it. *"You'll just know. It won't even be a question."* I was too young to understand what she meant. But looking back, I saw true love shining in her eyes whenever she looked at Dad. I don't know if I'll ever find someone who looks at me like that, but I know it's not Gastonia.

A dry, rattling cough interrupts my thoughts. I move without thinking, my feet carrying me across uneven floorboards to Dad's room. He's sitting up in bed, his cheeks bright red in his gray-tinged face. His shoulders shake violently as he coughs into a scrap of cloth.

"Dad!" I fly to the bed. Leaning a hip against the thin mattress, I slip an arm around his shoulders. "Deep breaths, remember? Just like the doctor said." But that was over a year ago. And I'm not even sure he was a real doctor—or even human. Not that the latter makes any difference, but some species of the Myth enjoy tricking humans.

"It's…all…right," Dad says between coughs. He catches his breath and slumps against me. "I pulled you from your work. I'm sorry, son."

"You didn't. I'm just about finished for the morning." I ease him to the pillow, trying to ignore how frail he feels under his nightshirt. He releases a reedy sigh as he settles into the bed, his white hair like cotton candy on the pillow. I smooth it back. "Can I get you some water?"

His brown eyes twinkle. "No, but I'll take whiskey if you're offering."

"Maybe for dinner."

"With shepherd's pie," he says, playing our old game. "And one of your fruit tarts."

"Strawberry or apple?"

"Apple. With whipped cream on top." His lids slide to half-mast, but his smile remains as he keeps the game going. "Your apple tarts are better than your mother's." One eye pops back open. "Don't tell her I said that."

I return his smile even as my heart squeezes. "I won't."

He pats my hand. "You're a good lad, Beau. The best son any parent could hope for. Your mother is proud of you. She'd tell you herself if she were here, but..." His eyelids droop, and he finishes his sentence on a sigh. "You'll just have to trust me."

"I do," I murmur. I watch him fall asleep, my fingers entwined with his. When his breathing stays even, I rise and pull the quilt to his chin. The scrap of cloth falls to the floor, a bright-red splotch of blood in the center.

My hand shakes as I retrieve it. He's dying. The knowledge sinks into my bones. But maybe it's been there for a while. Since last winter, when his cold became pneumonia and then settled in for good. If I could keep him warm, maybe it would go away. If he had enough to eat or the right kind of medicine. But I don't have access to any of those things. Medicine is impossible to find. It would be easier to raid Lord Fuoco's apple orchard than to find—

I jerk my head up.

Options. Marrying Gastonia isn't the only avenue open to me. The apples in the Fire Lord's orchard have magical properties. John Robinson smuggled me some about six months ago. I baked them into a pie and for two weeks, Dad walked with a spring in his step.

But the orchard is forbidden land. For all I know, Lord Fuoco executed John for stealing from it. If I get caught...

Dad lets out a sudden cough, his whole body jerking. His eyes stay closed as he gasps for breath. After a tense moment, he settles down again. His chest rises and falls steadily.

But now blood flecks his lips.

One apple. How hard can it be to grab one apple?

Bending, I stroke the cloth over Dad's mouth, wiping away the blood. Then I tuck the quilt more snugly around his shoulders and rush from the room with new determination pounding through my veins.

∽

It's a twenty-minute walk to the orchard. By the time I reach the hedge that grows tall around the rows of trees, my heart pounds so hard I think it might burst from my chest. One silver lining? I'm sweating so much the cold doesn't bother me.

I walk quickly, pausing every few steps to glance at the sky or look over my shoulder. The village is a blurry collection of buildings on a slope in the distance. If Lirem or Varden catch me, they'll probably kill me on the spot. The yellow-eyed enforcer, Nazzar, always has a knife on him. Rumor has it he carves his initials on his victims before putting them out of their misery.

Sweat trickles down my spine as the hedge looms. The road is deserted. No footprints mar the the dirt. *Because no one is stupid enough to come here.*

The sweet scent of apples teases my nose. Between a gap in the hedge, a thick ribbon of green grass stretches into the distance. Trees line either side, their branches teeming with fat, red apples. Dozens lie on the sun-dappled ground. Even at a distance, the first signs of rot are visible. Anger kindles in my gut as I approach. All of this fruit going to waste when people in the village are starving.

Right on cue, my stomach rumbles. My mouth waters uncontrollably, and the orchard darkens at the edges as a wave of dizziness sweeps me. Swaying, I stop and brace my hands on my knees as I fight to stay on my feet. I skipped dinner last night—and lunch before it. But if I can pull this off, Dad and I will dine on stewed apples tonight. And maybe I can sell enough to buy wheat and other supplies.

The dizziness passes, and I straighten, the determination I felt at Dad's bedside propelling me forward. Just as I reach the gap in the hedge, a shuffling sound makes me freeze. A second later, a white head appears in the gap, and a horse with a platinum mane stares me down.

No, not a horse. Awe spreads through me as I fix my gaze on the mother-of-pearl horn protruding from the center of the beast's forehead. It's a unicorn.

Without warning, it opens its mouth and releases a wet burp. A tiny rainbow-colored cloud puffs in the air.

I blink, my feet rooted to the ground. Did it...? Did it just burp a rainbow?

The beast snorts and tosses its head. It shuffles around, a pair of stubby wings flapping in the center of its back. A snow-white tail swishes as it clip-clops down the strip of grass between the trees. A moment later, a wet squelch splits the air, and a rainbow puffs from its hindquarters.

My awe shifts to amusement. A smile tugs at my lips as I walk forward. I hesitate at the break in the hedge, then hold my breath and step through it.

Nothing. Lirem doesn't appear. Dragon fire doesn't rain from the sky. A gentle breeze picks up, stirring the apple trees' leaves and sending the scent of fresh fruit into my lungs.

The unicorn's broad hips sway as it meanders the path in front of me. Moments later, a second beast noses its way from between a pair of trees. It gives me a bored look as it chews rhythmically. Its pale wings flap, and if I didn't know better, I'd think it was happy to see me. Or maybe just happy to see anyone.

Another wet squelch echoes down the rows of trees. Ahead, the first unicorn pauses and releases a long, thin rainbow-hued stream of flatulence.

"Oh, *really*, Cornelius," a deep voice scolds.

The air leaves my lungs. My brain screams at me to run, but I can't move. I stand frozen as a cloaked figure shifts at the base of one of the apple trees. His legs stretch before him in a casual pose. His hands are folded in his lap. His cloak is brown like the bark at his back, the long folds of cloth covering him from head to toe. Maybe that's why I didn't see him. I'm so stupid. I was distracted by the unicorns, and now I'm going to die. Any second, the man is going to spring up and slit my throat.

"I'm not going to hurt you," he rumbles. Bright green eyes study me from inside the hood of his cloak. Sunlight slants over him, illuminating features that loosen my knees.

And tighten my cock.

Oh gods. *Not now*. Of all the times to be attracted to a man... But *this* man is gorgeous. There's no other word for it. High cheekbones shaded with dark stubble lead into a firm jaw. Sensual lips curve at the corners. Something about those corners makes me want to move closer.

They're mysterious and perfect—little hollows I want to explore. He's big. His position on the ground makes it hard to tell just how big, but he's not a small man. His cloak stretches over wide shoulders and a broad chest. Heat snakes through me as I continue to gawk, every teenage fantasy I tried to suppress flashing bright in my mind.

The ghost of a smile plays around his mouth as he studies me. "There is nothing to fear." A languid hand gestures to the first unicorn, which is busy tugging an apple from one of the trees. Green eyes gleam with humor. "Unless you're afraid of intestinal discomfort."

"I…" My throat is so dry, I have to gulp a couple of times. "I'm not."

His smile spreads to his eyes. "A fortunate coincidence, then." He looks at the first unicorn. "Honestly, Cornelius."

The beast pauses its tugging. Its pot belly trembles, and it releases another rainbow-sheened belch. The second unicorn sidles up to a tree and drags its flank over the bark. Its deep-blue eyes go half-mast as it releases a sound somewhere between a honk and a purr.

"Terrible manners," the stranger murmurs. He meets my gaze with something like exasperation in his eyes. "They're supposed to guard the orchard. But I'm afraid they're quite drunk."

"Drunk?"

"Mmm. Apple juice will do that to unicorns." He keeps his eyes on me as he raises his voice. "Especially when they can't control themselves."

The first unicorn snorts as it snaps an apple off the tree.

The stranger and I continue our staring contest. When he seems content to simply watch me, I blurt, "Who are you?" He's not a dragon, thank the gods. If he were, I'd already be dead. Probably, he's some kind of Myth creature. An incubus, perhaps. Or maybe one of the elves. Although, the books I've read say the elves mostly live in Europe.

Green eyes sweep down my body, raising goosebumps on my skin. As they travel back up, I swear I can feel their caress. My breath hitches, and my erection pushes against the front of my pants. For once, I'm grateful for my oversize coat, which conceals the effect the stranger has on me.

"A passerby," he says in that low, rich rumble.

It takes me a second to realize he answered my question. Partially answered it, anyway. Maybe he doesn't want to give a proper name.

Maybe he's here to steal too.

"Do you have a name?" he asks, green eyes making another lazy trip over my chest. As they linger, my nipples tighten. My heartbeat pounds in the taut peaks the same as it throbs in my dick.

"Beau," I rasp. Right away, regret sweeps through me. *Stupid.* So stupid to tell him my name. He could be a spy or—

"Beau," he says, rolling the vowel like he's tasting it. Sensual lips curve, those tempting hollows growing deeper. He tilts his head and his hood gapes, exposing a strong, brown neck and the graceful arch of his cheekbone. "That means handsome, does it not?"

Somehow, I will my tongue to move so I can say, "Yeah."

"It suits you." His eyes darken, the green as rich and deep as the leaves on the apple tree above him. "It's perfect for you."

My heart slams against my chest. My cock aches, the tip wetting the front of my briefs. Gods, I have to get out of here. It's been a long time since I lost control like this. Years ago, when denial and confusion swirled like poison in my veins, I avoided touching myself. At night, I lay in bed and ignored the images of broad shoulders and thick biceps that tried to rise in my thoughts. All that denial led to a few close calls —one too many scenarios that nearly exposed me to everyone in the village.

I feel exposed now, desire burning so hot I wait for smoke to waft from my skin. The stranger is definitely an incubus. There's no other explanation for my lust.

"I…" I back up a step. "I have to go."

"So soon?" The man frowns, his disappointment so seemingly genuine I almost believe it. Almost.

I jerk a thumb over my shoulder. "I'm needed—" I suck in a breath. "Someone is waiting for me."

Green eyes sharpen. His voice dips dangerously low. "A man?"

"M-My father." Fear spikes then wanes as his eyes soften once more. "Um…nice meeting you." I turn, my eyes on the gap in the hedge and the tiny view of the village beyond it.

"Hold."

The stranger's deep command wraps around me like a whip, jerking me to a stop as surely as if he'd clamped a hand on my shoulder. Heart in my throat, I slowly turn.

In one graceful movement, he rises from the ground and steps away from the tree.

My heart skips beats as I crane my head back…and back some more so I can meet his gaze. Even with the distance between us, he *towers* above me. In his hood, his glittering eyes appear to dance with green flames.

Not an incubus.

My knees loosen as he slinks forward, moving with that same inhuman elegance. Because he's not human. He's a dragon. Bigger and taller than the enforcers. The voice of the elderly farmer echoes in my head. *"…taller than a tree with hair like green fire."*

The dragon's hood conceals his hair, but as he advances toward me, the two halves of his cloak part, revealing golden-tan skin covered in emerald-green scales.

Green fire.

Lord Fuoco.

"Please," I croak, nausea rising as death stares me down. "I-I'm so sorry…" Speech deserts me as tears burn my eyes. *Dad.* He'll be alone in the world without me. Who will make his tea exactly the way he likes it? Who will tug him away from his workbench when he falls asleep in the middle of scribbling notes?

Lord Fuoco's shadow falls over me. Unable to face the flames in his eyes, I drop my gaze to his chest. A spicy scent wafts around me. It's dark and masculine, like expensive cologne mixed with herbs and incense.

No. *Smoke.* He smells like smoke, I think dumbly as I stare at the scale-covered skin exposed by the gap in his cloak. Against my will, my gaze travels down, and my breathing stutters as I take in rippling abs and a line of dark hair that leads to…

Oh gods. He's nude under the cloak.

As I struggle to catch my breath, he curls a finger under my chin and forces my head up. Burning green eyes capture mine. Then his expression shifts, something like wonder dancing among the flames in his stare.

"*You.*"

I blink. He doesn't sound like he wants to kill me. He sounds...enthralled.

Slowly, he rotates his hand so he's cupping my chin. One big thumb strokes my cheekbone, the tender touch raising goosebumps on my skin. Inside his hood, his eyes soften. His voice gentles. "You *never* apologize to me, selsara."

The strange word trips around my mind. His scent floods my senses, crowding and overwhelming until every breath is drenched in dark, smoky spices. His thumb continues its sweeping caresses, each brush of his skin against mine streaking a frazzled path to my throbbing dick.

His touch welds me to the ground. Holds me immobile. But I'm no longer frozen. Now, a delicious warmth spreads through my limbs, loosening tense muscles and sapping tension. My lips part and my breath shudders out.

"There you are," he whispers, eyes glittering. "Beautiful."

Beautiful? People have called me handsome. Good-looking. But no one has ever called me beautiful. No one has ever looked at me like this. Like I'm a diamond they unearthed from the dirt. Confusion swirls, joining the fog of desire in my head. Before I can puzzle it out, he steps back. In another elegant move, he bends and retrieves an apple from the ground. Then another. His big hands gather half a dozen, then he straightens and tucks them into my pockets.

"What...?" I drag in a breath. "What are you doing?"

Tenderness and humor mix in his gaze. He pats my laden pocket with one hand. With the other, he runs his thumb across my lower lip. "This is what you came for, yes?"

Fear pierces the thick, spice-scented cloud of desire. "I'm not supposed to take anything." As if he doesn't know that. This is his orchard. The one I'm forbidden to enter upon penalty of death. Fear spikes higher. "I'm s-sorry—"

"No," he rasps, big palm cupping my cheek once more. Glittering green eyes sear mine. "Whatever is mine is yours. Anything you need, selsara, you come to me. Understand, Beau?" The flames in his eyes flare higher. "Tell me you understand."

The spices in my lungs form a hook that sinks deep into my soul. It tugs, drawing me closer. Making me want *more*. "I understand," I breathe, unsure what I'm saying. My head spins, the heat in my limbs curling into pleasure.

A rustling sound is my only warning. Before I can react, Lord Fuoco whips his head up and blurs. One second he's in front of me, the next he's gone, leaving me swaying. I stumble, regain my balance, and spin around.

The spike of fear becomes a lance that pins me in place.

Nazzar stands in the gap in the hedge, his bulk obscuring the view of the village behind him. He moves forward, pulling a long, wicked-looking blade as he enters the orchard. Bright yellow eyes fix on Fuoco, who stands between us.

"My lord," Nazzar says, inclining his dark head. His citrine stare flicks to me, and his mouth twists in a sneer that exposes his fangs. "Allow me to remove this vermin from your sight."

My blood freezes in my veins, all the hazy heat evaporating. *It was a set up*. Fuoco toyed with me. Now he'll let Nazzar chop me into pieces. I take a swift step backward, the primitive part of my brain kicking into overdrive. Urging me to turn and run.

"No," Fuoco says, stopping me. But he doesn't turn around. Instead, he advances on Nazzar, his brown cloak flaring around his ankles. The enforcer's eyes go wide, surprise flitting through them as he furrows his brow.

"My lord, you shouldn't concern yourself with filth from the village—"

"He's not *filth*," Fuoco says sharply, and I can't see his face but his tone is enough to make terror slosh in my gut. "This one is off-limits. No one touches him. Is that clear?"

Nazzar ducks his head like he's a marionette controlled by a puppet master. His frown stays put but deference enters his voice as he rasps, "Clear, my lord."

Fuoco turns, his emerald eyes latching onto me with a predatory stare. He jerks his head toward the hedge. "Go," he says, his deep voice touched with a little of the tenderness from before. "Quickly now."

I don't hesitate. Clumsy and inelegant, I lurch forward. Steering a broad path around the dragons, I rush to the gap in the hedge. Fuoco's stare burns in the center of my shoulder blades as I scramble through the gap and rush into the street. *No one touches him.* Somehow, I know he tells the truth. Nazzar won't hurt me. At least not this time.

But I don't wait around for Lord Fuoco to change his mind. I sprint toward home, apples bobbing in my pockets. The village looms larger but I hardly see it.

My vision fills with a pair of burning green eyes. The rhythmic pounding of my footfalls disappears, replaced with a deep voice rumbling a foreign word wrapped in a tone that shivers into the deepest, most secret corners of my soul.

Selsara. I don't know what it means. I don't know what just happened. But I'm alive. That's good enough for now.

CHAPTER 5
FUOCO

Nazzar clutches his knife tighter, his yellow eyes trailing Beau through the hedge. His predatory focus yanks my dragon to the surface. When I snarl, flames curl out of my lips. Nazzar's gaze flits back to me, and his pupils blow wide. He offers a respectful nod, but his fingers twitch on the knife handle.

I saw Beau enter the orchard and knew he was mine.

And Nazzar seeks to take that from me.

My blood boils knowing my selsara is running, slipping farther away by the second. Nazzar was going to hurt Beau. My Beau. Fierce anger heats my skin, flames dancing just beneath the surface as fury and protective instinct take over. I *need* to ensure my selsara's safety. To eliminate the threat Nazzar poses. I stride across the grass and tower over my enforcer.

He's careful not to show me his throat as he lifts his chin to meet my gaze. Confusion clouds his citrine eyes. "Why did you stop me? You burned a human for stealing from this orchard this very week, Fuoco. If you allow it once—"

I shove him, knocking him backward a step. "That *human* is my selsara. You will not touch him!" The words come out on a roar. Frenzied outrage rises, urging me to rip Nazzar limb from limb for even thinking of pointing his knife at Beau.

Nazzar's yellow eyes go wide as his mouth drops open. He raises his knife. "No, it can't be! He's just a—"

I lurch forward and grab his throat, digging my claws into his neck as rage builds. Red descends over my vision as I squeeze, choking off the insult he was about to deliver.

"What?" I demand. "Only a human? Just a thief? Tread carefully, Nazzar. I've waited centuries for him. I wouldn't touch a hair on his head if he took every fucking apple in this orchard." I glance at the knife Nazzar still holds between us. "I won't allow you near Beau," I growl. "Not now, not ever."

Anger flashes in my enforcer's eyes. The trust we've built over many decades crumbles to ash. Time slows as apprehension tingles down my nape. I look at the knife just as he slashes upward, aiming for my side. I shove him into the hedge, but the knife slashes my forearm, fire following in its wake.

Snarling, I smash my fist into his jaw, snapping his head back. He recovers quickly and comes for me again, slashing with the knife.

I dodge him easily, tapping superior speed as I grab his wrist, jerk him into me, and pin his arm behind his back. I yank up, and a sickening *pop* echoes around the orchard as his shoulder dislocates. The knife drops to the grass at our feet.

Nazzar screams. Eyes burning with anger and agony, he snaps his long fangs, missing my neck by less than an inch.

Spinning, I toss him into the nearest tree, relishing the crack of his spine when he hits the broad trunk. He lands in a heap at the base of the tree, his legs flung out at odd angles.

"You threatened my selsara, Nazzar." I stalk toward him, scooping the knife from the ground as I go. I flip it and point the tip at my enforcer. "No one threatens my mate. No one."

"You're a fool," he spits through bloodied lips. "An insufferable fool sent here to babysit beings far beneath you. And now you wish to take a human thief for your selsara? I can't serve you another fucking minute."

I stare down at him. Grief for what I'm about to do sinks in my stomach like a ten-pound stone. I trusted him for years. But that's gone now, evaporated like smoke over cinders.

Nazzar's breathing grows more labored as I lift his knife higher. Red draws my gaze to the blade. Dried blood crusts the metal. Unease buffets me as I step back and turn the knife over. It's an unremarkable piece, the blade worn and scratched. The handle is simple and unadorned. More dried blood gathers in the groove between the blade and the handle.

I look at Nazzar. "This isn't a blade for your hoard. Why would you even carry this?"

"Attacks. Highwaymen." He licks his lips, wariness flitting through his gaze. "Justice when the situation calls for it."

"Bullshit. Your job is to protect the humans. I handle lawbreakers. You've never meted out punishment." I sniff at the blade, a sickening feeling roiling my gut as the scent of iron fills my nose. "This blood is human."

Nazzar laughs—a cruel sound like he's enjoying a joke at my expense. When his laughter dies, his lips curl in a vicious sneer. "This plane is ripe for the taking, *my lord*, if one knows how to keep a secret."

Maybe it's true that some dragons are cursed to go mad, because madness threatens to overtake me. It rises in my chest as the implications of the bloody blade and his words sink in. Wrath hovers just out of reach, urging me to tear Nazzar apart.

He laughs again. "You never could see the truth, could you? Dragons are *better* than everyone else." His eyes glitter with a viciousness that steals my breath. Bloody spittle flies from his lips. "We could have ruled this plane like the kings we are had you not insisted on helping the humans. It's ridiculous. It's—"

The knife thunks into his chest, the handle vibrating just below his collarbone. The pain hits him a second later, and he screams hoarsely. He claws at the blade, but it's useless. He's pinned to the trunk.

I go to the tree and kneel at his limp knee. "How far does this rot go, Nazzar?" I ask, gripping the handle of the knife and twisting. "Is it just you who holds this opinion of humans? Or Lirem and Varden as well?"

Nazzar screams, throwing his head back against the tree as tears stream from his eyes.

"Answer me." I stop twisting, and his screams fade to heavy, labored pants. He grits his teeth and shakes his head. When it's clear he won't say anything else, I rise and cast my cloak to the ground. Glacial fury replaces the sinking realization that Nazzar isn't the male I thought he was.

He wanted to hurt Beau. It's my privilege to protect my selsara. As long as Nazzar lives, Beau isn't safe.

A trickling sensation like boiling water trails down my spine and spreads along my limbs. It climbs up my neck, a searing hand spreading its fingers over my scalp. Hot, ruby-red rivulets coat my vision as I call the orchard to attention.

Nazzar watches me, disbelief stirring in his eyes.

"I've kept a secret too," I murmur.

As my power builds, Nazzar makes a choked sound. "It can't be," he rasps. "There hasn't been an elemental dragon for hundreds of years. They died out in the Old Country!" His breathing goes fast and hard. He claws at the knife again, struggling even as his body below his waist remains limp.

Power swells in the forefront of my mind. Cool clarity illuminates the world around me. I sense every element—the fire in my chest, water that trickles in an aquifer far beneath us, the air that dances around my body in the form of a cool breeze.

The ground under Nazzar.

Swirling my hands, I summon the earth, willing the ground beneath my enforcer to crack.

"It can't be!" he insists, panic twisting his features as he struggles to free himself. "We heard the rumors. We watched you for years. There's never been a single fucking sign of elemental power!" He yanks at the knife, grunting.

Snarling, I snap my fingers, calling to the air and forcing it to press the knife harder into his shoulder. He screams and writhes against the pain.

I don't bother explaining why I hid my power. Nazzar betrayed me. He wanted to hurt Beau. Nobody touches Beau.

The ground beneath Nazzar opens, and his useless legs fall into the widening crack.

"No!" he shouts. "I didn't realize! I won't touch him. I'm sorry, my lord! Please! Let's talk about this!" He scratches at the tree behind him, trying to find purchase.

I cleave the ground in front of him, creating cracks that splinter out from the base of the tree. The dirt heaves and sways. It shreds apart, the opening growing wider. Nazzar shrieks as his lower body sinks into the hollow. A crack splits the tree trunk, releasing the knife. He drops, then catches himself on the crumbling edge of earth and grass. He claws at the ground, desperate yellow eyes boring into mind. "Please, Fuoco! We're *friends*."

He wanted to hurt Beau. Unacceptable.

I wave my hand, setting the ground quaking. "Would you have made Beau plead for his life? Would you have drawn his blood?"

Nazzar's long claws scratch at the dirt as he clings to the heaving ground. Sweat dots his forehead and darkens the neck of his blood-stained shirt. He dangles over the hole, the muscles in his shoulders bunching as he tries to haul himself up. "No, my lord, please!"

"Would you have hurt Beau like you've obviously hurt others?" My dragon simmers just under my skin, ready to burst from my human form and burn my betraying enforcer to ash.

Nazzar shakes his head, clawing at the ground and tearing up chunks of grass and dirt as he slides deeper into the abyss. "Fuoco, don't do this."

Red flames streak along the cool fingers wrapped around my mind. Nazzar will never touch my mate. I bellow, the sound ripping from my throat when I think of what could have happened if I hadn't visited the orchard today.

The chunk of ground under Nazzar's claws turns to dust. He drops out of sight, his scream spiraling up until it cuts off with an abrupt squelch.

Panting, I call the dirt back, filling the holes and covering Nazzar's broken body. I smooth the earth into place until the ground is flat and whole. Exhaustion nips at the edges of my mind as I mend the crack in the tree's trunk, leaving no scar behind.

Silence descends on the orchard. The apple trees dance and sway on a slight wind. Over my shoulder, Cornelius and his brother snore. There's no sign of Nazzar. No sign that anything happened here.

He wanted to hurt Beau.

My selsara.

Grabbing my cloak, I swing it around my shoulders and sprint from the orchard. I race toward the village, instinct urging me to protect my mate at all costs. I've lost crucial minutes fighting my enforcer. The need to protect my mate outweighs every other emotion. If I can just get my hands on him, I can keep him safe. I can ask him why he needed to steal. I can give him the *world*. I've planned and prepared for him for centuries.

I reach the village in under a minute. For a tense beat, panic rises as I think I've lost my quarry. Then I spot Beau's chocolate-brown waves and ratty coat. He dips between two tall cottages and into the village.

Too late. Godsdamnit.

Red-hot fury rises again, clouding my vision and filling my mouth with the taste of cinders. Madness beckons, its long, bony fingers scrabbling at me. I stand in the road and suck in a deep breath, willing the insanity to recede. My heart pounds. My selsara is close—so close—and yet I can't touch him. I've finally found him after so many years of dreaming and longing. By rights, I should carry him back to the castle and declare him my mate before the entire court. Instead, I cling to the shadows, fearful of being seen.

Swallowing a growl, I skirt the edge of the village. I can hardly stride into the town square wearing nothing but a cloak, yet I'm not ready to give up the chase. The need to see Beau eats at me. Frustration builds, my instincts urging me to abandon caution and go door to door until I find him. As quickly as it comes, I squash that impulse. Beau is mine. He'll still be mine tomorrow. I know where to find him. Now I need to know why he entered the orchard with theft on his mind.

Stalking along the outermost buildings, I peer down every alley, hoping to see him. After half an hour, I've rounded the entire village, but he's nowhere to be found. I slip into a dark space between two buildings and let the shadows swallow me. Huddled in my cloak, I lean against the cool bricks. Humans pass, heads down and shoulders hunched against the cold.

Dozens of homes and buildings dot the village. Shops form a circle around an old water fountain, although there's no water this time of year. At first glance, the village appears clean and orderly like any other.

A mother and several small children hurry past. The breeze picks up, ruffling their clothes and making the mother pull a threadbare shawl more tightly around her thin shoulders. The children follow like ducklings, worn boots ringing out against the pavers. A tiny girl with pale ringlets brings up the rear. Suddenly, she stops and looks down my alley. Blue eyes lock with mine and go wide.

Slowly, I lift a finger to my lips. Some wild impulse compels me to let my beast rise. As flames wreathe my head, I wink at the child.

Wonder fills her eyes. Her bow of a mouth curves into a sweet smile. Just as she starts toward me, her mother appears and tugs the child back into line with the others.

I shove my dragon down, pressing into the shadows as the mother and children hurry past.

More villagers pass. People going about their business. A few call out greetings, but no one pauses to speak. "Open" signs hang in shop windows, but no customers come and go. And every villagers' clothing is as worn and tattered as my selsara's.

Something's wrong. From above, this town would appear to be cared-for and thriving. But standing here at street level, I see another story and it sours my gut.

Treasure-hoarding thieves, the lot of you.

The memory of the thief's penetrating sea-blue eyes hits me like a punch.

Lirem, Varden, and Nazzar reported an exceptional harvest. The humans should have been ready for winter. The villagers should be relaxing before their fireplaces with full bellies and fat bank accounts.

The scene before me doesn't match my enforcers' reports. Not at all.

The sun dips behind the treeline and casts long shadows across the town's square. The number of humans criss-crossing the street dwindles until the streets are bare. My skin prickles with the need to stalk the village and find my selsara. But it's clear I won't catch another glimpse of chocolate-brown waves tonight.

With a final look at the square, I leave the alley and return to the orchard. The unicorns doze beneath the trees. A half-eaten apple dangles from Cornelius's lips. I pull it out and toss it away lest he choke. Then I find a clearing, fling my cloak off, and call to my beast.

It answers right away. The change roars through me, claws and wings replacing my weaker form. Now, the ground is dozens of feet below. Soil flies as I take a running leap and burst into the sky. On the horizon, my selsara's village sparkles with light as dusk slides into true night.

Treasure-hoarding thieves, the lot of you.

Beau's village is one of many in my syndicate. Nazzar said this plane is ripe for the taking. What has he been taking from my people? Are Lirem and Varden party to his deception?

As I beat my wings against the frigid wind, icy resolve fills me. Nazzar was right about one thing. I've been a fool. I kept my distance from my people, and now it looks like they've suffered for it. My *selsara* has suffered for it. The wind gusts harder as I wheel in the sky, my gaze on the distant lights that mark the next village. Before this night is through, I'm going to find out just how big of a fool I've been.

CHAPTER 6
BEAU

The scent of cinnamon and nutmeg fills the air of the bakery. Humming, I pull a sheet of hot cross buns from the oven. The golden-brown crusts glisten, the butter-and-sugar glaze sparkling in the morning sunlight.

Perfect.

Bits of diced apple peek from the bread as I place the sheet on a cooling rack. Whirring sounds drift through the bakery's back door, which I propped to release some of the hot air from the oven. Shuffling backward, I look through the doorway to Dad's workshop on the edge of the cottage's tiny garden.

The whirring echoes across the short distance. Worry gnaws at me as I stare at the shop's closed door. Although, maybe I shouldn't worry. Dad woke at dawn and practically skipped from the cottage. One bowl of spiced apples cured his cough and restored his energy.

"Where did you get apples, son?" he asked when I handed him the bowl last night. A tremor went through him, and he glanced at the window before lowering his voice to a whisper. "You didn't go to the orchard, did you?"

"Of course not," I said, the lie like acid on my tongue. I nodded toward the bowl. "*Eat before it gets cold.*"

As the whirring continues, I return to the buns. The oven pops and creaks as I grab a knife from the counter and scoop a dollop of frosting from a mixing bowl. As I spread frosting over the cooling buns, I eye the bowl that holds the apples I diced when I returned from the orchard yesterday.

I made twenty batches of stewed apples last night, and the bowl never emptied. As cinnamon wafted from the bakery, neighbors appeared. Within minutes, I had enough coin to buy flour and butter. The ten pies I baked sold in under an hour. After another trip to the grocer's, I filled the bakery's shelves with cakes, apple muffins, and loaves of bread.

And the bowl of apples stayed full to the top.

Glittering green eyes appear in my mind. Lord Fuoco's words echo through my head. *"Whatever is mine is yours. Anything you need, selsara, you come to me."*

The orchard is a forbidden place. The dragon lord executes people for taking apples, yet he stuffed six of them into my pockets. He stood between me and Nazzar when the yellow-eyed dragon would have carved me up—or worse.

And Fuoco called me that strange name. *Selsara.* What does it mean? He didn't look like he wanted to kill me yesterday. He looked like he wanted to…devour me—and not in a way a dragon might ordinarily devour someone.

Frosting splats on the counter. Shaking myself, I grab a rag and wipe up the mess. *That's my Beau*, my mother always said. *If his head's not in a book, it's in the clouds.*

I have no business daydreaming about Lord Fuoco. Whatever his reasons for giving me the apples, he didn't…desire me. My cheeks heat as I dip the knife and spread more frosting on the buns. But even as I work the sugary confection into the grooves, phantom hands brush my legs. When Fuoco touched me, I forgot to be afraid.

The oven creaks, but I ignore it as I finish the buns and load them onto one of my mother's round serving platters. The "old beast" as Dad calls it has been temperamental today, heating up too quickly and taking forever to cool down, but I've got too many orders to fuss with it now.

"Hello?" a voice calls from the front of the bakery. Grabbing the platter, I hurry from the kitchen and into the main part of the shop.

A slender young man with pale hair and bright blue eyes stands before a shelf of muffins. He's dressed head-to-toe in black leather that hugs his lean but muscular body. His black, fur-trimmed coat looks like it was tailored just for him. Slits in the fabric allow a pair of iridescent wings to rise gracefully from his back. His ears are pierced, and a studded choker circles his neck. He turns as I enter. Immediately, his jewel-bright eyes drop to the platter of hot cross buns in my hands.

"Buns!" Smiling, he strolls to me, plucks a bun from the platter, and holds it up. He gives it a squeeze and winks at me. "And they're glazed. You naughty boy, you."

"You're a pixie," I say stupidly. He's beautiful. Ethereal. But not my type. As quickly as the thought comes, I shove it away.

He turns slightly, showing his wings that flutter and stir the air. "Guilty as charged." He peers at the bun in his hand. "Are these apple-flavored?"

Words stick in my throat. I curl my fingers around the edge of the platter as my heart beats faster. "Yes." *I did nothing wrong.* And I have no reason to fear this stranger. Pixies are known for mischief, not murder. I nod toward the shelves. "I have other flavors, too, if you don't like apples."

"Oh, I love apples." He waves his bun toward the broken window, which I tacked a sheet over. "Kid throw a rock?"

"Something like that."

"Bummer." He waves his bun again, gesturing around the shop. "Looks like business is booming, though. Kind of unusual for this neck of the woods, huh?"

"We had a decent harvest this year." Face flaming, I heft the platter. "I should put these out for display."

He steps aside. "Be our guest."

I start forward. A beat later, I stop as his words register. "Our?" My nape prickles. Fun-loving party-goers they might be, but pixies are part of the Myth. And no creature from the other side of the Veil is completely trustworthy.

Something squeaks. Before I can locate the sound, the pixie bends and scoops something from the floor. As he straightens, small, dark eyes peer at me from between his fingers.

"It's all right, little guy," the pixie says softly. "Beau is a friend."

I startle at his use of my name, which I definitely didn't tell him. Before I can puzzle it out, he opens his hand to reveal a small, gray mouse perching on his palm. Long whiskers twitch, and a pink nose wriggles as the mouse appears to take my measure. Abruptly, it turns to the pixie and releases a series of high-pitched squeaks.

The pixie raises sculpted brows. "Well, how should I know?" Another squeak, and the pixie gives the mouse a stern look. Behind him, his wings flutter rapidly, the delicate edges turning red. "No, and it's rude to ask."

The mouse sticks its head in the air and curls its tail tightly around its furry body.

"Fine," the pixie sighs. "Be that way." He looks at me. "I'll take some raisin bread if you have it." The mouse perks up, its whiskers twitching once more. A smile plays around the pixie's mouth. "Raisin bread is Bert's favorite."

For a second, I can only look between the pixie and the mouse. Then I clear my throat. "Of course." Nodding, I back up a step, bump into a display of muffins, then turn and go to the shelves where I keep the bread. I grab one, then look over my shoulder at the duo. "Uh...do you want the whole loaf?"

"Yes, please." The pixie angles his free hand against one side of his mouth and speaks in a stage whisper around it. "Bert's doing one of those low carb diets, but I know he'll bitch later if I don't buy the whole thing."

An angry squeak splits the air as I pull the loaf from the shelf and go to the cash register. After a few more bewildering moments, the pixie smiles as he accepts the paper bag of bread. "Thanks, gorgeous. This will come in handy when I'm waiting to speak to Lord Fuoco."

My stomach does a flip. "Fuoco?"

The pixie nods. "He was supposed to give me an audience yesterday, but he never showed up. And his courtiers were all sleeping off hangovers, so they were no help. Dragons, am I right?"

Curiosity blossoms inside me. I push the register drawer shut and will myself to keep my mouth shut too. But then I open it and ask, "Why do you need an audience?"

"Flight arrangements." The pixie jerks a thumb at his wings. "These are pretty, but they won't get me to Europe." He rolls his eyes. "And let me tell you, if I hear one more dragon make a joke about *endurance*, I will hex the everloving shit out of Fuoco's princess castle. A bunch of stand-up comedians, those metal-gazing nerds. And they have a lot of nerve because those horny fuckers…"

As he prattles on, my head fills with images of what Fuoco might look like in flight. Dragonback is the only reliable way to cross the ocean. After the Veil fell, human airplanes could no longer fly. The magic in the air warps the metal.

"Would Fuoco take you?" I blurt, interrupting the pixie's tirade. For some reason, the thought of the elegant male on the dragon lord's back fills me with a heavy, uncomfortable heat.

"Doubtful," the pixie says, tucking the mouse in his front shirt pocket. He points a manicured nail decorated with a tiny pink heart at the rodent. "Stay in there this time. You know you can't tolerate the cold." The pixie meets my eyes, and something twinkles in his. "Fuoco isn't one to give rides. But you never know. He might make an exception for the right man."

My heart pounds, the heavy heat streaking to inconvenient places.

The pixie's wings beat the air, shedding glitter that sparkles in the sun. "Gotta run. Dragons get so shitty when you keep them waiting." He goes to the door. On the threshold, he turns and gives me another wink. "Thanks again for the bread, gorgeous." With a final swish of his wings, he leaves.

I stand at the counter, staring blindly after him. The right *man*, he said. Not person. Is Fuoco…gay? The pixie certainly was. Although, maybe I shouldn't assume. But something tells me the leather-clad male would be perfectly fine with the assumption. He wasn't ashamed. He definitely wasn't interested in hiding. A smile pulls at my lips as I picture him strutting through the village with his painted nails and a mouse in his pocket. I look at my hand on the counter—at my plain, square fingernails and my hand covered in tiny, waxy burns from various oven accidents. Even if I wanted to, I could never be like the pixie.

With a sigh, I turn toward the kitchen.

BOOM.

A gust of wind picks me up and hurls me backward. Time slows, and glass spins around me as I fly through the air. A second later, I land hard and sprawl on my back. For a second, I just lie there, my head spinning and my lungs trying to inflate. The fall knocked the wind out of me. What the *hell* just happened?

"Beau!" My father's voice reaches me, and then he kneels at my side. "Beau… Oh gods." Panic fills his eyes as he shakes my shoulder. "Speak to me, son. Are you all right?"

"Fi…" I swallow, tasting copper. "I'm fine." I wiggle my toes and then hold back a sob of relief when they move in my shoes. My back isn't broken. That's a good sign, right?

My father's face crumples. "This is all my fault."

Footsteps and the crunch of glass fill my ears. Cold winter wind gusts over me, raising goosebumps on my skin. The grocer and his teenage son appear and gaze down at me with troubled expressions. A second later, the cobbler shows up, his face smeared with something bright green and sparkly. It glints in the sunlight as he shoots my father an angry look.

"This was your doing, Maurice!" The cobbler points to his green-streaked jaw, then to me. "That explosion took out the wall of my barn and almost killed your son."

Explosion?

Dread rises as I sit up. The cobbler steps back, revealing the rear of the bakery. As I take it in, nausea burns my throat.

The kitchen is *gone*, nothing but gray winter sky beyond the bakery. Smoke billows around the hole where the kitchen used to be, the tendrils floating up and into the air. Bright-green sludge covers the floorboards and splatters over my loaves, muffins, and cakes.

Bright green. I've seen that color before—in a beaker in my father's workshop.

Slowly, I turn to my father. "Dad," I say carefully, "what did you do?"

Tears fill his eyes. "I was only trying to help." As he wrings his hands, several more villagers step through the hole in the wall. Great. Now a crowd is forming.

"Dad," I say more loudly. "What. Did. You. Do?"

My father bows his head. "It was supposed to fix the oven," he says in a small voice.

My breath catches. "The fuel?" Anger surges, turning my voice into a growl. "You put *experimental* fuel in my oven? Magical fuel?"

The cobbler sucks in a breath. "We don't truck with magic around here, Maurice."

My father lifts his head and gives the cobbler an indignant look. "There is nothing wrong with magic."

"There is when you blow up my fucking bakery!" I yell. As all heads swing toward me, I clamber to my feet. Pain shoots through my skull—and just about every other part of my body—but I push it aside as I limp to the wreckage. Silence reigns, the only sound the occasional whistle of wind coming from outside—or I guess *inside* now, since my father just destroyed my livelihood.

Despair chokes me. There is no coming back from this. I can't bake without an oven. Not even a bowl of bottomless apples can save me.

I freeze, and a single word pounds through my head.

Selsara.

Lord Fuoco's voice was soft and reverent when he called me that. *"Whatever is mine is yours. Anything you need, selsara, you come to me."*

The dragons are rich. An oven is nothing to a male like Lord Fuoco. *Whatever is mine is yours.* That's not the sort of thing someone says when they want to roast you alive. Maybe he meant it. Maybe I should go ask him. What else do I have to lose? Because right now it feels like I've already lost everything. The pixie didn't seem frightened about having an audience with Fuoco. Why can't I have one too?

Anything you need, selsara, you come to me.

As bright-green sludge creeps toward the toe of my shoe, I square my shoulders. Time to find out if Fuoco is a man of his word.

∽

A half hour later, I stare up at Lord Fuoco's castle with my heart trying to pound its way from my chest. The castle's pale stone sparkles in the late morning sun. Towers of various heights soar above a main keep so large it could house the village a hundred times over. Mullioned windows glitter like diamonds. As my gaze wanders over the imposing structure, I'm fairly certain I've lost my mind. The explosion knocked me senseless, and now I'm going to walk into a dragon's castle and ask him to replace my oven.

Hysterical laughter bubbles in my throat. I force it down as the wind picks up, its icy fingers delving under the jacket I threw over my rumpled clothes.

Clothes that are now splattered with sparkly green goop. Angling my head down, I pick at a drying spot on my shirt. I should have changed before leaving the village. Lord Fuoco might interpret my sloppy appearance as an insult.

But it's too late to turn back now. And if I do, I know I won't work up the courage to try this again. So, I run my fingers through my hair, doing my best to smooth the thick waves without the benefit of a comb or mirror. That task complete, I draw a deep breath and move forward.

The castle gates loom, the scrolling metalwork like something out of a fairy tale. Until today, I've never ventured close enough to Lord Fuoco's home to see the gates. As a child, I sometimes climbed the hills on the outskirts of the village so I could stare at the castle and dream of living in something so grand one day. That was before I realized ordinary boys from tiny villages don't grow up to live in castles.

The gates are flung wide, and no one stops me as I continue my approach. Colorful gardens border the path to the castle, the blooms as bright as gemstones. No...they *are* gemstones I realize with growing awe. Rubies curl into tight rosebuds. A few others are in full bloom, the multifaceted petals casting a red glow over their neighbors. Amethysts and sapphires mimic foxglove and hydrangea, their petals glittering in the sun. The blooms shouldn't be able to stand upright. In an ordinary world, the gems would be too heavy to wave in the breeze. But these are magic flowers. Dad would love them.

The thought of my father sobers me, and I tear my gaze from the flowers and pick up my pace. A thick curtain wall surrounds the main keep. In the center, an open archway shows a glimpse of a large, airy courtyard. My heart pounds harder as I head toward the opening, nerves prickling as I wait for guards to appear.

But no one comes, and I pass through the arch and enter the courtyard unmolested. As I stop and look around, a sense of unease lifts the hair on my nape. The castle is enormous, and the courtyard is sized to fit. Gray flagstones stretch as long and wide as one of the old football fields that dot the ruins of human settlements from before the War That Ripped the Veil.

Fuoco is rumored to command an army of servants. But no one moves about. Aside from sunlight streaming through patches of blue sky, the courtyard is deserted.

The cavernous space is beautiful but austere, with high walls made of smooth white marble. Dragon statues stand sentinel at every corner, their wings folded around bodies that glint with jewels. The nearest statue depicts a blue dragon with wings veined in gold. I don't need to venture closer to know the gold is real. As I wander deeper into the courtyard, the beast's eyes appear to track my progress.

Blood rushes in my ears. Movement in my peripheral vision makes me whirl toward the source. On the far side of the courtyard, a thick metal post rises from the ground. Manacles dangle from a chain fastened at the top. Around the base of the post, the flagstones are solid black.

From being repeatedly scorched by dragon fire. A cold sweat breaks out on my forehead as I realize I'm staring at the spot where John Robinson died.

The spot where Lord Fuoco burned him alive.

Trap. This is a trap. And I'm an idiot. Just as I turn to run, a hand clamps down on my shoulder. I'm spun around, and then shoulder-length blond hair and a pair of glittering ruby-red eyes fill my vision.

Lirem's mouth twists in a malicious smile. He holds my stare as he lifts his voice. "Look what I caught."

Booted footsteps ring out. A second later, a dragon enforcer with dark hair and bright purple eyes appears next to Lirem. My heart stutters. It's Varden. He's even bigger than Lirem, with a broad chest and a square jaw shaded with stubble. Dark-purple scales peek from the collar of his shirt, which strains over thick biceps. His gaze is cold and hard, and his voice drips with contempt as he rakes his gaze down my body.

"This one looks like he got into some magic."

As I bristle at being spoken about like a misbehaving dog, Lirem tightens his grip on my shoulder. He hauls me closer and uses his other hand to flip my coat open. He gives a vicious chuckle as he takes in the green mess staining my clothes. "What happened, boy? You wander into the path of a spell gone wrong?"

"It's nothing," I grind out. And I'm an even bigger fool than I thought. If they find out Dad was using unauthorized magic, there's no telling what they'll do.

"Looks like something to me," Varden says. He widens his eyes and places a gloved hand over his chest. "You wouldn't lie to us, would you, human?" He turns to Lirem. "I think our friend here is lying to us."

Lirem's red eyes gleam, little fires dancing in the ruby depths. "We don't like liars, boy."

I'm not a boy. The words stick in my throat as fear sinks its claws deep. Swallowing my pride, I lower my gaze. "I-I'm sorry. I didn't mean—"

"Didn't mean to lie? Or didn't mean to trespass?"

I jerk my head up. "I'm not—"

"Yes, you are," Varden says. "You entered the castle grounds."

"Without permission," Lirem adds.

Varden heaves a put-upon sigh. "I think we have to teach him a lesson, Lir."

"No," I gasp, tugging at Lirem's grip. "No, please—"

"Shut up," he growls. As if they rehearsed it, he and Varden hook their arms under mine and drag me between them, sweeping me off my feet as they hustle me backward. I can't see where they're taking me, but I already know. Seconds later, my back hits the post. Metal clanks and then Lirem yanks my arms above my head. Cold steel burns my wrists. My bowels go watery as visions of fire and torture dance in my head. These two can't burn me with dragon flame, but they're capable of hurting me all the same.

They step back, their eyes burning with hatred. Varden yanks one of his leather gloves off and slaps me across the face with it. I cry out, not from pain but the sheer humiliation of it. I'm not good enough—not man enough—for a punch.

But that comes a second later. Lirem's arm blurs. Pain explodes in my gut. I jerk, instinct driving my shoulders forward as I try to curl over the pain. But the manacles bite into my wrists, keeping me upright. Before I can catch my breath, my head snaps back. Metal clanks as my vision blurs and numbness spreads through my jaw. It's going to hurt later. Everything is going to hurt so much.

The blows keep coming, fists pummeling me. My feet scrabble on the blackened flagstones as I twist and turn, helplessly absorbing the enforcers' punches and slaps. Deep, masculine laughter accompanies my hoarse cries. Flashes of purple and red punctuate the bursts of agony. The enforcers' gem-bright eyes shine with hatred that sinks almost as deep as their fists.

Endure. I have to endure. This can't go on forever. Dad needs me. I do my best to dodge their fists, but the hits come too quickly. Darkness huddles at the edges of my vision. It beckons, and I want to answer its call. In the darkness, I won't feel any pain.

The dull thuds of the enforcers' fists grow fainter. My screams seem to echo, as if they come from someone else. The darkness swells, and I reach for it. A roar builds, the sound louder than anything I've heard. Louder than the oven exploding.

The ground shakes, but I pay it no mind as I stretch toward the blackness.

CHAPTER 7
FUOCO

Bulleting through the early morning sky, I focus on my castle's stony spires when they come into view. I built a territory and home where my people and the humans were supposed to coexist peacefully. After what I've seen over the past several hours, that false peace tastes like ash in my mouth.

I flew all night going from village to village, hiding in shadows to observe the human towns. Each village was more destitute than the last—empty storefronts with ragged interiors and homes that only appeared well-tended at a cursory glance. Rage simmers under my skin, fire building in my throat. The ominous black clouds overhead match the stony sensation in the pit of my belly.

Sometime in the night, I decided I'll confront Lirem and Varden in front of my court versus privately. Their demise will send a message, and I'll pick off anyone else who shares their beliefs. I'll trace the rot all the way through my people, and only those who truly believe in equality can remain.

Treasure-hoarding thieves, the lot of you.

Those words haven't stopped ringing in my ears. I don't know if they ever will—or if they should. They'll hang like a weight around my neck, reminding me of my neglect.

My shadow looms over the open courtyard as I swoop low to land. Lirem and Varden stand before the post, their fists clenched at their sides as they step away from a chained, limp man.

No. Not just any man.

Beau.

My selsara. Bloody and groaning, his head lolls from side to side.

Lirem and Varden look up as I race toward the ground. Varden waves a hello, as if beating a man is commonplace.

Bellowing, I snap my wings close to my body and land with a thud, shoving my head between Beau and my enforcers. Lirem and Varden stumble backward, twin expressions of shock on their faces.

My mate groans, a pained sound that yanks at my soul and has me spinning around. Protective instincts burst through my rage as I snuffle Beau gently, running my snout up his neck. Blood flows freely from a wound along his hairline, and I scent my enforcers' hands all over him.

Die.

As it did with Nazzar, the red madness descends over my vision. Roaring in fury, I spin and swipe my tail in an arc, knocking both Lirem and Varden to the ground. In a flash, I curl my tail behind them, trapping them where they lie.

Varden leaps to his feet and throws both hands in the air. "My lord, this man came onto castle grounds without permission."

Lurching forward, I open my mouth and let a stream of fire erupt from my throat. Varden screams as he burns, skin melting from his bones, blood dripping to sizzle on hot stones. His voice fails as his throat caves in, bone turning to liquid.

I jerk my head toward Lirem. He's burned but he moves quickly, dipping under my chin as Varden crashes to the ground. I swivel, catching sight of Lirem as he darts behind Beau. Lirem's red eyes glitter as he glances around, looking for a way out.

There is no way out for him. No survival for the sin of touching my mate. If I were in human form, I'd cackle like a madman.

Madness beckons now, red tendrils snaking into my veins. Urging me to call the elements and dispose of this vermin as I did with Nazzar. I could do it. I could call *everything*. Water and earth. Air and fire. I could make sure no one ever touches what's mine again. The rage builds, its call growing louder. *Do it*, the rage whispers. I should. I'll summon the air to cleave Lirem's limbs from his body. Then I'll present the pieces to my selsara like bloody jewels.

Beau's grunt punches through the rage. My selsara sways against the pole as he struggles to lift his head. Lirem hovers behind him, the skin on one side of his face blackened and bubbled. Fucking coward, using my mate as a shield. Growling, I whip my tail around the pole, stabbing the sharp tip into Lirem's side and knocking him sideways. The moment he's away from Beau, I slap him again, tossing him across the courtyard like a rag doll. He hits the far wall with a scream and slides to the black stones, unconscious.

I'll deal with him in a moment.

Shifting quickly to human form, I rush to Beau and rip his manacles in half. He falls forward into my arms, his head dropping to my shoulder. Chocolate hair is matted with blood. His face is swollen, his handsome features distorted.

They beat him for daring to enter my home. Knowing what I know now about how the enforcers have treated the humans, I'm amazed he had the bravery to come here.

Fury storms through me, the red madness threatening to overtake my reason. I hoist Beau higher in my arms and turn back to the courtyard.

The spot where Lirem fell is empty. He's gone.

I roar as my beast rises, intent on finding Lirem so I can shred his muscles from his bones. He hurt my Beau, my selsara. The red tendrils of my elemental power slither up my spine like snakes.

Beau stirs, the movement drawing my attention to him. His eyelashes flutter, and I hold my breath as he opens his eyes. He stiffens, his pupils blowing wide as he stares up at me. A second later, he comes alive, pushing against my chest as he tries to squirm from my arms.

"Easy, selsara," I croon, crossing the courtyard. "I will keep you safe."

He pauses, one hand on my chest and his gaze locked with mine. His eyes are so fucking beautiful—the color of melted chocolate in the center with flecks of black and gold along the outer rim. I could lose myself in his eyes.

But he reeks of fear, the scent acrid and bitter in my nostrils.

"Y-You can put me down. I'm able to walk." His voice wavers, his lower lip trembling.

I don't slow as I enter the castle. "I don't think so, selsara. You need a healer."

His throat works as he swallows. "I shouldn't have come here. I didn't mean to cause you trouble." He keeps his hand on my chest, his skin warm against mine. I wonder if he realizes he's touching me? Seeking me.

I shift him higher, curling my arms around his lithe frame. His thighs and back are strong and supple under my palms. "You could never trouble me, Beau. It's my pleasure to be at your service."

He does more wide-eyed staring. "But…" He clamps his mouth shut, another gust of fear lifting from him. He's clearly terrified of me. Watching me burn Varden and fling Lirem across the courtyard probably didn't help. He doesn't know how I spent last night, or the deception I uncovered.

And he doesn't understand why I spared his life—or why he's in my arms right now.

I'll remedy that as soon as possible. Desire spikes as I head toward the castle's infirmary. First, I'll make sure Beau is healthy and whole. Then I'll deal with Lirem. After that, I'll court my little mate, replacing his fears and doubts with pleasure.

I hook a right down a candlelit hall and stop in front of a glossy black door. I shoulder inside, calling for the healer as I move down two rows of empty beds.

A tall dragon strides from an antechamber, surprise filling his gaze as he sees me naked with Beau in my arms.

"Dieter," I say, giving him a nod. "I require assistance."

"Of course, my lord." He moves briskly, rolling up his sleeves as he gestures for me to set Beau on one of the beds.

I lower him carefully onto a plush mattress and step back. "Dieter has served my house for hundreds of years. He's an excellent medic. In my castle, he treats not only the dragons but also my human servants."

Confusion moves through Beau's eyes as he shifts backward, propping his shoulders against the bed's metal frame. "You give your servants health care?"

"Yes." And his confusion makes sense. Now that I know the depth of my enforcers' betrayal, any gesture of goodwill toward my servants probably comes as a shock. I hold my selsara's gaze. "We have much to talk about, Beau."

Dieter clears his throat as he hovers on the other side of the bed. When I meet his stare, he looks from me to Beau and back, curiosity in his diamond-bright eyes.

"Selsara," I murmur, folding my arms.

Dieter says nothing but he lifts a brow as he finishes rolling his sleeves. When he turns to Beau, there's none of the typical dismissive, casual dragon arrogance. He's yet another excellent asset I stole from my father's court. Like me, Dieter wanted a new world with new rules.

He smiles at Beau as he sits on the edge of the bed near Beau's hip. "Many dragons are blessed with magical gifts. As you've probably guessed, mine is healing." Dieter runs an assessing gaze over Beau's face. "I can treat your injuries, but I'll need to place a hand on your stomach and another on your forehead. Is that alright?"

Beau looks up at me. My heart squeezes as I give him a nod of encouragement. He draws a deep breath and turns back to Dieter. "Yes. Go ahead." He holds himself stiffly, and he jolts when Dieter lays hands on him.

Having been on the receiving end of Dieter's skills a time or two, I know Beau will feel the heat of the magic coursing through his veins as it mends his injuries. Sure enough, his cheeks flush a brilliant scarlet, and his plump lips fall open. His brows knit together as the wound on his temple closes, but he remains still as Dieter works his magic.

A long moment later, Dieter pulls his hands away and stands. "You need rest. Healing magic takes its own sort of toll. But you'll be right as rain come morning."

Wonder spreads over Beau's face as he touches his temple. He lowers his hand and stares at his fingers. "No blood." He gives a bemused laugh as he extends his arms, moving and stretching like he expects to feel pain. Finally, he looks at Dieter with wonder in his eyes. "Can you heal everything?"

Dieter smiles. "Not everything. But most human ailments." The healer's smile fades. "Although, the servants don't come to me as often as I'd like."

My blood freezes, because the truth is far worse than Dieter knows. The humans in my syndicate avoid him because they've been taught to fear dragons. And their terror is justified. My enforcers have stolen and taken and ravaged, and it happened while I distanced myself so I *wouldn't* terrify people I swore to protect.

Beau offers Dieter a shy smile. "Well, that's amazing. I'm so grateful for your help. Thank you."

"You are most welcome." Dieter rounds the bed, a knowing look in his eyes as he claps my shoulder and makes a quick exit. Beau watches him go, nipping at his lower lip as the door closes behind the healer.

I have to touch him. Now that he's healed, the instinct to pleasure and protect is overwhelming. I settle on the mattress, my thigh brushing his. When he sucks in a breath, I plant one hand on the other side of his hips and lean forward. "Why did you seek me out today, Beau? How may I serve you?" My gaze drops to his lips. The upper one is slightly plumper than the lower.

And I'm still naked—and getting harder by the second. I'm also tall enough that he can't get away, so I surge forward until my lips nearly brush his. "Anything," I murmur. "Ask and it's yours."

He darts a look down my body, his gaze landing on my dick before bouncing right back up. A flush spreads over his cheeks. He gulps, and the bob of his throat makes me bite back a groan. "My father is sick," he blurts. "And my oven exploded." Another gulp. "I'm a baker."

A smile spreads through me. "Ah, the apples are making sense. Tell me, sweet one, did you bake him an apple pie after we met?"

Beau's flush grows deeper, trailing down his neck into his threadbare shirt. He clutches at the bedding, twisting the sheet in his hands. "Yes."

I place my hand on both of his, stilling his nervous movements. "It's okay. Whatever you need, I'll provide for you." I brush my fingers over his knuckles and place the lightest kiss on the corner of his mouth. *"Whatever* you need," I say as I draw back.

His breath hitches. A delicious scent fills the air—something sugary and spicy all at once. I drag it into my lungs, letting it fill me up. If I'm not mistaken, my beautiful mate is just as affected as I am. His blush deepens, highlighting the tiny golden freckles that dust his nose.

He's so sweet for me. So shy. Fucking irresistible.

I put a finger under his chin. "I love the colors your skin turns, selsara. Reading your emotions is like reading my favorite book."

Black eyelashes flutter. "You can read my mind? Is that"—he sucks in another breath—"dragon magic?"

"It's not *my* magic," I say. "Mine is something else entirely, and I can't wait to show it to you. For now, let me help your father and see to your oven."

Hope fills his eyes. "You really think your healer will be able to help my father?"

I move my fingers to his jaw, stroking along the firm curve and then down the side of his neck. Soft, supple skin begs for my fangs and claws. I can't wait to introduce him to the pleasures of being mine.

But I won't lie to him either. "I can't say with certainty, selsara, but dragon healing magic is very powerful."

He licks his lips. "What does that mean? Selsara?"

I drag my thumb over his plump lower lip, touching the spot he swiped with his tongue. His mouth is so soft, so kissable. It would be easy to lean in and claim his lips. My dragon rumbles under the surface, eager to taste him. I force my beast back as I hold Beau's gaze. "Selsara is an ancient dragon word for mate."

Beau pales. "Mate?" he croaks, his jaw dropping before he snaps it shut. He presses himself against the bed frame, making the metal squeak in protest. "What, exactly, does that mean?"

Regret pummels me. He's afraid. Wariness I might understand. Few humans mingle extensively with creatures of the Myth. And mating a dragon would give most people pause. But Beau's fear stems from experience. His tattered clothing is a glaring reminder of the hardships he's endured at my enforcers' hands. And he has no reason to believe I'm any different.

I can tell him things will be different now. But words are empty vessels. They mean more when they're filled with action. I have to earn his trust before I can win his heart.

That realization brings a fresh wave of yearning. How long will I have to wait to have this beautiful, gentle man in my bed? Under my hands?

The answer comes right away. *As long as it takes.* I want to fuck him. Kiss him until he's breathless and begging. Instead, I ease back and let my longing seep into my voice. "It means we belong together," I say quietly.

His lips part. He draws a shaky breath, then speaks in a voice as low as mine. "You… You're…gay?" That fierce blush surges back, and he bites at his lip again. "You like men?"

"I like you," I rumble, staring at his mouth. When he makes a choking sound, I tear my eyes away from temptation. His cheeks are so red, I might almost think he's inexperienced. But that's ridiculous. He's not a teenager. I smile and lift a shoulder. "I suppose humans would call me bisexual. I've taken both female and male lovers over the centuries. Dragons call them consorts. But that's all in the past, Beau. Now that I've found you, I'll take no others."

His lips part again, but no words emerge. He's not recoiling in horror. On the contrary, the spicy-sweet scent of his arousal reaches me, curling into my lungs and getting under my skin. Good. That's where I want it.

I grasp his knee as I hold his gaze. "So to answer your question, selsara, yes. I am very, *very* gay."

CHAPTER 8
BEAU

The next morning, I cling to Fuoco's long, black claw as my breakfast tries to escape the confines of my sloshing stomach. My whole life, I thought coming face to face with a dragon was the most terrifying thing I could experience. Now I know I was wrong.

Flying through the air in the curve of a dragon's paw is definitely the most terrifying thing a person can experience. I grip Fuoco's claw as we soar over the syndicate, the world reduced to neat squares and thin ribbons of road beneath us. Up here, his territory looks rich and peaceful, with green fields dusted with snow. Mountains loom in the distance, their snowy caps wreathed by clouds. I huddle in my borrowed cloak, which keeps the chill at bay. But I hardly need the garment with Fuoco carrying me. His massive body is like a furnace, his scales hot to the touch. Warm and rested, I'm free to enjoy the view.

But it's not like I have a choice. Ever since I entered Lord Fuoco's castle, I've been under his command. Or as he put it, his "care."

"I can't allow it, selsara," he said last night when I asked to return home to check on my father. "Not when you're still weak from your injuries." He scooped me off the bed in the infirmary and tucked me under the blankets. He stood back, the brilliant green scales on his upper body shimmering in the light streaming through the windows. "You heard Dieter. You need rest."

"But my father—"

"Will be well. I'll send someone to check on him."

Alarm bolted through me. "A dragon?"

Fuoco gave me a tender look as he brushed my hair back from my head. "He won't be disturbed. You have my word. Now, what are your favorite things to eat?"

He ordered a feast from his kitchens. Then he watched me dine, his green eyes following every forkful until I protested that I couldn't possibly eat anymore. Afterward, he excused himself only to return moments later fully clothed and carrying a lute. He arranged his big body on the bed next to mine and strummed beautiful, haunting songs that lulled me into a peaceful sleep.

This morning brought another delicious meal—and his announcement that we would fly into the village to fetch my father.

"Would that please you, selsara?" he asked, his voice husky with dawn's first light.

It did please me. But as I followed him to the courtyard and watched him shed his clothes and shift, apprehension twisted my gut.

It twists again now, nerves joining the brewing revolt. Lord Fuoco has been nothing but courteous. But how long is that courtesy going to last? If I'm really his mate—and I have no reason to think he's lying—he's not going to be content sleeping in the bed next to mine. He's going to want us to share a bed…and do a lot more than sleep. He's twice my size. If he wants me that way, I have no hope of stopping him.

Heat blasts my cheeks, then runs a fiery path down my limbs. Memories of Fuoco's nude body fill my mind, images of his golden skin, broad chest, and pierced nipples popping into my head like they're spring-loaded. But the vision that jumps to the front of the line is his heavy, round penis. His *pierced* penis.

As blood pumps to my very ordinary, very unmodified member, I squeeze Fuoco's claw. His wings beat the air, the great whooshing sound keeping time with my heart, which pounds as I recall his long shaft and the bulbous tip decorated with a golden, bejeweled ring.

More gems glittered at his wrists and in his ear, but I barely noticed. And as I drifted to sleep with the sound of his lute in my ears, my mind supplied me with other visions. Fantasies. Forbidden things I had no business picturing. Like me on my knees pressing my lips to that ring. Maybe licking it. Licking him. Would he let me do that? A whimper escapes me as I imagine taking him into my mouth and tasting all that he has to offer.

Without warning, a massive wing swoops into my vision. Fuoco's claws curl more tightly around me as he wheels in the air. His other wing beats steadily, rotating us slowly as he lowers his head and peers at me with glowing emerald eyes. As we hover in the sky, a question forms in the gem-bright depths, and the tiny row of horns above his brow lift in an arch. His expression is unmistakable, as is his inquiry. *Are you all right?*

"Yes," I rasp, then clear my throat and raise my voice over the roar of his flapping wing. "Yes! Fine!"

He huffs, sending warm air gusting over my face. His snout looms closer, making panic jump down my spine. But he merely snuffles me, sending more hot air rushing through my hair and down my neck. The sensation is mild and more than a little ticklish, and I release an embarrassing giggle before I push his snout away.

"I said I'm fine!" His scales around his snout are smaller than the ones on his flank, and I run my fingers over the rough, bumpy ridges. He groans and leans into me, nudging his face against my hand in a universal gesture. *Pet.* Laughing, I smooth my palm over his snout. When his green eyes go heavy-lidded, I do it again. And again. I spend a few moments like that, nestled in the safety of his paw as I stroke his face.

"Better?" I ask after a minute.

Green eyes gleam with gratitude that warms me more than his body heat. With another gentle snuffle of my hair, he spreads both wings and propels us through the sky. Moments later, we touch down on the outskirts of the village. He deposits me carefully, and I clutch the packet of his clothes as he lumbers away and shifts.

The transformation is magical, which makes sense considering it's pure magic. But as he rolls his shoulders and shakes out his arms, his human form seems just as magical as his beast. For one thing, he's just so *big*. Everywhere. I run my gaze over his lats and delts, heat prickling through me as I take in the thick curves of his biceps. He runs both hands through his hair, smoothing the strands that are several shades darker than mine. But when he rescued me in the courtyard, his hair was *fire*. Crackling green flames that glowed as brightly as his eyes.

Goosebumps lift on my skin as he turns and strides nude toward me, his thick shaft bobbing against his thigh.

"Here," I blurt, thrusting the packet of clothes toward him. He takes it, tosses it on the ground, and cups his hands around my jaw.

"You okay?" he asks softly.

"Me?" I blink rapidly, a hundred different emotions firing in my brain. Shock, confusion, and arousal. More than a little stupidity. "Yeah," I gasp. "I'm good. Thank you."

His eyes stay serious. Steady. "Good," he rumbles, stroking his thumbs over my cheeks. "I'm glad." He doesn't move. Just continues gazing into my eyes, the pads of his thumbs tracing my cheekbones in tiny caresses that make me suddenly aware of every cell in my body—and *acutely* aware that he's nude in the road with the village a mere shout away.

"Um." I swallow thickly. "Are you going to get dressed?"

"No."

I blink again. "No?"

He shakes his head.

"But…why not?"

"Because I'd rather do this." He bends and slants his mouth across mine. I gasp, and he pushes his tongue into my mouth—gently at first and then deeper as I tilt my head and open under the pressure of his lips. He spears his fingers through my hair, his touch sending shivers down my spine, and then he strokes his tongue along mine in a hot, wet caress.

It's a passionate kiss. My *first* kiss. And it's everything I ever wanted. A man's lips on mine. A man's tongue in my mouth. A moan winds its way up from my throat, and I clutch at his shoulders as he answers my moan with one of his own. He slides his big hand to my nape and squeezes as he slides his tongue against mine, his strokes bold and demanding.

At last, he pulls back, sucking gently at my bottom lip before cradling my face in his hands. My heart thumps wildly as he regards me with bright emerald eyes. "Forgive me, Beau. I promised myself I would woo you properly. But you're so damn tempting I couldn't resist."

Heat floods my cheeks. I bite my tongue so I don't tell him I wouldn't mind if he kissed me again. I lick my lips, tasting mint and something dark and rich. I want to twine my arms around his neck and pull his head down so I can taste it again.

He steps back, releasing me with a sigh. "We should go before we're discovered." Humor gleams in his eyes as he scoops the packet of clothes from the ground. "We don't want to cause a scandal."

I look away as he dresses, my face flaming with a different kind of heat. It's too late to avoid a scandal. Walking through the village with Lord Fuoco at my side will start tongues wagging right away. And the second people learn I'm his mate, the whole village will know I'm—

A low noise escapes me before I can stop it.

"What is it?" Fuoco asks, instantly alert. When I press my lips together, he takes my arm. "Beau?"

"I..." Words stick in my throat, but I force them out. "Could we... Would it be all right if we wait to tell people about the selsara thing? Or at least keep it from my father for a little while?"

Understanding spreads over Fuoco's features. "Your father doesn't know you are gay."

"No," I murmur, dropping my gaze to the ground. "No one knows."

He tips my chin up, and his green eyes are soft as he says, "It's okay. We don't have to tell anyone else about our relationship until you're ready. You can take as much time as you need."

I nod, some of my anxiety ebbing away. But it rushes right back when we enter the village. As predicted, Fuoco turns heads. People I've known my whole life stop and gawk as the dragon lord prowls at my side. Several people gasp, turn on their heels, and flee in the other direction. But most simply stare as if they've seen a ghost.

I receive my share of stares, too. Eyes move from Fuoco to me—and then over my new cloak that probably costs more than everything in my cottage combined. Shock and disapproval radiates from familiar faces. I lower my gaze, my cheeks burning.

"Steady, Beau," Fuoco murmurs beside me. He matches my pace as I hurry us through the square and down the narrow alley that leads to the bakery. When we reach it, he stops me with a hand on my arm. He looks over the storefront with its simple stone walls, wooden shutters, and thatched roof that leaks during heavy rains. Broken glass litters the sidewalk. The sheet I tacked over the broken window hangs limply, exposing the interior. Fuoco's gaze fixes on the sagging cloth. "You live here?"

"Yes." Movement inside has me starting forward again. As I cross the street, Gastonia's face appears in the open window. She gapes at Fuoco, her mouth falling open. By the time I step inside, her shock has transformed to wariness—and something that might be anger.

"Beau," she says, swallowing hastily. She sets a half-eaten pastry on a shelf behind her and dusts sugar from her fingers. "Where have you been?"

"With me," Fuoco rumbles, entering behind me and resting a warm palm in the small of my back.

Gastonia's blue eyes shoot there like a laser. Her mouth tightens as she lifts her gaze and gives me a piercing look. "Everyone wondered where you went. People have been talking." She glances at Fuoco's hand on my back and offers a tight, humorless smile. "I expect they'll talk even more now."

My gut clenches but I keep my mouth shut as I gaze around. If possible, the place looks worse than yesterday. Broken crockery litters the slime-splattered floors. Flour sifts in the air. A blue tarp stretches across the back of the shop, blocking the view to the garden.

"My father brought it over," Gastonia says, following my gaze. "He wanted to help."

"And then you helped yourself to Beau's inventory," Fuoco says, stepping forward. His boots crunch over broken porcelain, and his long cloak swings around his leather-clad legs. He's so big he takes up half the bakery.

Gastonia's cheeks color as they face off. She lifts her chin, her blue eyes defiant. "My father always said *you* were the thief."

My heart lodges in my throat. "Gastonia—"

"Your father is right," Fuoco says. As I stare, speechless, he steps closer to Gastonia, who has to tip her head back to meet his eyes. Emerald-green scales spread down his neck as he speaks in a quiet voice that's somehow more terrifying than a shout. "But Beau belongs to me now. And I don't share what is mine."

The hair on my arms lifts as his words hang in the air, the warning unmistakable.

Gastonia's nostrils flare. Just when I think she might actually be stupid enough to insult Fuoco, she turns to me. "My father's help doesn't come for free. You owe us for the tarp."

Anger kindles in my chest. I pay my bills. I might have to ask for more time, but I've never shorted anyone. And I didn't ask for her "help."

The floor vibrates. Somewhere in the bakery, dishes rattle. Fuoco leans toward Gastonia, his voice even softer than before. "If there is a fee for your *services*, madam, send the bill to the castle."

Tension fills the air. Gastonia stands her ground even as hints of fear swim through her eyes. At her side, she curls her hand into a fist. I'm not entirely certain she won't swing it. When Cory Lannigan called her "Trash-tonia" in third grade, she knocked his tooth out. But Fuoco isn't Cory. The dragon lord is utterly still, his big body throwing off enough menace to collapse the bakery's three remaining walls.

A cough echoes from behind the tarp.

Dad.

I move without thinking, crunching over pottery as I race to the rear of the shop and fling the tarp aside. Dad shuffles toward me, his head down as he picks his way across our sorry excuse for a garden.

"Dad!" I rush to his side and take his arm. His shoulders are rounded, his straight posture from yesterday gone. His worn-out sweater hangs on him, the once-brown yarn gone tan from hundreds of trips through the ancient washing machine he rigged up. White tufts of hair stick out from his head.

But his eyes light up as he places a gnarled hand over mine. "Beau! I was so worried, son."

Guilt swamps me. Out of habit, I smooth his hair back, tucking the tufts into place. "I'm sorry. I got…caught up."

Dad's smile fades as he looks past me. Surprise spreads over his features. "You've brought company."

I sense Fuoco before I see him. Heat warms me from head to ankle, the force of the dragon lord's presence cranking higher as he appears at my side and offers my father a bow straight from a medieval court.

"Fuoco of House Drakoni, sir. I am most honored to meet you."

Dad's snowy eyebrows soar to his hairline. He recovers quickly, offering Fuoco a nod as the dragon lord straightens. "Maurice Bidbury of…well, this garden. And I'm honored to meet you, as well, my lord."

"Fuoco," Fuoco corrects softly, his tone filled with the kind of respect a polite young man might offer an elder. Except Fuoco is no such thing. He has to be hundreds—maybe thousands—of years old. Which is almost as surreal as the fact that he thinks we're destined to be together.

Dad coughs suddenly, his shoulders shaking. Fuoco reacts before I can, wrapping his big arm around Dad's shoulders. I hover helplessly, equal parts worried about my father and mesmerized by the sight of Fuoco supporting him as Dad's smaller frame is racked by a coughing fit. The apples' magic should have lasted longer. Which means my father's cough isn't just a cough. I gnaw at my bottom lip as tears burn my throat.

Eventually, the rattling sound subsides. Dad wipes at his brow. "Forgive me. The winter is never kind to my old lungs."

Fuoco's voice is gentle as he eases Dad away from him. "You should see the castle healer. Dieter's gift is powerful. His services are at your disposal if you wish it, sir."

Dad looks at me, questions in his eyes. "Is that where you went last night, Beau? The castle?"

Discomfort squirms through me. "Yes," I say, feeling like a teenager who sneaked out of the house in the middle of the night. "I, um, met the healer. He—" I cut myself off before I can admit Dieter helped me after the other dragons beat me up. "He's really nice," I finish lamely.

More questions fill Dad's eyes. For a second, I think he'll demand to know just what is going on here. But then he smiles and gives a little shrug. "What do I have to lose?" He turns his smile to Fuoco. "If this healer of yours can fix me, I'd love to meet him."

Fuoco's smile is warm enough to heat the whole garden. "It will be my pleasure to fly you and Beau to the castle."

Dad gathers a few things from his bedroom. Gastonia is gone when we walk through the bakery, and there's no sign of her in the village. But as we cross the road, something makes me look over my shoulder.

Gastonia stands in the shadows under the awning of Robert's bookshop, her blue eyes narrowed. As our gazes collide, she gives me a look filled with so much malice my blood runs cold.

Then she turns and walks away.

CHAPTER 9
FUOCO

Beau's father is dying. Whatever ails him fills my mouth with a sickly, acrid taste. Air doesn't flow through his lungs like it should. They're obstructed by disease. He doesn't have long. Urgency drives me to rush Beau and his father to the closest clearing.

I throw my clothes off to shift, ignoring how Maurice stares in shock at my nude body. My dragon rises, and I let the change flow over me. When I tower over my selsara and his sire, I uncurl one claw in invitation. Beau tucks my clothing under his arm and helps his father carefully into my palm.

When I dreamed of him over the centuries, our flights together were sensual. He should be astride me now, his thighs gripping my back and his long fingers stroking my scales. The sky should belong to the two of us and no one else. Having him near and being unable to touch him the way I wish is a particularly brutal torture.

The need to pursue Beau gnaws at me from the inside out. It's selfish, but my beast doesn't care about manners. My selsara is within my grasp—literally—and I've yet to claim him. Every instinct I possess urges me to fly to my mountain lair and make the gorgeous man in my palm *MINE*. But I shove instinct away and streak toward the castle.

When we arrive, I swoop down to the courtyard and deposit Beau and Maurice on the stones. When I shift back, Beau is waiting with my clothes. He averts his eyes as I pull them on, his high cheekbones stained with pink.

Maurice studies the blackened stones where Varden's ashes have settled into the cracks. He lifts wary eyes to Beau, who glances at me.

"I burned one of my enforcers there," I say, buttoning my pants. "That's why the stones are black."

Maurice swallows but says nothing. He and Beau exchange another cautious look.

"He hurt Beau," I say, fresh anger searing my gut. "I'd burn him again without a second thought." *And zero remorse.*

Maurice pales. He opens his mouth—

"It was nothing, Dad," Beau says. "We'll talk about it later. Right now, you need a doctor."

Anger moves through Maurice's eyes as he stares at his son. "It doesn't sound like nothing." He looks at me. "This enforcer is dead?"

"Very."

"Good."

Understanding passes between us. Maurice nods, and I return the gesture as I go to him and sweep him into my arms.

His anger drops away, replaced with sputtering indignation as I stride toward the castle. "My lord, this is most unnecessary! I may be old but I can still walk."

I look down at my selsara's father. "Maurice, you're very ill. You have a disease of the lungs, and I'd rather you not strain yourself walking to the infirmary."

Beau jogs to catch up to us, his brow furrowed in worry. "You're certain that's what's wrong?"

I look at my mate and nod. "I can hear the air in his lungs." Nobody in the castle knows I'm an elemental dragon, and now isn't the time to divulge my gift. I'll tell Beau when we're alone and he's not focused on his father.

Neither man speaks, but anxiety is a cloud around us as we move through the castle. Servants catch sight of us and gasp, quickly dodging from my path and disappearing like ghosts.

By the time we reach the wing that houses the infirmary, anger dogs my steps. Anger that the humans are terrified of me. Anger that I didn't see what my enforcers were doing. Anger that I tried to rule kindly and ended up failing the syndicate despite it. Maybe because of it.

I was the weakest egg in my clutch but my mother's favorite because of my kindness. She saw it as a strength instead of a weakness. But it doesn't feel that way now. Perhaps if I'd been a little more bloodthirsty and untrusting like my father or brothers, none of this would have happened.

I'm growling by the time I shove through the infirmary door.

Dieter stands at the ready. From the look on his face, he heard me stomping down the hall. His diamond-bright eyes go to Maurice right away.

"Dieter," Beau says, worry thick in his tone. "This is my father, Maurice. He's—"

"Dying," I finish bluntly. "Please do what you can, Dieter." I set Maurice carefully down on an empty bed.

Beau rushes to his side. He grabs one of Maurice's hands and brings it to his chest.

My heart aches at my mate's distress. I want to whisk him to bed and banish his worries with my mouth. But I keep my hands to myself as I face my selsara across the bed.

As he did with Beau, Dieter explains his process to Maurice, then lays hands on the sickly man. Maurice hisses in a breath but holds steady as Dieter's magic probes.

"Easy, Dad," Beau says quietly.

After a moment, Dieter straightens and regards Maurice with serious eyes. "You have cancer of the lungs." His voice gentles. "Untreated, you won't survive the winter."

Both men gasp. Beau's eyes fill with tears.

"Selsara," I whisper, aching to touch him.

Maurice regards me with a curious expression before focusing on Dieter. His lower lip wobbles slightly. "You said untreated? Do you have a treatment? Or do I need to make arrangements—"

"Dad!" Beau rasps, clutching Maurice's hand to his chest. "Don't even say that!"

Dieter inclines his head. "I can heal your cancer, Maurice. But you'll need multiple treatments over the course of two or three weeks. If you agree, we'll get started right now."

Tears spill down Beau's cheeks. Maurice releases a shaky breath. "Of course. I'd be incredibly grateful. I'm in awe that you can do this." He frowns. "I don't know how I'll ever repay you."

"You won't," I say gruffly, and all eyes turn to me. "There's no charge for this."

Surprise covers Maurice's features. "But—"

"No charge."

Maurice studies me, confusion and gratitude in eyes that remind me of Beau's. Then he turns to his son, something like hope filling his voice. "If this works, we can go home and fix the bakery. I'll be able to help this time. And things will be different, Beau. No more experiments with magic."

Beau squeezes his father's hand. "Don't worry about it, Dad."

"But I want to…"

Panic grips me as Maurice continues, his expression earnest as he explains how he'll help Beau restore the bakery. Beau listens patiently. Receptively.

Is he actually thinking of returning to the village?

Leaving me?

Panic blooms into something thick and hot. My beast rises, fire crackling just under my skin. My selsara—the mate Fate promised me —is thinking of leaving my home. *Our* home. Doesn't he realize that everything I own is his? Every possession, every gemstone, I've procured over the centuries is for him. And now he'll walk away from the life I've built for us so he can bake apple tarts?

He can't. He *won't*. The panic claws at me, digging bloody furrows into my heart, which my selsara is doing his best to break. A growl brews in my throat. My hands curl into fists as he stares at his father with love beaming from his eyes. He's never looked at me that way. That look is *mine*. He should be lying in our bed, his gorgeous brown eyes shining with love. With obsession.

Fear beats at me, the prospect of Beau rejecting our bond washing over me in acid waves until I want to pull the castle down around us brick by brick. I can't lose him. Not for his father or any other reason. Maybe the old legends are true. Maybe elemental power is a curse. Because the horrible dread simmering under my skin doesn't give a shit about Maurice or Dieter or any of the fucking villages that dot my syndicate. It wants Beau, and it doesn't care if it has to burn the world to ash to claim him. The waves pummel me...and then shift into icy, pitch-black focus.

It centers on Beau, propelling me around the bed just as Maurice says, "We could go back sooner if—"

"Absolutely not," I snap, grabbing Beau's arm and hauling him up. He stumbles into me, his eyes wide. Dimly, I'm aware of shocked gasps and Dieter moving out of the way. Beau gapes at me, his gaze traveling up...

"Your hair," he says hoarsely.

Flames crackle around my head. My beast moves restlessly beneath my skin. The hot, acidic panic chokes me, turning my voice to gravel as I look at Maurice.

"Beau isn't going anywhere. Dieter will heal you, and then you can go home if you wish. But Beau stays."

The old man shrinks against the pillows.

Fears me.

Beau is stiff at my side, reluctance rolling off him. He would leave me if he could. He was *planning* it.

"Come," I bark, tugging him to the door. I throw Dieter a look over my shoulder. "Heal the father. We'll be back later."

"Beau!" Maurice calls. Dieter's deeper voice rumbles assurances behind me as I clench my teeth and hustle Beau from the infirmary. It takes everything I have not to toss him over my shoulder—or shift to beast form and fly him to the mountains. I settle for keeping him locked against my side as I move through the labyrinth of corridors. Beau struggles to keep up, his breathing growing labored. I slow my strides but I don't look at him. I can't. Not until I get him alone. Not until I regain control.

But the sharp scent of his fear clogs my throat. *My fault.* He has every reason to be terrified, and I've just made it worse.

I stop before the next chamber and fling the door open. As it crashes against the wall, a maid whirls from where she stands polishing a candelabra. She fumbles the piece, almost dropping it as she stutters. "L-Lord Fuoco! Oh gods, I'm so sorry."

"Out!"

With a squeak, she rushes from the room, trailing more of that sour stench of fear. *Always* fear.

And now my selsara smells of it.

He wants to leave me.

"You *can't*," I growl, pushing him against the wall. I trap him there, my hands on either side of his head. My chest heaves as I bury my nose in his neck, hunting for his natural scent under the layers of worry and fear.

There.

Rich spices and hints of sugar. He must bake with it often. Sweetness clings to him.

He trembles against the wall, his heart a rapid beat in my ears.

"You can't leave," I croak against his skin. "I won't allow it." I drag his essence into my lungs, letting it soothe me. Slowly, the panic and the rising haze of madness recede. I keep my hands on the wall as I lift my head and meet Beau's gaze. "Lirem is still out there. I can't let you return to the village."

"But you'll let me go once you find him, right?"

Never. I don't say it. But my silence says it anyway.

He raises his chin a fraction of an inch. "Am I a prisoner, then?"

"No." *Maybe.*

Probably.

His dark brows angle into an irritated vee. "If I can't leave, I'm a prisoner."

The panic roars back, obliterating my tenuous calm. I shove my larger frame against his lithe body, pressing him hard against the wall. Dipping my head, I brush my lips over his. "Not a prisoner." As if I'd ever lock him away. No, I want to show him everything. I want to court him properly—to guide him through the elaborate mating rituals of my people. But he's definitely not ready for *that*. Not just yet.

I move my lips to his jaw and slowly drag my mouth over his stubble. When he shivers under me, my cock goes painfully hard. "You're mine." I lift away so I can see his eyes. "And I'm yours."

He winces. "You said you wouldn't tell my father about the selsara thing. But the way you acted in the infirmary…"

Regret sluices through me, bringing clarity with it. "I'm sorry. Do you think he'll guess?"

Beau offers a wry smile. "My father is eccentric, but he's not a fool." Beau's smile fades. "Life hasn't been easy for him. I worry this will only make it worse when he returns to the village."

"Then he won't. He'll live here in the castle."

Beau frowns again, anger stirring in his eyes. "You might be able to force me to stay here, but you can't impose your will on my father. We have a life in the village—"

"Not *we*. You're not going back to that miserable place." Gods, how could he even consider it when he can live in luxury with me?

He lifts his chin, chocolate eyes sparking with defiance. "It might seem miserable to you, but it's my home. I have a business to run."

"What business?" I demand, frustration rising. "Your oven is blown to pieces. Your supplies are covered in broken glass. Tell me, what are you rushing back to? Slime-coated floors and tarp-covered walls?"

His defiance turns to anger. "The walls can be repaired. As for supplies, I'll get apples from the orchard."

"Not from mine, you won't."

His nostrils flare. "You would really do that to me? Bar me from the orchard?"

"You know the penalty for stealing." Gods, I'm such a dick. But I can't stop. Words pour from me like poison, threats spilling out as I fight the urge to do exactly what he accuses me of wanting to do and lock him away so he *cannot* leave me. "There's nothing for you in that village, Beau. Your place is here. Your father requires my help. Stay and I'll see to it he receives it."

The color drains from Beau's face. "You're blackmailing me into staying with you? Are you serious? You'll hold the threat of my father's *life* over my head unless I do what you want?"

It's wrong. So, so wrong. But if I have to threaten him to secure his compliance, I will. Because he can't run from me. If he tries, the whole fucking world could be in danger.

From me.

"My beast is…restless," I say. *An understatement.* "I need time alone with you." I stroke chocolate waves away from his face as I scan his gaze. "Stay and Dieter will heal your father. Maurice will want for nothing."

Beau jerks his head, evading my caress.

I grit my teeth and straighten, putting space between us. "You don't need the bakery. Anything you desire, I will provide. You're my selsara. Everything I own is yours."

He folds his arms, his lean muscles bulging against his borrowed shirt. "Do most dragons capture their mates and lock them up until they agree? Is that how this is going to go?"

This is all wrong. This is how other dragons behave. I know better. I should be wooing him, not forcing him. Then again, I didn't anticipate having him inches away and still out of my reach.

"Yes," I rasp, the admission scraped from the back of my throat. "Most dragons are cruel, selfish, and possessive. I've always thought I was better than that, but the idea of you returning to that run-down cottage is more than I can bear."

He regards me with a stony expression, his jaw tight as he stands against the wall.

"Dragons dream of our selsara before we meet them," I say, hoping he can hear the truth in my words. "I have been dreaming of you for centuries. Daydreams. Dreams in the middle of the night. For so long, it was just glimpses of you from behind my closed lids. Flickers of your form in the fire. But now I see you, and I am *enraptured* by what I see."

His lips part. Slowly, he unfolds his arms.

"To have you here in my home and asking to leave is…" I grope for an adequate description. But seven hells, there isn't one. I capture his hand and place it over my heart. "This beats only for you, Beau. And for the rest of my life it will *only* be you for me. Allow me to woo you properly. We'll take it as slowly as you wish, but please don't ask me to watch you leave."

His fingers curl against my chest. Seconds pass, each one an eternity as he appears to think it over. Then steel enters his eyes. "You'll heal my father?"

"Stay with me."

"And you'll heal him?"

I nod. "I swear it."

Beau inhales deeply, then jerks his head once in agreement. "I'll stay. Just…heal him. Please."

Triumph unfurls in my chest. Humans don't make binding vows like creatures of the Myth, but I know he means it. Then again, his father is the center of his world right now.

It should be me. *All in good time.* Beau hasn't dreamed of me for centuries. I can tell him what he means to me, but it'll be a lot more effective if I show him. Deeds over words.

I lace my fingers with his. "Come. Let me give you a tour of your new home."

After a moment's hesitation, he nods. "All right."

The castle is quiet as I lead him through the various chambers. Servants move about, but the members of my court are absent. Of course, word of me finding my selsara has likely spread. My courtiers are creatures of the Myth. They understand how dangerous it is to get between a dragon and his mate.

When Beau and I reach the Great Hall, I gesture to the long table that sits on a dais before the massive hearth. "This is where I take my meals with the court. Everyone usually eats together."

His stomach rumbles. He slaps a hand over it, a blush spreading over his cheeks.

"Are you hungry?" I guide him to a sideboard where servants have set out trays of fruit and cheese. "Take whatever you want."

He doesn't wait. Pulling his hand from mine, he plucks a pear from the tray and takes a healthy bite. His eyes slide shut as he chews, and he gives a low groan that streaks straight to my dick. Juice dribbles from the corner of his mouth.

I can't help myself. Surging forward, I cup my hands around his jaw. Brown eyes fly open as I lick the juice away. When he gasps, I trail my lips down the column of his neck. *So fucking sweet.* I suck at his skin, groaning at the taste of him. His pulse throbs against my mouth, the beat thumping faster. My cock presses painfully against the front of my trousers.

Beau freezes in my grasp, his throat bobbing. His erection brushes mine. I want nothing more than to reach down and grip his hard length. Stroke him to release. But he's clearly starving, and I need privacy for the things I want to do to him. Releasing him, I run my fingers down his throat before stepping back.

"Forgive me, Beau. I was overcome." I gesture to the pear in his hand. "Please finish."

Once again, he doesn't hesitate. He sinks his teeth into the fruit, taking oversize bites and chewing quickly. He devours the pear and then darts his eyes to the tray.

"Another one?" I ask. I point to a platter stacked with small mountains of cubed cheese. "Or maybe some cheese?"

He gives me a grateful look and takes a cube. He eats it—then another…and another. I take the pear core from him so he can grab more food. He finishes off a cheese mountain, along with a second pear. He eats like a man possessed—or someone who's known the gnawing, aching pain of true hunger. When was the last time he enjoyed a full meal?

"Easy, selsara," I murmur as he reaches for a second cheese mountain. "You'll make yourself sick."

Beau nods, his flush reappearing as he withdraws his hand. "You're right. I don't want to overdo it. It's just… I've never seen so much food in one place."

I follow his gaze to the table. Three meager platters sit there. The servants leave the fruit and cheese for courtiers to tide them over between big meals. Few bother with it. Most of the court keep to their rooms during the day, only emerging at night to feast and make merry. *While the rest of my people starve.*

Gods, what have I done?

Choking back regret, I take his hand. It's sticky with pear juice, so I lift it to my mouth and suck his fingers clean.

Beau grunts, his pupils blowing wide as his flush spreads down his neck.

I finish cleaning him, never pulling my gaze from his. He watches my mouth with parted lips, his breaths rapid and shallow. His arousal drifts around me, the scent sweeter than the fruit.

He wants me—but he also wants to leave me. And why shouldn't he? I made his father's treatment contingent on Beau agreeing to remain in the castle.

I'm a monster.

"Beau," I murmur, nipping at one slim fingertip.

He flicks heavy-lidded eyes to mine. "Yeah?" He clears his throat, a frown forming between his brows as he tugs his hand from my grip. "Yes?"

"Come on." I tip my head toward the big double doors on the other side of the Hall. "There's a lot more I'd like to show you."

There are tasks ahead of me that I don't relish—hunting Lirem chief among them. But for the next few hours, I'll pursue Beau. I have to make him understand why he belongs here, with me.

I show him the rest of the main castle, and then I lead him to the greenhouse. His eyes go wide as we step through the doorway. He stops and stares at the rows of fruit and vegetables like they're chests full of gold coins.

"You grew all of this?"

"The castle is self-sustaining. We grow everything we need."

"Gods," he mutters. "This is incredible. All this food."

Guilt burns my gut. "My enforcers told me the villages brought in a record harvest. I didn't know things were so dire."

Beau's expression is guarded. "You really didn't know?"

I shake my head. "When I first took over the syndicate, I attempted to rule alone. I carried on like that for almost 150 years, but the humans were terrified of me. I brought my enforcers on board because they were from lower houses. They're smaller and less intimidating. And I thought they were different from other dragons." Bitterness wells as I offer Beau a tight, humorless smile. "I was wrong."

"Is that why you burned the one and attacked the other when you found me in the courtyard?"

The guilt in my gut threatens to twist into rage. "Not entirely. They touched you." *Put their hands on what's mine.* "I trusted them, and now I know it was blind trust. That won't happen again."

Beau watches me, the sunlight streaming through the glass walls highlighting the golden flecks in his chocolate irises. "It's not a bad thing to trust, Fuoco."

"It is when it leads to abuse. I killed Nazzar after he threatened you in the orchard. I burned Varden to ash. Lirem will die for what he did to you and others. Once that's done, I can figure out how to make amends."

He gives no response, and he seems lost in thought as we wander the rows of plants. When we reach a line of peach trees, I pluck a fat, fuzzy fruit from a branch and hand it to him.

"If you'd like to bake, all of this is at your disposal. The castle's kitchen should have everything you need."

He studies the fruit, then hands it back. "Why bake if I can't sell anything?"

My heart sinks. He's still angry. And he still thinks he needs to work—that he should repair that decrepit cottage he considers his home.

His home is here. The sooner he accepts it, the better.

I tuck the peach in my pocket. "Maybe you could bake for pleasure and not because you have to in order to survive."

He holds my gaze, his brown eyes steady. "Maybe."

Tension arcs between us. Anger, mostly. But there's desire in there, too.

I can work with that.

I hold my hand out. "Come, selsara. There's one last room I want you to see."

Despite the moment's tension, he places his hand in mine. "What is it?"

I turn toward the doors that lead to my private wing of the castle. As we leave the greenhouse, I slant him a look. "Our bedchamber."

CHAPTER 10
BEAU

Fuoco's bedchamber is even more opulent than the rest of the castle. It's also the size of the village.

Well, maybe half the size of the village. I pause on the threshold, my senses overwhelmed by the decadence sprawling before me. The room is all rich, dark colors and sumptuous-looking fabrics. Heavy drapes adorn the windows. Candles flicker on various surfaces. A marble-topped vanity with an enormous jeweled mirror stands in one corner. In another corner, a grand piano with glossy black lacquer reflects the candlelight. A crystal chandelier descends from a large medallion in the center of the ceiling.

But it's the bed that makes my mouth go dry. It dominates one wall, its four posts rising like regal sentinels. A purple canopy drapes around them, the thick panels descending to the plush carpet. The black headboard is carved with symbols that lift the hair on my nape.

"Does it please you?" Fuoco asks, moving around me. He means the room but that doesn't stop my face from heating as I tear my gaze from the bed. He's as beautiful as his bedroom, his green eyes flickering with remnants of the intensity he displayed in the infirmary. His hair is normal again, thankfully, the eerie flames snuffed out. But he's still intimidating in leather pants and a white shirt unbuttoned enough to show the emerald-green scales that cover his broad chest. His nipple piercings are shadows under the finely woven fabric.

Before I can stop myself, I lower my gaze to the thick bulge between his legs, my head filling with images of the shiny ring that adorns the tip of his dick.

"I want you to like it," Fuoco adds softly, stepping toward me.

I jerk my head up, my gaze colliding with his. The intensity is back, the green depths glittering. My heart skips a beat as I realize he's not talking about the room anymore. He moves closer, his body heat caressing mine. He's always so warm. Of course he is, I think, nervous laughter bubbling up. He's a dragon. A big, powerful dragon who says he's *enraptured* with me.

I swallow hard. "Does it matter if I like it?"

"It matters," he says, curling a finger under my chin. He tilts my head back gently. "But I don't just want you to like it, baby."

My breath shudders out, my lungs deflating as that *baby* slides under my skin.

"I want you to love it," he murmurs.

Desire beats a hard rhythm inside me. My knees loosen, fear and arousal swirling as I stare into his glittering green eyes that promise all sorts of wicked, forbidden things. Warmth spreads through me, chasing away the tight, frozen anger I *know* I should be feeling. He deserves it. He kidnapped me but says he wants to protect me. He dangles love before me when his most recent actions have been anything but loving.

And yet...

"Are you doing this?" I ask. "Making me feel this way?"

Slowly, he shakes his head. "That's not my magic, selsara. And even if it was, I would never force your hand in this."

But you'll force it in other things.

He waits, little flames dancing in his eyes. Something hot and absolutely ancient hovers there, its gaze so possessive it steals my breath. *His beast*, I realize. A dragon has me in its sights. Memories rise—snippets of passages I've read about dragons in the books Robert lends me. Dragons hoard treasure. They covet glittering, shiny things. But they reserve all their avarice for their beloved, fated mates. *And woe betide the fool who steps between a dragon and his most precious treasure.*

"Selsara," he says, the word delivered in a broken whisper. And then he lowers his head and claims my mouth. The kiss is gentle at first, his soft lips brushing against mine as if testing the waters. When I gasp, he deepens the kiss. He skims his hands up my sides to my hair as his tongue teases its way into my mouth. After a few easy caresses, he strokes his tongue boldly, his long fingers cradling my head. When I move my tongue tentatively against his, he gives a low groan—the sound undeniably needy.

He wants me. Desperately, I think of all the reasons I shouldn't want him back. He's holding me hostage. He barred me from his orchard. He won't help my father unless I stay.

He groans and sucks at my tongue. Need clenches in my belly. Dimly, I'm aware he's walking me backward across the carpet, his thighs brushing mine. His *dick* brushing mine.

And I'm hard—harder than I've ever been. I shouldn't want this, but my body doesn't seem to care that I've been blackmailed and bullied into this arrangement. Not at all. For only the second time in my life, I've got a man's tongue in my mouth and a man's body—a large, muscled body—driving mine backward, and all I can think about is getting more.

Fuoco gives it to me, pulling me tightly against him just as my back meets the wall. His kiss turns hot and demanding, his tongue plunging deep as he grinds his erection into mine. He seizes my hips and rocks against me, letting me feel every hard inch. I grip his shoulders for balance as I melt into him, my self-control spiraling away.

His heat seeps into my skin. Sweat beads on my forehead. I'm going to burst into flames and I don't care even a little bit. My head goes fuzzy, lust and anticipation obliterating rational thought. His hand works between our bodies, and then he palms me through my pants.

Gods. Maybe I say it, the word swallowed by his tongue and the lust that's drowning me. He pulls back, and I chase his mouth, a broken whimper breaking from me as he takes his heat with him.

But he keeps his hand on my dick. He braces his other hand on the wall and stares at me with swollen lips and eyes dancing with green fire. We're both panting, our breaths mingling.

He looks at me for a long time, his big hand cupping my erection. Then he leans closer, not stopping until his lips graze mine. "Do you love it?"

The question rumbles against my mouth and streaks straight to my cock.

"Yes," I whisper, the admission wrung from the bottom of my soul. I've fought so hard not to like this, but I can't deny it. And I don't want to anymore. He moves his hand from the wall to my jaw. Easing back a bit, he trails his fingers to my mouth and presses a thumb between my lips.

I suck on his thumb, tasting salt and fire. Imagining sinking to my knees and sucking his cock this way. The mere thought of it drags a deep groan from my chest.

"Baby," Fuoco breathes, his eyes narrowing to burning emerald slits. He pushes his thumb deeper, forcing my jaw wider.

A shudder rolls through me. My heart races as I swirl my tongue around his thumb. I'm in uncharted territory and I'm probably messing this up.

But Fuoco doesn't seem to think so. His breathing grows ragged as he watches me suck and lick. His hand on my dick tightens…and then begins to stroke, his fingers digging in just enough to make me moan as he pumps up and down in a slow, steady rhythm.

"*Ungh*," is all I can manage as I buck my hips, thrusting my dick into his hand with an eagerness I should be embarrassed about. And if he keeps touching me, I *will* embarrass myself.

He seems to understand my predicament, because he steps back and pulls his hands away. Gaze still locked with mine, he fists the bottom of his shirt and yanks it over his head. Hard pecs and washboard abs covered in dragon scale reflect the candlelight. His skin is sun-kissed, the hollows of his muscles dark spaces I want to explore with my hands and tongue. I want to touch him everywhere—to feel all that heat and muscle under my palms. Fuoco claims he's dreamed of me. Well, maybe I've dreamed of him, too. Alone at night when no one can see, I've dreamed of feeling a man's body against mine.

Touching flat, broad chests. Kissing a man's stomach. A man's cock. Feeling the weight and heft of one other than my own.

Fuoco's big hands go to the button of his pants. And tires screech in my mind, spiky nerves throwing up barriers that make me suck in a breath.

Fuoco frowns, his hands stilling. "Beau?"

Words stick in my throat. My erection flags as fear and frustration grip me. Just when I finally have an opportunity to do all the things I've fantasized about, my courage deserts me. Because I don't know what to do. I don't know the first thing about anything. Fuoco is hundreds, maybe thousands, of years old. Experienced. And I'm...me.

Fuoco's expression changes, understanding spreading through his eyes. He steps into me again and cups my jaw. "You've never been with a man."

I swallow hard. "Or...anyone."

His eyes go wide. "Never?"

"Never," I whisper, and the sound is pitiful. *I'm* pitiful—and so far out of my depth it's laughable.

Fuoco doesn't laugh. He brings his other hand to my face and feathers his thumb over my burning cheekbone. Tenderness shines from his eyes as he gazes down at me. "Beau," he murmurs, and his voice is as soft and gentle as his hands on my face. He lowers his head and brushes his lips over mine in a kiss that's over almost before it begins. But it's enough to make my heart flutter.

He brushes his nose against mine. "You have no idea how beautiful you are, do you?"

I shake my head, my face flaming. I know I'm not ugly. Plenty of women have looked my way. It would have been so much easier if I wanted to look back.

But no one has ever looked at me like this dragon.

"Let me show you," he says. Slowly, he reaches down and grasps my hand. Gaze locked with mine, he places it on his cock, which is rock-hard and burning hot through his pants. At my swift intake of air, he gives a shaky laugh. "*That's* what you do to me, Beau."

My heart pounds. Fuoco's heat sears my fingers.

"What do you want?" he asks. "Tell me and I'll help you explore it." His thumb strokes my cheek, his touch featherlight. "You can trust me, Beau. I'll never hurt you."

He won't. I've never been more certain of something. He's violent and dangerous. He burned his enforcer before my eyes. But he'll never turn that brutality on me.

"Yes," I rasp, and I don't know what I'm agreeing to—or asking for. Maybe I'm asking for everything.

He gives me another tender smile. "Come on," he says softly, taking my hand and leading me to the bed. He pulls the bedding back and pats the white, pristine sheets. "Lie down."

Heart racing, I obey, crawling into the center of the mattress that's as big as my bakery. He follows, stretching on his side with his elbow propped and his head resting on his hand. With another smile, he extends his free hand in invitation. "Come here."

I can hardly breathe as I let him tug me against him. My head lands in the crook of his shoulder as he wraps me in his arms, holding me close against his bare chest. His scales are softer in this form, the brilliant colors ranging from the lightest green to the deepest emerald. His heartbeat thrums beneath my ear, the beat steady and strong. For several long moments, he simply strokes my hair. Then, when I sigh and settle more deeply into his embrace, he starts his exploration.

He touches me everywhere—soft brushes of his fingertips against my temple, my neck, my chest just under the collar of my shirt. He unbuttons it with quick fingers, then lifts me and whisks it away, leaving us chest to chest. My skin tingles, heat spreading through me so swiftly I wonder if *my* hair might turn to flames.

"Gorgeous," Fuoco murmurs, circling one of my nipples before pinching it lightly.

"Oh!" I squirm against him, little rivers of pleasure flowing under my skin.

Fuoco does it again, his gaze riveted on my face. He watches me closely, as if he's waiting for any sign of discomfort or regret.

But those things don't exist to me. They're impossible. And I'm *lost* in his arms, my body perched on the edge of something unknown and intense. I'm no stranger to orgasms. But this is so very different from the way I touch myself.

"You like that?" he murmurs, plucking at my other nipple.

"Yeah." I shudder and grind my hips into his, feeling his dick and needing *more* and *now*.

But he takes his time, tracing patterns that feel like he's painting stories on my skin. My dick aches as desire rushes back, and it's not long before I'm panting and aching. Then I'm begging.

"Please," I moan, my breath hitching.

He rolls me under him so quickly I gasp. My back arches as he presses my hands over my head. "Leave them there," he says, a playful smile on his face. The playfulness fades as he unbuttons my pants. He pauses, his glowing green eyes lifting to mine. "Do you want this?"

I give a jerky nod. "Yes. Yes, I want it."

He pulls my pants off, then my underwear, and then I'm nude beneath him, my dick hard and red. Moisture clings to the tip. He pushes my thighs wide and settles between them.

"I want to touch you," he murmurs, leaning in and pressing a soft kiss to the thatch of dark curls above my shaft. He nuzzles the base of my dick, and his breath tickles my heated skin. "Let me touch you."

"Yes," I croak, and I couldn't look away if I tried. I stare down my body, scarcely able to believe the sight of him between my legs. I bite my lip hard as I study the bulge straining the front of his pants. "Can I see you?"

He flashes a quick grin. Equally fast, he strips off his pants and pitches them past the foot of the bed. He resettles on his knees between my thighs, his hand on his dick. The ring in his cock head glints in the candlelight. As he gives himself a languid stroke, more metal glints under the thick shaft.

Oh, gods. He's pierced there, too.

He reaches for me, and I forget all about his piercings as his fingers wrap around my dick. He swirls them along my shaft and strokes from base to tip and back again, each pass wringing hoarse moans from my throat. It's everything, his big hand gripping me. Stroking me. He knows what he's doing. When I get too close to that shimmering edge, he eases the pressure. When I need more, he squeezes harder, tugging me up so I'm arching and moaning his name. He fondles my balls, his big hands tugging and caressing the delicate skin.

Then he goes to his stomach and sucks my balls into his mouth.

I cry out as pleasure courses through me and my hips lift off the bed. Fuoco sucks and licks, his tongue swirling around and around one tender globe…then the other. He mouths at my sack, planting soft kisses before flicking his tongue over the seam. He teases the sensitive area between my sack and my hole, sending shivers rippling through me. I bend my knees, my thighs splayed wide as the air fills with the sound of my harsh breaths and his wet kisses.

He lets my damp balls fall back against my skin, then slowly moves his tongue up my shaft. Gripping me at the base, he licks my slit, teasing the tiny opening. Lapping at the moisture with a satisfied-sounding hum. He sucks my tip into his mouth and swirls around the crown with long, slow licks that make me shudder and gasp and claw at the sheets. Green eyes sear mine as he closes his lips around my cock head and suckles me, that *hum* rumbling down my dick and into my balls. I writhe beneath him, my hips bucking as I barrel toward the edge.

Just as I'm about to plunge over it, he pulls back. "Not just yet, selsara," he rasps, stroking his big hand up my glistening length.

I thump my head hard against the mattress, both hating and loving his teasing.

With a chuckle, he bends and licks down my shaft, tracing the veins that run along my engorged length. He holds me in an iron grip as he sucks and bites gently. And I'm helpless. Trembling and desperate, I can only watch as he worships my dick with his talented, devious mouth. My muscles clench. I cling to the edge by my fingertips.

Then he swallows my dick.

"Ahh!" I shout, hips thrusting. I bite my lip, trying not to scream as he deep-throats my shaft, taking me all the way to the back of his throat and swallowing loudly around my length. Hot, wet pressure engulfs my cock. He hums around me, the vibrations making my toes curl. He bobs on my dick, sucking and *sucking* me. Swirling his tongue over my head before licking down my shaft. He slurps at my cock, letting the tip hit the back of his throat over and over until I'm reduced to guttural, incoherent moans. His hand massages my balls. And I fly apart.

My orgasm shatters through me. I shout his name and thrust into his throat, my release pumping from me. It's so much—too much—and I squeeze my eyes shut as I ride the waves. His throat works around my dick as he swallows my cum, that deep growl of his rumbling the bed. And he knows when I grow too sensitive because he takes a final lick at my cock head before pulling off and collapsing beside me.

I stare at him, panting and shivering in the aftermath. "Gods, Fuoco…" I gulp breaths, scarcely able to believe what just happened.

He brushes hair off my sweaty forehead. "Was it okay?"

"Are you kidding? It was great."

He grins, his emerald eyes gleaming with satisfaction. "Good."

I stroke his arm, the intense warmth of his skin sending a pleasant tingle up my spine. "Could I…? Would you let me…?"

He knows what I'm asking. Satisfaction turns to anticipation as he takes my hand and presses his lips to my knuckles. "Of course, selsara. Anything you want."

Oh, I want. Nerves rising, I guide him onto his back. He watches me with hooded eyes as I kneel between his legs and wrap my hand around his dick. It's as big as the rest of him, and my thumb and forefinger don't touch as I give him a tentative stroke. The gold ring through the tip catches the light as I work him. Another piercing decorates the smooth skin under the base of his dick. A small, golden ring adorns the area between his balls and the pink, puckered skin of his asshole.

My fingers tighten around his dick. He grunts, and I snatch my hand away. "I'm sorry—"

"No." Lifting onto one elbow, he grabs my hand and guides it back to his shaft. "Keep going, Beau. You're doing good." He flashes a rueful smile. "*Too* good, if you catch my meaning."

Emboldened by this praise—and the idea that I can make him as needy as he makes me—I quicken my strokes. He grows harder under my hand. His ridged abs twitch, his green scales glittering as his breath hitches. A bead of moisture swells at the prominent slit in his cock head. Unable to resist, I lower my head and swipe my tongue over it.

His taste is exquisite. Salt and fire and man. I mimic what he did to me and fasten my lips around his tip. Immediately, more of that delicious taste fills my mouth. I swallow every drop as he begins to move, bucking his hips gently against my mouth. I take that as encouragement and suck him deeper into my mouth, licking and swirling my tongue over his shaft as I go.

"Oh, Beau," he murmurs, his voice thick with appreciation. "Yes, baby. Just like that." He threads his fingers through my hair and guides me with gentle hands as he whispers praise and encouragement. I probably don't deserve it. My moves are clumsy and uncoordinated. My jaw aches from his cock, which is far too big to fit down my throat. But my enthusiasm must make up for my lack of skill because he bucks harder against my mouth.

I keep sucking, my eyes rolling back in my head at the taste of him. He clenches his fists in my hair, and I know he's close. Saliva coats my chin but I don't stop. I want this for him. I want to make him come. I take him deeper, pushing him over that cliff. He shudders beneath me, his entire body shaking as his release erupts in my mouth. I swallow convulsively, gulping him down, my senses spinning.

I don't pull away even after he softens in my mouth. I keep kissing him, licking and nipping at his tip—at the golden ring that's warm against my tongue—until he stops shuddering and finally exhales. Then he moves in a blur, surging up and wrapping his thick arms around me. We collapse in a sweaty tangle, my head on his chest. Exhaustion tugs at me, threatening to close my eyelids.

After a moment, Fuoco shifts so he's facing me. He leans in and kisses my forehead. "You amaze me, selsara," he whispers against my skin. "You always have."

Impossible. He barely knows me. But if the stories are true, and he dreamed of me for centuries, maybe he knows me better than I think. But do I know him?

Can I trust him?

I must drift off because the next thing I'm aware of is a warm cloth wiping me down. Fuoco's deep voice murmurs something I don't catch, and then a sweet-smelling blanket covers my nude body. The bed is so soft—soft enough to sink into. So I do, letting the waves of exhaustion pull me under.

CHAPTER 11
FUOCO

I sit in a velvet chair next to the bed watching Beau sleep. One of his arms is shoved under the pillow, the other slung off the side of the bed. His fingers twitch now and again as he slumbers. His legs are pressed tightly together like he's trying to take up the least amount of space possible. Perhaps that's accurate. His cottage in the village was tiny. His bed was probably little better than a cot.

Regret is a heavy weight in my gut. I'm not foolish enough to believe that one well-timed orgasm is enough to make Beau drop the subject of returning to his bakery. I coerced him into staying with me. Used his father's illness as leverage. That sort of dominance can force cracks into any relationship—even a fated one. If I try to compel Beau's love, I'll break us.

I prop my elbow on the chair and rest my chin on my hand. I keep my free hand on the chair's other arm, my fingers stroking the velvet. Beau is right in front of me and yet he's not totally mine. When I dreamed of my mate, I never imagined I'd have to convince him to accept our bond. For me, our connection is clear as day—bright and beyond certainty. But Beau isn't a dragon. Maybe he doesn't feel the same pull that I do.

The panic of the infirmary is a painful undercurrent to the sated, hazy afterglow of having his mouth on me. As much as I tell myself I *shouldn't* force him, I know I'll do anything to keep him.

Treasure-hoarding thieves, the lot of you.

The words ring through my mind for the hundredth time, along with the growing realization that the old man was right. Because if Beau returns to that village, I'll find him. Steal him. Make him the jewel of my hoard.

Perhaps I'm exactly the monster that human accused me of being. I thought myself better than other dragons—certainly better than the enforcers who betrayed me.

A growl rumbles in my chest. Lirem is still out there, and that won't do. He's dangerous. He could hurt Beau…

The chair's arm creaks under my hand.

A knock at the door pulls me out of my thoughts.

My beast screams to the surface, the dragon riled at the thought of anyone disturbing our sleeping mate. I rise and cross the room, ripping the door open with a scowl.

One of the human servants flinches on the threshold, then quickly drops her gaze to the carpet. "My lord…" She gulps a breath and speaks in a rush. "I'm sorry to bother you at this late hour but there's a pixie in the Great Hall asking for an audience." She hesitates, her blue eyes darting from the carpet to my face and back again. "He said something about you missing an appointment—"

"Jasper Lilygully," I bite out. The meddlesome pixie is the very worst of his kind, always sticking his nose in other people's business. But perhaps I can use him to my benefit. Pixies always seem to know more than they should. Jasper in particular has a knack for digging up gossip.

I look down at the human. "Thank you, Tess."

Startled blue eyes lift to mine. Her cheeks go red. "You know my name?" She sounds shocked—and slightly horrified—at the prospect. Another problem I can lay at my enforcers' feet.

But…no. I'm the master of my castle. I can't blame Varden and the others for this. Gentling my tone, I offer the woman what I hope she interprets as a kind smile. "I know the name of every human in the castle. You're Tess Greenlee. Your mother works in the kitchens and your father assists in the greenhouse. You have two younger brothers." I search my memory, recalling something Dieter told me a few years ago. "The eldest broke his leg climbing a tree."

Her lips part as she places a hand over her heart.

After a moment of awkward silence, I clear my throat. "I'll find Lilygully. Was there anything else, Tess?"

Big eyes blink a few times. "N-No, my lord. Nothing else." She curtsies, then whirls and hurries toward the main castle. The stench of fear lingers in the hall, but maybe it's a bit lighter than before. That scent kept me away from the servants in the past. Another mistake.

With a sigh, I shut the door and return to the bed. Beau slumbers on, his dark lashes long and thick against his cheeks. I drink him in greedily, plans spinning through my head. I'll spoil him. Show him how much he means to me. In time, he'll understand that every decision I've made throughout my long life was with him in mind.

Unable to resist, I lean down and stroke chocolate waves away from his forehead. He's relaxed in sleep, the signs of worry absent from his face. Our bedplay was a first for him—another gift I don't deserve. But I'll take it. Cherish it. I have so many other firsts to share with him.

But right now I have to go see about a pixie.

That's enough to bring the growl back to my throat as I make my way to the Great Hall. I hear it before I reach it. A late-night party is in full swing, raucous music spilling through the Hall's massive double doors. Laughter bounces off the thick stone walls as I push through the doors and pause between them.

None of my courtiers notice my presence. Myth creatures lounge around the long tables, several in various states of undress. Pitchers of wine sit among platters heaped with food. My stomach clenches as my head fills with images of Beau tearing into a pear like he worried someone might take it away from him.

A burst of laughter rises from the head of the table.

Lilygully. The fucking pixie sprawls in my chair, his pale wings fluttering behind him. The dragon seated at his right leans in and whispers something in the pixie's ear.

A slow smile spreads across Jasper's face. He turns to the dragon and nods. The dragon's expression grows heated as Jasper strokes a hand down the male's square jaw. After a second, Jasper swings his legs over the chair's armrest. He tips his head back, and the dragon dangles a bunch of purple grapes over his waiting mouth.

Gods, he's insufferable.

Stalking up the length of the table, I kick the leg of my chair. "Get up, Lilygully. You try my patience." My beast roars to the surface, wreathing my head with green flames.

Jasper sits up, a slow grin splitting his face. Brilliant blue eyes fix on my hair. "Aww, did I upset you, flame daddy?" He plucks a glass of wine from the table and takes a hearty swig, his eyes never leaving mine. Mischief rolls off him in a thick wave that's almost tangible, the sensation like beetles scuttling over my skin.

"You requested an audience," I say. "I'm granting it." Without waiting for his response, I turn and stride to the far end of the Hall. A chair scrapes behind me, followed by his soft footfalls and the flutter of wings that sets my teeth on edge. The sooner I get him out of the Great Hall the better. If he hasn't already noticed my enforcers' absence, he will soon—and he'll undoubtedly start asking questions. My courtiers don't know Nazzar and Varden are dead, and I'm not ready to explain it.

Plus, Lirem is still out there. He should have never escaped in the first place. He slipped away while I was distracted and desperate to tend to my wounded mate.

Jasper trails me down the darkened hall and into one of my private meeting rooms. A large, round table dominates the center of the space. A fire dances in a hearth big enough for several men to stand inside. Diamond-paned windows take up the far wall, offering a view of the moon that sits high and bright in a pitch-black sky.

Jasper sighs loudly behind me. When I turn, he clasps his hands together, a look of delight on his face.

"A private room, Fuoco? Moonlight and a roaring fire?" He moves to the table and hops onto it. "Gods, if you wanted me that badly we could have done it in the Great Hall." He winks. "You dragons are into that sort of thing, I hear." His delicate wings flutter, scattering silvery glitter onto the table's surface. He crosses one leg over the other and gives me a seductive smile. "Here I am, m'lord. Ready to be defiled."

I fold my arms. "What can I do for you, Jasper?"

He cocks his head to the side. "You're such a sweet talker, Fuoco." He glances around the room, his tone turning airy. "I do need something from you. But we'll get to that in a second. All this cloak and dagger business tells me you need something from me, too." The firelight flashes in his blue eyes as they travel down my body. "How can I be of service?" he asks breathlessly.

"My selsara sleeps in my bed as we speak, pixie." I gesture to my body. "*This* is not available to you."

He studies me. "Arrogant, but you're hot enough to pull it off." He nods to himself. "I'll allow it."

I speak through clenched teeth. "State your business."

He hops down from the table and leans against it. "The rumors are true, then? A certain pretty little baker is warming your bed?" A sigh lifts his chest. "Tale as old as time."

I give him a stony stare. Under the crackle of the fire, a snuffling sound reaches my ears.

"I met him, you know," Jasper says, examining his short nails adorned with some kind of symbol. *Hearts.* He looks up at me with a grin. "He's got gorgeous...apples."

I lean forward. "I'll ask you a final time why you and your mouse require an audience."

Jasper looks down at the pocket of his leather jacket. "You can come out." After a moment, he rolls his eyes. "Of course he heard you, he's a dragon. And no, he won't eat you." Jasper gazes into his pocket as he appears to listen intently. "Well, what do you expect? Your damn breathing is so fucking loud, Bert. It's like an elephant, honestly."

A tiny gray head pops out of his pocket. Round, black eyes peer at me.

"I never said I won't eat you," I tell the mouse.

Bert lets out an indignant-sounding squeak. He scurries up Jasper's chest and perches on the pixie's shoulder, his long tail flicking agitatedly against Jasper's jacket.

"Don't you usually travel with another one?" I ask Jasper. Immediately, I regret the question. The last thing I need is Lilygully thinking I'm interested in hearing details about his life.

But the pixie merely smiles. Bert shifts on his shoulder. The mouse's ears twitch as he releases a series of squeaks. Jasper heaves another put-upon sigh. "Fine, I'll ask him." He strolls forward, his wings batting the air lazily. "I need to go to Paris, and dragon back is the only way to get there."

"What's in Paris?" I demand. The elves maintain their strongholds in Europe but it's unlikely Jasper has business with any of the elven houses. Despite their common ancestry, pixies and elves have long harbored animosity toward each other. Like many among the Myth, the pixies view elves as stuck-up and sanctimonious. The elves regard pixies as irresponsible troublemakers.

Of course, the elves have a point…

Jasper lifts a shoulder. "I hear the men are gorgeous."

"You're going there to stir up trouble," I say flatly. "Aren't you tired of meddling in other people's love lives?"

He presses a hand to his throat. "Me? Meddling? You wound me, flame daddy."

Bert chatters in Jasper's ear, his whiskers twitching.

Jasper nods. "Excellent point, Bert." Jasper closes the distance between us, not stopping until he's close enough for me to see the tiny laugh lines radiating from the corners of his eyes. He tilts his head, his expression abruptly serious. "Now, what do you need from me?"

I debate how much to tell him—or if I should tell him anything at all. But he always seems to possess information others can't obtain. Like the elves, pixies commune with animals. For all I know, Jasper has a rodent army at his disposal. And mice can run through even the thickest castle walls, sniffing out secrets and tracking down those most determined to hide.

But more than anything, I can't help but think that Lilygully is up to something. He's been lurking around the various syndicates. *Meddling.* But maybe there's a method to his scheming. There's something in the air around him.

And I learned a long time ago to listen to what the air tells me.

I unfold my arms as I lower my voice. "I recently learned my enforcers weren't carrying out my wishes when dealing with the villagers in my syndicate. They've been terrorizing the humans, stealing and leaving my people to starve. Two of the three have paid for their crimes, but the third has gone to ground."

Jasper stays silent, his face unusually somber. On his shoulder, Bert appears just as attentive.

"It's my responsibility to fix this," I say, "but first I need to find Lirem. And quickly."

Jasper cocks his head. "Your court is full of dragons. They won't help you search?"

"My court is full of courtiers, not warriors. My enforcers earned their positions because they were skilled fighters. No one here is qualified to take on Lirem." I hesitate, then voice the second reason I haven't asked my court for help. "Lirem has friends among the Myth. It's possible some of those friends reside in this castle. If he has inside help, I don't want anyone alerting him to my plans."

"What will you do once you find him?"

"Kill him." My beast stirs as visions of Beau's bloodied face float through my mind. "I'll make an example of him so everyone in the syndicate knows humans are off-limits. They deserve to live in peace like everyone else." Heat crackles under my skin and rushes up to my head. "And *no one* will ever touch my selsara again."

Bert leans toward Jasper's ear, but the pixie lifts a forestalling hand. He glances at the flames leaping off my scalp. "We'll help you. We'll start tonight."

Relief spreads through me—and I don't know whether to be surprised or worried that a partnership with Jasper is producing feelings of well-being. "Thank you."

"No problem, flame daddy."

It's my turn to sigh. "Please stop calling me that."

He leans back, his gaze critical as he runs it down my body. "You know, you're right. It's more of a *zaddy* thing you've got going on."

"Do I want to know?"

"Probably not." He holds his palm to his shoulder. Bert hops into it, and Jasper lowers the mouse carefully to the ground. Bert scurries across the floor, squeezes into a crack in the wall, and disappears.

Jasper straightens and sticks out his hand. "So I'm good for a dragon ride?"

"Yes," I grunt, not taking his hand.

He waggles his palm. "Come on, Fuoco, it's just a hand. It hasn't even been anywhere scandalous." He seems to rethink that, then chuckles. "Well, not *today* anyway."

Grimacing, I shake his hand, sealing our bargain in the human fashion even though magic bound us the moment we uttered our exchange. "Let me know when you want that ride."

His blond brows go sky high. "Flame zaddy! Aren't you the impatient one."

I grit my teeth. "You know what I meant."

"I know what I wanted you to mean."

Gods, what was I thinking, making a deal with him? "Are we finished here?"

He makes a show of looking around. "I mean, *I* didn't finish, but—"

"Never mind," I growl, turning and stalking to the door. "Come find me if you hear anything about Lirem."

"Aye aye, captain," comes his cheery reply. "Say hi to Beau for me!"

Beau. I want nothing more than to return to my bedchamber, climb into bed, and pull his warm body against mine. But as I move down the hall, I head toward the courtyard instead. Jasper will honor his word and search for any trails Lirem might have left. But it's my duty to search for Lirem—and I have an opportunity to start while Beau is asleep in the safety of the castle.

Smothering a groan of longing, I walk into the moonlight and begin stripping off my clothes. I have all night to search. Lirem is out there.

And I'm going to find him.

CHAPTER 12
BEAU

"Is there anything else you might like, sir?"

I look up from my plate to find the woman, Tess, hovering in the doorway of Fuoco's bedchamber. She appeared when I woke at dawn to find Fuoco absent. A note lay on the pillow that still bore the indentation from his head.

Attending to syndicate business, the elegant handwriting read. *Sleep as long as you wish. The servants will bring breakfast.*

Tess made good on that promise, carrying in platter after platter of steaming food. Apparently, "breakfast" in the castle is slang for "every breakfast food ever created." Because Tess brought enough for an army.

The table before me practically groans with an endless array of dishes. Scrambled eggs. Waffles smothered in syrup. A dozen different kinds of toast. Fluffy pancakes wrapped in bacon and sprinkled with sugar. Omelettes stuffed with spinach, tomatoes, and onions. The French toast topped with currant was too sweet for my taste. A platter of cinnamon rolls as big as my head sits untouched.

I smile at Tess as I try to ignore my rising panic. "No, thank you. I honestly couldn't eat another bite."

She worries at her bottom lip. "Are you certain? Lord Fuoco won't like it if you go hungry. He said to make sure all your needs are met."

The panic blossoms into something hot and uncomfortable. If he can't make me his prisoner, Fuoco seems determined to make me his pet. Even if I could accept that kind of arrangement, I'd never be able to show my face in the village again. I look down at my plate, where egg yolk spreads in a yellow, cloying puddle. The bacon and coffee that made my mouth water half an hour ago now sets acid churning in my gut. The breakfast before me could feed half the village.

Is it really possible that Fuoco didn't know his people were starving? How could he have spent so many years surrounded by wealth when the village had nothing?

"Sir?"

Tess's soft voice yanks my head up. I stand, rattling the dishes in the process. "Sorry," I say, steadying a coffee cup before it can tilt off its saucer. I step away from the table and tuck the chair into place. Squeezing the back, I attempt a reassuring smile. "The breakfast was lovely, but I promise I'm stuffed. And please, call me Beau."

Tess returns my smile with a hesitant one of her own. "Okay... Beau." Her blue eyes flick to the rumpled bed behind me.

Heat climbs up my nape. "Um..." I clear my throat. "Have you eaten?"

Her eyes go wide. "Me?"

I gesture to the table. "I'm not going to eat this. I mean..." Oh gods, is it rude to offer her my leftovers? "I just thought..."

She eyes the platter of cinnamon rolls. "Varden doesn't like it when the servants eat food prepared for the court."

"Well, he's not here." When she looks at me, I use my chin to point toward one of the platters. "He's as crispy as that bacon."

She slaps a hand over her mouth. *"What?"*

My stomach twists. I shouldn't have let it slip about Varden. The enforcer was an asshole, but he probably had a family. People who care about him. Maybe Fuoco doesn't want news of his death getting out just yet.

But it's too late now. As Tess gapes at me, I square my shoulders. "I can't say anything else. But you don't have to worry about Varden anymore. He's gone, and I don't think Lord Fuoco will have a problem with the servants eating this food."

Above her hand, her eyes flicker with doubt. "Truly? You don't think he'll be angry?"

Fuoco's voice runs through my mind. *"I didn't know things were so dire."*

"No," I tell Tess. "He won't be angry." And if he is, well, I'll stay until Dad is better, and then I'll figure out a way to leave the castle for good.

Tess lowers her hand. Emotions play over her pale face. Curiosity and relief and, finally, something that might be a spark of happiness. She gazes at the spread of food before lifting smiling eyes to mine. "Thanks…Beau. The kitchen staff are going to love you for this."

More heat creeps over my nape. "Do you happen to know the way to the infirmary? I'd like to check on my father."

Ten minutes and a few dead-ends and U-turns later, I find Dad sitting up in bed enjoying a miniature version of my breakfast. A smiling Dieter perches on the bed next to him, opalescent dragon scales visible under the collar of his dark sweater. The two men break off what sounds like an animated conversation as I enter.

"Beau!" My father sets his biscuit down and wipes his mouth with a white cloth napkin. "Come in, come in." He waves me over, his brown eyes sparkling. "Have you eaten? There's more than enough here for two."

"I have, thanks." I move to his side and nod to the healer. "Good morning, Dieter."

"Morning, Beau. I hope you had a restful evening."

Memories of Fuoco's bed flood my brain. His big hands undressing me. His hot mouth on my dick. "I d-did, thank you," I say, backing to the bed behind me and sitting so hard the springs squeal in protest. As Dad's brow furrows, I squeeze my hands together in my lap and focus on Dieter. "How is my father?"

The healer leans forward and places a big hand on Dad's shoulder. "Maurice is doing even better than I expected. His lungs are clearer this morning." The dragon's smile spreads as he meets my father's gaze. "We might even try taking a walk through the gardens later if he feels up to it. Exercise is excellent medicine."

Dad laughs—the kind of deep chuckle I haven't heard him make since his illness last winter. "Just admit it, Dieter, you're tired of answering my questions about dragon magic."

The healer stands. "Never. We'll continue our discussion when we take our walk." He turns his smile to me. "I'll let you and your father catch up, Beau. Let me know if you need anything." He sweeps from the room, his long coat flaring out behind him.

Dad watches him go, then turns to me with serious eyes. "How are you, Beau? And don't give me the answer you think I want to hear."

Nerves tighten my gut. I rise and move his breakfast tray to a nearby table before sitting near his hip. "I'm fine, Dad. Really."

All signs of merriment vanish from my father's eyes. He lowers his voice. "Did Lord Fuoco hurt you?" My father's expression darkens. "Or force you to do something you didn't want to do?"

"What? No!" I glance around the empty infirmary. "It's not like that. He didn't... We didn't..." My face grows as hot as my ruined oven. "He would never hurt me."

Dad nods slowly. "I see." He takes a deep breath, then reaches out and grasps my hand. "You don't have to hide who you are, son. Not from me."

I freeze. For a moment, words fail me. I force myself to hold his gaze. "I...don't?" I whisper.

His expression softens. "I've known you were gay since you were nine years old, Beau. And I've loved you since the moment your mother told me she was pregnant with you. Maybe before." A tear slips down his weathered cheek. "We tried for a long time, you see, and we'd almost given up hope. But then you came along, so unexpected and such a joy. When your mother saw you for the first time, she said you were beautiful. And you were. So we named you Beau." Dad squeezes my hand. "You are a beautiful person inside and out, son. I can see why Lord Fuoco is taken with you."

My throat closes as tears fill my eyes and spill over, forming hot trails down my face. "I had no idea," I rasp. "I thought I hid it so well."

My father laughs lightly. "Oh, I'm sure you did from most people. But I know you pretty well." His smile fades, replaced with a fierceness I've never seen on his face. "I don't want you to ever hide again. You don't have to be afraid of judgment or punishment—not from me or anyone. I just want you to be happy and safe. That's all that matters to me, my son."

More tears streak down my face. Dad grabs his napkin and dabs at my cheek.

I recoil as something cold and squishy drops into my lap. "Ugh, there's egg on your napkin." We dissolve into watery laughter as I bat the napkin away. Then Dad grabs my arm and pulls me into a hug that smells like parchment and axle grease and cinnamon oatmeal cookies baking in the oven.

Home. He smells like home.

"I love you," I whisper, my chin on his shoulder.

He pulls back and regards me with love and pride shining from his eyes. "I love you, too." As he wipes the last of the tears from my eyes with his thumbs, a hint of the fierceness returns. "Dragon or no, if Fuoco ever hurts you I'll kill him with my own hands."

"I would expect nothing less," a deep voice says behind me.

I spin around to find Fuoco leaning against the stone doorway, his arms folded and a slight smile on his lips. A long, black coat stitched with brilliant green embroidery hangs from his broad shoulders. Black boots climb up his legs, which are once again wrapped in black leather. Between the halves of his coat, a shiny green corset hugs his waist. A green stud winks in his ear. He's a menacing figure of muscle and power. But his eyes are alight with amusement. And approval.

He straightens and walks to the end of Dad's bed. "I trust you're feeling better this morning, Maurice."

Dad returns Fuoco's gaze steadily. "Much better, thank you. If you break my son's heart, there will be hell to pay."

"Dad!" I half rise, ready to smother my father with a pillow.

But Fuoco bows at the waist, one hand sweeping elegantly in a courtly bow that should look ridiculous but steals my breath instead. He straightens, the look in his green eyes for my father alone. "I assure you, sir, my intentions toward your son are entirely honorable. I vow to care for him and protect him with my every breath." He turns his gaze to me, and the intensity of his stare makes my heart skip a beat. "Fate has given me the most precious gift in Beau. I'll never take him for granted. I'll make sure he has all the happiness he deserves." Fuoco turns back to my father. "And if you permit it, I would love nothing more than to court Beau. Assuming I have your blessing."

Heat suffuses my cheeks as my heart tries to beat from my chest.

My father's face creases into a smile. He glances at me, then nods. "I have faith you'll do right by my son. If that's what Beau wants, you have my blessing."

Fuoco offers another bow. "Thank you, sir. I won't disappoint you." His lips twitch. "Or provoke your ire." He moves around the bed and extends a hand to me. "Or yours, selsara," he adds softly.

My breath hitches as I let him pull me up, and my stomach flutters as he tucks my arm through his and turns to my father. "I'm taking Beau to visit the castle tailor. She's exceptionally skilled at her craft. I can have her stop by later to measure you for some new clothes."

Dad hesitates.

"She uses magical thread," Fuoco says.

Dad's face lights up. He shoots me a look.

"Go ahead, Dad," I say softly. "You didn't bring much with you from the village." *Because he doesn't own much.*

"That's true..."

"I'll send her around once she's finished with Beau," Fuoco says. He bids farewell to my father, then leads me from the infirmary with my hand tucked firmly in his elbow.

"I don't need any clothes," I say, the memory of the sumptuous breakfast spinning through my head.

Green eyes gleam as they travel down my body. "Nonsense, selsara. You need everything I can give you."

∾

Twenty minutes later, I stand on a small round platform wearing an unbuttoned shirt and a pair of suit pants. A slender woman with a blond ponytail and a pair of delicately curved horns squats in front of me with several straight pins bristling from the corner of her mouth.

"Feet apart," she says through the pins. "I need to measure your inseam."

I bite my lip and do as she says. In the mirrors that line the workroom walls, a dozen copies of me do the same.

And a dozen Fuocos observe from a plush chair in the corner. In the mirror, his glowing green eyes study my ass. Then, as if he feels me watching him, he lifts his gaze to mine.

Slowly, he pulls a peach from his coat pocket.

My breath catches. Is that the same peach from the greenhouse?

"Perfect," the tailor murmurs. "Stay just like that." She lifts a hand, and a measuring tape flies from a table and into her palm, its long tail thumping against the platform. She gives it a stern look, a red sheen rolling over her blue eyes. "Settle down."

The measuring tape droops.

The tailor softens her tone. "Oh, go on, then. Do both inseams, his waist, and his shoulders. Make it snappy." She opens her hand, and the measuring tape flies out of it and dives between my legs.

"What the—?" I yelp, stumbling back.

Fuoco chuckles.

"Stay still," the tailor scolds. "He'll just be a minute."

"He?" I ask, my voice an octave higher than normal as the measuring tape wriggles around my groin, snuffling like a golden retriever.

"You can call him Gordon if you want," the tailor says, pulling pins from her mouth. Her horns catch the light as she tugs at the cuff of my trousers.

Suddenly, the tape snaps into a straight line that extends to my ankle.

"Good boy, Gordon!" the tailor says. On the table, a feather pen springs upright and begins scribbling in a notebook. A second later, the measuring tape becomes fluid again. Tail waving, it whips itself around my waist and pauses. The feather pen continues its scribbling.

"Don't move, human," the tailor says, her tone matter-of-fact as she glances up at me. With a snap of her wrist, the pins fly from her fingers and embed themselves in a perfect circle around my cuff.

I gape at the pins, then look at Fuoco in the mirror. He grins and toys with the peach. His long fingers curl around the fruit, his thumb lodged in the crease. His movements deliberate, he drags his thumb up and down the cleft.

Heat blasts me, making sweat prickle under my arms. I jerk my gaze from his and study the workroom instead. Dad would love it. Magic practically oozes from the stone walls. Under the mullioned window, an invisible hand plies a needle and thread, the stitches neat and precise as they wind around a cloth-draped mannequin. On a distant table, a pair of scissors cut along a seam, the rhythmic sound steady and oddly soothing. Bolts of sumptuous fabrics in all shades and textures line the walls. The air is thick with incense and the charcoal-like scent of brimstone.

"Hurry along, Gordon," the tailor says, standing and giving the measuring tape an expectant look.

Snuffling and wagging, it winds around my chest and stretches across my shoulders. The feather pen scribbles, then drops back to the table. The measuring tape shivers, the loose tail beating against my hip.

"Good boy," the tailor says, extending a hand tipped with red claws the same shade as her lips. The tape shivers, then zips into her palm and curls into a coil. The tailor looks at Fuoco. "Do you want to see fabric swatches?"

"No," Fuoco says. Peach in hand, he unfolds his big body from the chair, his tall form filling the mirrors. "Just make one of everything."

The tailor props a hand on her hip. One arched eyebrow climbs high on her smooth forehead. "I have over twenty thousand bolts of fabric."

I suck in a breath. "I don't need that much!"

Fuoco ignores me as he addresses the tailor. "That will do nicely, Zara. Please deliver the garments to my quarters as you make them."

"Will do." Zara slants me a look from under her lashes. "I'll start with pajamas." Before I can say anything, she winks out of sight. A thin, black cloud hangs in the air for a moment before dissipating.

"Demons," Fuoco says, strolling to me. "Theirs is a dry humor."

I avert my eyes from the peach in his hand. "I thought they were like the cops of the Myth."

"Some are. But there are several daemonum. Zara is a *precisor* demon. Her stitches never unravel."

"Then I don't need twenty thousand outfits," I point out. Even with the platform, I have to tip my head back to meet his stare. "I don't even need a hundredth of that."

"You need clothes." His gaze roams down the strip of bare skin exposed by my unbuttoned shirt. "Although, I prefer you in nothing at all."

Desire blisters through me, tightening my dick. But I can't be distracted by lust. I tug the halves of my shirt together. "It's not fair for me to have so much when the villagers have so little."

Fuoco steps closer, his body heat searing my skin. His fangs flash as he growls, "We've already established that you're not returning to the village."

Fear and arousal twist through me. Before Fuoco, I wouldn't have found that combination particularly compelling. But it's as if the former fuels the latter. The same instinct that tells me Fuoco won't harm me also whispers that I might enjoy feeling a little afraid of him. Might revel in playing the role of his prey.

At the same time, a little voice warns me that there's a difference between sex and everyday life. It's one thing to capitulate in bed—quite another to surrender outside of it. If I don't stand up to him now, the power balance between us will be forever skewed.

I draw an even breath. "I understand that you want to give me things—"

"Everything."

"—but you have no idea what life is like in the village. If the townspeople find out how much breakfast you waste every morning, they'll storm the castle with pitchforks."

Green eyes flash. "They can try."

"They might if you antagonize them."

Exasperation flashes across his features. "I have no wish to antagonize them. I only ever wanted to help." He glances around the workshop. "I'll have Zara make them coats. She can use her most expensive fabric."

"They don't need fancy clothes." My voice climbs, and I fling an arm out, making my shirt gape wider. "They need their roofs repaired and enough firewood to get through the winter. They need to know the food they work hard for won't be snatched out of their hands by your enforcers."

Fuoco moves in a blur, his big arm snagging me around the waist and pulling me against him. His lips brush my forehead, and he breathes a word against my skin. "Done."

I put a palm on his chest and fight the urge to curl my fingers against the soft fabric and the hard muscle underneath. Drawing back, I stare into his emerald-green eyes. "You won't send new enforcers into the village?"

"Not if you don't wish it."

"I don't."

"Then, as I said, it won't happen." He slides his hand under my shirt and rests his palm over my ribs. "It's as simple as that, selsara."

My breath catches as the heat of his hand sinks into my skin. Slowly, he draws me forward, helping me step down from the platform. Then he turns us so he's standing behind me, both of us facing the mirror. Green flames dance in his eyes as he tugs the shirt from my shoulders. He wraps his arms around me, the peach still clasped in one hand that he rests over my pectoral.

"Look at yourself, Beau," he murmurs in my ear. He bends his head and drops a kiss on my shoulder, then slides his lips up my neck to nip at my earlobe. "How can I deny you anything?"

My heart slams against my ribs. I want to turn and look at him, but I can't tear my gaze away from his hands in the mirror. The air around us crackles, tiny currents of electricity licking over my skin.

He slides one hand down my abs to squeeze my aching cock, which is leaking all over the suit pants. Ordinarily, I'd be mortified but it's the last thing on my mind as he curls his long fingers around my dick and strokes. At the same moment, he lifts the peach to my mouth and whispers, "Bite."

With a whimper, I obey. Sweet, sticky juice explodes in my mouth. More trickles down my neck. Fuoco unzips my fly and pulls out my dick.

"Look at that," he rasps, pressing a kiss to my temple as he begins working my cock. He doesn't have to tell me. Because I'm already looking everywhere. At his hands. At his big body behind mine, the contrast between my nudity and his fully clothed form so surprisingly hot I think I might combust. The trousers slip down my legs and puddle at my feet. I can't muster the energy to care. I lean into Fuoco's chest, letting him support me as pleasure pumps through my veins.

He tugs me harder against him, pressing his rigid erection into my cleft. With his other hand he lifts the peach to my lips again. "Bite," he grunts, jerking me faster.

I cry out as I sink my teeth into the peach. Juice courses down my neck and forms little rivers that traverse my chest. I let my head flop back on Fuoco's shoulder as juice trickles over my nipple, making me moan wantonly.

He sucks the peach juice from my neck, the emerald stud in his ear winking as he sinks his dark head lower and laps at the nectar. All the while, his big hand continues flying up and down my dick, which is hard as granite and shiny with precum. He grinds his dick into my ass, his thick cock rubbing up and down my cleft and the place I desperately want him to be.

"Please," I whisper.

He lifts his head and locks eyes with me in the mirror. With a grunt, he walks me forward, half-lifting me when I stumble around the trousers at my ankles. "Hands against the glass," he murmurs, tossing the peach aside and cupping my ass with both hands.

Nerves run a quick, fraught path down my spine, but I do as he says, my breath puffing against the mirror.

Fuoco drops a kiss on the spot where my neck meets my shoulder. "Anything you don't want, you stop me. Understand?"

"Yeah," I rasp. But I want it. Whatever he's willing to give, I'll take it. I've waited so long for this.

He palms my cheeks, squeezing lightly. Letting me feel the heat of his hands. He traces light patterns over the quivering muscle, then pushes my cheeks apart and slips his fingers between them.

"Gods," I gasp, resting my forehead on the mirror.

"No, selsara," he rumbles, running his fingers up and down my cleft. He strokes around my pucker, teasing the most sensitive part of me. "No gods, my love. Only your mate."

My love. He can't mean it that way.

He pushes the tip of his finger inside me, and the thought spirals away as my spine turns to liquid. I groan against the mirror, my hips rolling and my breathing growing ragged. He pulls his finger out and rubs slow, firm circles around my entrance. His other hand finds my cock and strokes.

"Yes!" I gasp, thrusting my hips. "Please don't stop."

"I won't," he says, a smile in his voice as he brushes his lips over my nape. "Open a little more for me, Beau. I want to show you something." He works my dick faster, slicking my precum up and down my shaft. His finger against my hole disappears.

I lift my head in time to see him suck it into his mouth. Green eyes flash with heat and promise as he carries his damp finger back to my pucker and pushes inside.

My mouth opens but no sound emerges. I'm beyond speech. All I can do is watch his face in the mirror as he fingers me, filling me with delicious pressure while he strokes my dick.

"There you go," he says softly, pushing deeper. "Relax." He withdraws and then pushes inside again—and strokes something that makes pleasure crash through me in a thick, hot wave. *My prostate.* I've nudged it before when I play with myself. But my fumbling experiments have never felt like this—like everything good in the universe bundled together and injected directly into my veins. My eyes roll back in my head as I release a long, shuddering groan. My ass spasms around his finger, my muscles clenching tightly.

"That's it," he breathes against my neck, his hand flying up and down my dick. "So tight for me. Come on, baby." He pumps his finger, nailing that magical spot over and over. With each thrust, lightning shoots through my dick and balls.

The pleasure builds until I can't take any more. I cry out, my toes curling as I come, shaking and gasping against the glass. Fuoco holds me steady, one hand gripping my spurting dick. His thick finger still lodged inside me. I moan his name, shuddering with aftershocks as he slows his strokes and gently pulls his finger from my ass. When I sag, he turns me in his arms and guides my head to his shoulder.

"That was perfect," he whispers, his breath tickling my cheek. "How do you feel?"

"Tired." As his chest shakes with laughter, embarrassment floods me. I lift my head. "I didn't mean—"

"I know," he says, taking my lips in a slow, easy kiss. When he pulls back, he's smiling. "Would you have dinner with me tonight? There's something else I'd like to show you."

My face turns pink in the mirror. Even with my pants around my ankles and my leaking dick soft against my leg, I'm apparently capable of embarrassment. "Something better than that?"

Fuoco's smile grows as he strokes his knuckles down my jaw. "Oh yes, baby. Something much bigger and better than that."

CHAPTER 13
FUOCO

The Great Hall is even louder than usual. Laughter rings out, mingling with the upbeat tune the musicians play from the gallery. The full court is present, a buzz of excitement in the air. It's not every day a dragon formally takes a selsara. The *formally* part promises to be the main event of the evening.

I just have to hope it's not too overwhelming for Beau.

"Everyone is staring at me," he says under his breath, looking around the tables of dragons and other Myth creatures before pinning his gaze to his plate.

I place my hand over his on the arm of his chair, which the servants positioned next to mine at the head of the table. "Because they can't take their eyes off you." I fold my fingers around his. As he lifts an uncertain gaze to mine, I squeeze his hand. "And neither can I."

His cheeks turn pink, and my cock tightens at the sight of him clothed in a manner befitting his station. Zara outdid herself. Navy leather pants hug his lean thighs. A snowy white shirt peeks from the top of a jacket the same chocolate shade as his eyes. Twin rows of emerald-studded buttons march down his chest. Swirling green embroidery decorates his collar and flows down his sleeves, forming dragons in flight. He'd turn heads in rags. In court clothes, his masculine beauty is breathtaking.

But he's clearly uncomfortable with the attention he's receiving. If the night goes as planned, most of that attention will shift to me. My beast rises, eager to begin the ancient ritual I've waited my whole life to perform.

Beau's pulse flutters rapidly in his neck. He tugs at the collar of his jacket, exposing the hollow of his throat.

My mouth waters. I want to lean forward and lick the delicate skin at the base of his neck. Press my lips against his pulse and taste the sweetness that clings to him.

But I can't. Not yet.

"You've barely touched your plate," I say, gesturing to the dinner before us. I pick up a piece of warmed fig dripping with honey butter and hold it to his lips. "Let me help you."

His pupils dilate. The beat in his neck jumps faster, and the air seems to sizzle as he parts his lips. I slide the fig into his mouth, brushing my fingers against his tongue as I withdraw. A growl rumbles in my throat as he licks honey from his lips.

"More?" I rasp.

He nods, his dark eyes glittering with candlelight and anticipation. I bring a second fig to my own mouth and take a bite before offering him the rest. When he opens obediently, I drag honey over his bottom lip, then dip my head and lick it away before pushing the fig between his lips. When I keep my fingers in place, he whimpers and closes his lips around them.

"Suck," I murmur. Another sexy whimper breaks from him as he obeys, his dark lashes fluttering and that pretty blush stealing down his neck. Gaze locked with his, I pull my fingers away and suck my thumb into my mouth. He grips the arm of his chair, his eyes going heavy-lidded.

I reach for another fig when movement at the far end of the Hall catches my eye. Jasper appears in the doorway, his gossamer wings on full display. He's dressed to kill in a red suit that hugs his body and leaves nothing to the imagination. He's shirtless under his jacket, his smooth chest glowing faintly. The light glamour he typically wears is pulled back, revealing his tapered ears and otherworldly beauty.

He strolls through the Hall, pointing at courtiers and calling out greetings as he passes the tables. When a trio of muscle-bound ogres catcalls him, he blows them a kiss. A second later, one of the horned males yelps as red spots spread rapidly over his skin. His buddy next to him shoots Jasper a menacing look.

"You're asking for trouble, Lilygully!"

Jasper smirks. "You asked first, Krug the Ballbiter."

"It's Warhammer!"

"They both sound stupid."

At my side, Beau stiffens. "I've seen that man before," he says under his breath. "He came to the bakery."

I grunt, irritation prickling over my skin as I observe Jasper's progress. "He's a pixie," I mutter. "And a pain in the ass."

Jasper makes his way to the head table, where he sweeps me an insolent bow. He winks at Beau as he straightens, then looks at me and pulls his lapel aside, exposing his nipple bisected by an emerald-studded barbell. "I asked that dreamy jeweler in your basement to make me something special." He angles his head down and stares at his nipple, his brow furrowing. Almost to himself, he murmurs, "Although, maybe it's taboo to wear green piercings tonight?" He looks at me, his frown firmly in place. "I don't want to upstage your big, sexy dragon strip tea—"

"Get lost, Lilygully," I growl, my voice dipping lower than any human could speak. At a table under a row of banners, a group of centaurs launches into a rowdy song. A chimera seated behind them turns and spits fire over her shoulder, searing the beard of the loudest reveler.

"Oh, I would, flame zaddy," Jasper says, strolling forward. With a quick gust of his wings, he sails over the table and plops into the chair next to mine. As the unfortunate centaur's companions pour a pitcher of wine over his smoking face, Jasper lowers his voice. "But if you recall, you asked me to gather certain information."

It's my turn to stiffen. Slowly, I lift my goblet and speak behind the rim. "And do you have information for me?"

"Mmm." Jasper keeps his gaze on the centaurs as he says, "The male you seek has been sniffing around a certain bakery in the village."

I tighten my fingers on the goblet. Taking a sip, I swallow the rage that rises in my throat. "You're sure of this?"

Jasper slants me a slightly offended look. "My sources are solid." His blue eyes flick to Beau, who's a still, watchful presence on my other side. Across the Hall, the centaurs break into another song. Jasper pushes back from the table. As he rises, he speaks just above a whisper in my ear. "I'd keep my baker close if I were you."

My blood turns to ice in my veins. Jasper rounds the table, his wings scattering pixie dust as he reenters the throng of food and merriment. He flings his arms wide. "Somebody get me a drink!"

Cheers go up. The music continues to pump. Wine flows as the party continues, my courtiers unaware of the danger flowing like poison around us. At least, it appears that way. I sip my wine and let my gaze wander over the crowd, my senses primed for hints of treachery. Any sly looks or covert glances.

But there's nothing. Just bawdy laughter and colorful celebration. One of the centaurs snags Jasper around the waist and pulls the pixie into his lap. Jasper laughs and runs his hand down the male's broad chest, his sober expression from a moment before replaced with his usual insouciance.

"Fuoco?"

When I turn to Beau, worry brims in his eyes. He glances at Jasper and starts to say more, but I lean in and kiss him. He hesitates for a second, then opens under me with a deep moan that rumbles against my lips. I slide my tongue over his, tasting figs and honey, and then I move my mouth to his ear. "Later," I murmur. We'll have no secrets between us, but this isn't the right time.

Suddenly, the music changes. The strings go silent, leaving a rolling, rhythmic drumbeat. *Boom. Boom. Boom.* It shivers around the Hall, the sound primitive and impossible to ignore.

Beau pulls back as all eyes turn to us.

To me.

I stand and gaze down at my uneasy-looking mate. "When a

dragon finds his selsara, there is always rejoicing." I turn to my court and lift my voice. "Am I not right?"

Shouts of affirmation rise from those assembled, the cheers echoing off the stone walls and momentarily drowning out the sound of the drum. When the noise dies down, I leap onto the table. "But we don't leave it at that," I say.

"Take it off!" someone yells from the rear of the Hall. Laughter follows. The heckler's tablemate smacks him good-naturedly on the back of the head.

"Patience," I admonish, smiling as I nudge platters of half-eaten food out of the way with the tip of my boot. Servants spring forward and help, quickly clearing a space. When they retreat, I turn to Beau, who stares up at me with wide brown eyes. The pulse in his neck flutters more rapidly than ever.

"We don't leave it at that," I repeat softly, unlacing my corset. A dragon rises from a nearby table and moves to help me.

Beau sucks in a breath.

"When a dragon takes a selsara," I say, "his selsara must take him, too."

Anticipation ripples through my courtiers, but I pay them no mind as my corset drops to the table. Beau's brown eyes follow the path of my fingers as I unbutton my shirt.

The drumbeat rises around me, vibrating across the stone floor and shaking the table beneath my feet. I slip my arms from my sleeves and toss my shirt away. Scales shimmer over my chest in a hundred shades of green. The bars through my nipples wink in the candlelight. Murmurs rise behind me as the drumbeat grows faster. Wilder.

Beau's lips part. He grips the arms of his chair, his knuckles going white.

I bend and remove my boots. The murmurs swell, becoming chants. Magic crackles in the air.

Ritual.

Beau swallows hard as I unbuckle my belt. I fling it aside and unlace my pants, my dick straining against the leather. My selsara's dark eyes go to my groin. He licks his lips.

My dragon hums in my chest as I push my pants down my hips,

freeing my shaft that leaks for him. It bobs, my Prince Albert catching the light as I step out of my pants and stand nude before my mate.

The drumbeat pulses around the Great Hall. The courtiers' chants climb higher and higher. Beau's chest rises and falls faster as his gaze roams my body, returning again and again to the golden ring through my glistening cockhead. Precum beads at my slit and drips onto the table.

"I'm dripping for you, selsara," I purr. "Touch me. Accept me. Allow me to be yours."

Beau bites his lip, his white teeth digging into pink skin. Gods, I want to bite him there. Bite him everywhere.

I lift my arms away from my sides. Pitching my voice low, I look into my mate's eyes. "What do you say, selsara? Will you take me?"

CHAPTER 14

BEAU

I can't breathe. I can hardly think as I stare at Fuoco standing above me. His shaft sticks out from his hips, the thick, round head dripping with arousal. The drumbeat stops abruptly. Silence reigns.

Will you take me?

The Great Hall seems to hold its breath—the various monsters of the Myth waiting for my answer. Thank goodness my father isn't present. The shock might actually kill him. Hell, the shock might kill *me*. My heart thumps wildly, each beat echoed in my dick, which is embarrassingly hard. This scenario shouldn't be enticing. It should be scandalous.

And it is...but it's also titillating in a way I can't deny. Fuoco stands before me, completely unashamed of his nudity. Tiny flames dance in his eyes as he holds my stare. His body is perfection, every line taut and powerful. Broad, thick shoulders. Trim waist and rippling abs. His biceps flex as he holds out his arms, his palms turned up. Brilliant green scales cover him from neck to thigh, his golden skin still faintly visible underneath. It's like the two halves of his spirit mesh and coexist within him—and his beast is never too far from the surface. His beautiful cock thrusts proudly in my direction, the thick length curving upward. The head is deep crimson, the wet slit pierced cleanly by the golden, emerald-studded ring that fills me with a mix of lust of apprehension.

"Beau," he rasps, stepping forward, his feet as elegant and perfectly formed as the rest of him. For a moment, visions flood my head. Me on my knees pressing a kiss to one of his high arches. Me sprawling in a big chair with my legs flung apart, Fuoco dragging his bare foot up and down my dick…and then delving lower, his strong toes wriggling under my sack to stroke the sensitive skin around my hole. Me crawling up the foot of an oversize bed and playfully nipping at his ankle.

My breath catches as I blink rapidly, banishing the images from my mind. But the reality before me is just as riveting. Fuoco waits. Behind him, the whole court waits.

"Selsara," Fuoco murmurs, lowering himself to his knees. His scent—fire and spice and man—spins around me, invading my lungs. The piercings through his nipples and cock head wink in the Hall's soft light. "Say you'll take me, selsara. Say yes."

Time stops. The world stands still, the only two beings me and the dragon lord kneeling before me. Slowly, I nod. "Yes."

The Hall erupts into chaos. Cheers split the air. The musicians strike up a new song, this one fast and boisterous. Chairs tumble backward as Myth creatures stand and pull partners into a dance. Others pour wine. Jasper Lilygully throws his head back and laughs as a male with shiny black horns leans close and says something in his ear.

These things happen in some distant universe. Because the only thing I see is Fuoco's grin. It spreads wider as he rises, steps down from the table, and pulls me to my feet.

"What are you—?" My question ends in a gasp as he swings me into his arms. Hoots and applause follow us as he strides down the rows of tables to the big double doors.

"I can walk," I protest, fighting the urge to squirm. Something tells me that'll only make things worse. Knowing Fuoco, he'll simply toss me over his shoulder and keep going.

Green eyes gaze down at me with satisfaction—and a healthy dose of lust. "I'm aware, selsara. But you'll have to indulge me, because I like carrying you. And I'm too impatient to wait."

Wait for what? The question hovers on my tongue, but I hold onto it. Because I already know the answer, and it sets my heart fluttering as I settle deeper into his arms.

He walks quickly, the castle walls blurring as we wind our way through corridors and chambers. Within moments, we enter the courtyard. The stones are soaked in moonlight, the dragon statues around the perimeter stretching toward the night sky.

Fuoco sets me down and gives my forehead a quick peck. "Wait here." He strides a few dozen steps away and shifts, the transformation no less spectacular than the first time I witnessed it. His tail sweeps over the stones, striking sparks as he lumbers back to me. His glittering scales rival the moon. His claws are longer than my body.

But his eyes are gentle as he lowers his head and gently thumps his snout against my stomach. Warm breath puffs from his nostrils. He draws back, then offers an upturned paw. When I scramble into it, he nuzzles the top of my head and curls his claws around me protectively.

Then he launches us into the sky.

We soar high above the castle grounds, the cold wind whipping my hair. Once again, his body heat prevents me from getting too chilled. Below us, the village sparkles, its lights twinkling in the darkness. Fuoco spreads his wings wide, turning us and flying North. We cross rivers and streams, passing through fog banks and clouds. I cling to his claw, my heart racing as we climb higher and fly faster.

Finally, after what feels like hours of flight, a mountain range appears, its slopes shrouded in mist. Fuoco circles twice, then lands in a narrow valley tucked between two peaks. As he shifts, I drag crisp mountain air into my lungs, my head tipped back as I take in the blanket of stars winking overhead.

"It's beautiful," I murmur as Fuoco returns to my side.

"It's yours," he says, taking my hand and leading me to a stone door hidden behind a cluster of boulders. The door swings open at his touch, revealing a large corridor carved from the rock. Crystals as big as my fist sparkle from the floor to the ceiling, where chandeliers dance with blue flames. Fuoco tugs me inside, his hand warm in mine. "Everything here is for you, Beau. Come see it."

He leads me deep into the mountain, but it doesn't feel like we're underground. The air is warm. The ceilings soar overhead. The crystals in the walls turn to gemstones—rubies and garnets and sapphires as blue as the ocean. After several minutes, the corridor opens into a sprawling chamber.

And I freeze in place, my jaw dropping open as I look upon splendor that's like a gateway to another world. The walls shimmer with ribbons of silver and gold. More sparkling chandeliers hang overhead. In the center of the room, a massive fountain carved from black marble spouts crystal-clear water toward the ceiling. Plush rugs cover marble floors. Chairs and sofas are arranged in groups around tables carved from stone and studded with gems. High overhead, a window reveals the sky with its blanket of stars. A roaring fireplace crackles, its blaze setting all the gems in the room twinkling.

It's a room fit for a king—or a dragon lord.

"Come over here," Fuoco says, leading me to a sunken sanctuary of enormous silk and velvet pillows. His bed, I realize, goosebumps lifting on my skin. He's still nude and aroused, his cock bobbing as we descend to a cushioned platform softer than a cloud. Tiny diamonds sparkle along the golden ring that dangles from the tip of his dick.

"Your piercings…" I clamp my mouth shut before I can voice my errant thoughts.

But it's too late. "What about them?" Fuoco asks, pulling me down to the pillows. A smile plays around his mouth as he brushes his fingertips over the blush I can feel in my cheeks. "Let me guess, you noticed they disappear when I shift?"

"Yes," I rasp, trying not to stare at the monster between his legs.

"It's dragon magic. The metal is spelled to adapt to my beast form. It doesn't truly disappear. Just grows small enough to tuck behind my scales." His eyes shimmer with amusement as he eases me onto my back and comes down beside me. "And if you're wondering, my curious little selsara, my cock retreats into a sheath when I take dragon form. If it didn't, I'd probably have a hard time flying."

"I—" I gasp as he flips the button of my trousers and slips his hand inside to grasp my dick. "I wasn't wondering."

"Liar," he whispers, smiling.

I bite my lip. "Why do you have it?" I clear my throat. "That, um, piercing."

His smile spreads. He rolls me under him and grinds his dick against mine. "Because it feels fucking amazing."

"*Oh*," I gasp, my hips lifting on their own, my body eager for more friction. More *him*. "That's a good reason."

His laugh puffs over my face. "Indeed, it is," he murmurs, then lowers his lips to mine.

The kiss is slow and languid, as if we have all the time in the world. He teases me with his tongue, exploring my mouth until pleasure eddies through me in dizzying waves. His big hands roam everywhere—stroking my sides, pulling me closer, tugging at my beautiful clothes like they're rags instead of precious leather and silk.

My trousers go first, followed by my jacket and shirt. Then I'm nude beneath him, my feverish skin pressed against his. He kisses his way down my body, dipping and swirling over each nipple before moving to my abdomen and tracing feathery lines along the ridges of my abs. When he reaches my cock, he grabs my hips in both hands and sucks my cockhead into his mouth. He tongues my slit, dipping into the tiny opening over and over before taking me straight to the back of his throat.

I moan loudly, my head thrashing back and forth as he bobs up and down on my dick. He caresses my thighs, pushing them up so I'm splayed open, my knees pulled to my shoulders. Then he shoves them higher and buries his face in my ass.

"*Fuoco!*" I gasp, lifting my head as the exquisite and unfamiliar sensation barrels through me. His eyes glint with heat—and hints of mischief—as he pushes my cheeks wide and laps at my rim. It's slippery and hot and so, so good. "Fuck," I whimper, my head flopping back.

His chuckle drifts up to me as he teases my hole, swirling his tongue around my entrance. Pushing it inside me and getting me so wet his saliva drips down my crack. I rush toward that bright edge of bliss, my toes curling as he works me, thrusting his tongue so deep I claw at the pillows and scream his name. He slides a hand between my legs to cup my balls as he pumps his tongue, driving it into my hole over and over.

"You—" I writhe, panting and struggling to string words together. "You have to stop!"

He pulls back, rising to his knees and flashing a teasing smile as he wipes the back of his hand over his mouth. "You really want me to stop, baby?" He flops on top of me, his hips snug against mine. He rolls them against me, grinding our dicks together. As I shudder, he brushes my hair off my sweaty forehead. "No," he whispers gently, "I don't think you want me to stop."

I groan, rutting against him because I can't stay still. Not when his dick is so hard and perfect between us. "No," I say in a ragged voice. "I don't want you to stop."

"Do you want me to make love to you?" he murmurs, brushing his lips over mine. The look on his face is so tender that tears burn my eyes.

My heart hammers in my chest as I nod, unable to form words around the lump in my throat. He smiles against my lips, a satisfied sound rumbling from his chest as he captures my mouth in a slow, easy kiss. He rummages under a pillow and produces a little bottle of lube, then grins when I fail to muffle the mortified sound that escapes me.

"Do you know what this is?" he asks, drizzling moisture on his fingers.

I give him a look. "I'm not *that* inexperienced."

His soft laughter vibrates my chest as he tosses the bottle away and slicks himself. As he settles back over me, he fingers the rest of the lube into my hole. He kisses the tip of my nose. "Well, you're about to be a lot less inexperienced, selsara."

I stroke his shoulder, anticipation making me bold. "Get inside me."

"Yes, sir," he murmurs, rocking his hips against mine as he nips at my bottom lip. He slides a hand between our bodies and lines up the head of his cock with my entrance. He hesitates, his eyes soft. "The piercing won't hurt you. I'll go slow." He plants a gentle kiss on the curve of my eyebrow. "Do you trust me?"

I nod, breathing him in. Feeling the slick head of his cock poised at my quivering entrance. I'm soaked and open, my most private muscles twitching from the things he did with his tongue. I spread my legs wider, drawing my knees to my shoulders. "I trust you."

"Good boy," he whispers, and those two words strike like a bolt of lightning, hot forks of electricity licking through me. I cling to his shoulders as he starts to push inside. I expect pain, but it never comes —just a slow, delicious pressure as his cock stretches me. Then the blunt edge of his piercing brushes the spot that makes me see stars.

I moan and dig my fingers into the muscle of his shoulders as he rocks in and out, giving me shallow thrusts. "More," I beg, needing it. I want to be filled.

"Beau," he rasps, rising to his forearms and rolling his hips. He slides deeper with each thrust, filling me inch by glorious inch. I gasp and tremble, my eyes squeezing shut as he pushes all the way inside. He bottoms out, his warm, heavy balls snug against my ass.

He pauses, giving me a moment to adjust to his size. But I don't need to adjust. It's like I was made for him, my body designed to accommodate his. He must know it, because he pulls back and thrusts into me again, nudging my prostate and sending a burst of ecstasy pinwheeling through me.

"Yes!" I cry, opening my eyes. We stare at each other, and I see my wonder reflected in his green irises. "Fuck, yes," I breathe.

A shaky laugh warbles from him. "Selsara," he whispers, his voice reverent. He repeats the movement, withdrawing until only the head of his cock remains inside me before ramming himself home once more.

I moan loudly, my ass clamping hard on his dick. Acting on instinct, I throw my legs around his waist, hooking my ankles together and digging my heels into his back so I can pull him deeper. Pleasure blisters through me, and we both groan.

Bracing himself above me, he closes his eyes on a long blink. "You feel so good," he says, his voice shaking. "Gods, Beau, I don't know how long I can hold out."

Pleasure and astonishment mingle in my veins. He's the most powerful being I'll probably ever meet, but right now he's helpless.

Because of me.

Swallowing hard, I brush my fingers over his cheek. "Then don't," I say. "Don't hold out. And don't hold back."

His lips seek mine for a deep kiss. And then he *really* moves, letting himself off whatever chain he kept himself on. He drives his hips against mine, fucking me harder with each thrust. He moves faster and faster, our bodies slapping together as he pumps his length in and out of me.

My orgasm tightens in my belly—a tempest poised to unleash. And he must sense I'm close, because he reaches between us and strokes my dick, jerking me in time with his thrusts. "Come for me now," he says, his voice husky with desire.

That's all it takes. Half a dozen strokes and I'm done, a hoarse bellow ripping from me as I clutch his shoulders and spurt all over my stomach. Streaks of cum lash my chest, one splashing as high as my chin.

He gives a shout and thrusts a final time, pumping hot cum deep inside me. We stay like that for a moment, my legs locked around his waist and his spent cock twitching in my ass. Then he pulls out carefully and rolls us so we're chest to chest, our legs tangled together.

"Are you okay?" he asks, stroking his thumb over my cheek.

"Mmm," is all I can manage, my limbs weak with pleasure. His cum seeps from me in a hot slide. Sweat cools on my skin. Sleep tugs hard at my lids. Once again, he's worn me out. I'm going to be sore as hell tomorrow. But I loved every minute of it. Already, I can't wait to be filled again.

He kisses me softly on the forehead. "That was everything I dreamed of."

A response floats in my consciousness—words that bob gently as I drift off, warm and secure in Fuoco's embrace.

It was everything I dreamed of, too.

The next time I wake, it's morning. Fuoco sleeps on his stomach next to me, his arms hugging a pillow and his face turned away. Light streams through the window in the ceiling and plays over his body, highlighting the elegant dip of his spine and the firm, round curves of his bare ass. His long legs are slightly spread, giving me a glimpse of the piercing behind his heavy sack.

I rise, my face heating as my body aches in places that have never ached before. Taking care not to step on Fuoco, I clamber nude from the sunken pit. My clothes are folded neatly on a nearby chair. Pulling on my pants and shirt, I take a minute to gaze around at Fuoco's hideaway. It's no less spectacular in the daytime. Gemstones wink at me from a variety of surfaces. The marble veining in the walls glitters in the sunlight. The fountain splashes gently, water bubbling toward the vaulted ceiling before falling into the large bowl at the base.

And on the far side of the chamber, a stone archway offers a glimpse of something that makes my heart rate pick up.

Books.

I'm across the room and through the archway in seconds, and I stifle a gasp at the sight that greets me. Not just books—a full library. Bookcases climb up the walls, every shelf lined with leather-bound volumes. I run my fingertips down one row of spines, then turn and admire the rest of the room.

And there's a great deal to admire. Colorful tapestries hang in the spaces between the bookshelves. A large mahogany desk sits near one marble-veined wall, its surface piled high with papers and parchment. A globe with a carved dragon curled around its base perches on the corner. Several plush armchairs scatter through the room, each one inviting me to curl up and lose myself in a story.

Heavy footsteps vibrate the floor under my feet. A second later, Fuoco bursts through the archway and staggers to a halt.

"Beau!" Instantly, green flames wreath his head. Tension radiates from him. The dragon scales across his chest gleam as he heaves a breath. He steps forward, his eyes narrowing. "You left without telling me."

I back up, my shoulders bumping the bookcases. "I d-didn't—"

"You can't do that." He slashes a hand through the air. "You can't leave."

Confusion swamps me. I point to the archway behind him. "I came from the—"

"What were you thinking?" The flames around his head leap higher. "You could have been hurt! Don't you ever do something like that again, do you understand?" He leans forward, his fangs showing between his lips as his voice climbs to a roar. "If you don't go places with *me*, you don't go places at *all*."

In a flash, anger replaces my confusion. My feet carry me forward until I'm close enough for the heat of his flaming hair to warm my skin. My voice is deadly low in my ears as I stare up at him. "What did you say to me?"

His eyes go wide. For a moment, he seems speechless. And maybe I'm imagining it, but I can almost swear that fear flickers in his eyes.

But my blood is pumping too hot for me to care. "I asked you a question," I say quietly.

The flames around his head dim. He drags in a breath, his big chest swelling. As he releases it, he rubs a hand over his mouth. "You're right," he mutters behind his palm. When he lowers his hand, his voice is tight with regret. "I had no right to speak to you that way. It's just that…" He stares at me, and flames flicker among the dark waves of his hair. "You mean more to me than you know. My dragon is…unsettled by any threat to you."

I glance at the main chamber through the arch behind him. "It's a threat when I walk from one room to another?"

"I woke and you weren't there," he says tightly. "I couldn't find you." He sucks in another deep breath. "Last night at dinner, Jasper Lilygully told me he scented Lirem around your bakery."

Memories surface—Lirem's grating laughter as he slammed his fist into my jaw. "You think he wants to hurt me?"

"I think he wants revenge." Fuoco clenches his fists. Then he seems to catch himself, because he forces his hands open. Anguish fills his green eyes. "Lirem knows you're the most important part of my life." Fuoco's gaze searches mine. "You *must* know that by now, Beau." He rubs the center of his chest, wincing as if his heart pains him. "I can't breathe without you."

Fear and wonder tangle within me. All those years denying who I am and what I want. I never thought I'd find someone to share my life with, let alone someone who wants me as much as Fuoco does. But he wants so much...

"Dragons are possessive about their mates," he says, "but my beast is even more so when it comes to you." He takes another step, closing the distance between us. "My magic is powerful, and it produces powerful emotion in those who wield it."

Despite the weightiness of the conversation, curiosity sparks. "What is your magic?"

"Everything," he rasps, taking my hand in both of his. "I'm an elemental, Beau. I command earth, air, wind, and fire."

My heart beats faster. "What do you mean by command?"

"I can manipulate the elements around me. Speak to them in a fashion. Bend them to my will. I can make it rain when I want. Make the wind blow as hard as I wish. And I can bring fire to life with a thought." As if to demonstrate, he slides his hand up my arm, leaving a trail of heat in his wake. "But the emotions that come with my gift are overwhelming. If I'm not careful, they'll consume me. If that happens, it won't take long for my mind to break."

The hair on my nape lifts. "And what happens then?"

"The world burns."

Coming from anybody else, such a statement would sound grandiose or even a bit silly. But seeing him now—his eyes wide and stark—I know he means it. He's capable of burning everything down.

He stares at me a moment longer before stepping back. He draws an even breath, and the flames in his hair wink out. "My gift is both a blessing and a curse. I have to keep my emotions in check, especially now that I've found you. Even the *thought* of losing you could tip me over the edge. And now that I know Lirem seeks you, my need to protect is overwhelming."

"Okay, but do you really need to protect me from your library?" I wait for him to deny it—maybe laugh and dismiss such a notion as absurd. Instead, he says nothing, his gaze deadly serious. Alarm bells clang in my head. "Fuoco, I can't live my life glued to your side."

"Would it bother you to spend that much time with me?"

"Honestly, *yes*." I gesture at the books around us. "I want to be with you, but I have interests of my own. I love reading—"

"Which you can do here."

"—and baking. I have a business I worked hard to build."

He folds his arms, his expression mulish. "I've spent centuries amassing wealth. You don't have to work anymore."

"I *like* working. And I don't just bake for profit, Fuoco. I enjoy it."

"You can bake here," he insists, frustration lacing his tone. "Or in the castle. You can have anything you want. Anything." His fingers twitch at his sides like he's just barely managing to keep himself from reaching for me. His voice climbs again. "I want to give you the world but I can't do that if I can't keep you safe, and I can't keep you safe while Lirem is out there!"

"So you'll tether me to your side until you find him?"

"If that's what it takes."

"What about after?"

His jaw is tight, the look in his eyes so stubborn and unyielding I want to slap him just to shock him out of this ridiculous mindset. How can I make him understand that I need more than nice clothes and pretty books? The apprehension I felt over breakfast in his bedchamber resurfaces.

"I can't be happy as a pet," I say firmly. "A gilded cage is still a cage." I square my shoulders. "I'm not a warrior. Not even close. But I'm not a coward, either. I don't want to be coddled, Fuoco. I need to be able to make my own decisions, and that includes taking risks. I'm not saying I want to run into the village and wait for Lirem to find me. But I need freedom of movement. If you lock me in your castle and dress me up in outfits, it'll wear me down until there's nothing left of me. And then you won't have me at all."

"Don't say that," he whispers, pain flitting through his eyes.

"Then don't treat me like a piece of jewelry you own. Treat me like an equal."

He takes my hand. "You *are* my equal. All I've ever wanted was for you to rule by my side."

I exhale slowly, the tension in my chest easing a bit. If he wants me to rule with him, maybe I should show him what that looks like. "As a ruler, what's the most pressing issue in front of you right now?"

"Protecting you," he says without hesitation.

I fight the urge to punch him. "Okay, the thing after that."

"Finding Lirem."

I smile and squeeze his hand. "Let's start with that. We should probably go to the village, right? If Lirem was around the bakery, we should check it out."

He frowns, clearly not liking the idea of me anywhere near a spot where Lirem might be lurking.

"You'll keep me safe," I say. "You're the only dragon shifter in the syndicate, right? The other dragons can't best you in a fight."

He grunts.

"Does that mean yes?"

"Yes," he says, his expression so sulking I could almost laugh. Then inspiration strikes. "We can take food from your greenhouse to the village. I've distributed bread for years. If the people see you doing it, it'll go a long way toward shifting their opinion of you."

Surprise—and something that might be respect—flares in his eyes. "You really think so?"

"It's worth a try."

He hesitates for a moment before finally nodding in agreement. He pulls me against him, his mouth inches from mine. "We'll go, selsara. But you are never out of my sight."

"I wouldn't dream of it," I say, and then I melt under his kiss.

CHAPTER 15
FUOCO

I swoop over Beau's village, my emotions rocketing back and forth between dread and hope. Beau perches carefully in my claw, looking out at the world below us. In the other claw, I carry a large wooden wagon laden with all the things he thought the humans might want—cured meats, canned and fresh fruit, salted seeds, and plenty of freshly baked bread.

His insistence on being by my side for this visit has my dragon simmering just under my skin. I imagine Lirem around every corner, although I don't think he'd be foolish enough to target Beau in front of me. But the idea of it has me bristling, fire building and curling in my throat. I huff out a stream of smoke to dispel it. I've got a lot to make up for when it comes to the humans. Setting their village aflame wouldn't be the most auspicious start.

I glide swiftly down to the village square, dropping Beau and the wagon to the ground and shifting fast. He hands me clothing and I yank the pants and shirt on before swinging a dark cloak around my shoulders. Faces appear in windows. Astonished eyes goggle at us.

An odd sensation flutters in my gut, like butterflies struggling to fly out of my mouth. Am I...nervous?

I'm ready for whatever response the villagers throw at me. Anger, fear, accusations. Not that my preparation will make today any easier. I've avoided humans for over half a century. Aside from Beau, I have no clue how to interact with mortals.

"Remember what we talked about," Beau says softly at my side. "Just be yourself. Talk to them." He brushes his hand against mine as if he can sense my discomfort. As villagers emerge from the buildings, he waves at a small girl peering at us from a window. A few men step into the street, their gazes wary and their bodies tense. One grips a pitchfork in a tight fist.

"A little on the nose," I say to Beau under my breath.

"Behave," he murmurs back, a smile in his voice. Then he lifts a hand in greeting. "Henry! Bartholomew! Join us. We come with aid."

Slowly but surely, the square fills with villagers. The little girl from the window darts out the door only to be yanked back inside by a heavily pregnant woman.

Tangible tension floats over the group. It's in the men's tight shoulders and the women's hostile stares. I remind myself what Beau told me before we left the castle—winning the people over isn't going to be easy, but each town we visit and every step we take to mend past wrongs will help.

Clearing my throat, I shove my hands into my broad cloak sleeves, doing my best to appear smaller and less threatening. "Beau and I have brought food and supplies. I recently learned that my enforcers were stealing from you. For too long, they terrorized the people of my syndicate. I didn't know, and I'm deeply sorry for what happened. I've come to make amen—"

"You expect us to believe that when all you've done is lie and steal?" The harsh feminine voice cuts across the courtyard. A second later, a young woman steps out from between two buildings and stops at the edge of the crowd. Her dark curls gleam in the sun. Bright blue eyes narrow as she looks from me to Beau.

It's the woman who helped herself to Beau's pastries when he wasn't around to stop her.

She accused me of thievery then, too.

I hold her stare. "As I was saying, I've come to make amends."

"What have you done to Beau?" she demands. "Just days ago he hated dragons the same as the rest of us. Now, he stands by your side. This reeks of dark magic."

A chorus of shouts rises among those assembled. The man with the pitchfork tightens his grip around the handle.

Elemental power stirs in my chest, sharpening my senses. Chilly air curls against the stones. The water in the fountain behind the woman trickles through old, leaking pipes. The earth below the courtyard calls to me, ready to do my bidding. It would be so easy to answer its call—to command the ground to open its jaws and swallow her whole.

Beau puts his hand on my forearm as he addresses the crowd. "Two of the three enforcers are dead. The third is in hiding. Lord Fuoco killed the others for their crimes against us. I saw this with my own eyes. He killed them the moment he found out what they were doing." Beau gestures at the wagon behind us. "This isn't enough to make up for the years we endured Lirem, Nazzar, and Varden, but it's a start. Please, take what you need."

Pride blooms in my chest. The elemental madness recedes as the heat from Beau's hand seeps under the sleeve of my cloak and into my skin.

"Is it poisoned?" someone shouts from the back.

"No," Beau calls out. He gazes around the crowd, meeting villagers' eyes one by one. "You all know me. Trust me when I tell you there's nothing to fear."

A man in the front looks at the wagon. Then he turns to the people around him. "We could use the food."

Several villagers nod. Rumbles of agreement move through the crowd.

I lift my voice. "There is more where this came from. If you give me a list of what you need for the winter, I'll bring it from my own stores."

"Been hoarding it, have you?" It's that fucking dark-haired woman again, shoving through the crowd to glare daggers at me. The cloying scent of rosewater sears my nostrils as she props her hands on her hips. "You took it from us and now you'll give it back?" She releases a short, bitter laugh. "How generous."

My beast moves under my skin. At the same moment, Beau

tightens his grip on my arm. His touch steadies me, soothing my dragon and curbing my tongue.

I offer the woman a stiff nod. "You're right. My enforcers stole from you. I take responsibility for their actions, which is why I'm here. I want to give back."

The tiny girl from the window darts through the crowd and runs up to me, skidding to a stop. Several villagers gasp.

I drop to a knee so I'm closer to eye level with the child. "How may I help you, little one?"

"I saw you before," she whispers. "Your hair was green!"

I smile. "That's right." I gesture toward the wagon. "Is there something special you'd like from what I brought?"

She holds her arms out in the age-old gesture demanding to be picked up. More gasps ascend from the crowd as I lift her. Swinging her high, I place her on the wagon.

"Pick anything you want," I tell her, and she flashes me a bright, gap-toothed smile as she perches on the edge and surveys the goods within. After a moment's consideration, she chooses a giant loaf of pumpkin bread and clutches it to her chest. I help her down, and she darts back into the crowd.

For a moment, the square is silent. Then an elderly man steps forward. "Got any meat in there, Beau?"

Beau is quick to help the man, reaching into the wagon and withdrawing a shoulder of cured pork bundled in twine. "Here, Archibald. Enough for a roast and then some."

The man dips his head as he accepts the meat. Then he turns to me, his gaze wavering between distaste and watchfulness. Eventually, he offers a curt nod before shuffling back into the crowd.

A few beats pass. Then the floodgates open. Villagers surge forward, calling out requests. Beau and I busy ourselves hunting for items and parceling them out. The dark-haired woman retreats into a store, where she stands at a window and glares at us with folded arms. I receive plenty of glares from other villagers, but I grit my teeth and stay the course.

As I work across from Beau in the bed of the wagon, he meets my gaze, his eyes shining with affection. "You're doing a wonderful job," he murmurs. "I'm proud of you." The words are so low they're scarcely audible, but they ring loud as a bell in my chest. He's proud to be here. With me.

He's worth every moment of discomfort.

When the last of the food is gone, the villagers disperse. Several clap Beau on the shoulder as they depart, offering gratitude and a smile. The smiles fade as their eyes stray to me, but a few mutter "thank you" before they walk away. Then Beau and I stand alone beside the wagon.

He slips his hand into mine. "I think it went well. How about you?"

"They don't like me." The words sound sullen, and I smile ruefully as I lift Beau's hand and place a quick kiss on his knuckles. "Not like you do."

His cheeks turn pink, and he glances around like he's making sure no one heard. "It'll get easier." Chocolate eyes reflect the green flames in mine as he smiles up at me. "One step at a time, right?"

I nod. "One step at a time."

∼

A WEEK PASSES IN A BLUR. Every day, Beau and I deliver food and goods to the towns in my syndicate. Some are less welcoming than others, but we always promise to return with the things they need. Beau keeps a running list, and watching him diligently add to it thaws something cold inside me.

He answers every question and listens to every request. He handles complaints with incredible grace. He's a natural with the people, who flock to him as soon as he flashes his warm smile.

I'm another story. Most of the villagers are still wary of me. Some are outright hateful. At best, they're indifferent. But they're all smitten with my selsara.

At every stop, we hear stories about what my enforcers did to my people. In a village in the far north, Beau asked a farmer what he needed to get his farm back on track.

"A new windmill," the man grumbled. "Varden set mine on fire for not paying taxes, 'cept I had paid them. He just wanted more, always more."

I placed my hand on the man's shoulder and turned him to face me. "I'll return every coin he stole with interest, and I'll see about getting a new windmill built immediately."

Fear sparked in the man's gaze. He stepped out of my grasp, but nodded and offered a clipped "thank you."

And so it's gone on for a week. Nazzar drowned someone's cow. Lirem broke all the windows in a tailor's shop and the man's leather-making supplies were ruined in a rainstorm. Varden took all the gold from one village's bank, loading it into big sacks and disappearing.

My enforcers' crimes make my stomach churn with shame. My dragon paces constantly in my chest, desperate to rip Lirem to shreds for his treachery.

Jasper checks in several times but offers no substantive updates on my missing enforcer. If the pixie's mice can't find Lirem, then he's gone so deeply to ground it could be years before he shows his face. I can't let that stand. So I begin every evening by pleasuring my mate—and afterward, while Beau sleeps, I take to the sky and scour my territory, hunting for any sign of Lirem.

As the days wear on without progress on that front, my mood sours.

Like tonight. Beau sits at my side in the Great Hall, his spicy-sweet scent doing nothing to chase away the stench of failure that burns my nose. My court is as rowdy as ever, but I can't seem to muster the energy to join in their revelry. A week of seeing hatred and disgust on the humans' faces sits like a weight around my shoulders. I'd love nothing more than to grab Beau, shift, and spin up through the clouds to leave my problems behind.

But that won't solve them.

I pick at the food on my plate, pushing it around before shoving it away. Maurice Bidbury's rich laughter brings my head up.

Beau's father sits beside my selsara, his wrinkled face glowing with good health. Maurice is clearly enamored with my court. He's constantly introducing himself to any magical creature who will speak with him. Fortunately, the courtiers reciprocate his interest. It turns out my selsara's sire is as endearing as my mate.

"Yes, Maurice," the dragon on Maurice's right rumbles with a throaty chuckle. "It's simple enough magic. The cobbler suggests what the tools should do, but they carry out the work themselves."

Beau turns to his father. "I've seen it, Dad. You should visit the cobbler to watch for yourself. And you could use some new shoes. I'll go with you if you want."

Maurice smooths his wisps of white hair. "I might take you up on that, son. Although, the ladies around here can't stop complimenting me on my new clothes. If I add shoes, they won't be able to keep their hands off me."

"Dad!"

The dragon who spoke of the cobbler gives a hearty laugh.

I toy with my wineglass as I observe them, my rings winking in the candlelight.

Beau meets my gaze, and his smile falters a little. *You alright?* he mouths.

I nod, forcing a smile. I didn't expect to fix everything immediately, but it's clear now that making inroads is going to take a very long time. The bright light at the end of my tunnel is Beau.

"As long as I have you, I'm perfect, selsara." I reach under the table to squeeze his knee. He ducks his head—but he also spreads his legs, allowing me to slide my hand all the way up his thigh. I grip it tightly, thankful I've got him by my side to sort through the messes I've made. "You amaze me," I murmur.

He's been tireless this week, never once complaining about the hard work of traveling from village to village.

My equal.

Chocolate eyes crinkle at the corners as his smile deepens. It's the seductive smile of a lover becoming comfortable. He no longer cares if someone sees that smile, or if his father observes us holding hands.

On Beau's other side, Maurice launches into an animated conversation about some fresh topic, waving his hands around as he illustrates a point.

But when I hear Lirem's name, I snap my head up to eye a dragon sitting farther down the table.

"What was that?" I demand. "What did you say about Lirem?"

The dragon gives me a wary look. "Just that I haven't seen him around in a few days." His brow furrows as he appears to contemplate it. "I haven't seen Varden or Nazzar either, come to think of it. Gods, they've missed out on quite a bit, but I suppose they're busy."

Maurice and Beau freeze.

Across the table, a pretty female dragon named Riselle sits forward, her amethyst eyes serious. "There's been talk, Fuoco. Rumors about why the enforcers aren't here."

Jasper hasn't uncovered anything to indicate Lirem has allies here in my court. And I can't keep Nazzar and Varden's deaths a secret forever. If anything, coming clean will lift one of the burdens that plague me.

Rising, I plant my hands on the table. "Nazzar and Varden are dead."

The dragons closest to me gasp, then a flurry of rushed murmurs carries the news down the tables. I draw myself up, letting my voice boom through the Great Hall. "They're dead for the crimes of theft and torture. They were stealing from the humans, hurting them and worse."

Another round of gasps peppers the air.

"What about Lirem?" someone calls from a nearby table.

A growl rumbles in my throat. "Lirem escaped after attacking my selsara." Every head swivels to Beau, who presses back into his chair, his throat bobbing.

Riselle stands. "He touched your selsara? He hurt Beau?" The look on her face tells me she finds it as shocking as I do. Harming another dragon's mate is a crime punishable by instant death. She tosses her hair over her shoulder, danger glinting in her purple eyes. "What's our next move, my lord?"

"I'll hunt him and then I'll kill him," I say, flames wrapping around my head. "And we're finished with enforcers. From now on, I'll work with all of my people directly."

Around the Great Hall, every human servant stands rooted to the ground. The familiar scent of fear fills the room.

Riselle gazes around at them. "This is not our way. Dragons didn't come to this plane to hurt people. I'm sorry."

For a moment, no one speaks. Then the dragon who spoke to Maurice stands. "Riselle is right. We aren't here to take advantage." He touches his fist to his broad chest and bows his head. "I'll do whatever I can to right this wrong."

One by one, dragons stand, their eyes gleaming as they echo the sentiment. After a moment, other Myth creatures join in.

Awe spreads through me as my court of partiers and merry-makers put down their wineglasses and commit to serving the people.

Riselle turns glittering amethyst eyes to me. "How do we get started, my lord? Tell us what you need and we'll do it."

Before I can answer, Tess crosses the Hall with a serving platter in her hands. She pauses before my table, her cheeks brilliant red as she darts a quick look at Riselle before staring at the ground. She speaks in a hushed voice that nevertheless echoes around the quiet tables. "Lord Fuoco and Beau have been delivering supplies to the villages. They've been making regular trips, but the people still need food and firewood to get through the winter." Tess tightens her fingers around the platter. "I just thought… Maybe you could…" She trails off, a mottled blush spreading down her neck.

Beau stands, rounds the table, and goes to Tess. He takes the platter from her and puts his other arm around her shoulders. They stand among my court of Myth creatures, both mortal and seemingly powerless. But their courage shines as brightly as any gem.

"Tess makes a great point," Beau says. "Fuoco and I have made a lot of progress, but we could use more help. I've got a list of items each village needs. Perhaps we can split up the responsibilities to distribute them more quickly."

The screech of chairs being pushed back fills the hall. As one, my courtiers raise their glasses.

"We are with you," Riselle declares. She swings toward me and inclines her head. "Whatever you require, my lord, we'll make it happen."

"I'll help, too," Tess says, her voice stronger as she looks at me from under Beau's arm. "If it pleases you, my lord."

I nod. "It would please me very much, Tess."

Her smile transforms her pale face from meek to lovely. Beau releases her, and she slips among the tables, her steps lighter than before.

As Beau returns to my side, Maurice rises and puts a hand on Beau's shoulder. "Your mother would be so proud of you, son." Eyes brimming with tears, he pulls Beau into a hug.

"I love you, Dad," Beau says. Around the Hall, courtiers glance their direction and smile. At a table near the double doors, Jasper catches my eye. The pixie winks, his wings flicking silvery dust into the air as he stands and walks from the Hall.

Probably up to something. I try to scowl after him, but I can't stop the smile that insists on spreading over my face. The atmosphere in the Hall is more subdued now, the wild carousing replaced with earnest conversation as courtiers discuss plans for taking food to the people. The transformation is so complete, it's like a spell descended over the court.

But as my gaze settles on Beau, I realize that's not quite right. The change is magical, but it's not a spell.

It's Beau. *He's* the magic. He's bringing humans and dragons together. He's flourishing by my side, not locked up in a glittering tower like my most prized possession. He's nothing I expected and everything I needed.

I'm going to tell him that tonight as soon as we're alone.

Maurice wipes tears from his face as he eases away from Beau. "It's been a wonderful evening, but I need to get to bed." Maurice's brown eyes twinkle as he looks from me to his son. "And I think that's where you two need to go, too."

"Oh my *gods*, Dad," Beau says, burying his face in his hands.

Maurice grins at me. With a chuckle, he claps Beau on the back before heading for the doors.

Smiling, I pull Beau's hands away from his face. "You heard your father." I tangle my fingers with his, then lift our joined hands to my mouth and bite his knuckle. "Bedtime."

We set a record getting to our bedchamber, and we stumble through the door locked in each other's arms. I stroke my tongue deep into his mouth, shoving my hips against his as he rips my shirt from my shoulders.

We fall into the bed and I yank his pants down, tossing them to the floor. He climbs on top of me with a big smile, then gasps when I flip us, flinging him to his back and pushing his legs up. With a wicked smile of my own, I dip down and suck his balls into my mouth, swirling my tongue around one swollen globe, then the other. I reach up and find his cock, which already drips for me.

"Fuck, Fuoco," he moans, gripping his knees and pulling his legs higher. "Don't stop."

Chuckling, I trail my tongue down to his pucker. I lap at his quivering hole as I stroke his hard length, teasing him until he's panting and rocking his hips to meet my mouth. When his thrusts grow wild and desperate, I sit back on my heels.

"Nooo," he whines, shooting me a faux glare from eyes gone glassy with lust. "Teasing was never part of our bargain, my lord."

"That bargain is finished," I say. I'll never threaten him again. My beast curls in my chest, content in the knowledge that I don't have to worry about Beau leaving me. He's *chosen* to stay, which is more precious to me than any treasure.

The lust in his eyes flares higher when I reach under a pillow. But as I withdraw two brilliant green gemstones, he sits up with a gasp.

"These are beautiful." He strokes the stones with careful fingers. Their light plays over his chest, scattering green sparks across his skin and making me bite back a groan.

"They're mating jewels." I give him one, and his hand dips under the gemstone's weight. "Dragons consider them sacred. If you accept mine, I'll bind it to your chest. Then I'll bind my own and our mating bond will be sealed."

He looks up at me, his chocolate eyes wide. "And what happens once we're bound?"

"We live together for eternity," I murmur, anxiety stirring. I'm asking for everything. What if he's not ready to give it? "This binds us soul to soul. If one of us dies, the other will as well. There is no greater bond among creatures of the Myth."

He studies the jewel, brushing his thumb over the glossy green surface. Just as my anxiety threatens to blossom into full-blown panic, he looks up and gives me the brightest, most beautiful smile. "I'd be honored, selsara."

Pleasure frazzles through me. My dragon roars under my skin. "You called me selsara," I rasp.

Beau hands me his gemstone. "Claim me. I accept."

Growling, I grip his shoulders and flip him into the pillows. Straddling his hips, I rub at a spot in the center of his chest. "I'll place this here while I take you. And when we come together, the jewel will bind itself into your skin."

A hint of unease enters his eyes. "Will it hurt?"

"No." I smile. "You'll come harder than you ever have."

Humor and heat shine in his eyes as he bites his lip. "That's hard to believe."

"I swear it. Are you ready?"

He nods, and the humor in his eyes fades, leaving only heat. "Yes."

I place his jewel carefully in the divot just under his pectorals. Then I hand him my stone and show him where to hold it against my skin. "Don't let go."

"I won't."

I grab the lube and drip a sticky string onto his bobbing cock. Then I toss the bottle aside and stroke moisture over his shaft. Precum beads at his slit as I coat him from base to tip.

He grunts, rocking his hips and bowing his spine.

"You need more, selsara?" I tease, slipping my hand down to his sack and slicking his balls. When he's shuddering, I work a finger into his hole. His cock leaks all over his rippling abs. "It's a wonder you need lube at all," I say. "You always get so wet for me."

"Fuck," he whispers, clenching so hard around my finger I almost lose my grip on his jewel. "It's too good." He groans when I push a second finger inside. "I'm losing my mind."

Smiling, I play with his hole a bit longer, stroking and teasing in and out of his tight heat as I work him open. Then I grip my cock and slap it playfully against his before taking both of our dicks in hand. I rock my hips, stroking us together. Gripping our shafts, I fuck his cock with mine until we're both panting. As Beau cries out, I know I don't have long. My mate is ready.

"I've waited for you my entire life," I say, guiding my cock to his entrance. I push inside slowly, perfect heat and pressure engulfing me.

Beau's cries stretch into a full-on wail. He squeezes his eyes shut, but his hand pressing the jewel to my chest remains steady. "Fuuuck," he groans, the tendons in his neck taut.

I jerk my hips, burying my dick to the hilt inside him as white-hot pleasure streaks down my spine. Under the jewel, a burning sensation like a thousand tiny pinpricks stabs at my skin. I rock out of Beau, then slam back inside, jolting his body against the pillows.

"The jewel," he bellows, dropping a startled gaze to his chest. Just as quickly, his eyes roll back in his head and a wanton moan escapes him. "Gods! Fuck!"

I thrust harder, pumping my hips faster. My breaths come in short gasps as I lose all sense of time and place. The intensity between us mounts. With every thrust, the jewels glow brighter.

Beau opens his eyes, his gaze wild as he stares up at me. His breath is ragged, his skin flushed and slick with sweat. The jewel sears my chest as we approach our peak together. I push and pull in time with Beau's choked cries, sweat sheening my skin as the stone grows even hotter.

My vision tunnels, focusing solely on Beau as pleasure builds like a wave inside me. The burning sensation intensifies, and I keep going, my thrusts jerky and uncoordinated as my balls tighten and the bright, shiny edge of release speeds toward me.

Beau gets there first. He convulses, his cock spurting across his heaving abs. My mouth hangs open as I watch cum paint his skin. Then I'm coming, too, a scream ripping from my throat as I line Beau's ass with my release. I roar, the sound somewhere between my human voice and the animalistic, predatory bellow of my dragon.

Red and green galaxies burst behind my eyelids as I ride the wave of ecstasy with my mate. He writhes beneath me, his hand never moving from the jewel he presses to my chest. The crescendo ebbs and rises again, and I'm obliterated from the inside out, my orgasm so powerful my teeth gnash together, my jaw locking tight as I curl over him, shuddering so hard I swear I can feel my bones grinding to dust.

Long minutes later, I blink my eyes open. Beau pants beneath me. His lips are parted, his chest rising and falling as he takes great, gasping breaths. In the center of his chest, his mating jewel glows as if lit from within.

My mouth falls open as a cascade of green light shines from the gemstone, illuminating his face and bouncing off the walls around us. I pull out and fall onto my ass, tears pricking my eyes as I gaze at my mate.

Beau sits up. As he looks down at his chest, I brace myself for the worst. I wait for him to panic or demand I remove the bond, which I can't do. We're locked in this together now.

He lifts his head, his eyes shining with unshed tears as he gazes at the matching jewel in my chest. Going to his knees, he brushes his fingers over my pecs and the glittering edge of the gemstone. "This is the most beautiful thing I've ever seen."

A split second later, he gasps as I tackle him to the pillows. I stretch my body over his, my hands pinning his wrists next to his head. "I love you," I blurt. "I've loved you for my whole life, but having you here with me..." I drag in deep breaths as I struggle to finish the sentence. "I can't imagine anyone else I'd want this with, Beau. Selsara." My voice breaks as emotion overtakes me. So I stop talking. Burying my nose in his neck, I suck in deep breaths of him. Cinnamon. Sugar. All the smells of his bakery are imbued in his skin.

"I love you, too," he says.

"I will always protect you," I vow. "No matter what comes."

"I know," he says, rubbing a hand over my back. He turns his face into my shoulder and smiles against my skin. "I'll protect you, too. You're mine, Fuoco."

Bound for eternity.

I've never been happier.

CHAPTER 16
BEAU

Fuoco's light snores fill the room. As usual, he lies on his stomach with his legs flung apart. Smiling, I stroke my fingers through his hair. Poor dragon. I wore him out.

For once, I'm too worked up to sleep. But maybe that has something to do with the jewel embedded in my chest. Its green light is dimmer now—because Fuoco is sleeping. My selsara. After our second round of lovemaking, he explained that my gemstone will always reflect his state of mind. Likewise, his will echo mine. When he's at rest, the jewel in my chest will rest, too. *"And when I'm aroused, selsara, you'll feel it everywhere."*

He wasn't kidding.

Moonlight pours through the window and splashes over the bed, joining the light cast by my jewel. *Bound for eternity.* Fuoco and I didn't exchange vows in the traditional sense, but we're as good as married now. Maybe *more* than married. It's not like I can divorce him.

My heart thumps faster, and something that feels a little bit like panic scrabbles down my spine. I didn't hesitate when Fuoco presented me with the mating jewels. But maybe I should have? How many people marry the first person they fall for? Fuoco is immortal, and now that my life is linked with his, I'll live as long as he does.

What happens a hundred years from now? A *thousand* years from now?

Fuoco stirs, the muscles in his back rippling as he snuggles the pillow more tightly. I hold my breath while he moves, then slowly release it when he finally settles down. Slipping from bed, I go to the big wardrobe and pull on the first clothes I find. There's one person in this castle who knows me better than I probably know myself. Maybe he can give me some advice.

Ten minutes later, Dad offers me a startled smile as he opens his door. "Beau! What are you doing up at this hour?" His snowy brows pull together. "Is everything okay? Are you sick?"

"No," I say quickly. "I'm totally fine. But I need to talk to you about something."

He nods and steps back so I can enter. A familiar whirring sound greets me as he shuts the door. A large worktable sits against one wall, its surface covered in test tubes, mechanical contraptions, and other equipment.

"You've got a whole lab in here," I say, wandering toward the display.

"Isn't it great?" Excitement bubbles in my father's voice as he steps beside me. "Fuoco had everything delivered this morning. Dieter gave me a clean bill of health, so I can start inventing again."

Gratitude swells my chest. Fuoco didn't mention any of this to me. He just did it—he took care of my father because that's what he does. My *husband* takes care of the people he loves.

"Beau?" Dad moves in front of me, concern in his eyes. "What did you want to talk to me about, son?"

I take a deep breath as I struggle to find the right words. "Fuoco and I… We're together now. Permanently." I tell my father a censored version of what happened this evening, explaining the jewels and how Fuoco and I are bound. "It all happened so fast, and now I wonder if I rushed into it?" I shove a hand through my hair, my heart thudding in my chest as doubts ripple through me. "I mean, Fuoco has been dreaming of me for longer than I can wrap my head around, but I don't know. Maybe I'm just infatuated. It's not like I've dated—"

"Beau," my father says, interrupting my rambling. Smiling gently, he tips his head toward the balcony. "Why don't we go outside and get some fresh air, hmm? I have some thoughts on your predicament."

We step into the brisk night and sit at the table and chairs by the railing. Dad takes a moment to look at the stars, and I can almost see his thoughts turning as he gazes at the sky. Finally, he turns his attention to me.

"I remember when your mother and I first met. I felt like I'd been knocked over." He flashes me a self-deprecating smile. "I'm sure I acted like a fool. But she never seemed to mind. Or maybe she felt just as ridiculous and out of her depth as I did. This is a tired cliche, but we were like two magnets drawn together by invisible forces neither of us could control."

"Sound like Fate," I murmur.

"It was." Dad's eyes go soft, his face suddenly years younger. "I knew Evangeline was special from the very start. My gut told me this was it, that I was going to love this woman forever." He pauses, studying me for a moment before continuing. "Not everyone has the privilege of finding the person they're meant to be with. It's an uncommon gift. Those old wedding vows say it all, really. You're with them through good times and bad, sickness and health."

A low sound breaks from my throat. I reach across the table and grab his hand. "Dad..." I say softly.

He places his other hand atop ours on the table. "Love isn't always easy, son. In a lot of ways, it's a leap of faith. A great deal has happened to you in a short period of time. But I think if you listen closely enough, you'll hear your heart speaking to you. It has a way of cutting through all the noise in your head. It'll tell you what's right."

I smile, remembering how I felt the first time Fuoco and I met in the apple orchard. "Yeah. My heart has already spoken."

Dad grins and squeezes my hand before releasing it. "Anyone who looks at you and Fuoco together can see you're meant for each other. But what I told you in the infirmary still stands. If you ever feel like your heart is telling you something different, I'm here for you."

I swallow a lump in my throat and nod. "Thank you, Dad. I'm so grateful that you—" My throat closes up, tears burning my eyes. "I used to worry..."

"Beau," he says gently, taking my hands again. "No matter who you love, I will never turn away from you. You can trust me in this for the rest of your life. That's a promise from your father to his son, and it can never be broken."

Throat burning, I can only nod. Dad might not possess dragon magic, but his vow is just as powerful as the one Fuoco and I made.

He stands and ruffles my hair the way he used to when I was a boy. "I think I'll make a few notes before I turn in. And you should probably go find your husband before he comes looking for you."

I snort. "He's out cold. Snoring." Abruptly, I realize I'm absolutely right. The jewel in my chest is subdued—almost drowsy. And somehow, I know that if I focus on it, the drowsiness will spread through my limbs.

Dad chuckles. "Well, that's marriage for you."

"Do you mind if I sit out here a bit longer?" I want to study the feeling hovering in my chest, to explore whether it changes depending on how far away I am from Fuoco.

"Stay as long as you like." Dad kisses me on the forehead and disappears inside.

Alone, I close my eyes and focus on my chest—on the feeling of Fuoco inside me, connected to me through our bond. It's like a steady heartbeat, each thrum warm and reassuring. I bask in the feeling, letting it chase away the chill of the winter night. My father is right. Love is an uncommon gift. I'm not a dragon, but I've found a treasure all the same.

A faint, sweet scent rises in the air. Rosewater.

Startled, I open my eyes just as a cloud of glittering dust fills my vision. It rushes up my nose and into my lungs, squeezing them tight. Clawing at my neck, I flail, tipping my chair back.

A hooded figure leaps over the balcony railing. I get a glimpse of glittering red eyes before the figure throws an arm around my neck and drags me over the edge and into the night.

∼

THE NEXT TIME I open my eyes, I lay on my side on the ground with my wrists bound in front of me. As I struggle to get my bearings, boots crunch. A second later, a hooded figure emerges from the gloom and thrusts a torch in my face. Heat sears my cheek, and flames sizzle in my ear. I recoil, wriggling backward as best as I can. "Hey! What—" Pain explodes in my side, and air leaves my lungs in a whoosh.

Torch in hand, the hooded figure kneels in front of me and throws back the cowl.

My heart races as I take in Lirem's glittering red eyes and mangled face. Healing burns cover him from forehead to shoulder, the skin on his left side red and waxy. Tufts of blond hair sprout from his blackened scalp like new vegetation struggling to grow. On his right side, his blond hair dangles to his chin in dirty, matted clumps.

Lirem stares at me, the disgust in his eyes so potent I can't stop myself from cringing away. His lips twist into a sneer, one side of his mouth curling higher than the other as scar tissue stretches. "You think you can escape me, you worthless little shit? I don't even need to tie you up."

"Then why did you?" I ask before I can think better of it.

His hand flies out, tangling in the front of my shirt. He yanks me roughly off the ground and onto my feet. Dizziness swamps me, and I stumble, wincing as the rope around my wrists abrades my skin. Lirem jerks me against him, his fist digging into my throat. My stomach churns as the stench of charred flesh invades my nostrils.

He leans in close, his breath hot and foul on my face. "Because I like it," he growls. "I like watching you weak, disgusting mortals struggle in the dirt where you belong."

Contempt gleams so strongly in his eyes, it loosens my knees. He wants to kill me. The desire is there right alongside the contempt. Fear grips me as the memory of Fuoco's voice flows through my head. *"Even the thought of losing you could tip me over the edge."* Oh gods, what have I done?

Lirem's red eyes narrow. Abruptly, he thrusts me away just enough to claw my shirt open. Green light spills from my chest, illuminating the small clearing and drowning out Lirem's torchlight. He stares at the jewel, then gives a low bark of laughter. "Fuoco certainly didn't waste any time. I guess congratulations are in order, baker."

A gasp sounds from somewhere, followed by rapid footsteps. Gastonia emerges from the darkness and stops at Lirem's shoulder, her gaze glued to the jewel.

"Gastonia?" My voice is a thread of sound. Confusion pummels me even as my heart thumps harder. I look between her and Lirem, who maintains his stranglehold on my shirt. Why is she with him? Her normally immaculate appearance is the worse for wear. Dirt smears her forehead. A twig pokes from her dark hair. Did Lirem kidnap her from the village before coming for me?

But she doesn't appear under duress. She continues staring at the jewel, her creamy skin bathed in its green glow. Then she lifts hard eyes to mine. For a second, something that might be pain glimmers in her blue irises. But it vanishes so quickly, I wonder if I imagined it. "So it's true. You let Fuoco bind you."

My confusion turns to shock. "How…?" I swallow against a dry throat. "How could you know that?"

Lirem's laugh is cruel. "You should see your face, baker. Did you really think a village blacksmith could afford the kind of lifestyle Old Man Legum enjoys?" He jerks his head toward Gastonia. "She knows plenty about dragons. She and her father have been in league with us for years. They fleeced your people like sheep."

"And turned the profits over to you!" Gastonia protests, clenching her fists at her sides.

"You profited plenty, too." Lirem keeps his gaze on me as he taunts her. "Sadly, Miss Legum, it appears your luck has run out. Your pretty boy here is very much taken. I tried to tell you. Fuoco's reaction in the courtyard made it clear what the baker is to him. But you wouldn't listen. Just like a human."

Gastonia vibrates with obvious fury. "I've had enough of your insults." Viciousness laces her tone. "You've always loved talking about how powerful you are. Where was your mighty dragon's strength tonight when you forced me to scale the side of the fucking castle?"

The torch bobs dangerously close to my face as Lirem swings

toward her. "You know the rules, you spoiled little bitch. *You* serve *me*. Not the other way around. You wanted the baker, so you helped me get him. You could have saved yourself the trouble if you'd listened to me." The scars on his face pull taut as he grins at her. "But I enjoyed watching you struggle up that rope." As rage boils in Gastonia's eyes, his grin widens. "I hoped to watch you fall but, alas, it wasn't meant to be. Just like your romance."

"Get fucked," she spits.

"Gastonia," I gasp, desperation cutting through my fear. "Please, don't do this." I hesitate, not even sure what I'm trying to stop her from doing. But if she's with Lirem, her plans can't be good. "If we could just talk—"

"Shut up!" She turns to Lirem. "Kill him."

My stomach drops. I struggle against Lirem's grip. "Gastonia—" My plea ends in a pained grunt as Lirem drives his knee into my stomach. When I double over, wheezing, he seizes the scruff of my neck and yanks me right back up.

"You heard her," he growls. "Keep your mouth shut."

"Kill him," Gastonia repeats, her tone ice cold. "You said killing one soul-bound mate will kill the other." She glances at me like I'm a bag of garbage. "If you want Fuoco dead, you should slit his throat and be done with it."

"Not yet," Lirem says, his grip on my neck like iron.

"You're a fool," Gastonia says, venom in her voice. "There's no reason to wait."

Lirem lunges toward her, dragging me with him. "I've done nothing *but* wait, woman. For *decades*, I've bowed and bent, babysitting humans because Fuoco was too much of a coward to rule as he should have." Lirem's red eyes glow as he stares Gastonia down. "Fuoco is going to pay for what he did to my friends and my face. Before he dies, he's going to hurt. So we go to the mine first, where we'll take care of your boyfriend."

"He's not my boyfriend," Gastonia says, giving me another cold look. "He's nothing to me."

"Glad to hear it," Lirem says. "Now shut up and don't fall behind." He tosses the torch to the ground, then stomps out the flame. Tightening his grip on my neck, he marches me across the clearing. When we reach the tree line, he hauls me against him, his arm banded around my throat. My feet barely touch the ground as he plunges us into the woods. Branches whip my face and yank at my clothes.

"How far is the mine?" Gastonia demands, scrambling after us.

What mine? I've never heard of any mines in the syndicate. Questions spin through my head, but I can hardly concentrate on them as I struggle to stay upright. If I go down, I have no doubt Lirem will make me sorry.

"Don't fucking worry about it," Lirem growls. "Just move faster."

"I'm moving as fast as I can," Gastonia fires back, panting as she struggles over a fallen tree. Worry enters her tone. "You said Fuoco won't be able to feel him underground, right?"

Lirem grunts. He tightens his grip as he splashes us into a ravine. With my hands bound, all I can do is stumble along with him, freezing water filling my shoes. Moonlight pours down on us, giving me glimpses of Lirem's scarred face tight with determination.

Terror drags an icy claw down my spine. Tears sting my eyes. I should have listened to Fuoco. He warned me it was dangerous to stray from his side. But I was too stubborn. And now Lirem is taking me underground. With every step, he carries me farther away from my mate.

Please, my love. Find me.

CHAPTER 17
FUOCO

Urgent knocking at my door rips me out of a sensual dream about my selsara. I shoot upright in bed, reaching for Beau. Instead, I grasp his empty, cold pillow. He hasn't been here in a while.

Pain lances through the jewel buried in my chest—a knife blade so hot and sharp that I arch in the bed, screaming as rhythmic waves of agony radiate from my sternum. It takes everything I have just to force oxygen into my lungs.

Beau is in danger.

Choking for air, I lurch out of bed and stagger toward the door, jerking my pants on as I go. I don't need to look around the room for Beau. Because he's *not here*.

And wherever he is, he's fucking terrified. That terror throbs in the jewel—a horrible, raw feeling like a predator stripping my flesh from my bones. But that terror isn't mine—it's his.

Bellowing at the pain, I rip the door open to find Maurice on the other side, his features twisted in desperation. "She took him! Gastonia! Beau was with me and—"

"Come!" I command, gripping his wrist. Another sharp stab of pain hits me square in the chest and I stumble against the wall, crying out.

Maurice hovers, his voice vibrating with worry. His eyes fall to where I clutch my mating jewel. "What's wrong? Do you know where Beau is?"

"She's hurting him," I gasp. *The dark-haired woman from the village.* "We've got to find him!" I straighten, shoving the agony away as I grip Maurice's arm and hurry him toward the courtyard. "Tell me everything!"

Maurice wheezes as he runs to keep up with me. "Beau and I were talking on the balcony in my room. When I went inside, Gastonia appeared. She had a hooded figure with her. I didn't get a good look, but whoever they were, they were bigger than a human."

"Lirem," I snarl. I whisk Maurice into my arms and run faster. The frantic need to find Beau slices through my pain like a lance through a festering wound. Cool tendrils of power snake through my veins, my gift rising like a leviathan spiraling up from the depths. Wind whips behind me, shoving at my back and speeding me forward. The ground trembles as I fly over the flagstones. Doors loom ahead.

OPEN THEM, I tell the currents that flank me. Wind screams down the corridor and flings the doors wide. Clutching Maurice to my chest, I burst into the courtyard and collide with Jasper.

The pixie flies backward, his wings fluttering wildly. He catches himself in mid-air and crashes to the ground. Chest heaving, he points in the direction of the village. "They've got Beau in a cart. They're taking him through the woods outside the village. I've got Bert following them but I have to stay close or I'll lose my connection."

I move in a blur, setting Maurice down and sprinting away. I shift in a flurry of shredded clothing before returning to Maurice and Jasper. They scramble into my paw, and I leap into the sky.

"Hurry!" Jasper shouts from inside my grip. "They're moving fast. Get me close so I can hear Bert and the others!"

Some part of my brain acknowledges what I've long suspected—Lilygully has more than one animal helper. But that's a mystery for another day. Right now, my only concern is finding Beau and *annihilating* those who dared to touch him. I streak toward the village as Maurice fills Jasper in on the details of Beau's kidnapping. At the mention of Lirem, my outrage sizzles higher.

But confusion joins my wrath. Lirem despises humans. Why would he work with one to take Beau?

The jewel in my chest burns like it's trying to burrow through my skin into my chest cavity. Rage and regret swirl in a toxic cloud in my mind. If only I'd been selfish. If I'd kept Beau locked away, Lirem could have never gotten to him.

Even as I think it, I know I could never do that to Beau. My sweet, independent selsara would never stand for it—and I couldn't live with myself if I trampled his spirit.

Pain hits swiftly, spearing my chest like a sword burying itself through the center of my heart. It comes so suddenly, I falter in the air, plummeting forty feet before thrusting my wings wide and righting myself.

Jasper and Maurice cling to my claws.

"Fucking hells, Fuoco!" Jasper hollers. "Keep it together!"

I scream into the night, releasing a stream of fire I can't hold back. Lirem and the human are hurting Beau. Possibly, Lirem wants my mate as a way of getting to me. Now that Beau and I are soul-bound, his death would also be mine. And without me to rule, Lirem would undoubtedly attempt to take over the syndicate.

Rage coils around me, wrapping tight as the elements respond to my fury. The air goes hot and stifling. As I streak over the forest, trees fall flat in great rows behind me. Water bubbles up from the ground, creating pools of steam that follow us toward Beau's village.

"Circle!" Jasper shouts from my claw. "I need to find Bert!"

Panic chokes me as the ground underneath Beau's village quakes.

"Calm down, Fuoco!" Jasper orders, leaning out from between two of my claws to scan the woods. "You're going to flatten your mate's village!"

STAND DOWN, I urge the soil. I claw back my anger as I widen my circle. If they fucking hurt him—

"There!" Jasper points to a small footpath that cuts through the woods. A tiny pinprick of gray scurries up the trail. "Bert has an update! Get me closer!"

I wheel in the sky, swooping over the footpath. Jasper cocks his head to the side as if he's listening. Desperation claws at my throat as I wait for the pixie to receive word.

"Straight ahead!" Jasper points in front of us. "There's a series of caves that used to be mines. Bert says they went in there!"

The jewel in my chest throbs. As I streak forward, I focus on my connection with Beau. *Pain. Terror. Fear.* His emotions pour through the link, each one stoking my rage higher. *I'm coming, selsara.* I can't speak to him through our bond, but I try to channel comfort back to him. If he can just hang on…

But in the span of a second, the connection snuffs out.

The bond is gone.

CHAPTER 18
BEAU

We don't walk long. Within minutes, Lirem drags me into a dark cave with a ceiling supported by thick wooden posts that march down a narrow tunnel. Moonlight spills into the entrance, illuminating a rusted set of tracks that snake into the distance. My jewel casts a dull, emerald glow. Several large, wooden carts with equally rusted wheels sit on the tracks. Others huddle against walls dripping with water.

Gastonia swings toward Lirem. "*Now* will you kill him?"

I struggle against Lirem's grip, then cry out when he cuffs me against the side of my head. My vision blurs, and my ears ring as nausea burns my throat. As my stomach threatens to revolt, Lirem produces a knife and cuts the rope that binds my wrists. Before I can process my newfound freedom, he drags me to one of the carts that sits on the tracks. He shoves me hard, and the world tumbles over itself. I crash into the bottom of the cart, striking my shoulder and elbow as I land in a heap. The stench of rotting wood invades my lungs. My stomach pitches, and I swallow bile as I struggle to rise.

"Stay down," Lirem barks, shoving me. My forehead scrapes the wood, and I tuck my chin in case he strikes again. "We're not killing him yet," he mutters. "I want Fuoco to feel it."

"This is stupid," Gastonia says above me, derision in her tone. "You have a chance to kill Fuoco, and you're wasting it—" Her sentence ends in a strangled scream. Choking sounds and the crunch of stone echo around the cave as Lirem forces her away from the cart.

"Fuoco won't survive this night, bitch," Lirem snarls. "Make no mistake about that. But I've waited a long fucking time for this." The choking sounds grow louder. "Fuoco will feel everything I do to his selsara, and he'll die with his mate's agony in his chest. And that's exactly what Fuoco deserves for being a traitor to his own kind. So unless you want to join the baker in the cart, keep your mouth shut and do as I say."

The choking sounds cut off. Gastonia's labored gasps reach me, along with the crunch of stone as Lirem moves around the cave.

RAGE. Out of nowhere, black fury fills my chest. It obliterates my aches and lingering dizziness, leaving only cold, calculated anger. The emotion is so thick I could almost choke on it. But it's not mine.

Fuoco. Tears prick my eyes as I cup my hand over the jewel in my chest. *He knows.* My mate knows I'm missing, and he's furious.

"And what happens then?" I asked him when he spoke of the danger of losing control.

"The world burns."

But the rage in my chest isn't hot. It's icy cold. My vision clears, and I swear I can see my breath puffing against the wood in front of me. Some instinct compels me to hold my hand over my jewel, muffling its light.

Stone crunches, and then Lirem looms over the side of the cart. His red eyes glitter as I dare to turn my head and meet his gaze.

"You look lonely, baker. It's a long ride to our destination." His lips curve, his scarred cheek pulling in a grotesque parody of a smile. "But I'm a kind male. I've brought you some company. They're dying to meet you." He lifts a wooden crate. Faint scrabbling sounds emanate from the interior. "You might even say they're hungry to make your acquaintance." Just as fresh terror squeezes my heart, he tips the crate, spilling its contents.

Hot, furry bodies rain down on me. As I scream, my new companions scream, too. Lirem has filled the cart with rats.

"No!" I cry, slapping the wriggling bodies away. "Please!"

Lirem disappears, then returns a second later with something big and wooden in his hands. *A lid.* He slams it onto the top of the cart.

Plunging me into blackness.

∼

Pain. Movement. Darkness.

I don't know how long these things last, only that they've become my world. I claw at the box and the rats claw at me, digging into my skin as I thrash. Their teeth nip and pinch. Fur fills my mouth. Tails whip my legs and flick against my skin. High-pitched screams fill my ears. Some are mine. Some belong to the rats, which dig at my flesh like they're trying to burrow down to my bones.

The wooden cart creaks and shakes, its wheels squeaking as I roll toward some unknown destination. I can only assume Lirem set it on the tracks, but I'm not entirely sure—and I'm not sure I care. All I know is pain, movement, and darkness.

The latter bothers me the most. At some point—and I can't remember when—the jewel's light dulled to almost nothing. And now I fight so hard I'm not sure I see it anymore. Shadows squirm over my eyes, which I try to squeeze shut as I flail against the teeth and claws that writhe and scratch mercilessly. I scream again and again, pounding against the wood as I try to dislodge my tormentors.

But they won't let go. Tears wet my face. Or maybe it's blood. As soon as the thought enters my head, the coppery scent registers in my nostrils. The rats are shredding my flesh. If this goes on much longer, they'll kill me.

Sorrow wraps around me, and it's worse than the pain and the darkness. *"If one of us dies, the other will as well. There is no greater bond among creatures of the Myth."*

If I die, Fuoco will die, too.

No. The thought rises in my mind as clear and bright as a shooting star. Fuoco will *not* die. It's not happening, not even if Lirem dumps a thousand fucking rats on my head.

Gritting my teeth, I pound on the side of the cart. Claws dig more frantically into my back as I bellow so hard my throat aches. "Let me out, you fucking coward!" I rock back and forth, throwing my shoulder against the rotted wood. My thoughts run in circles as I grope for the insult most likely to get under Lirem's skin. "You're so afraid of a human you have to put me in a box! Face me like a man, asshole!"

No response. Just pain, movement, and darkness. I kick at the side of the cart, rage building in my chest. And this time, the rage is *mine*. My whole life, Lirem has stolen from me and the people I love. I won't let him steal my future. Fuoco said he spent his whole life looking for me. Now I know I was looking for him, too. I won't let him go.

I kick harder, grunting with my efforts. The cart continues rolling and creaking. And then, finally, it stops. A second later, the cart tips violently. Light floods my vision as I tumble onto the ground. Wood splinters, and rats scatter in every direction. Squinting against the harsh light, I struggle to my hands and knees. Stinging pain covers me from head to toe. Blood seeps from dozens of wounds on the backs of my hands. More blood drips from my chin to form tiny red craters in the dirt.

"Not so loud now, are you?" Lirem asks, his boots appearing in front of me. One flies in a blur, catching me under the chin and sending me sprawling onto my back. A soaring ceiling spreads above me. Then Lirem blots it out, his scarred, twisted face even more shocking in the harsh light. He steps on my shoulder, grinding it into the ground. His red eyes gleam like rubies. "What was that about facing me like a man?"

My jaw throbs, which makes it easier to keep my mouth shut. He didn't kick me as hard as he might have. He held back, which means he's not ready to kill me just yet. The longer I can delay, the more time Fuoco has to find me.

I cringe away from Lirem, doing my best to appear cowed and meek. It's not much of an effort with pain stabbing at me from all angles and the stench of my fear thick in my nostrils.

DESPERATE. The emotion comes out of nowhere, nailing me in the center of the chest. It frazzles through me, the feeling so powerful and frantic it's a struggle to lie still. Fuoco is searching for me. But I have no idea how to tell him where to find me. Tears burn my throat as I picture his green eyes that crinkle at the corners when he teases me. Green eyes that burn with possessiveness when he lowers his mouth to mine.

I hold his image in my mind as I stretch my senses toward him. *Come find me, selsara.*

Lirem's lips pull in a sneer as he presses his boot harder into my shoulder. "You're like the rest of your kind," he says, contempt coating his tone like oil. "Weak and worthless."

My heart thumps hard. Sweat stings the cuts and bite marks that cover me. I swallow the urge to point out the hypocrisy of calling me weak when he's got his boot on my shoulder. And anyway, I want it there. I want his eyes on my face. Anything to keep him from looking at the jewel in my chest. If Fuoco is connecting with me, the gem's light is probably growing brighter.

"Please," I croak, injecting as much obeisance into my voice as I can muster. I blink rapidly, letting tears spill down my temples. "Please don't hurt me."

"Get up!" Lirem steps back, and I roll to my side and struggle to my feet before he can kick me into doing his bidding. Gastonia stands a few steps away, her arms folded and her blue eyes cold and flat. As I look past her, I forget how to breathe.

We stand on a cliff in an underground cavern twice the size of Fuoco's Great Hall. A narrow rope bridge spans the width of an inky black chasm that appears to have no bottom. On either side of the rift sit riches almost too vast to contemplate.

Torches line the walls, the firelight dancing over the enormous hoard. Marble statues of gods and goddesses stand among chests piled high with glittering coins. Gilded weapons lie across tables inlaid with mother of pearl. Jewels, crowns, and necklaces sparkle in a rainbow of color. Everywhere my gaze lands, priceless treasure greets me. Silver goblets, golden trinkets, tapestries, and paintings worth more than a small kingdom.

Or a village.

Because it's not just gold and gemstones. Sacks of grain sit among the riches, the burlap bags so fat the seams strain to contain their contents. Rocking chairs and plain, sturdy farm furniture peek from among the austere Chesterfields and elegantly sculpted tables. Lirem's hoard is a storehouse of the villages' wealth.

I look at Gastonia. "You knew he was taking all of this. You helped him steal from us."

She holds my stare, her gaze unflinching. "It was my only way out." Her voice is tight, her tone as frosty as her eyes. "You could have come with me, Beau. Together, we could have escaped and lived a *real* life."

My heart drops into my stomach. I knew she wanted to leave the village, but not like this—not by stealing from everyone she knows and loves. She saw what the enforcers did to people. She watched the theft and abuse up close. Broken windows and broken bones. Children so hungry the teacher had to send them home because they couldn't concentrate on their lessons.

"People were starving," I rasp, disbelief pounding through me. But no, it's not disbelief. The proof of her betrayal glitters all around me. Her guilt is written across her face—and in her actions tonight. No, what I feel isn't doubt. It's anger.

Her lips curve in an acid smile. "So earnest, Beau," she says softly, strolling toward me. "Such a *good* son, always doing the right thing. Taking bread to hungry kids in the village." She reaches me, and the malice in her eyes glitters as brightly as the plundered riches around us. "But that didn't stop you from running to the castle at the first opportunity. And when the dragon lord summoned you to his bed, why, you jumped right in."

Heat suffuses my cheeks. "That's— It wasn't like that—"

"It wasn't?" She tilts her head. "Tell me, then. How was it?" She runs a scathing gaze down my body, her eyes lingering on the jewel visible between the two halves of my shirt. "You mean you and Fuoco sit around and play chess?" She throws her head back and laughs, the brittle sound bouncing around the cavern. But when she lowers her chin and meets my gaze once more, her eyes are devoid of emotion. "I would have taken good care of you. But that's over." She drops her voice to a hiss. "You missed your chance."

I draw a deep breath and step forward. "Gastonia, please. It doesn't have to be this way. There's still time to do the right thing."

She shakes her head. "It's too late. I've made my choice, and you've made yours. There's no going back now."

"Please think this through—"

"I am *tired* of thinking!" she screams, her face twisting with so much abrupt rage, I suck in a breath. She advances on me, blue eyes blazing. Spittle flies from her lips. "I'm tired of waiting and hoping for things to be different! I'm done with the fucking village, and I'm done with you!"

Madness dances in her eyes. I stumble backward just as Lirem clamps an unforgiving hand on my shoulder. He steers me around and propels me forward.

"Time to go, pretty boy. You and I have unfinished business." He pushes me to the rope bridge. A rat streaks from the splintered remains of the cart, its beady eyes reflecting the torchlight. Lirem snarls and kicks the rodent, sending it screeching into the abyss.

A whimper escapes me before I can stifle it.

Lirem chuckles as he forces me onto the planks, which creak and sway immediately. "Face you like a man, huh?" He digs his fingers into my shoulder, pressing hard into the bite wounds that throb in sync with my racing heart. "We'll see how long that tough guy act holds up once we reach the other side." He leans close, his hot breath searing my nape. "Nazzar left a lot of knives behind. I think I'll carve out your liver first."

As we make our way across the bridge, my gaze is drawn to the fathomless gorge beneath us. There is no bottom in sight, just impenetrable darkness. Sharp gusts of frigid wind buffet my face. If I fall, nothing will catch me. And once Lirem gets me to the other side, he's going to make me regret my words in the cart. I focus on my jewel, straining for any glimmer of Fuoco. But there's nothing.

Only silence.

CHAPTER 19
FUOCO

Gone. Beau is gone.

I bellow my fury at the sky. The air responds, whipping violently as I bullet in the direction Jasper points me.

Can't feel Beau.

Can't feel Beau.

Can't feel Beau.

The desperate refrain beats in time with my heart, which threatens to pound from my chest. Power surges through me, tearing away layers of reason until all that's left is the unyielding drive to find my selsara. It speeds me forward—faster, faster, faster—as Jasper shouts directions.

A ravine twists and curves like a snake below us, moonlight sparkling over the water. As I pump my wings, Lirem's scent slams into me so hard I tumble in mid-air. Clenching my paw tightly around Maurice and Jasper, I quickly right myself. With a roar, I dive for the ground, my wings flat against my body. As the trees rush up, I fling my wings wide and land, depositing Jasper and Maurice at the edge of the ravine.

"Follow Bert!" Jasper shouts, pointing to a trail of mice and other rodents who scurry along the embankment. They're all headed in the same direction.

Lirem's scent is everywhere, his anger and frustration soaking the air. Underneath that cloying, tart stench is something light and sweet. *Beau.* As I drag his essence into my lungs, I sense a third scent signature—rosewater, fear, and bitterness. *Gastonia.*

Nostrils flared, I lumber forward, careful not to trample the mice as they lead me up the edge of the ravine. Maurice and Jasper hurry in my wake. For five harrowing minutes, we race along the leaf-strewn water's edge, the scents growing stronger. Yet my jewel remains dull and silent. That can only mean one of two things—Beau is so deep underground that I can't feel him, or he's locked behind iron where Myth magic can't reach him.

Or both.

But my beast scents him, and that keeps me moving until the mice lead me around a bend to find a dark tunnel tucked among fallen trees and tangled brush. It would have been invisible from the sky. The opening is supported by twin wooden beams. A rusted sign over the entrance marks it as a former mine. The opening is far too small to accommodate my beast. Frustration rises hot and fast as I pace, my tail swishing and my talons clawing up the soil. The ground shakes, the earth itself responding to my anguish.

"Easy, Fuoco," Jasper says, his eyes flashing in the moonlight. "If you collapse the cave, we'll never get to Beau."

Grunting, I shove my head into the cave's entrance and suck in a deep breath. The sickly scent of Beau's fear fills my nostrils. But there's something else.

His blood.

I shift so quickly I'm still a dozen feet above the ground when I take human form. I hit the dirt already striding forward, rage bubbling so close to the surface I can almost taste smoke in my mouth. Flames wreath my head, and green scales descend from my shoulders to my knees. When Jasper and Maurice jog inside, I round on them.

"You can't follow. Lirem won't hesitate to kill you."

Maurice lifts his chin, determination shining in his brown eyes. "If he hurts my Beau, I'll kill him first." He draws himself up to his full height, which is more than a foot below mine. But he seems taller as he defends his son. And it's clear he won't be pressured into staying behind.

Jasper steps forward. "We should go with you." A mouse skitters past him and scurries down a set of rusted tracks. Water drips down the mine's walls. The wind buffets the flames dancing around my head.

My power slithers under my skin, the elements ready for my command.

"Stay close," I tell Maurice and Jasper. "And if I tell you to run, you do it."

We follow the tracks, which lead us deep into the darkened mine. Empty sconces line the walls, any torches they held long gone—or removed by Lirem. A few dozen feet into the tunnel, Jasper stops me with a hand on my arm.

"Maybe we should do this with the lights off." He gives my head a pointed look. "If Lirem has any kind of lookout posted, they'll see you a mile away."

The pixie is right. But my dragon is so close to the surface, I'm not sure I can rein it in.

"It's for Beau," Jasper says softly, squeezing my arm. "You'll do anything for him."

My throat tightens. "Anything," I echo hoarsely. And holding onto my temper is the least I can do. Gathering every bit of self-control I possess, I close my eyes and drag in a deep breath. Then another. After a moment, the heat licking around my head goes cold. When I open my eyes, my night vision kicks in, revealing Jasper and Maurice. Behind them, tiny, furry bodies hurry up the tracks.

Without another word, I rush after them. Power hums under my skin. The elements answer, racing alongside me as I move faster and faster. Dripping water and the crunch of dirt. The chilly breeze that swirls around my feet and ruffles my hair. Embers whisper from the empty sconces, begging to be coaxed into flame.

The ground dips, the tracks marching down an incline. The mice scamper over the rails, little feet flying. Behind me, Maurice's breathing grows labored. But Beau's sire doesn't fall back. He and

Jasper stick to my heels as I surge forward, following the mice. The dark plays tricks on my mind, sending phantom voices bouncing off the rocky walls as I rush through the tunnel's twists and turns.

But then I hear it. Lirem's sneering baritone echoes down the tunnel, followed by a woman's angry shriek. A second later, a masculine whimper reaches me.

Beau.

They've hurt him.

Cold, black fury fills my mind. My beast thrashes against my ribs, struggling to break through flesh and bone to rain fiery vengeance on Lirem and Gastonia. But I can't shift in this tunnel. I'll cave the whole thing in.

As I race forward, a small circle of light appears in the distance. I run at it, urgency pounding harder as the circle grows broader. The mine track veers off to one side and ends in a cluster of wooden carts. The light swells. I speed toward it, and now it's so bright it hurts my eyes. But the pain is nothing. Beau is *everything* as I push myself to run faster, faster, faster, finally stumbling to a halt as the tunnel opens upon a vast cavern. Panting, I gaze over the largest dragon hoard I've ever seen.

The cavern is huge, its walls lined with torches. The light dances over chests spilling with gold and jewels. Marble statues of kings and goddesses stand amid the treasures, their expressions passive. And directly ahead, Lirem drags Beau across a swaying rope bridge suspended over a black chasm. The human woman, Gastonia, follows, her dark hair tangled down her back.

Rage builds in my chest, the pressure so intense it overshadows all other emotions—and likely my connection to Beau. But that's probably a good thing. If I sense his pain right now, I'm not sure I'll be able to keep my power in check.

My beast pushes harder, straining to break free. The cavern's ceilings have to be at least a hundred feet high. Plenty of clearance. Stepping farther into the cavern, I let the shift take me. In dragon form, I look back to see Maurice and Jasper huddled at the mouth of the tunnel.

I peer at them, doing my best to convey my wishes through my expression. *Stay put.* Swinging back around, I snake forward, my gaze pinned to Lirem as he pulls Beau farther across the bridge.

The hoard's scents fill my sensitive nostrils. Gold and furniture and expensive perfumes. The earthy aroma of grain. But the strongest scent is the one that makes my lips peel back from my fangs.

My selsara's terror.

Ahead, Lirem and Beau reach the end of the bridge. Lirem grips Beau by the hair as he forces Beau onto the rocky cliff that juts over the chasm. Piles of treasure rise around them. Gastonia picks her way across the last few wooden planks and exits the bridge.

Hold on, selsara.

Moving as soundlessly as possible, I unfurl my wings as Lirem reaches for a long ax handle sticking out of the pile of treasure in front of him.

He turns.

Not an ax.

A lever.

"Hello, Fuoco," he snarls, jerking the lever down. The biting scent of iron fills the air as forty-foot spikes rain down from the ceiling, slicing through my left wing and burying themselves in the rock beneath me.

Agony obliterates conscious thought as I lunge forward, only to come up short. I'm pinned in place, trapped by the metal impaling me. Worse, it's iron. My magic dims, power slipping away.

Beau screams, but the sound is distant and muffled, like someone tossed a thick blanket over my senses. The iron seeps into my body, stealing my magic and sucking it into a void so depthless I can barely sense the elements. My bond with Beau stays dark even as he shouts for me across the cave. With every breath, pain skewers my wing and ripples through my body in sickly waves.

Across the bridge, Lirem wrenches Beau tightly against him, Beau's back to Lirem's chest. My former enforcer reaches into a chest of weapons and withdraws a long, jagged knife. He flips it once, then places the tip under Beau's chin.

I roar, struggling against the stakes impaling my wing. But every move tears muscle. With each labored breath, more iron seeps under my skin.

Beau. My Beau.

My hind legs give out, straining my trapped wing more tightly. My power drifts farther away. Huffing out a pained breath, I push forward, testing the iron, but it doesn't give.

Across the chasm, Lirem twists the tip of his blade. Blood rolls down Beau's neck.

Roaring, I pull harder. Blood pours down my wing, sticky rivulets coating my scales.

Lirem thrusts Beau away from him, then grabs him by the shoulder and spins him around. As Beau staggers, Lirem backhands him across the face. Beau flies into a pile of treasure, smashes his head against a wooden chest, and crashes to the ground.

Red covers my vision. I open my jaws and roar, the vibrations shaking the ground. As dust sifts from the ceiling, Lirem grabs Gastonia. He shoves her toward Beau, barking instructions to keep an eye on him.

Then Lirem whirls and stalks to the bridge. His red eyes glitter as he crosses, his gaze locked with mine. He stops just out of my reach, his lips curving in a cold smile that pulls his scars taut. "You're fucked now, Fuoco," he murmurs, twisting the tip of his blade into his thumb. He watches the blood drip down his finger, then licks it off and smiles up at me. "You killed Nazzar, didn't you?"

When I don't answer, he shrugs. "No matter, all the more treasure for me."

I surge forward, snapping at him, but the iron stakes hold me tight. I can't shift—not with iron sapping my magic. I am, as Lirem says, fucked.

"That last man you burned called us thieves," Lirem says, studying his blade. "I don't think of it as thievery, though. We deserve everything we take from this godsforsaken plane. We sacrificed our world for this one, and you want us to serve the vermin who inhabit it? You're out of your fucking mind." He spits the last word, his ruined features twisting into rage.

In my peripheral vision, Maurice and Jasper sneak around the outer edge of the cavern, hugging the shadows among the treasure.

Beau's moan echoes across the chasm, pulling my attention back to him. Gastonia stands over him, her fists balled at her sides. When he tries to sit up, she delivers a swift kick to his shoulder. He cries out and falls onto his back.

I bellow and jerk against the spikes, gritting my teeth when agony halts me.

Lirem watches Gastonia over his shoulder for a moment, then turns back to me with an acid smile. "She thought she could help me snatch him and then she'd actually get to keep him. Stupid cunt." He tilts his head. "What's it like, knowing you'll never taste him again? I think I might like a little taste before I rip that fucking jewel from his chest."

Mine.

Beau.

Selsara.

I stretch my neck out, snapping at my former enforcer. He sidesteps easily, raising a blond brow as he offers another mocking smile.

Just don't look back, I pray. *Keep your eyes on me, you fucking asshole.* Over his shoulder, Jasper flies across the chasm with Maurice in his arms. The pixie's wings beat the air as Beau's sire clings to his neck. Gastonia catches sight of them. Before the men land, she screams and sprints to the bridge.

Lirem whirls around. "No! You useless fucking bitch!" Knife in hand, he charges across the bridge.

Beau. He's going to kill Beau.

I need my magic. I've got to get to Beau.

Lirem reaches Gastonia. He tries to shove past her, but the planks are too narrow. The bridge sways wildly. Jasper touches down with Maurice.

Lurching forward, I screech, agony blooming as the spikes tear through my wing. Muscles and tendons rip from bone, iron cutting through me like a blunt knife. My wing snaps, the momentum almost sending me sprawling. The wing dangles uselessly. But I'm free.

Lirem tangles with Gastonia, shoving her down and stepping over her. She screams, grasping at the ropes as the bridge swings from side to side. As Lirem scrambles onto the cliff, Jasper steps in front of Beau. The pixie grips a knife, his expression deadly cold as he faces off with Lirem.

Agony lances me, my wing hanging limply. Now that I'm free of the iron, my power rushes back. In a flash, I shift into human form and stalk across the bridge. Gastonia scrambles her way to safety, but I pay her no mind. No, I only have one quarry at the moment.

"Lirem!" I shout, leaping over the last few planks and onto the cliff.

He spins. Red eyes go wide.

"It's over," I say, power surging through my veins and closing the wounds on my arm. "You were a dead man the moment you touched my selsara. But you also tortured and stole from the people you swore to protect. You betrayed your vow. And for that, you must die."

Lirem raises his knife. "You are the betrayer! We are meant to rule this plane! But you were too weak to see it!"

"Perhaps," I say, power spiraling higher. It climbs up and up, filling me as I hold Lirem's stare. "But I'm stronger than you." I lift my arms out to my sides and let my power spill over.

EARTH, COME TO ME. Instantly, the ground shakes. The piles of treasure tremble, jewels spilling onto the ground and shivering to the edge of the chasm. Coins tumble and bounce. Lirem gasps as a ruby-studded diadem falls into the chasm and winks out of sight.

WATER, JOIN US. Steam hisses above our heads. A second later, water shoots downward in great streams that soak the tumbling, bouncing coins. Little rivers form, ferrying more of the hoard into the abyss.

"No!" Lirem shouts, panic twisting his features as he watches his treasures stream toward the edge and disappear. "Stop it!"

FIRE. With a flick of my hand, I summon it from the torches. Plumes form a line at the edge of the cliff, cutting Lirem off from the rivers of flowing treasure. MORE, I command, and another round of flames leap from the torches and into my hands. They warm me. Soothe me. Old, familiar friends. Power I've spent my whole life keeping at bay. But no more. Now, I embrace my power—and I have one final friend to call.

"AIR!" I roar aloud, my bellow toppling treasure. In a blink, wind whips through the cavern, screaming around the walls like a hurricane. In some corner of my mind, I'm aware of Jasper and Maurice helping Beau to his feet. The men cringe against a large chest, their hair tossed around their heads. *Selsara.* I should go to him.

Lirem staggers, jerking my attention back to him.

I step forward, wrath forking like lightning over my skin. "You touched him!" I shout. "And now you die! Nobody will ever know where your bones lie. Your name will be wiped from the history books."

"No!" Lirem cries. He falls to his knees.

Reaching a hand toward him, I call the air from his lungs. It whooshes from his lips in a great rush of breath. He claws at his throat, his eyes rolling wildly.

My power climbs to new heights, fury curling into madness. "YOU FUCKING TOUCHED HIM!"

Lirem's mouth stretches on a silent scream. The cliff rocks, boulders tumbling from the walls. Water flows around Lirem's knees. Wind roars, streaks of fire joining the maelstrom that spins around the cavern.

I stand in the center of it all, the cavern coated in the red haze of my fury.

NOW, I tell the air.

Lirem's lungs implode. His body jerks, back arching. His skin wrinkles and splits as I suck every bit of air from his body. I call it until there's nothing left of him but a dried husk. It drops to the ground and explodes into fine powder.

Satisfaction thrums through me—a shivering note in the jangling, swirling power that spins faster around the cavern.

Good, I tell the elements.

More, they respond.

Yes. I tip my head back and close my eyes. Red paints the inside of my lids.

Yes. *More.*

CHAPTER 20

BEAU

I gape at Fuoco as I struggle to stay on my feet.

He stands in the center of the inferno that surrounds us, his arms outstretched and his face tilted toward the ceiling as if he's basking in the sun. But the sun is a distant memory in this place. Now, there is only screaming wind and flashes of fire. A tempest whips around the cavern, scooping up coins, jewels, and pieces of furniture. Weapons clatter over the trembling ground, knives and swords tumbling like driftwood. Sofas and statues join the fray, spinning in an ever-faster moving circle.

"He's lost it!" Jasper shouts, his blue eyes narrowed against the wind. His wings tremble violently as we cling to the side of an oversize chest. Dad huddles at my back. Jasper grips my shoulder. "You have to talk to him!"

"What? How?"

"Show him you're safe! Make him see reason, Beau. You're the only one who can."

My heart stutters. Drawing a shaky breath, I push away from the chest. I stagger toward Fuoco, my progress sluggish like I'm moving through water. Sweat drips down my back, stinging my myriad cuts and bite marks. With every step, a thousand aches and pains assail me.

But I keep moving, sidestepping coins and jewelry that fly over the ground.

Behind Fuoco, the rope bridge swings, wood creaking as the wind tosses it from side to side. Movement on the ropes catches my eye, and I stop as I try to puzzle out what I'm seeing.

Mice. Over a dozen of them scurry up the ropes. A few drop to the planks and begin chewing at the knots that hold the wood in place.

What the…?

"Selsara?"

I jerk my gaze to Fuoco, who stares at me with glowing green eyes. Green flames leap around his head. But nothing gleams as brightly as the jewel in the center of his chest. Its glare flashes across my vision, and I gasp as my jewel throbs hard enough to make my breath hitch. As connection sizzles between us, I raise my voice over the storm.

"It's me, Fuoco! It's Beau!"

The wind ebbs. Around the cavern, coins and furniture crash to the ground. Fuoco holds my gaze, blinking as if waking from a trance. He takes a step toward me, and then another. The flames around his head shudder, waves of his dark hair flickering among the fire.

"Beau?" he rasps.

"Yeah." Joy bursts like a firework in my chest. I swallow against a suddenly thick throat. "It's me, baby."

Tears fill his eyes. His big shoulders slump as he draws a ragged breath. With a hoarse cry, he reaches for me.

At the same moment, Gastonia streaks out of nowhere, a jeweled broadsword in her hand. Her face is a mask of fury as she pounds toward Fuoco, who's angled away. He can't see her coming.

Everything slows down.

I move without thinking, launching my body across the short distance separating me from Fuoco. With a bellow, I hurl myself in front of him, my muscles screaming. The blade grazes my shoulder, and then clatters to the ground as Gastonia slams into me. We flail, our limbs tangling, as she claws at my face.

"How dare you!" she screams, dark hair flying. "How could you want someone like *him* when you had someone like *me*?"

My lungs burn. Everything hurts, but the pain is nothing compared to the anger that punches through me. It lends me strength, and I growl as I fling her away. She goes flying, landing with a grunt on the first few planks of the rope bridge.

Chest heaving, I stalk forward and stand over her. "I never had you," I snarl, "and you certainly never had me."

For a brief moment, her face crumples. Then she hauls herself to her feet, murder in her eyes. The bridge sways as she claws her way toward the cliff, her dirt-streaked hands on the rope railing. "No one humiliates Gastonia Legum! You and your *beast* will pay—" She shrieks as a mouse scampers over her hand. As more mice race along the ropes and leap onto the cliff, she yanks her hands close to her body. "Get the fuck away from me, you disgusting rats!"

An ominous groan swells, echoing through the cavern.

Gastonia freezes, fear flashing in her eyes. "What—?"

The bridge snaps. For a fraction of a second, her terrified gaze collides with mine. Then she plunges into the abyss.

Silence reigns. Jasper appears at my side, his wings gently waving as he cuddles his mouse close to his chest. Stroking the creature between its pink ears, the pixie directs a mild look into the chasm. "Bert's a mouse, not a rat."

I get one second to stare at Jasper. Then strong arms seize me, and I'm spun around and pressed against a sweaty, bare chest.

"Beau," Fuoco breathes above me, and then his mouth is on mine, his kiss wild and desperate. The world spins as we cling to each other, our tongues exploring hungrily. He slides his hands down my back, gripping my ass and pulling my hips into his. He deepens the kiss, ravishing my mouth.

Eventually, we break away, both gasping for air. Tears fall unchecked down Fuoco's cheeks as he grips my arms. "I couldn't feel you. I thought I'd lost you."

"Right back at you," I say through my tears.

His eyes go stark. "You...did. I lost control, selsara." He swallows hard, and then he frowns, confusion entering his green eyes. "I'm not sure why, but I feel like that won't ever happen again."

"It won't," Jasper says beside us. When Fuoco and I both look at him, he smiles and gives a little shrug. "Beau broke the curse."

Stunned silence rolls off Fuoco. Then he straightens. "What are you talking about, Lilygully?"

Jasper gives Fuoco an exasperated look. "The *elemental* curse." An unspoken *duh* hangs in the air as he looks down at Bert. "These dragons really are as thick as fence posts."

Tension ripples through Fuoco. "That's a legend."

Jasper cants his head up, a smile playing around his mouth as he meets Fuoco's gaze. "Is it?" Bert wriggles into Jasper's front pocket and disappears. The pixie's smile blooms brighter as he looks at me. "I knew you could do it, Beau."

It's my turn to be confused. "Uh...thanks." I clear my throat. "What, exactly, did I do, again?"

"You stepped between Fuoco and the sword. The blade wouldn't have killed him, but it doesn't matter. The point is, you were willing to give your life for his. An act of true love is old magic. When it's done right, it can be powerful enough to break a curse." His smile softens. "Even a very, very old one."

Fuoco stares at Jasper. "How do you know this?"

For one brief moment, it appears like Jasper might say something profound and earth-shattering. But then his lips quirk. "That's what I do, flame zaddy. I'm hot, and I know things."

A muscle twitches in Fuoco's jaw. "Being hot isn't something you do."

"It is when I do it."

"Listen here, Lilygully—"

"We should get moving, my lord." Jasper casts a dubious look at the ceiling. "I'm not feeling an abundance of confidence about the structural integrity of this cavern after you played hurricane in here." He rolls his eyes as he looks between us. "You two are probably going to make out again, and then Beau really needs to hug his dad. After that, we can head back to the castle, where I intend to drink myself into the lap of the first strapping centaur I see."

The mention of my father has me whirling around. He stands a short distance away, his hair sticking up at odd angles and a patient smile on his face.

"Dad!" I rush into his arms, inhaling his familiar scent. "Are you all right?"

"Never better, son. And never more proud." When we ease apart, wonder moves through his eyes. "You were like a warrior."

My face heats. "I don't know about that…"

"I do," Fuoco says, taking my hand. "You were magnificent."

We hold hands the whole way out of the mine, only breaking apart when we emerge to find most of Fuoco's court—and more than a few human servants—waiting at the entrance with weapons in their hands. Tess meets my gaze from the back and gives me a little wave.

The female dragon Riselle steps forward, relief in her eyes as she looks from me to Fuoco. "Oh, thank the gods you're safe!" Her purple eyes sharpen. "Is Lirem dead?"

"Very," Fuoco says.

A cheer goes up among the crowd, shouts of "let's party!" and "drinks are on me!" rising from the chorus of jubilant celebration. "The drinks are free, you idiot!" someone calls out. Two ogres attempt to high-five and miss. Riselle winces, then offers us an apologetic look. "They're a little drunk."

"It's fine," Fuoco murmurs, his eyes shining as he gazes over his court. "They came."

Riselle smiles. "We could start a training program, my lord. You don't have to defend the syndicate all alone."

I slip my hand into Fuoco's. As he looks at me with love in his eyes, I squeeze his fingers. "She's right, selsara. You don't have to do anything alone anymore."

He lifts my hand to his lips. Just before he presses a kiss to my knuckles, he murmurs, "Not with you by my side, I don't. You're a dream come true."

EPILOGUE
FUOCO

Early spring

I swoop through the greenhouse in dragon form, Beau riding atop my back with a sack of seeds in his hand. He dumps them in a steady stream, hanging onto my neck spines as I wheel and fly down the row we just planted. Crackling power surges through me, and I call the earth to cover the seeds by just a few inches. By the time we reach the end of the row, the seeds are warm and snug in their spots.

In the next field over, I sense the seedlings straining to rise from the ground. I'd help them along, but the struggle seems to make them stronger. Just because I can control them doesn't mean I should.

Beau taught me that.

Everywhere, plants and people thrive. As I wheel in the air, Tess looks up from a row of tomatoes and waves. Beside her, Ellen does the same. Her cap is gone, her hair swept back into an elegant bun. Soft tendrils frame a face that's now rounded with good health.

I trumpet a greeting, smoke rolling from my nostrils. The women laugh as I soar toward the front of the greenhouse, my selsara's happiness humming in the jewel in my chest.

My wing twinges, and I wince as I descend and land. The wing is fully healed, but still aches on occasion, especially when the weather changes. Dieter has done what he can, but dragons heal more slowly when we're injured in beast form. I stretch the wing once before folding it close to my body.

The front wall of the greenhouse is gone, the space open to the outside. Humans and creatures of the Myth work alongside one another to expand the fields and erect a new wall. When they finish, the greenhouse will be triple the size it is now.

Beau slides off my back with a quick stroke down my scales. "This place will be amazing next winter, my love." He plants his fists on his hips and looks around, pride shining in his dark chocolate eyes. "Think of all the seeds we can give the farmers in another month or two." He tips his head back, meeting my gaze with one of his soft smiles. "You're changing lives with this, Fuoco."

I shift into human form and loop an arm around his waist, pulling him close. "This is all your doing, you know. I wanted to throw the people a party."

Beau rolls his eyes good-naturedly. Parties are the one thing we disagree on. I always want a party—it's the perfect chance to show off my beautiful mate. But I'm the first to admit that my selsara's idea of opening the greenhouse to the whole syndicate was a stroke of genius. The more time people from the villages spend around me, the more at ease they are in my presence. I've been getting my hands dirty helping to grow food. Even better, I've been getting to know the humans who depend on me to lead them. Already, I can sense them shifting from depending on me to trusting me.

"Did somebody say party?" Jasper strolls in from outside, his wings shimmering in the sun pouring through the glass walls. He stops and gives my hips a pointed look. "Oh, *that* kind of party. I should have known."

Beau tosses me a pair of pants with a laugh.

"Didn't you say you had somewhere to be?" I ask Jasper, pulling the leather over my hips. The meddlesome pixie has been a permanent fixture in the castle since Beau's rescue.

Jasper shrugs noncommittally. "I suppose I could claim my dragon ride now. I'm overdue at court."

My senses sharpen. "And what court would that be?" There are only so many "courts" among immortals. If Jasper is overdue for an appearance of some kind, he's most likely visiting the pixie court. Its location is one of the best-kept secrets of the Myth. Queen Mab might be as mischievous and wayward as her subjects, but she takes security seriously. On the other hand, there's a decent chance the pixie monarch simply enjoys keeping people guessing.

Jasper winks at me. "Wouldn't you love to know, flame zaddy."

"For the last time, Lilygully, I asked you not to call me—"

"I can leave as soon as tomorrow if you two think you can manage without me." He gestures around the greenhouse. "I mean, it looks like you've got things well in hand." He waggles his brows at Beau.

"Very well in hand," my selsara says with a laugh, taking Jasper's teasing in stride.

Jasper returns Beau's smile, the expression softening as it reaches the pixie's blue eyes. "It's good to see you happy, Beau. You deserve it."

"What about me?" I grumble, folding my arms.

"You too, of course, my lord. You two are couples goals for sure."

Beau bumps Jasper with his hip. "Wanna see something? It might change your mind about sticking around a few more weeks."

Jasper's lips curve in a devious grin. "Show me everything, cutie."

I glance at the ground under Jasper's feet. A small hole opens, and he lets out a startled yip as he drops into it up to his ankles. He flutters his wings furiously, shooting me an exasperated look. "Are you really that possessive?" When I raise an eyebrow, he waves a dismissive hand. "Yeah, yeah, stupid question."

I jerk my head toward my selsara. "Beau's been excited to show you this. Get out of my hole and—" I clamp my mouth shut as Jasper bites his fist, devilry dancing in his eyes. "Forget I said that," I growl.

The pixie makes a strangled sound.

"Lilygully..." I warn.

"All right, all right!" With a flick of his wings, he clears the hole and flits to Beau's side. My selsara just shakes his head, a smile twinkling in his eyes as he leads Jasper through the greenhouse.

Pleasure lights up the mating jewel in my chest. Beau's happy, so incredibly happy. I trail him and Jasper as they round a field of half-grown corn. At the end of the row, a piece of wooden machinery sits in a small clearing. A metal tube pokes from underneath the contraption, leading to a large wooden bowl.

Maurice appears around the side of the machine, Riselle close behind him.

Beau goes to his father and places a hand on the older man's shoulder. "Well? Is it working, Dad?"

"Like a charm," Maurice says, beaming. He turns his bright smile on Riselle. "But only because of Riselle's advice. I couldn't have done it without her."

Riselle pats the side of the machine. "Nonsense, Maurice. It's your fuel that powers this, and hopefully many more like it." She winks at Beau's sire. "We're good partners."

The tips of Maurice's ears turn pink. Jasper looks from Maurice to the female dragon, silvery dust falling softly from the edges of his wings.

Beau gestures toward the big wooden machine. "Well, Dad, tell everyone what you've invented."

Maurice claps his hands together, pride shining from his eyes as he gazes at the machine. "It's a wine press! Fuoco is already growing grapes on the other side of the greenhouse. By the end of the summer, we should have a full production line going."

For the next half hour, I listen as Maurice explains the inner workings of the press, along with the magical fuel that powers it. But I reserve the bulk of my attention for Beau. He watches his father, and I watch him, my selsara's joy tangible in my jewel. The powerful emotion spreads through me, warming me from within.

Eventually, Maurice and Riselle wander to the rear of the machine, their voices animated as they debate the merits of adding some kind of filter before the press fills the final bowl.

Beau grins as he turns to Jasper and me. "We can probably head back to the castle. They're going to be at this for a while."

A tiny head pops up from Jasper's shirt pocket. The pixie stares down at his mouse as it releases a long stream of chatter. "How in the world do you know that, Bert?" Jasper demands. When the mouse's chirping grows louder, the pixie throws up his hands. "Okay! I'll tell him." He looks at me. "Bert says you should use that press to make elderberry wine. It'll speed the healing of your wing."

I blink. Then I meet the mouse's dark eyes and offer a bow. "Thank you."

Beau reaches out, and Bert hops into his open palm. "Thank you for everything, friend," Beau murmurs, stroking the top of Bert's head. "I wouldn't be here without you. I'm forever grateful."

Jasper sniffs as he retrieves Bert and tucks the mouse carefully back into his pocket. "I hate goodbyes."

"Is that why you've moved into my castle?" I ask.

"Fuoco!" Beau scolds. "We owe Jasper as much as we owe Bert."

As usual, my selsara is right. Softening my voice, I place my hand over the jewel in the center of my chest and bow over it. "My apologies, Jasper. You have my thanks...and my help if you should ever require it." When I straighten, Beau gazes at me with love shining in his eyes. I make a mental note to apologize to Lilygully more often.

Jasper smiles. "You'll probably regret that."

"I don't doubt it," I say, returning the expression.

We stay like that for a moment, friendship and affection swelling among the three of us. Well, four of us, I mentally amend with a glance at Bert. Then Jasper flutters his wings.

"Gotta run. I need to pack." He blows us a kiss and heads toward the front of the greenhouse.

My heart sinks. "He's got *so* much luggage."

Beau laughs and links his arm with mine. "You can handle it, selsara."

I snag him around the waist and bury my face in his neck. "I never get tired of hearing you say that." I bring my lips to his ear and nip his lobe, then trail a row of kisses down the vein throbbing just under his skin. Dragging his collar aside, I kiss my way to the hollow of his throat. "You taste like the most sumptuous of wines, selsara," I murmur. "Have dinner with me tonight."

Beau's laugh rumbles against my lips. "I have dinner with you every night, my love."

"But tonight I want to show you off."

He tangles gentle fingers in my hair and forces my head up. "You got new jewels, didn't you?"

I pretend to be affronted, but I can't keep up the appearance. "I'm not the least bit sorry for lavishing you in riches, Beau Bidbury. Now come, I want to show you what I got you."

His plump lips curl into a smile as he follows me to our bedchamber. When we reach it, I grab a stack of clothes Zara delivered earlier.

Beau smiles. "Another corset. Color me surprised."

Grinning, I place the clothing in his arms and grab a blood-red collared shirt off the top. I slip it over my shoulders, then step back to give my selsara an eyeful.

Pink steals across his cheeks as he sets the clothing down and plucks the corset from the pile. "Face the mirror." His husky command sends a trill of anticipation down my spine. Beau and his commands are something new we're trying in the bedroom. Turns out my sweet baker has a deviant streak. Exploring it has been so much fucking fun.

Literally.

"Hands on the mirror," he murmurs. When I obey, he slips the corset over my shirt and makes quick work of the laces at the back. As he yanks them tight, I meet his eyes in the reflective surface.

"Perfect," I whisper.

His smile grows bigger, and he ties the laces at my lower back. The mirrored tie comes next, and he turns me to face him, his fingers working deftly to knot it around my neck.

And I can't stop looking at him.

"You're fucking beautiful, Beau," I murmur. "As beautiful as the day we met."

"You're not too bad yourself." He chuckles, one dark brow rising. "You planning on wearing pants? I didn't see any in that stack."

I grumble. "They're not ready yet, so I'll wear something I have." I gesture to an ornately jeweled box on a stand by our door. "Open the box, Beau. Your present is inside."

He tosses a flirty look over his shoulder as he goes to the door. When he opens the box, his gasp fills the room. "It's beautiful," he breathes, turning the vambrace in his hands.

I cross the room and take it from him. Flipping it over, I show him the scrolled design on one side. "The House Drakoni crest, my love. I had this made before I ever met you."

Eyes bright with tears, he leans forward and places a tender kiss on my lips. When we part, he strokes the glittering metal. "I love it."

"I want you in nothing but this after dinner," I say, slipping the vambrace around his forearm. As he shivers, I pull the laces tight and knot them.

Beau turns his arm over, the vambrace's metal surface catching the light. When he lifts his gaze to mine, his expression is so open and loving it steals my breath. "You ready to go see our people, my lord?"

Our people. I love the sound of that. I stroke my fingers along his stubbled jawline. "Yes, selsara. But you're the only thing I'll see."

"I love you," he murmurs, dark eyes shining. He reaches up and brushes the back of his hand over my cheek. "But you know you don't have to get me things. I already have everything I need."

I pull him against me. "Well, that makes two of us, selsara. I've got everything I need right here."

Happily ever after.

I can't imagine a more perfect ending.

~

BONUS CHAPTER
TEMPER THE FLAME

BEAU

"Are you sure this is necessary?" I ask, squinting against the black fabric over my eyes. I can't see anything.

Which, considering I'm blindfolded, is understandable. It's not the first time I've been blindfolded around Fuoco. On the other occasions, however, I was also naked...and tied to his bed.

My dick tightens, lustful memories forming behind my eyelids. And this is most definitely not the time and place for it. We're in the village. I know that much. The familiar scents of home invaded my nose as soon as we landed on solid ground after a hair-raising flight from the castle. The sweet smell of the honeysuckle that climbs the outside of Robert the bookseller's shop still clings to my nose as I take another cautious step forward.

Fuoco's low chuckle caresses my ear. His lips graze my cheek as his warm palm spreads over my lower back. "Absolutely necessary, selsara. Because you always complain when I give you presents."

"That's not true." Even as I say it, I know it's true. Fuoco spoils me. After a lifetime of poverty, however, it's hard to accept gifts. Which is...strange. An outsider would probably expect me to gobble up any generosity I can get my hands on. But it doesn't work that way. Maybe part of me thinks I don't deserve it. Being poor was like putting on an old but familiar sweater. I didn't love it, but I was used to it.

But I'm not poor now. Neither is the village—or any other part of Fuoco's territory. Once he realized his people were suffering, he put a stop to it. He's spent the past year making amends and getting to know his subjects. And he doesn't limit his generosity to me. Over the past twelve months, Fuoco has showered the Fire Syndicate with wealth.

I've helped him every step of the way. Together, we've built new schools, distributed food, and repaired houses. If I'm being honest, my reasons for lending a hand haven't always been altruistic. Seeing Fuoco in jeans and a tool belt does *things* to me.

"A little farther," Fuoco says, still guiding me. "One small step up, my love. Be careful." A bell tinkles, and Fuoco moves his hand to my elbow as he stops me from stumbling over the step.

The scent of flour hits my nose. And…sugar? Lifting my head, I sniff at the air. Other scents follow. Vanilla. Cinnamon. Chocolate. A couple of mystery scents hang in the air. I don't need to figure them out to know we're in a bakery. But that can't be right. My bakery was destroyed when Dad accidentally blew up my oven. Fuoco and I have been too busy to do more than clean up the mess and help Dad salvage the scrap metal. He's been happy as a clam in the castle, his suite filled with bubbling beakers and plans for new inventions.

Turning my head, I strain toward my husband. "What's going on?"

Fuoco's fingers fumble at the blindfold's knot on the back of my head. Then the cloth drops from my eyes, and sunlight blinds me all over again. Wincing, I drop my chin.

"Easy," Fuoco murmurs, resting a hand on my nape. As he strokes my hairline, emotion shivers across our mate bond, each feeling pulsing in the mating jewel embedded in my chest.

Contentment.

Excitement.

Anxiety.

The last brings my head up—and my jaw drops. A bakery spreads before me. But it's not just any bakery. It's enormous. Gorgeous.

The pristine space glistens with polished copper fixtures and marble countertops. Glossy wooden shelves line the walls. Glass cases rise behind the counters, the domes sparkling in the sun. As I gaze around, my brain identifies the mystery scents. The smell of fresh paint and cut lumber mixes with the aroma of sugar and spice. Everything is new and perfect. It's a bakery fit for a king.

Or a king's mate.

"It's yours," Fuoco rumbles beside me.

I turn to him, gratitude swelling my chest. "Fuoco... This is..."

He smiles, his brilliant green eyes alight with a mixture of excitement and nervousness. "I know how much you loved your bakery." His throat bobs, and something vulnerable moves through his eyes. "You value your independence, Beau, and I want you to have it. This bakery is more than a fresh start. It's my promise to you that I'll never stand in the way of you doing what you love. But I still want you to make this place your own. That's why the walls are white. You're in charge, selsara. Whatever you want, just tell me, and—"

"Fuoco," I rasp, emotion clogging my throat. Tears burn my eyes as I step into him and lay a palm on the mating jewel that pulses in the center of his broad chest. Even under the layers of his embroidered jacket, silk shirt, and leather corset, the gem heats my skin. "It's amazing. Better than anything I could have dreamed up."

Fuoco strokes beringed fingers over my cheek. "That's fitting," he murmurs, "because I dreamed of you for centuries, and the reality of you exceeds every precious glimpse I hoarded over the years."

My breath hitches, disbelief making my head spin. But maybe that's just Fuoco's effect on me. Somehow, this big, beautiful dragon wants *me*. Scratch that, he's obsessed with me. Any doubts I've harbored have been obliterated by the way he worships my body every night in our bed. And in his lair in the mountains. And inside the greenhouse. And against the walls of his castle. And in the apple orchard where we first met.

Now that I think about it, Fuoco has worshipped me in just about every location possible.

Green flames wreath his head as he runs jewel-bright eyes down my chest, and the pulse in his throat flutters faster as he moves his hands to my ass, his long fingers spreading over both cheeks. He tugs me against him, the long, hard length of his erection prodding mine. Desire—and *intention*—frazzle across our bond, lighting up my mating jewel. Its green glow glimmers through my shirt at the bottom of my vision as Fuoco grinds his cock against mine.

Blood pumps to my shaft, and my breath hitches as I spread both hands over Fuoco's chest. Lust makes me bold as I tip my head back and let challenge enter my tone. "I love this present, but it's missing something."

He freezes, dismay flitting through his eyes. "Name it. I'll take care of it today."

Moving my hands to his hips, I jerk *him* into *me*. As surprise widens his eyes, triumph surges through me. Keeping my dragon shifter husband on his oversized toes has been an unexpected and delightful facet of our marriage.

I have to remember to do it more often.

Pressing my cock harder against his, I stroke his mating jewel through his clothes. As a deep purr rumbles in his chest, I rise on tiptoe and brush my lips over the dark stubble on his jaw. "I want you to show me the kitchen. And then I want you inside me."

Fuoco's nostrils flare. His lips part, but no sound emerges. Poor thing. I've rendered him speechless.

"Can you do that for me?" I ask, working my hips against his.

My feet leave the floor. The bakery spins, and I'm suddenly clasped against a broad chest, my legs dangling as Fuoco strides toward the back.

"Anything for you, my love," he growls.

~

FUOCO

THE FLOORBOARDS SHIVER as I carry Beau to the bakery's kitchen. He gasps as he gazes around at the gleaming appliances and veined marble walls. He gasps again when I deposit him on the nearest counter and start on the buttons of his shirt.

"Someone will see!" he protests even as he tilts his head back to give me better access.

I shake my head. "The village is empty."

Beau's chocolate brown eyes go wide. "What?"

I toss his shirt aside and start on his belt. "They're waiting for us at the castle. We're having a banquet to celebrate the new bakery." The belt makes a *zipping* sound as I yank it from Beau's trousers.

Beau seizes my wrist. "Wait. Shouldn't we be at the banquet, too?"

My hands shake as I rip his fly open. "I told them not to expect us for a few hours." Freeing his cock, I wrap my hand around his hot, silky length. We groan together, our gazes colliding. "The banquet can wait," I add, stroking him. "Right now, I only want to feast on you."

A hungry look sheens his dark eyes. The mating jewel glitters in the center of his lean, muscular chest. His arousal pulses through our bond in thick waves, every loop urging my own lust higher.

"I love you," he whispers, something like wonder in his eyes. "Sometimes, I can't believe you're real."

Tenderness wells, a lightning bolt of need on its heels. Sliding my hand under his sack, I finger the small jeweled hoop that pierces the silky skin of his perineum. The adornment is another reminder of our commitment to each other. Another mark of my possession.

No, *obsession*. My people love shiny, glittery things. It's no wonder we lavish our mates with jewels and riches. I'd crawl under Beau's skin if I could. The naughty little ring is as close as I can get.

He shivers as I stroke widening circles around the ring, my finger questing closer to his hole. His thick, dark lashes flutter as he arches on the marble. He swipes a pink tongue over his bottom lip, and I have to hold my breath against a surge of need so powerful it scares me.

"More," he says, spreading his thighs. Sunlight from the window picks out the red highlights in the neat thatch of dark curls around his cock. "Gods, Fuoco, give me everything."

Within seconds, I have him stripped and bent over the counter. His body is a dream, his tight, muscular ass flexing as he cranes his head over his shoulder.

"I want to see you," he says, his tone bashful as an adorable flush stains his cheeks.

"Everything you see belongs to you," I tell him as I unlace my corset. Appreciation gleams in his dark eyes as he watches me strip.

Nude at last, I grip my cock, presenting it to him as I did the night I stripped for him in the Great Hall. The bars through my nipples wink in the light. More sunlight catches in the tiny diamonds that glitter in the Prince Albert piercing in my cockhead.

Beau's gaze lingers on the barbell under the base of my erection. Memories of his tongue swirling over the metal put a groan in my throat, and I let it emerge as I slide my fist down my shaft. Green scales spread down my arms. Fire crackles around my head.

And precum drips from my slit, tiny droplets splatting on the marble floor.

"This isn't very sanitary," Beau says, his brows pulling together.

Despite the arousal hammering me, I can't fight a smile. "I had the workers install a cleaning closet, selsara. It's well-stocked." Bending, I scoop my trousers from the floor and pull a packet of lube from the back pocket.

Beau's cheeks turn a deeper shade of red. "You brought lube?"

Chuckling, I step behind him and lodge my dick in his crease. "Beau," I murmur, nuzzling under his ear, "I *always* bring lube." Running the tip of one fang down his throat, I roll my hips, working my cock deeper into his cleft. "Because I want inside this tight, warm ass of yours every chance I get."

Goosebumps pebble his skin as he catches his breath. "Oh gods," he groans. "I… I want that, too. Please."

I ease back long enough to coat my fingers. Then I urge him to his forearms and slip my hand between his cheeks. His moans and gasps fill the quiet kitchen as I nudge his legs wide and circle his hole, coaxing the ring of muscle open. My mating jewel casts prisms on his back. His passage squeezes and twitches around my finger.

"So hot," I rasp, thrusting deeper until I graze his gland. "So tight and hot for me, Beau." I lean back because I need to see him, and I dig my teeth into my lip at the sight of his pink rim stretching around me. His guiche piercing sparkles behind his sack, which sways as he rocks his hips, fucking himself onto my finger. "Can you take another?"

"Yeah," he rasps. "I want it."

"You'll get it." Gods, I'll give him anything. Everything. My cock weeps with need, but I ignore my lust as I sink another finger inside him, stretching and massaging. Pushing more lube inside him. The slick sounds war with his cries, which grow louder as I fuck him with my fingers.

"Fuoco!" he says hoarsely, rocking harder. Muscle ripples across his back as he spreads his hands on the counter and bends over the marble. He thrusts his ass back wantonly, his buttocks bouncing against my wrist.

"That's it, baby," I tell him. "Come get what you want. Gods, I can feel you opening for me. You're going to be so ready for my dick, aren't you? Stretched just the way I like you." I rub his prostate, stroking the spongy, slippery gland.

Beau moans and whimpers, his hips bucking uncontrollably. Sweat sheens his shoulders, and the little ring behind his balls trembles against his glistening taint. My cock throbs, but I force myself to hold back—to savor the sight of my mate's slick, pink opening swallowing my fingers.

"Take it," I growl, fire leaping around my head. "Take it all, babe." Beau's cries escalate as I push a third finger inside him.

"Now," he grits out, bucking harder. "Now, Fuoco, I can't wait."

The plea is music to my ears. Pulling my fingers from his body, I groan as his glossy entrance flutters, the muscle clamping repeatedly.

"Little hole missed me," I growl, slicking lube over my shaft. Lining up, I push inside him.

"Yes!" Rearing up, he turns his head, seeking me.

Another growl rips from my throat as I seize his lips, possession like a fire in my chest. Slicking my tongue against his, I push my hips forward, sinking into his tight, perfect heat.

He's so fucking ready for me. Always, Beau is ready for me. Twining an arm around my neck, he accepts my kiss as sweetly as he accepts my cock, his taste like sugar on my tongue.

"Love you," he moans against my lips as he begins to move. "Love you so much."

"I love you, too," I whisper back. "So much." Snaking a hand around him, I find his cock and stroke. My hips bounce off his cheeks.

His ass sucks at me, his passage rippling with every thrust. I plunge my tongue deep as I sink into him over and over, driving him onto his toes.

Moaning, he clings to my neck. And he moves with me, absorbing everything I give him. Our grunts and cries echo around us. Dust motes dance in the lust-soaked air. Fire sizzles in my veins. An inferno of lust crackles in my chest. I'm burning up, and I've never felt so alive.

So complete.

I can't hold on. "You feel too good," I mumble against Beau's lips. "I'm going to come."

"Do it," he gasps. "Come inside me. Fill me up, selsara. I want to drip you for the rest of the day."

The filthy talk is game over. My balls draw up, and I come on a bellow, my hips jerking wildly. Beau follows a second later, his body shaking as he spurts all over my fist.

I stroke him through it, smearing hot, sticky cum up and down his shaft. His gasps turn into a low, masculine whimper as he drifts down, shaking in the aftermath of our joint release.

When I can breathe again, I pull gently from his ass and turn him around. He rests his damp forehead on my chest, his warm breath gusting over my pecs.

"Are you all right?" I ask, stroking his back. "Was that okay?"

Beau lifts his head, a mischievous glint in his eyes. "You don't have to ask. I know you feel my satisfaction through the mate bond. Yours is vibrating hard enough to shake my bones apart, by the way."

I can't help my grin. "I'm a dragon. We love praise almost as much as we love jewelry and spoiling our mates."

Beau snorts, but he returns my smile as he cups my jaw. Feathering his thumb over my cheek, he gives me a tender look. "I love the bakery, Fuoco. Thank you."

"You're welcome. I'm sorry I got cum on the floor."

"Gross," Beau says, his shoulders shaking as mirth dances in his eyes.

"I'll help you clean it. I'm good with a mop."

The mirth dances higher. "I find that hard to believe."

Pressing him against the counter, I give his cock a firm stroke. As he sucks in a breath, I use my free hand to tip his chin up. "Cleaning makes me hungry. The pantry is fully stocked. You could bake me cookies." My mouth waters at the thought of Beau's considerable skill with an oven. "Maybe those semi-sweet chocolate chip kind with the chopped walnuts."

He tilts his head as if he's thinking it over. "Maybe," he says finally, love and desire replacing the humor in his eyes. "Or perhaps an apple pie?"

I know my smile is stupid and lovesick. And I don't care one bit. Cupping my hands around his face, I lean in for a kiss.

"That's exactly what I wanted."

KISS THE SLIPPER
AN MM CINDERELLA RETELLING

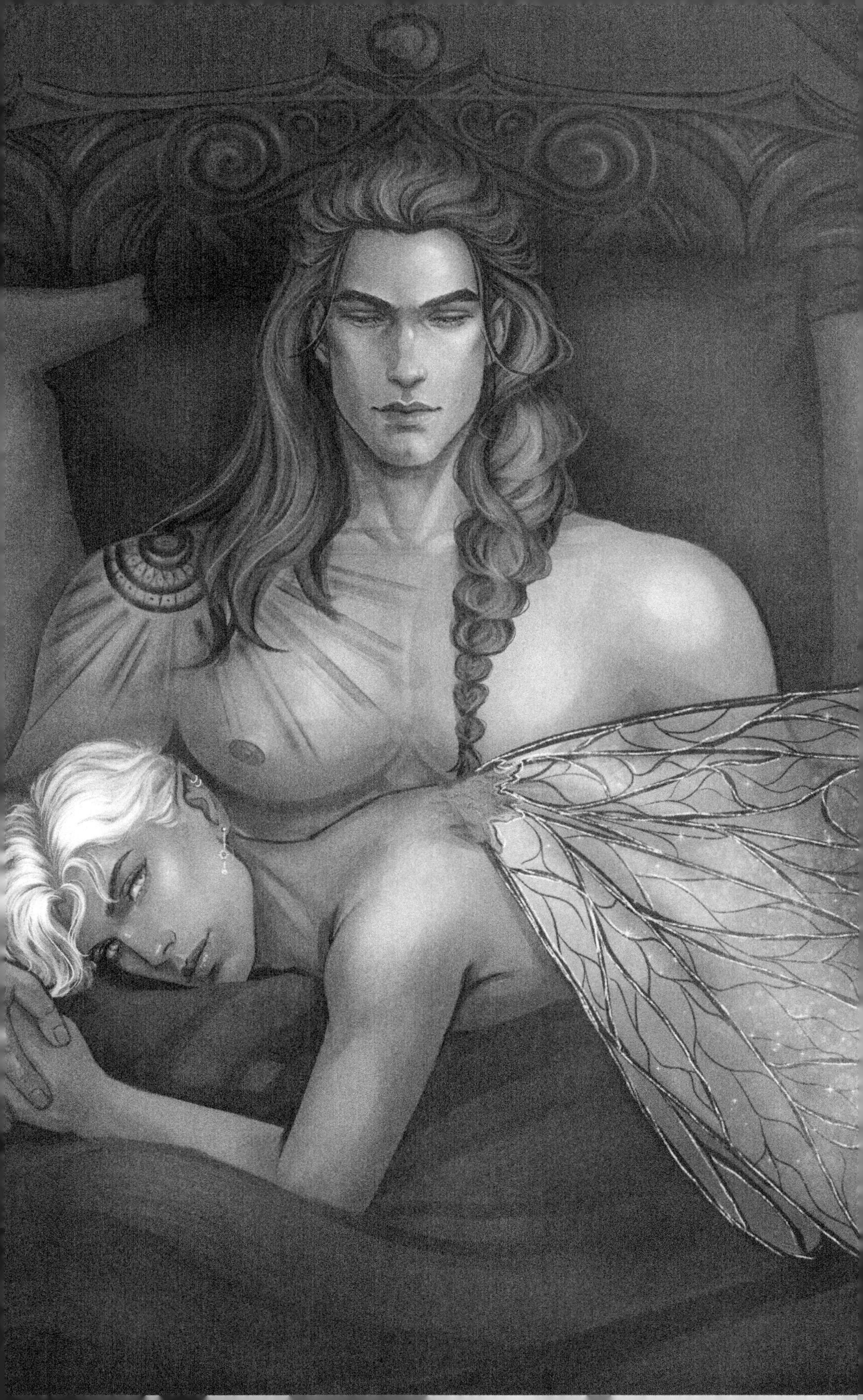

PART ONE
SPRING

CHAPTER 1
JASPER

"Paris in spring," I say with a sigh. "Has there ever been a bigger cliché?"

I wait a moment, my gaze on the twisted, warped Eiffel Tower piercing a pale blue sky. The heady scent of flowers fills the air. Even on the outskirts of the city, I swear I can hear someone swearing in French—a distinctive "merde" floating on the wind. "Well," I amend, "maybe pissed-off Frenchmen are a bigger cliche."

When my companion stays silent, I look up at him. "What, you don't agree?"

Fuoco swings his green snout toward me, the look in his reptilian eyes decidedly irritated. I can't communicate with him the way I can with some animals, but speech isn't necessary with this particular beast. Even in dragon form, the Lord of the Fire Syndicate has a knack for making his displeasure known without saying a word.

"Oh come on, flame zaddy, it wasn't *that* bad flying with me." I let a smile touch my lips. "Although, I confess I'm a little chafed. It's been a while since I had something that big and hard between my thighs."

Fuoco shifts in a blink. Before I can draw a breath, seven-feet-plus of muscled, nude syndicate ruler glowers down at me. A large emerald glows in the center of his chest. A green scale pattern ripples from his neck to the tops of his meaty thighs. Green flames dance around his head.

"Hot," I breathe, fanning my face.

His fangs flash as he leans over me and speaks in a growl. "I've lost count of the number of times I've asked you to stop calling me *flame zaddy*."

I stretch my wings, craning my head over my shoulder to study the edges. "You know," I muse, "before the Veil fell, human airplanes had flight attendants." I arch my back, savoring the stretch for a moment before I meet Fuoco's gaze and level a look at him. "They brought passengers alcohol and snacks, Fuoco."

"I'm aware, Lilygully. I was there." He folds his thick arms over his chest. "And rest assured, you would have been on every no-fly list in the world."

"You say that like it's a bad thing."

"It *is* a bad thing—"

"And anyway, it's not fair that you dragons have a monopoly on air travel these days." I wave a hand in the direction of the ocean. "Two days to cross the Atlantic, and you were a positive beast the entire time. I mean, I know you're eager to get back to Beau, who is probably at this very moment sitting in one of the castle windows pining for you, but they say distance makes the heart grow fonder. Don't you think you two could use a break?"

"Jasper…"

"Gods, your *bed* could use a break." I flutter my wings, sending a small gust of wind into Fuoco. As he grimaces and tosses the hair from his eyes, I inject mild reproach into my tone. "If wood could talk, m'lord, it would say *uncle*."

A muscle twitches in Fuoco's jaw. "Don't you have some kind of appointment?" He glances at the Parisian skyline. "I thought you were overdue at court."

"Admit it, you're going to miss me."

His tone turns long-suffering. "Are you okay on your own?" He flicks another look at the city, then narrows his eyes at me. "Do you need an escort to Mab's court?"

Cheeky dragon. I let it slip once that I was late for a meeting at court.

I didn't say which court, but Fuoco clearly put two and two together. Undoubtedly, he'd love to know where Mab keeps her throne. But Mab doesn't blab—at least not about our headquarters.

I smile and dust my wings together. "I can handle myself, thanks, Daddy. I've been to Paris a time or ten."

Fuoco grunts. Then his features soften. He unfolds his arms and gives my shoulder an awkward pat. "I, uh, wanted to thank you, Jasper." Another pat. "For everything you did to help Beau and me get together."

Satisfaction thrums in my chest. *If only you knew, you big, sexy oaf.* But he can't know. If there's a universal truth about the ancients among the Myth, it's that they don't appreciate being manipulated. The older and more powerful the monster, the less tolerant they are of other beings meddling in their business.

And, well, meddling is one of my primary charms. Literally.

I tilt my head. "From what I've seen—and heard—you and Beau get together just fine on your own."

He snorts and drops his hand. "Stay out of trouble, Lilygully."

"I always do."

For a moment, something shimmers in Fuoco's green eyes. His voice goes gruff. "I mean it, pixie. The Hallows would be less…colorful without you." His brows pull together as he glances at Paris once more. "I feel like maybe I should go into the city with you."

The hair on my nape lifts. A sense of unease drifts through me as I follow the direction of Fuoco's glance. Some dragons have the gift of precognition. But that's not Fuoco's talent. "Why?" I force a smile. "Do you know something I don't?"

"No." He clears his throat, and his eyes clear too. "I'm sorry. Just being fanciful, I guess. And maybe I got used to you being around the castle." He grunts again. "I don't know if I'll be able to handle the quiet."

"I'm sure you and Beau will think of something."

Shaking his head, Fuoco turns and walks the narrow path that leads away from the city. When he's a dozen steps away, he shifts back into his dragon form, his green scales shimmering in the late morning sunlight. With a powerful beat of his wings, he launches into the sky.

"Show off," I murmur, smiling as I bat my much smaller, less spectacular wings.

Bert wriggles in my breast pocket, and I unbutton my jacket so he can poke his head out. He watches as Fuoco shrinks into the distance, then lifts his dark eyes to mine. His high-pitched voice fills my head. *"Mab won't like it if you're late."*

Bossy mouse.

I roll my eyes. "Please. Like she's ever been on time in her life." Which is saying something, considering she's quite possibly older than dirt.

But Bert has a point. Besides, I'm in Paris for a very important reason.

Adulation. Today kicks off my victory lap, and I'm ready to accept my accolades, thank you very much.

"Let's go, then," I tell Bert. I take two steps, then stop and look down at him. "Are you wearing a sweater?"

"What's wrong with that?"

"Nothing." I scratch between his ears and continue toward the city. Bert scrambles from my pocket and runs up to my shoulder.

"You're smiling."

"I'm not," I say in his head. Because I'm definitely fighting a smile, and it'll be more obvious if I speak aloud.

Bert's voice in my head squeaks with indignation. *"Mert said it looked nice."*

"He would." Bert's twin brother has abysmal taste.

"What's wrong with the sweater, Jasper?" Bert demands, tugging sharply on my ear.

"Ow!" I jerk my head away. When he continues tugging at me, I pluck him from my shoulder and bring him level with my face. "Nothing is wrong with it," I say gently. "It's just that you're not wearing any pants."

He looks down at himself. Then he looks back up. *"You didn't wear pants to that party in the centaur's room the other night."*

I mull it over. "Hmm. Good point."

"I can think of at least fifty other instances where you spent the evening entirely pantsless."

"True."

"Then there was that whole month with the jockstrap thing—"

"Say no more."

"Luke calls it The Jockstrap Incident. When he's drunk, he calls it The Empire Strikes Crack."

"Does he, really?" Mice are naturally sarcastic, but Luke takes it to criminal levels. I place Bert on my shoulder. "I like to think of it as more of a saga."

Bert nods as I resume walking. *"Makes sense. You were dating a berserker."*

"Ugh, he was a handful. And not the kind of handful you want in a man." I glance at Bert. "The sweater is adorable, by the way."

"Shut up."

Twenty minutes later, we stroll along the banks of the Seine, which bustles with human and Myth creatures selling food and souvenirs. The Eiffel Tower looms large, its twisted spire warped by magic. According to legend, the iron structure was one of the first victims of The War That Ripped the Veil. Humans do a lot of finger-pointing, but no one really knows who started it. And it doesn't really matter, since no one can change the outcome. One now-extinct country launched nukes at another. The other retaliated. Their neighbors panicked and launched more.

And then everything went *kaboom*. The blasts were so powerful, they destroyed the Veil that separated the human plane from the magical realm. Magic rushed into places it was never meant to dwell, devouring human technology and reducing glass and concrete to dust. Airplanes dropped from the skies, which suddenly teemed with dragons, gargoyles, and griffins.

And pixies.

A smile tugs at my lips as I dip into an alley. Pausing, I look over my shoulder, my gaze on the passersby near the river.

"No one followed us," Bert says in my head. *"I kept an eye out."*

I reach up and tweak his tail. "You always do, friend."

"I don't have a choice. Not with you admiring yourself in every reflective surface we pass."

"Can you blame me?" I reach a small wooden door at the end of the alley. Stepping to the right of it, I kneel and loosen a pebble from the crumbling base of the stone wall. As I straighten, the wall turns transparent. Magic lashes from the other side, long fingers licking over my skin. Tasting me. An instant later, the wave of power bows.

Passage granted.

I reach up and fist bump Bert. Then I step through the wall into a corridor lined with will-o'-the-wisp lanterns. They bob greetings as I head toward the audience chamber. A thumping bass bounces down the corridor, the beat vibrating the stones under my feet.

"Sounds like a party," Bert says.

"The biggest in the Myth," I murmur. A pair of tall, golden doors loom before us. Just as we reach them, a pixie with a bushy red beard steps from an alcove. A squirrel rushes up his shoulder and gives me an arrogant look. The pixie holds a clipboard, his nails painted with polish a shade brighter than his hair and one shade darker than his lipstick. His wings sift silvery dust onto the floor.

"Hey, Rufus," I say. "How's it hanging?" I glance at his kilt, which hits well above the knee. "Not too low, I hope."

"Wouldn't you love to know," Queen Mab's steward rumbles in his thick brogue. He looks behind me as if he's searching for someone. "Your mum with you?"

"Not this time." I examine my own manicure in the lantern light. "She's in the Maldives with my fathers." I look up. "And their boyfriend."

Rufus lifts a brow. "Titania always did like variety."

"I don't see it lasting." I lean in and lower my voice. "He's a rage demon."

"Temperamental."

"You have no idea."

"Oh, I do."

I lean back. "That's right! You dated that tall drink of water from London."

Rufus grins. "Got a poke from a bloke." His grin fades as he scratches his beard. "That's an accurate description, actually. For a demon, he wasn't all that skilled at delivering his packages, if you catch my meaning."

The squirrel on his shoulder chatters in his ear, its bushy tail swishing over the steward's leather harness.

"Aye, I'm gettin' to it. Can't two old friends catch up?" Rufus lays a hand on one of the ornate door knobs and slants me a look. "You ready to join the party, Lilygully?"

Excitement shivers down my spine. I flick my wings and put my shoulders back. "It's not a party until I show up."

"Arrogant much?"

I wink at Rufus as I drop my glamour completely. In the doors' shiny surface, my ears taper to points. My hair, which I wore bright green today just to fuck with Fuoco, turns its natural shock of platinum. My features grow sharper and otherworldly, and a faint glow rises from my skin.

"You missed a spot," the steward snarks.

Gaze on the door, I give Rufus the middle finger.

"You wish," he says. With a good-natured snort, he pushes the doors open. The bass swells, the thumping beat interspersed with the chatter of hundreds of pixies. They cluster at the rear of the throne room's antechamber, where they wait to speak to Queen Mab. Color blooms everywhere, from the red, diamond-patterned walls to the fuchsia ceiling. More will-o'-the-wisps hang in strings across the antechamber, their flames bobbing green, orange, and red. Spun-sugar clouds drift overhead, illuminated from within by twinkling sparks of lightning someone must have charmed to stay within the fluffy confines. In an alcove covered in glittering quartz and spun-gold accents, a trio of musicians play instruments from beyond the Veil. A tall pixie with black hair and black-tipped wings shreds a bass guitar.

Heads turn as pixies catch sight of me. The crowd surges in my direction, and smiling faces and fluttering wings surround me as I move toward the throne room's doors.

I don't get far.

"There he is!" someone calls. As more heads swivel in my direction, exclamations ripple through the crowd.

"Jasper!"

"Ooh, he's here!"

"Nice work in the Hallows, Lilygully!"

"Yeah, baby, he matched all four of those dickheads."

Slapping sounds. "You can't call the syndicate lords dickheads!"

"Sorry. Cockheads."

Someone thrusts a marker at me. "Will you sign my tits?"

The marker-wielding pixie's companion elbows her in the ribs. "Not enough room on those mosquito bites."

"Not everything can be as big as your ass, Vivica."

Shaking my head, I murmur greetings and thanks. Slowly, I maneuver through the crush. After a few dozen handshakes, I make it to my destination. A female pixie in a purple minidress stands at the throne room's doors, a bubble of pink chewing gum slowly expanding from her mouth. Her blue eyes regard me impassively as the gum balloons.

"*Hi*, Dahlia," I say deliberately. Bert makes huffy noises in my head, his tail swishing against my shoulder. Mab's herald is notorious prickly. Most pixies are merry. Dahlia is…not.

Pop! Dahlia sucks the gum into her mouth. "What up."

"I have an audience with the queen." I wave a dismissive hand. "You know, to tell her all about how I matched the four syndicate lords of the Hallows with their mates. No big deal."

"Uh-huh." Dahlia's jaw works as she chews her gum. "Couple people ahead of you."

"*Ridiculous,*" Bert hisses in my head.

I give Dahlia my most winning smile—the one that charmed an entire horde of orcs into abandoning their weapons and joining an orgy that's supposedly still going on somewhere in the south of France. "Are you sure?" I sift my wings, gold glitter spilling from the edges. "Maybe you should check your list."

Dahlia blows a small bubble and pops it. "Oh yeah? Lemme check." She waits a beat. "Yup. Still a few people ahead of you."

Bert sputters in my mind. *"Preposterous! This is—"*

"It's fine," I say through clenched teeth.

His tail whips my arm. *"Maybe she misplaced the list in her gum."*

"I'll wait." Swinging away, I flick my wings as I move into the crowd. I'm in Paris to get my hero's welcome, and now I'm stuck in a fucking queue. Ignoring Bert's mental bitching, I let my gaze wander around the packed chamber. As the guitar riff changes, I make eye contact with the tall pixie playing the bass. Recognition tingles within me as a slow smile spreads across his face.

"Ugh," I say under my breath.

Bert halts his tirade and curls his tail around my shoulder. *"Hey, don't you know him?"* Bert waits a beat. *"Biblically?"*

"Don't remind me." The guitarist flutters his wings as he holds my stare. "Gods, I used to think those black tips were so edgy."

"Mmm, your bad boy era."

"More like just bad. No need to bring the boy into it." I tear my gaze away, my irritation growing. But another emotion rises, too. One I've done my best to ignore over the past few months. At first, I couldn't figure it out. For weeks, I delayed my trip to Paris as I grappled with the unfamiliar feeling—a mix of boredom and frustration. And not the sexual kind. Bert teased me about shedding my pants at the centaur's party. What he doesn't know is that I drank water all night and ducked back to my room to *read a book*.

For the first time in my life, flirting feels forced. Almost tedious.

"Bert?" I ask cautiously in my head. *"Am I getting old?"*

"You're ninety-three. That's like five in Myth years. I'm surprised you can wipe your own ass."

I sigh as the crowd continues its chatter around me. *"You say the sweetest things."*

Something bumps me hard from behind, making me lurch forward.

"Hey!" I whirl in a flurry of agitated wings—and suck in a breath.

A golden god stands before me, everything about him like honey melting on a summer day. I tip my head back—*way* back—as I take him in. Tall, ripped, hot as fuck. Golden-brown hair waves back from a broad, unlined forehead. Golden eyes blink rapidly, surprise in the thickly lashed depths.

"I'm deeply sorry," the god says, offering a slight bow. His dark suit hugs his body, which is muscled under the expensive cloth. And he is *very* expensive, this god. Spicy cologne and notes of sandalwood and leather reach me, making my toes curl in my boots. As he straightens, I bite back a groan. Sweet mother of Puck, he looks like he could break me over his knee.

He's also spilling magic like a poorly trained waiter with a water pitcher. It hovers around him, just barely contained by his glamour. If he's a pixie, he's an exceptionally skilled one. Few Myth creatures can hide their true form from me for long. And he's *got* to be a pixie. Mab never admits other kinds of creatures to her court.

The god's brows pull together as he searches my gaze. "Are you okay? Did I hurt you?"

"Don't ask him if he wants to," Bert chimes in my head.

"Why not?" I mutter.

"I beg your pardon?" the god asks, his frown deepening.

"Don't ask him if he wants you to beg," Bert says.

"Silence," I hiss.

The god blinks, confusion in his gorgeous eyes. As he opens his mouth, Dahlia's voice rises above the crowd.

"Jasper Lilygully, beloved nephew of Queen Mab!"

The music stops. All eyes turn to me.

Dahlia throws the doors open, her wings gone bright silver. As she turns back to the crowd, she spreads an arm toward the throne room visible between the doors. "Make way for Jasper, the most accomplished matchmaker in a generation!"

Applause erupts. Several pixies cup their hands around their mouths and whoop. Someone claps my shoulder. "Congratulations, Jasper!"

"Get 'em, baby!"

"J to the A," a burly pixie with a backward baseball cap hoots.

Smiling, I move through the crowd, the golden-eyed god slipping from my thoughts. Cheering pixies flank me until I reach the throne room's doors. As I step inside, Dahlia pops her gum before pulling the doors shut. The noise of the crowd and the thumping bass cuts off—and the sound of beating wings replaces it.

A purple runner sweeps up a black diamond-patterned floor. At the end of the runner, Queen Mab sits on a golden throne with crimson cushions, her leather-clad legs propped on one arm and crossed at the ankle. Spiky stilettos adorn her feet. Her white-blond hair is wound in two buns that perch precariously on either side of her head.

Hummingbirds flit around her, pausing briefly here and there to whisper in her ear.

"Jasper!" she exclaims, swinging her legs off the throne. Rising, she waves me forward, her gossamer wings shedding silver dust. "Get over here! I wanna hear everything."

"Aunt Mab," I say, striding up the runner with a grin splitting my face. When I reach Mab, she yanks me into a cherry-scented hug. Hummingbirds buzz around us, tiny wings beating the air.

Mab eases back and beams at me. "They said you couldn't do it, but I always believed in you."

"Thanks. Wait, who said I couldn't do it?"

She waves a hand. "Oh, everyone." A hummingbird darts forward and hovers at her shoulder. She tilts her head, listening intently as the bird speaks in her mind. "Sure, tell him I said it's fine, but if he fills the swimming pool with champagne again, I'll bring back the guillotine." As the bird darts off, she offers me a small smile. "The bubbles are terrible for the filters."

I nod solemnly.

Mab links her arm through mine and leads me away from the throne. "Soooo, spill it. Which one of those big, bad men was the hardest to deal with and why was it Wotan?"

For the next few minutes, we chat about my mission, which was top-secret until about a month ago. I still don't know why Mab was determined to see the syndicate lords mated. When I asked her the day she gave me the assignment, she lifted a casual shoulder and said, "Why not?"

Undoubtedly, my aunt has her reasons. Or maybe she just wanted to see the rulers of the Hallows brought to their knees.

Not that I tricked them in any way. Matchmaking doesn't work like that. No, I merely helped them along. Tipped my hand. Steered the ship through rocky waters.

"And what of Ari Razorfin?" Mab asks, her wings glowing more brightly. "Hot, right?"

"Scorching. But so angry. Hot angry. Hangry? You know what I mean."

Mab flings a hand out. "I mean, it's not *that* far off. What with the whole cannibalism thing."

"I know. And why is that also hot? Is something wrong with us?"

"I'm afraid to meet him in a dark alley, and I *like* it."

We both shiver. Then she tips her head to the side. "I'm proud of you, Jasper. With this accomplishment, you've cemented your status as one of Fate's most dependable helpers. Yours is an uncommon gift."

My insides warm. I brace myself for her to announce she's promoting me to a new position at court. Maybe even Chief Matchmaker, a role that has stood empty since my grandfather died.

Mab opens her mouth.

A hummingbird flits to her ear, its wings a blur.

"Oh!" my aunt says, facing the doors. "He is?" She looks at me with a distracted air. "Uh, I have to take this, Jasper. We'll talk later, okay?"

The doors fly open, and Dahlia's voice rolls through the throne room. "Prince Abelin Vale of the Summer Court!"

Gasps ring out from the antechamber. A second later, the golden god steps past Dahlia. Only he's not a god. He's an *elf*. Still hot as the sun, but now his glamour is down, revealing pointed ears and the perfect, glowing skin only the elves can achieve. His hair shimmers like molten honey.

Confusion pummels me. An elf in the pixie court? And not just any elf—a royal prince. As in, the highest and mightiest.

What in the hot fuck is an elven prince doing mingling among pixies? Our two peoples share a common ancestor, but the family tree split ages ago. In the intervening millennia, our differences have only grown wider. The snobs of the Myth, elves keep to themselves, rarely descending from their ivory towers. Immensely powerful, they look down their elegant noses at pixies. To them, we're the embarrassing distant cousin. A low-rent version of the real thing.

Mab slips past me, her wings suddenly trailing bright-gold dust. "Your Highness! Please, come in."

The prince darts a look at me before offering my aunt a stately bow. "Your Majesty."

"Oy!" Rufus appears out of nowhere and jabs me in the ribs.

I round on him, anger spiking. "What the fuck?"

Rufus jerks his head toward a small door behind the throne. "This is a high-profile visit. Mab'll take it alone."

Is he serious right now? I draw myself up, but murmuring pulls my attention back to the doors. Prince Abelin bows over my aunt's hand and kisses her knuckles.

"The pleasure is completely mine, Your Majesty."

Puck's beard, is that a slight French accent?

Mab's wings flutter, golden pixie dust spilling onto the throne room floor. I got silver.

"Jasper," Rufus says sharply under his breath.

"I'm going," I mutter, turning and stalking to the side door. Bert chatters in my head, but I ignore him as I wrench the door open and make my way down the dimly lit corridor.

I got silver.

It's the only thought that pounds through my head as I step through the portal that takes me back into the heart of Paris.

∼

THIRTY MINUTES LATER, I'm still fuming as I wind my way through the narrow streets of St. Germain. Humans and Myth creatures dine at sidewalk cafes. More than one hot guy gives me a second look as I pass. Normally, I'd look right back, but I can't talk to anyone right now. Not when my head is stuffed full of images of the elven prince.

"Abelin," I tell Bert through our mental bond. *"What kind of name is that?"*

"Elvish, apparently."

I clench my jaw. That fucker stole my spotlight. After months of planning and scheming, of hopping from syndicate to syndicate, I finally accomplished my mission. I watched other people fall in love. At heart, every pixie is a matchmaker. It's our thing. Well, that and hexing assholes who deserve it. But I'm damn good at shepherding Fate. It was no small feat to match all four syndicate lords. I was ready for a little recognition.

And then boom. Elf-bombed.

I glance down at Bert, who peeks from my jacket pocket. *"Who does he think he is, waltzing into our court? He flirted with Mab. That takes balls."*

"Which you were definitely thinking about."

I grunt as I slip into the shadows under a striped awning. *"Not anymore. I wouldn't touch him with a—"*

A hand clamps down on my shoulder. Before I can react, I'm spun around and faced with a familiar broad chest. Prince Abelin's glamour is back up, but he's no less stunning with the Parisian sun slanting over him. Spiky, black lashes cast shadows on his cheeks as he appears to catch his breath.

I pull from his grip. "How did you find me?"

Humor—and maybe a touch of arrogance—gleams in his eyes. "You're not the only one with an animal familiar."

Right. How could I forget? Elves commune with beasts the same as pixies. Of course, they do it better and fancier, bonding with one creature at a young age. Their familiars are usually some kind of mythical beast. I glance around, looking for a phoenix or a hellhound.

"I'm sorry to stop you like this," the prince says. "I hope I didn't startle you." He flashes a wry grin, showing perfect, white teeth. "You're faster than you look."

Anger sparks—along with a flash of heat I ignore. "Fast for a pixie, you mean."

His perfect brows pull together. "I, uh…no. I didn't mean it that way." His throat bobs. "Look, I'm really sorry about what happened back there."

I fold my arms. "Oh, yeah? You looked really sorry."

"I am. I had no idea the herald was going to announce me during your audience." Another throat bob, which is *not* sexy. "Would you let me make it up to you?"

Awareness tingles down my spine, bumping over the base of my wings, which are stuffed under my glamour. I've been hit on enough to know when a man is interested.

The prince's eyes fill with unmistakable anticipation. "Say yes," he says softly. "Have lunch with me. Make me a happy man today, Jasper Lilygully."

My breath hitches. If I had buttons, this elf just smashed the whole fucking panel. Still, I can't let him win that easily.

I raise a brow. "Does that line work on everyone, Abelin?"

"Not everyone." His gaze dips to my mouth. "But I'm really hoping it'll work on you." Golden eyes lift to mine. "And please, call me Vale."

Something inside me loosens. "Vale," I repeat, my voice sounding far away and sort of breathless.

The prince's lips curve. "Vale Gentry."

Gentry. A common surname the elves use when they move among humans.

But there's nothing common about this prince. And, dammit, I'm going to say yes. I shouldn't. I really fucking shouldn't. But fuck me, he's hot. And he owes me.

"Fine," I hear myself say. "I'll let you buy me lunch, Vale Gentry."

CHAPTER 2
VALE

"Great!" I say, my voice bright with enthusiasm. I clear my throat, admonishing myself to behave as the heir to the Summer Court should. But I've already accomplished today's mission. I did exactly what I told my father I'd do.

Jasper's startlingly blue eyes narrow, as if he thinks I'm somehow luring him into a trap.

He's so beautiful I can barely breathe. His glamour is up, but even that is stunning. Short platinum hair. A delicate but nevertheless masculine bone structure. Pouty lips that draw my gaze over and over. His eyelids are smeared with some kind of shimmery paint. His clothes hug his lithe body, hinting at muscle through his chest and shoulders.

The intense need to touch him courses through me—sunbursts of longing that radiate along my skin. I shove both hands in my pockets to avoid temptation. I really shouldn't be here, asking a gorgeous, definitely mischievous pixie to lunch.

Yet I can't find it in me to stop.

Instead, I smile. "Are you up for a walk?" I tilt my head toward the heart of the 17th arrondissement. "We can either go somewhere with a great view, or a place that serves my favorite dish in all of Paris. Your pick."

Jasper's expression hardens, although there's interest in the way he stares at me, like he's trying to sort out what puzzle all of my pieces go to. "Is this some kind of a trick?"

"No trick," I murmur. "Just lunch."

I'm not sure if I'm trying to convince him or myself. Maybe both. There's nothing *wrong* with me taking him to lunch. He's the pixie queen's nephew. It's a smart political move to learn more about him. I tell myself that's why I'm doing it, and not because I'm fucking entranced by his wings, or the cocksure expression he's worn since the moment I first saw him in Mab's court. It most definitely has nothing to do with how I want to strip every piece of clothing from his lean body and explore him with my teeth and tongue.

"Fine, then," he says. "Your favorite food." He lifts his chin. "But if it's something hoity-toity and disgusting, I'm not eating it."

I laugh. "Not hoity-toity. It includes fried potatoes, and I promise it's deliciously edible. You'll be licking your fingers." I can't help the look I cast him, and I don't miss the way his nostrils flare. I didn't mean it to sound so sensual, but I seem unable to hold myself back today.

Jasper's the one to clear his throat this time. He gestures up the street with one elegant hand. His nails are painted with purple and black diamonds—perhaps a nod to Mab's ostentatious throne room. "Lead the way, Your Majesty."

"Vale," I correct gently. "I prefer Vale. And majesty is reserved for my father. But maybe I should call you Your Highness?"

Jasper shakes his head. "Only Mab uses a title."

"But you're her nephew."

The tips of his wings turn pink. "Yeah, well, I guess we've let that cat out of the bag."

"Was it a secret?"

His blue gaze turns shrewd. "You're the Prince of the Summer Court. You know damn well it was a secret."

"But not anymore." I let a smile touch my lips. "People are going to want to know more about you, Jasper. And I'm the first in line."

The interest that's been brewing in his eyes flares higher. "You're a very forward man, Prince Vale."

"Just Vale. And you're right. I don't beat around the bush when I see something I want. So...lunch?"

Dark eyelashes flutter, but he gives me a quick nod.

I've always had the gift of reading people well. It's not Myth magic, per se, just something I've honed over years of dealing with my godsawful stepmother and difficult father.

Jasper wears confidence and snark as easily as he does his beautiful glamour. What would I find if I stripped all that away? Who lies beneath those layers of sarcasm and deflection?

I want to know.

I shoot him my broadest grin as I lead us up the street. "My favorite spot is in Villette, about a twenty-minute walk."

"I thought Villette was mostly residential."

I flash him another smile. "It is...mostly."

Twenty minutes pass in a blur. We talk about why he was in Mab's court and the matchmaking coup he pulled off in the Hallows. It's obvious he's incredibly proud of what he accomplished there. Guilt rips at my chest knowing my presence stole his limelight. If I'd known, I would have delayed my audience with Mab.

I duck off the main thoroughfare and onto a small cobblestone path, pushing through overgrown shrubbery to clear the way.

Jasper peers through the foliage and cuts me a sharp look. "You're not trying to murder me, are you? Mab would shit a brick if I got massacred. She loves me, you know."

It's on the tip of my tongue to joke that there's *something* I'd like to stab him with, and it's not a weapon, but I hold back. He doesn't know me, and despite his dry tone, he might actually be worried. I did just hold a shrub open and ask him to step through it.

"No murder, just moules-frites." I gesture ahead of us. About forty yards away, an ancient-looking wooden door stands open, propped in place with a bucket of oyster shells. The salty smell of seafood wafts up the alley toward us.

Jasper steps through the hole I made, his suspicious expression transforming into a stunning smile. I want more of those smiles, preferably aimed directly at me. I shove my hands back into my pockets. I'm going to touch him if I don't.

When he catches me checking him out, his expression grows cocky. "You're staring, Vale."

"Because you're stunning," I say. "And I can't take my eyes off you."

He tips his head to one side. "If you're just trying to get me into bed, Abelin, it's going to take a lot more than sweet words. That said, keep the sweet words flowing. I'm not entirely immune to flattery."

I grin at his teasing. I'd love for him to be in my bed. I bet he's absolutely radiant when he comes.

But he called me Abelin again. The not-really-Jasper mask is back.

Still, I'm a patient man. I'll pull that mask off piece by piece, starting with lunch.

"It's Vale," I remind him, gesturing toward the restaurant. "Shall we?"

~

Two hours later, Jasper grins as I pour him another glass of white wine. We've polished off nearly four bottles. Alcohol doesn't hit pixies and elves the way it does humans, but Jasper's cheeks are flushed and his shoulders are relaxed. The wine spreads through my veins, warming me from within.

But it's the pixie across from me who's responsible for the fire under my skin.

He waves his hand over a now-empty plate of moules-frites, the discarded shells piled high in a metal baking dish. We've long since devoured the fries that came with them. "You're telling me this moules-frites isn't even French?"

"Nope." I smile as I set the wine bottle down. "Moules-frites originated in Belgium, but they've become something of a French staple, to the point that the humans once ran a survey to find France's favorite food, and moules-frites lost by just a few thousand votes."

Jasper smirks and grabs a small chunk of the crusty bread we've been using to sop up the remaining garlic, butter, and chive. "Well, I can't be swayed. I'm still calling *this* French bread."

I snort out a laugh. "Baguette, Jasper. Doesn't that word sound so much more beautiful rolling off the tongue? Baguette!" I say the last with a flourish, my barely there french accent more pronounced.

He pops the bread in his mouth, obviously savoring it. The smile he turns on me is radiant, the mask gone. It disappeared two glasses of wine ago when he told me more about his exploits in the Hallows. Considering what he accomplished, he deserves every bit of praise he came to Paris to receive.

I rest my elbows on the table and lean forward. "So, why the secrecy with your lineage?"

Instantly, his eyes grow shuttered.

Regret nips at me. He finally lowered his guard, and now I've opened my big mouth and ruined it.

I reach across the table and touch his arm. "I won't spread the word. But as you said, *le chat est sorti du sac*." The cat is out of the bag.

His lips quirk. "Is that even a French saying?"

"No. Don't tell anyone I said that. They'll take away my passport."

Humor dances in his eyes, and relief flows through me. For a moment, we just smile at each other. I look at his mouth again because I can't fucking help it.

He notices, and the air between us grows thicker. More charged.

Finally, he settles more deeply in his seat. "I had to make my own way. I didn't want to trade on the family name."

"Ah." I pick up my wine glass. "You wanted to be known for your gifts."

"Precisely."

I raise my glass in a toast. "And you are very gifted."

He holds my gaze. "You could say that," he says softly.

My dick tightens. I drag in a deep breath as I will it to bide its damn time. Because I can't mess this up. And I shouldn't be doing *this*.

But I know I'm not going to stop.

A mouse pops its head out of Jasper's front pocket, breaking the tension. Smiling, Jasper plucks a small piece of bread from his plate and hands it to the tiny creature.

"Who is this?" I ask. Most pixies commune with animals, so it's hardly a shock to see one with him. But the rodent might be…an issue. My familiar, Sulien, is a Taranathen cat from beyond the Veil.

Jasper waves his hand at the mouse, who stares at me with round, black eyes as it munches the bread. "This is Bert. His brother, Mert, is usually with us, too, but he had business to take care of back home."

"Business, huh?" I stare at Bert, unable to help my smile. "What sort of business might you be into, Bert?"

The mouse looks up at Jasper, who tilts his head, obviously listening intently. After a second, Jasper rolls his eyes and meets my gaze. "Bert says he appreciates your thoughtful question, but we've been talking about me for hours and he'd like to know more about you." He shifts back in his seat, slinging one arm along the top of the booth. "Please," he adds, an insolent smile playing around his mouth. But there's heat in his eyes, too. Bert isn't the only one who wants to know more.

Got you. A real smile. I could eat up a million more of the same. I'm fucking fascinated by that smile.

But I can't say any of that. I shouldn't…for many reasons. Duty, honor, my people. All those responsibilities form an invisible weight on my shoulders, crushing me the way they have my entire life. Somehow, being with Jasper takes the weight away, if only for a little while.

I pick up my wine glass and swirl it, my gaze on the pale liquid. I can't tell Jasper everything about myself, no matter how much I might want to.

Don't embarrass us today, Abelin.

My stepmother's words from this morning clang around my head. I haven't embarrassed her or my father in nearly two hundred years, but she loves to remind me anyhow. Preferably in front of King Nylian himself.

I meet Jasper's gaze. I'll tell him as much of the truth as I can. "I've long abhorred the hatred between pixies and elves. Even as a younger man, it never made sense to me. We each have strengths and weaknesses. There should be partnership between us, not enmity."

Jasper's smile fades into something more cautious. But curiosity gleams in his eyes.

I barrel on. "Most elves are snobbish." Jasper snorts, and I flash a wry smile. "I know that's our reputation. I don't want it to be our future."

The curiosity in Jasper's eyes shines more brightly. "So you aim to change it?"

I nod. "For all that my father, King Nylian, is an ancient monarch, he's adapted well to modern times. Hundreds of years ago, when we still lived beyond the Veil in the Taranathen Forest, I petitioned to represent him at Mab's court. I had an idea to build a foundation of partnership between pixies and elves." Heat touches my cheeks, and I release a shaky laugh. "Unfortunately, I was something of a playboy in my first hundred years. No matter how much Father agreed with my ideas, he never allowed me to represent us anywhere."

Jasper grins. "Playboy? I like the sound of that."

"It was fun," I admit, running a hand through my glamour's golden-brown waves. "I didn't take my role seriously back then. Everything seemed like a problem for future-me to deal with. But I've worked hard in the last few hundred years to change my father's impression of me. Today was a big step."

Gods. Why did I tell him all of that? Father would be mortified at me showing my hand like this. Spilling my guts to Mab's nephew.

But I can't stop talking. Not when Jasper's looking at me like he wants to know more—and not because his mouse pushed him to ask.

"My mother died when I was very young," I say. "Father remarried shortly after. My stepmother and I aren't…close. I think some of my earlier rebellion was probably a reaction to that relationship." I huff a humorless laugh. "Or lack thereof."

"But you're reformed," Jasper says. A polite smile touches his lips. "A playboy no longer."

The polite smile sours my gut. I want the real smile again, the one that crinkles his eyes in the corners.

I pick up the wine bottle and top off his glass. "Not a playboy anymore." I set the bottle down and push the glass toward him. When he reaches for it, I brush my fingers over his. "These days, I'm much more focused."

Just like that, sexual tension springs between us again.

I withdraw my hand and sit back.

He lifts his glass and takes a slow sip. When he lowers it, his voice is slightly husky. "What convinced your father you were ready to assume more princely duties?"

"I'm smart and powerful. Every court's elves have some degree of command over their element." I grin. "The sun is very formidable. It takes a great deal of control to wield it. Once I demonstrated a mastery over Her rays, my father knew I was serious about my role as his heir."

Jasper glances out the window. "It's gotten cloudy outside, Vale. Bring a little sun back for me?"

I'm always cautious with my gifts. Summer Court powers are easy to abuse. Elves learn that from an early age. But I need more of Jasper's true smile. And gods help me, I want to see the sun light up his delicate wings.

I follow the direction of his gaze out the window. Then I turn back to Jasper and call the sun. My magic snaps taut in my chest. Anchored there, it tugs at Her, asking for a few of Her rays to shine light through the window next to Jasper. I don't need to look up to see the clouds part. Deep within me, light blooms as shadows roll back. A moment later, golden sunlight streams through the glass and illuminates the side of Jasper's face.

In my mind's eye, I pluck at the line that connects me to Her—and I ask for a little more light. Enough to blanket my pixie like a cat in a window on a summer's day.

At once, smaller rays join together. They radiate against Jasper's skin, which gleams luminously under Her caress.

He tips his head back, a contented sigh easing from his lips. Sunlight dazzles over his cheeks, chin, and neck. His perfectly arched brows and long lashes. That pouty, irresistible mouth.

I can't look away. And I can't get involved with a man right now. But when I think about watching him walk away after lunch, I know I won't let him go. Because this is Jasper. Whatever he wants, I'll give it to him.

I don't know how long I shine the sun on him. I'm too lost staring at him to keep track. But eventually, he lowers his head and claps slowly.

"Bravo, Vale. That was incredible. Usually, I'd have a snarky comment, but I find myself very impressed."

"Good," I murmur, my voice rocky and low. Needy. Does he hear the desire in my tone? I want him to. I jerk my head toward the door. "Walk with me. Please."

When he nods, I toss two crisp bills on the tabletop and reach for him. He doesn't hesitate, just takes my hand and lets me pull him to his feet.

His gaze locks with mine, his earlier caution gone. For a moment, we just stare at each other, neither of us moving. He must feel it, too, this pull like we're two magnets desperate to meld together and become one.

Grinning, I lace my fingers with his and lead him from the restaurant and into the alley. We push through the foliage and step onto the busy main road.

And then we walk for hours, covering every topic under the sun. The conversation flows more easily than it has with anyone my whole life. Jasper has an opinion on everything, and he's not afraid to share it. He holds nothing back, dispensing wit and snark in equal measure. But he's also an excellent listener—attentive and thoughtful. At the same time, he doesn't hesitate to poke fun at me. As the afternoon wears on, I find myself letting my guard down completely. In the elvish courts, every look has meaning. Too often, words are weapons. I've played those games my entire life. It gets old fast.

I get none of that with Jasper. It's just…easy.

My familiar, Sulien, trails us quietly at a distance. I sense his presence in my mind, and then his voice fills my head.

"What are you doing?"

I keep my gaze on Jasper as I speak to Sully through our bond. *"I'm going for a walk."*

My oldest, dearest friend hisses in my head. *"And where does the walk end, my prince?"*

"Don't worry about it."

Sully makes a disgruntled sound. *"This is folly. You should put a stop to it before it gets out of hand."*

Jasper cocks his head. "You okay? You seem distracted."

"I'm perfect," I say, proffering my arm. My heart soars when he takes it. Sulien falls silent even as his irritation vibrates along our bond. His advice is sound, but I can't follow it.

Because I'm following my instinct, and every instinct I have points me to the captivating pixie with his arm looped through mine.

Don't embarrass us today, Abelin.

Screw my stepmother and her cruel words. I *did* my duty today. Now I'm going to chase happiness, because I deserve it.

Eventually, night falls. Jasper and I stop at another restaurant for dinner, where we laugh and flirt over plates of pasta. Sulien peppers our familiar bond with misgivings and increasingly insistent demands that I return home—alone.

I shut the familiar bond down hard. Jasper isn't optional to me. I know where the walk ends now. From the look in his eyes, my pixie does too.

After dinner, we sit on a bench overlooking a small offshoot of the Seine. The moon plays peekaboo with clouds that drift over the inky sky. Stars sparkle on the water. Jasper finishes the ice cream I bought him, then watches me take the last few licks of mine.

"You like vanilla?" he murmurs, his blue eyes reflecting the moonlight.

I swipe my tongue over the cold, creamy dessert, and I let some of the lust in my veins leak into my voice when I say, "Sometimes, but I'm good with variety, too."

Smiling, he crosses one lean leg over the other. "I always say I'll try anything once."

I return his smile. "What about elves?"

His eyes sparkle with a mix of heat and mischief. "I thought we were talking about ice cream, Prince Vale."

My heart thumps harder. I lean forward and brush my lips over his. It's the lightest of kisses. Just a teasing caress. "We've shared two out of three meals today together, Jasper. Let's round it out with breakfast. Come home with me."

Dark lashes brush against his smooth cheeks. Jasper's breath mingles with mine. It's sweet, like everything else about him. I'm dancing on the blissful edge of taking that pouty mouth right here on a park bench. But I'd rather take him to my bed.

"Okay," he whispers into my lips.

I don't need further encouragement.

The sky chooses that moment to crack open, lightning forking through gray clouds. Thunder booms like a cannon. Sulien jumps in our bond, hissing his displeasure at being outside.

The clouds open and rain pours down in torrents. I grab Jasper's hand and pull him with me into a sprint, running across the park toward my place in Villette. We laugh as we run, hard rain peppering our faces. By the time we reach the stoop outside my building, we're both soaked to the skin. Jasper's hair is plastered to his head. Water droplets cling to his eyelashes.

"We're here," I say. "Let's get you dry."

He slants me a mischievous look. "Wet suits me just fine, Vale Gentry."

I snort. "I bet it does, Jasper Lilygully. But I'd rather wet you with my mouth. I'm jealous of the rain right now, covering your skin. That should be me."

His smile falls, his expression growing hungry. His heart throbs loudly in his chest. Elves—and pixies to a degree—were predatory beyond the Veil. His heartbeat is a call that pulls my dominance to the surface. Desire fills me as I wave a hand, opening my front door with magic.

Sulien darts through and disappears up the stairwell without a backward glance.

I shove Jasper through the doorway and into the wall, pressing my body to his smaller one. He's hard, his cock a rigid length against the front of his pants. I grind my erection against his as I grip his chin. Possession screams through me at how pliable he is beneath me. How his blue eyes darken with desire.

For a heated moment, we stare at one another. Unspoken words hang heavy in the air.

My breath comes hard and fast, like I can't pull it into my lungs quickly enough. The need to possess him in every way slams into me, battering my senses.

Surging forward, I take his mouth. I plunge my tongue inside, stroking it along his. When he groans, I suck on his tongue, then release it and drag my fangs gently over the tip.

Jasper pants into my mouth, and I angle my head so I can deepen the kiss. I kiss him like it's the first and last time I'll ever kiss someone. He shoves his hands under my wet shirt, caressing my stomach. I need more, I need his touch all over my naked body. And I need my mouth everywhere on him.

Growling at not being able to have everything at once, I swoop him into my arms and jog up the stairs to the second floor.

"Your neighbors," he gasps, grabbing at my shoulders like he wants to haul me closer.

"I own the building."

My butler, Izig, stands at the top of the stairs wearing a neutral expression. He's stout, his dark-green skin mottled and wrinkled. Like all ogres, he's also a fan of beautiful clothing, and he's as dapper as ever in a three-piece suit and black bowler hat.

I set Jasper down. His wings flutter softly as he waves to Izig. "Oh hey, are you Vale's familiar?"

He must not have noticed Sulien dash past us just now.

"Hardly," the ogre drolls. "I am Izig, Prince Vale's butler."

"Fancy," Jasper says, raising a brow at me. He returns his gaze to Izig and offers a short bow. "Pleasure to meet you, Izig."

Izig ignores him and turns to me with a warning look. "May I draw you a bath, sire?"

I grin when I think of Jasper in the tub, but he rises on tiptoe and speaks quietly in my ear.

"We don't need it." His voice dips lower. "I'm ready for anything you want to do."

My lust cranks higher as I meet his gaze. His meaning is clear—and it's a relief because I'm dying to get inside him. I address my butler without removing my gaze from Jasper's. "A fire in my room would be perfect, Izig, thank you."

Sulien stalks out of the shadows and sits next to Izig. Displeasure sparks in our bond. He's mad about being wet, and he's wondering what the hells I'm doing.

"Oh, a cat," Jasper murmurs, his tone laced with displeasure.

I gesture to Sully. "This is Sulien, my familiar. He's a Taranathen cat from beyond the Veil."

"Mhm," Jasper says. He sounds distracted. When he glances down at his pocket, seeming to listen to something, I realize he must be communicating with Bert. "No, of course not," Jasper murmurs. "I'd never let that happen."

I move closer so I can see into his pocket. Bert is barely visible, his dark eyes distinctly wary. When he catches sight of me, I offer what I hope is a reassuring smile.

"Bert, if you'd like to go with Izig, he'll get you dried off and find you some food. And I promise Sully won't eat you. I swear it on the sun."

Sully growls into the bond, but I caution him. *"These are our guests. You can't eat this mouse. Bert is Jasper's friend."*

"Fine," he snaps. *"But it's only this mouse I agree not to eat."*

I turn to Jasper. "Bert will be safe. Do you trust me?"

"That's up to Bert." Jasper looks down at his mouse. "What do you say, old friend?"

The diminutive rodent scurries up to Jasper's shoulder. His dark eyes narrow as he studies me. My nape prickles. For a moment, it's like standing before my father when I was young and awaiting his judgment after some kind of reckless decision.

After a second, the mouse nods.

I release a breath I didn't realize I was holding.

Izig steps forward, his palm outstretched. In an agile move, Bert leaps from Jasper's shoulder into my butler's hand. Sully's golden eyes follow every movement. He licks his lips.

"Sully…" I say through our bond.

My familiar gives me a lazy look as he rises and stalks away. *"I said I wouldn't eat him. I never said I wouldn't think about it."*

Izig grunts and clutches Bert to his chest. The squat ogre straightens his bowler hat, then turns and disappears down the hall without another word.

Jasper leans toward me. "Friendly fellow. I take it the stick up his ass was placed there in your court?"

I palm his nape and pull him into me. With my free hand, I stroke his erection. "I don't want to talk about Izig," I growl. "I want to talk about this, and how I can take care of it for you."

Blue eyes flash. His pink lips part. "How are you gonna take care of it, Your Highness?"

Smiling, I cup his balls through the fabric of his pants. "I'll take care of every inch of you, Jasper Lilygully. For as long as you let me."

His eyes drift shut as I move my hand to his dick and give him a slow stroke. "Who could say no to that offer…"

Izig appears at the edge of my vision. "Your fire is ready, Prince Vale."

"Thank you, Izig," I say without turning my head from Jasper. "Ignore the noise, please."

He lets out an incredulous snort before disappearing down the hall, muttering under his breath.

Jasper opens his eyes, which gleam with humor and a healthy dose of that mischief I'm already addicted to. "I think your butler disapproves of me," he whispers.

"He's a little more sullen than most ogres," I whisper back. "A little too mouthy. But I love mouthy, so here we are." I rub Jasper's bottom lip with my thumb. "Speaking of mouths, I need mine on you now."

He swallows hard and rocks his hips to match the rhythmic stroke of my hand. When I pinch the tip of his cock, his blue eyes go heavy-lidded.

"I'm yours," he grits out. "Take me to bed already."

I swoop him into my arms and carry him to my bedroom, where a fireplace crackles merrily. I lower him to his feet on the soft rug before the hearth, then grab a towel from the stack Izig left on a nearby chair.

Jasper's eyes glitter in the firelight as I dry his hair. I only get halfway down his neck when he pushes my hands away and reaches for the buttons of my shirt.

He undoes each one with deft fingers, shoving the fabric open as he goes. Sunbursts of pleasure sear me from the inside out. He pulls the shirt off my shoulders, then gasps as he spies the sun tattoo that covers my left shoulder. Her rays streak across my pec and end just over my heart.

"Into symbolism much?" he asks, but there's no snark in his tone this time. He strokes the tattoo, pulling goosebumps to the surface of my skin. He looks up, his eyes hooded. "Let me see all of you, Vale. The real you."

I pull my shirt off, tossing the wet fabric aside. My pants go next. Jasper's eyes drift down my body—and spring wide at the sun tattooed around the base of my erect cock. Rays fan out in a semicircle over my lower stomach, then extend down my rigid length to the tip.

Gripping my cock, I stroke it once, a thrill shooting through me as Jasper moans softly. "The tattoo is magical," I murmur. "The sun's rays are imbued with tiny filaments of steel. I can heat them or vibrate them with my power."

"You're shitting me, right? I've never heard of such a thing."

Grinning, I grab his hand and guide it to my dick. A ragged groan falls from my lips when he closes his fingers around me and strokes. His palm is soft and warm and *gods*, he's fucking perfect.

I want to show him all of me. Every bit, every inch, every angle. I rarely drop my glamour outside of the Summer Court, but I want him to see me without it.

So I cast it away. It falls in shimmering waves that dissipate into dust and vanish into the floorboards.

Jasper gasps, dropping my cock and rocking onto his heels.

I wonder how he sees me? I'm handsome enough, but more rugged than most elves. Mahogany waves tickle my ears. The barest hint of matching beard lines my jaw. My eyes are my father's pale gold shade, my skin a burnished tan—a gift from the sun Herself. If it wasn't obvious enough which court I'm from, my skin radiates faint sunlight, the rays illuminating me from within.

Jasper's eyes rove over me. My chest swells with pride as he looks at me like he can't drink me in hard or fast enough.

My dick twitches and bobs toward my stomach. My palms itch with the need to touch my pixie, to take this attraction and toss a match on it. We're like two volatile elements, he and I. Combustible. I want to watch the chemical reaction when he ignites underneath me.

"Get those clothes off," I command. The steel in my voice has Jasper obeying, something I suspect he's not typically accustomed to.

But he rips his soaked shirt over his head and shimmies out of his pants, tossing the wet clothing aside. It hits the parquet floor with a splat, and I get my first look at my pixie—in a black thong.

My breath seizes in my lungs.

Jasper smiles.

"Damn, baby," I say in a rush, reaching for him. He laughs softly as I take him in my arms and run my hands over him greedily. His body is long and lean, his skin pale and perfect. Silver bars pierce his nipples. His chest is smooth, that hint of muscle I glimpsed under his clothes more pronounced—and so fucking sexy. Iridescent wings flutter at his back, the curved edges sifting golden dust that sparkles in the air. His erection swells the tiny thong, and his ass…

"Gods," I growl, nuzzling under his ear as I palm the taut, round globes bisected by a strip of fabric. "Your ass is a crime."

He tips his head back and gives me a sultry smile. "Wanna commit some felonies with me?"

"Fuck, yes," I breathe, sliding my hands under the straps around his hips. I nip gently at his earlobe. "I want to commit some felonies inside you."

"Yes," he says simply.

A groan rises before I can stop it. But I don't really want to. Desire rides me hard as I slide the thong down Jasper's toned thighs. I straighten and pull his hips into mine, and we both gasp as our cocks rub together. His dick is as gorgeous as the rest of him, the thick length covered in swirling veins that throb in time with his heartbeat. The head is flushed dark pink, precum beading at the tip.

"You should know something about me, Jasper," I murmur as I pull him down to the rug and guide him onto his back. I shove his thighs wide and position myself between them. I look down at his cock, then back up. "I love giving head, sweetheart. I'm going to tease you until you're begging, and then I'll tease you until you're feral. And once you're wild, I'm going to put you on your hands and knees in my bed and own that pretty ass of yours."

Jasper's nostrils flare. "You kiss your stepmother with that mouth, Gentry?"

"No." I shift forward, bracing myself with a hand on either side of his thighs. Without breaking his stare, I plant a barely-there kiss on the very tip of his cock.

Jasper's mouth falls open. His brow furrows as I let my breath coast over his dick, then he groans as I swirl my tongue over his slit, lapping at the sweet honey he leaks for me.

When I stop, his eyes narrow. "Again, Your Highness."

I close my lips around his cockhead and suck hard, hollowing my cheeks.

"Gods," he grinds out. "You're fucking good at that."

I pop off him, and he rolls his hips, chasing my mouth with his dick.

"Are all elves such teases?" he huffs, arching his back and directing his cock toward my lips.

Surging forward, I put a palm on his chest and force him flat onto his back. He hits the floor with a soft grunt that turns into a wheeze as I wrap my other fist around his length and suck him down, swallowing his cock until my nose touches his white-blond pubic hair.

He cries out and spears his fingers through my hair. His knees fall wide, and he thrusts into my mouth, grinding against my face. I suck slowly, teasing my way back down his length with soft bites and swirls of my tongue.

His skin grows flushed. A series of escalating cries fall from his lips.

I've never seen anything so hot. And I've had plenty of scorching sex.

But it was never with *him*. It was never like *this*.

I slick my tongue over his tip, then take him into my mouth and suck rhythmically until his legs quiver. He's close. And I want to see him come. Reaching back, I fumble for a towel on the chair. My fingers brush something hard. It hits the floor and rolls into view. A bottle of lube.

Clever Izig. For all his snark and sass, he foresees my every need.

Smiling around Jasper's dick, I snap the bottle open and drip lube onto his balls. He grunts and cries out, and I deep-throat him again. Creamy precum flows from his slit, coating my tongue. He's salty-sweet and warm and he tastes like candy. It's perfect.

My cock drips sticky strings of arousal onto the carpet. Gods, I could come just watching Jasper underneath me. Slipping one hand to his sack, I cup and roll his balls, coating them with lube. Then I slide my fingers behind them, teasing the pucker of his ass with soft circular strokes.

"Beautiful," I murmur between licks.

"I know," he grits out. "I'm gorgeous, you lucky bas—"

His words die when I slide a finger into his ass, stroking in and out. He comes on a choked roar, his ass clenching around my finger. I swallow his cock, sucking down every drop of ecstasy. My name falls from his lips, and something inside me goes tight and loose at the same time. It's a knowing, a calling, an instinct so deep and ancient it can't be denied.

He's *mine*.

I swallow every bit of cum until he's wrung dry. Then I pick him up and toss him over my shoulder. When he rears up, I swat his ass playfully. "Stay down. You're going to my bed where I can fuck you properly."

"Give me a minute." He laughs when I deposit him gently in the middle. "I'm good, Your Highness, but not quite that good."

"I take that as a challenge," I say, grabbing his thighs and flipping him onto his stomach. When he curses softly, his voice thick with lust, I chuckle and climb onto the bed. "I promise you don't want to miss this, baby," I say, leaning down to kiss my way along his muscular shoulders. He rolls and arches like a cat, his gorgeous body covered in a sheen of clean sweat. The predatory side of my nature surges through me, and I sink my fangs into the side of his neck.

Jasper grunts, but the grind of his ass against my throbbing cock tells me all I need to know—he enjoys a little pain and pleasure mixed together.

"More," he whispers. "Give me more, Vale."

I release the bite. "I want to give you everything." And I do. I want every one of his sunrises and sunsets. I want every moment, good, bad, and in between. And I want to wring bliss out of him like it's my job. His happiness is mine. Gods, I'm going to enjoy this.

Pushing his cheeks apart, I set about loosening him up. I take my time with it, stroking and teasing. Pumping one finger and then two inside him while he moans and claws at the bedding.

"Fuck," he pants, turning his head and giving me a look at his pouty lips and long lashes. "I'm ready."

"You sure?"

My pixie shoots me a warning glare over his shoulder. "Get your dick in me, Prince, or pay the consequences."

Grinning, I give his prostate another stroke before guiding my cock to his ass and dragging the tip up and down his cleft. We look perfect together, my burnished shade against his paler skin.

He rocks impatiently beneath me, a soft whine urging me to hurry.

"You gonna come for me again?" I murmur, pressing my cockhead against the tight ring of muscle.

"Gods, yes," he says on a shudder. He tosses me an impish look. "I guess I'm better than I thought."

Smiling, I bend and kiss the corner of his mouth. Then I ease back. Bracing my weight on one forearm, I thrust carefully, pushing into him one painstaking inch at a time.

Jasper grunts as I fill him. His long, elegant fingers grip the sheets tightly. He drops his head forward onto the bed.

I trail the fingers of my free hand down his spine, following the delicate vertebrae between his gossamer wings. "You okay?"

"Fucking perfect," he groans. "Keep fucking going."

Laughing softly, I press forward until I'm fully seated in his ass.

He clenches around me, sending heat tearing through my body. But if I pride myself on anything, it's my control in the bedroom. I thrust once, watching a pink flush steal across the top of his shoulders. And then I call my magic to my tattoo. The tiny metal filaments begin to heat and vibrate.

Jasper sucks in a sharp breath. He gathers his arms under him and thrusts his body backward, rocking hard onto my dick. "Fuck! Is that your tattoo?"

Collaring his throat, I pull him up to my chest and put my lips to his ear. "Yes, and it's all for you. Enjoy this, sweetheart."

"Fuck," he groans, clamping around me. "I intend to."

Bliss rockets through me, and I have to take a few deep breaths before I can speak. "You take me so godsdamned well," I rasp, thrusting into him.

"More," he says. "Give me everything."

I shove him down, and he lands on his forearms, his beautiful body so open for me. His wings spill golden dust over my bed.

"You too," I grunt, picking up the pace. "Show me more of that pretty sparkle, baby."

His response is another groan. He rocks back to meet me, his tight passage rippling around my cock.

We both moan as I grind my hips slow and hard against his perfect ass. I slip my free hand over his hip and down his stomach to grip his cock. I stroke him in time with my thrusts, squeezing his lube-slicked shaft as I thrust faster.

When his cries rise into keening wails, I go wild, hand flying over his dick with rough strokes. Every snap of my hips sends his cock through my fist. I grunt as pleasure streaks down my spine. Heat fills me. I'm barely holding back. But I need his pleasure first. I need to drive him over the edge. Gripping him hard, I jerk him fast.

He detonates, spurting cum onto my fingers. His ass clenches hard, and I can't hold back. Bliss erupts, and I come with a roar that echoes through the bedroom. Ecstasy forces my eyes shut. Galaxies burst in my mind, a riot of colors exploding behind my lids. Sound fades to nothing as release carries me on swift waves. Jasper's ass pulses around me, coaxing more cum from my throbbing cock. Every muscle tenses tight, and the world reduces to Jasper. His scent. His perfect ass clamped around my dick like a fist.

As bliss fades, I collapse on top of him, my forehead pressed to his neck. I trail kisses along his flushed skin while he pants beneath me, his back rising and falling against my beating heart. But I'm probably too heavy for him, so I roll us, tucking him against me.

His blue eyes glitter as he catches his breath. "That was... Fuck, Vale, that was incredible."

"I didn't tease you like I said I would," I growl, nosing under his chin and nibbling at his neck. "I meant to do it for hours, but you obliterated my plans, baby."

Jasper huffs a contented-sounding laugh. "I tend to do that. Just ask the syndicate lords. I think I might have actually driven Fuoco crazy."

Ah, the Lord of the Fire Syndicate.

I roll Jasper under me. "I haven't done a good enough job if you can say another man's name in my bed."

He grins. "Jealous?"

I shake my head. "I'm not a jealous man. But I am possessive and determined. And I want you so satisfied, the only man on your mind is me." I grip him under one knee and shove his thigh to his shoulder. "Show me that pretty hole I just ravished, because I want to do it again."

Merriment—and more than a hint of challenge—dances in his eyes. "You think you have it in you?"

I sit back on my heels and stroke my hardening cock. "I absolutely do. But I'd rather have it in you."

"Damn," he murmurs, the merriment turning to lust. Slowly, he draws his other knee up. Cum seeps from him and slides down his cleft. "I'm all yours, Vale. Make love to me again."

I do. We make love for hours, until he's sated and limp. As the sky outside the window turns purple with predawn light, I tuck him into bed before donning a robe and settling in my favorite chair before the fire.

I want to keep him.

Sulien scratches at the edges of our bond, alerting me to his presence. A second later, he stalks gracefully into the room. He slinks over to me and rubs his dark cheek along my thigh, his long whiskers tickling my skin through the robe.

I stroke under his chin. *"You didn't eat the mouse, right?"*

He replies with a warning growl. *"Of course I didn't eat the mouse."* He glances at the bed. *"What are you doing here, Vale?"*

"What feels right," I respond honestly. *"I never knew he existed, Sully. I don't think I can give him up."*

Sully purrs softly, and like always, it's a reassuring rumble that wraps around my heart like a warm blanket. I stroke his long pointed ears, and his purr rises in intensity.

"You've only got eight months until the winter solstice," he reminds me.

I look at my bed. Jasper's long legs are tangled in the sheets. One muscular arm is thrown over his face. The other hangs off the edge of the mattress. His white-blond hair sticks up in the front. He's as uninhibited in sleep as he is wide awake. Everything about him makes me smile. I want to cherish him, protect him, adore him.

I return my focus to my oldest friend and confidante. *"I'll figure something out."*

A sorrowful look fills golden eyes that mirror mine. *"I hope you get what you want, Vale,"* Sully replies after a long pause.

"Me too," I say aloud, returning my gaze to the beautiful pixie asleep in my bed.

CHAPTER 3
JASPER

Two weeks later

Has Paris always been this beautiful? The city glows under a buttery sun, light sparkling over a nearby fountain.

Or maybe it's just the man next to me. Vale and I walk side by side, our fingers brushing as we make our way through an open-air market. He catches my eye and winks. The sun appears to wink, too, the market dimming for an instant. I peer at the sky, trying to figure out if I'm losing my mind. Then I glance at Vale, who does a poor job of hiding his smile as he steps around a basket overflowing with bouquets of flowers.

Pride and lust flare in my chest. My man is powerful. Something tells me he's only shown me a glimpse of his abilities. But he's not a snob. Arrogant, sure, but who wouldn't be? Besides, he wears it so well. When he returns my gaze at last, that cocky little smile spreads to his eyes, which gleam with promise I've quickly learned to decipher.

He wants me. Right on cue, my dick tightens.

"Stop it," I say, giving him a meaningful look.

All innocence, he raises his eyebrows. "What?"

Glancing at a knot of passing humans, I lean into him and lower my voice. "Looking at me like you want to get me all dirty."

His rich laugh rumbles down my side as he wraps an arm around my shoulders and pulls me against him. His glamour is dialed all the way up, but more than one human stares as we pass. He ignores them, his gaze on me as he slides his big hand down to my ass. "I don't want to get you dirty, baby," he murmurs.

"No?" I let disappointment lace my tone. This is a familiar game—pretending we aren't a couple of horny motherfuckers. Neither of us can pretend for long.

"*Jamais*," he says. Never. He stops us right in the middle of the market. Humans stream past us like water diverting around a boulder in a river. The promise in Vale's eyes gleams brighter as he bends his head to my ear. "I want to get you absolutely filthy. I want to be in your pores, Jasper Lilygully. In your blood and on your skin. No matter how hard you scrub, you're never going to get me off you."

A colony of fairy sprites takes up residence in my stomach. Heat sears me, blazing a fiery path to my dick. For a second, I consider playing it cool. But who am I kidding? I've never been cool around this prince. For the past two weeks, things between us have been one temperature only. Hot.

"Well, when you put it that way," I say breathlessly.

Vale eases back, a mix of humor and desire in his golden eyes. "You want ice cream?"

I almost burst out laughing. "I've never met anyone who loves ice cream as much as you." At first, I thought he was just treating me. Now I know Vale will use any excuse to eat ice cream. His favorite is chocolate chip. Abruptly, I realize I've known that for a while, just like I know he's a blanket hog and that he never picks up his towel after he showers. The second time I tripped over it, I snapped the wet length across his ass as he shaved—and promptly ended up flat on my back on his bed with a naked Summer prince between my legs. He put his tattoo to good use that morning, edging me with heat and light until I pleaded for mercy.

He shrugs now, looking boyish and so fucking hot I want to climb him. "I like sweet things."

"Don't you dare call me sweet."

"Wouldn't dream of it," he says with a smile. Then he takes my hand and tugs me back into the flow of the crowd. We get about a dozen steps when he leans close and adds, "But that sugary hole of yours tastes sweeter than any ice cream."

Bert makes a disgruntled sound in my head as Vale and I move toward the Arc de Triomphe. *"Does Prince Charming realize I can hear him?"*

I tip my chin down and meet Bert's dark eyes. *"You know, you don't have to come out with us. You can stay back at the house."*

"With that demon cat? No, thank you."

"Sulien isn't a demon. He's an elvish cat. And I don't think he ventures far from Vale's side." I glance around, but there's no sign of the waist-high feline. Of course, that doesn't mean he's absent. Taranathen cats are stealthy creatures. Despite their size, they find ways to remain unseen. And the cat is clearly devoted to Vale. On nights when Vale and I hit the town, it's not unusual for me to catch glimpses of black fur and a long tail out of the corner of my eye.

"Did Sulien come with you through the Veil?" I ask Vale now.

Vale nods, smiling. "Yes, he's been with me since childhood. Most elves bond with their familiars quite young." Vale's eyes turn the color of honey as his smile goes fond. "Sully passed up three of my cousins to claim me. And when a Taranathen cat declares you his, well, that's that."

"Sully?" Bert grumbles in my head.

"I think it's cute," I tell him, returning Vale's smile.

"Yeah, you get stupid when you're in love."

I suck in a breath. *"I'm not in love."* Am I?

"Yeah, right." Bert burrows more deeply into my pocket. Even without looking, I know he's curled up for a nap.

Vale tips his head back and gazes up at the soaring arch, which bristles with mushrooms. Vines trail from the top, where a large wooden house sprawls, its chimney belching smoke into the sky. Vale studies it for a moment, then looks down at me and smiles. "This place looked a lot different without a troll living on top of it."

I tilt my head. "How so?"

He returns his gaze to the arch, and his eyes grow distant like he's remembering. "Well, it was cleaner, for one thing. Bright white and surrounded by streets shooting from all directions instead of the labyrinth you see now. Back then, humans called it Arc de Triomphe de l'Étoile because the boulevards radiated outward like a star." Vale's chest lifts in a sigh, and his voice goes wistful. "The city was…alive. It's full of magic now, but it had its own kind of magic before the Veil fell." His expression turns melancholy as he gazes at me. "I wish you could see it the way I remember it."

"Show me," I say on impulse. "Take me around the city. Let me see it through your eyes."

Vale's face lights up, and he takes my hand. "Let's go."

We spend the rest of the day exploring Paris. Vale takes me to all the special places he loves—the backstreets that conceal traces of the city's ancient walls, the hidden gardens that smell of roses and jasmine, and the overlook high above Notre Dame where we can see all of Paris sprawled out below us. At each stop, he shares stories about how things were before the Veil came down—the cobblestone streets lined with shops, carriages pulled by horses instead of griffins, and a thriving business district instead of the crumbling office buildings of La Défense.

At 427 years old, he's young for an elf, but he speaks of an era I can only imagine, when humans wore powdered wigs and physicians believed illness was caused by bad humors in the blood. In those days, the Veil was thick, and elves lived in the vast forests of the Myth, their courts places of mystery and wonder.

"Do you miss it?" I ask quietly. "Your life behind the Veil?"

He stops next to a fountain where a street artist paints pictures of ducks swimming in a nearby pond. His expression turns thoughtful, and he takes a moment to answer. "I don't long for it—not like my father does. But he lived beyond the Veil for thousands of years. The Summer Court covered the whole Taranathen Forest. To hear him tell it, the magic was so strong there, even he feared its displeasure." Vale offers a sad smile. "I pity the ancients who were forced to abandon their world. It has to be difficult for them to adjust. To find meaning and beauty on this plane. I'm fortunate to have found both of those things."

Warmth tingles over my skin. It's obvious he means me. *I'm* the meaning and beauty he found. Sounds intrude—the splash of the fountain and the artist's scratchy brush strokes on the canvas—but they're nothing compared to the *thump thump* of my heart.

Am I in love? Is this what it feels like? I thought I knew. But I've never felt like this, like the ground beneath my feet is unsteady. I wait for some snappy comeback to appear in my mind. With anyone else, I'd flirt or deflect, tossing out a carefree remark like stones skipping over still water. But nothing surfaces. With this man, I'm out of my depth. I'm drowning a little, lost in a pair of eyes like honey.

Vale draws a deep breath. "Jasper—"

A bicycle bell splits the air. Vale jerks me out of the path of a cyclist who speeds past us, tossing a string of rapid-fire French over his shoulder.

Vale lifts his voice, shouting back at the man in the same language. Vale shakes his fist, his bellow so loud the ducks burst from the pond in a cacophony of honks and flapping wings.

"What did he say?" I ask, mirth bubbling.

Vale slants me a roguish look. "He told you to move your ass. I told him I'd shove his bicycle up his."

My laughter spills over. "You should have let me hex him."

"No," Vale says simply, tucking my arm in his elbow and pulling me into a stroll. "Anyone who wants to fuck with you has to get through me first. And trust me, baby, they're not getting through me."

Pleasure unfurls in my chest. Maybe I should push back on his macho posturing. I'm no prizefighter, but I'm capable of taking care of myself. On the other hand, it's hot as fuck watching him ready to throw down over me. Bonus points that he did it in his flawless French.

We move through the streets, sampling food from stalls and stopping to sniff bouquets wrapped in brightly colored paper. At one cart, he buys me a brilliant blue flower and murmurs in French as he tucks it behind my ear.

"What does that mean?" I ask, my heart thumping again.

"The same color as your eyes."

The cobblestone streets grow rougher, the buildings older. Creatures from the darkest corners of the Myth brush past us. I shiver as a male with bubbling skin and a face full of bulging eyes approaches and then steps around me at the last minute.

"What is it?" Vale asks, slowing and stroking his knuckles over my cheek.

"Nothing." I glance over my shoulder as the male moves away. "I've just never seen one like him."

Vale's eyebrows go up in apparent surprise. "You saw under his glamour?"

Smugness spreads through me. I smooth my hair and make my tone airy. "I'm better than most at seeing under glamour."

His smile is slow and full of delight. "Is that so?"

"Mmm." I flutter my wings and rake my gaze down his body. "One of my many, *many* gifts."

Vale laughs as he takes my hand and tugs me forward. "Come on, gifted one." He tips his head toward mine and lowers his voice. "Before you make me so hard I can't walk."

We stroll down streets so ancient they've been named and renamed and renamed again. Vale points out various landmarks, noting how magic has changed them, wearing away the technology and warping human progress. But magic hasn't conquered everything. Lacing his fingers through mine, Vale pulls me into a cathedral with gorgeous stained glass windows. Incense wafts in the air, and great shafts of multi-colored light slant across ancient floors. A brass plaque on the wall proudly proclaims the building is in its "original form since 1395."

"It's because so many of these places were built on top of pagan sites," Vale explains. "Before they discovered all their tech, humans believed in magic." His lips quirk in a sexy smile as he leads me down the side aisle of a shadowy cathedral. "Some of them even worshipped us."

"I bet you loved that," I murmur.

His eyes glint in the glow of the candles that cover a nearby altar. "I don't mind a certain type of man kneeling at my feet."

Instantly, my body burns as hot as the candles. I glance at the statue of a saint that looms over us. "Careful. You'll get us struck by lightning."

His low laugh echoes down the rows of empty pews. "Let's get out of here. I'm starving."

I heave a put-upon sigh. "You always are."

"Mmm." He tucks my arm through his and dips his head to nip at my ear. "Insatiable."

Dusk smears the sky in purples and reds as we emerge from the church. We end up on Rue Saint-Dominique, where Vale buys us croissants stuffed with warm, bittersweet chocolate that feels lighter than air on my tongue.

"Gods, I love these," I groan.

Vale smiles. "I know."

"You do?"

Heat flares in his eyes. "I pay attention, especially when it's something important."

Just like that, my dick goes hard. That "something important" is me. The Prince of the Summer Court pays attention to what I like to eat. It shouldn't be sexy, but it is. It might be the sexiest thing about him.

We eat right there in the street, laughing and swiping smears of chocolate from each other's mouths.

Halfway through our feast, Bert rouses and pops his head above my pocket. At the same moment, a trio of mice scamper around the corner of a nearby building.

"That's my crew," Bert says in my head.

I almost choke on a piece of croissant. "Did you just say crew?" I ask aloud, laughter warbling in my throat. When Bert's expression darkens, I switch to telepathy. *"I'm sorry, are you robbing a bank tonight?"*

"No, *asshole*," he says, jumping from my pocket and shooting down my leg to the ground. He hurries across the street, then stops and gives me a dirty look over his shoulder. *"I'm giving you some privacy. Not that you deserve it."*

One of the mice on the corner chirps, its tail swishing.

I offer Bert a short bow and soften my tone in my head. *"Thanks."*

"*Hmph.*" With a final withering look, he scampers off. Together, he and the other mice disappear into the shadows.

When I look at Vale, he stares at the corner with a bemused smile. "Your mouse knows Parisian mice?"

"No idea," I say, smiling. "I think all mice know each other everywhere, to be honest. Bert, Mert, and Luke seem to find friends no matter where we go."

Vale blinks. "You have other mice?"

"Oh yeah. Plus a few pigeons and a couple of chipmunks. But the others don't enjoy traveling. Mert suffers from terrible motion sickness, and Luke gets homesick, so—" I clamp my mouth shut as Vale's face splits in a grin. "What?"

"What?"

"You're smiling at me."

"Well, you're fucking adorable. Of course I'm smiling at you."

I flick the crumbs from my croissant at him. "We'll see how adorable I am when you want your dick sucked later."

At that, he throws his head back and laughs. Then he pulls me against him and kisses me, his mouth as warm and sinful as the chocolate. When I'm breathless and hard as stone, he pulls back.

"I have something else I want to show you. Are you up for one last stop?"

I'm up for anything as long as you're there.

"Yes," I say breathlessly. "Lead the way."

As night falls, the city's energy changes. Paris sheds its daytime skin and slips into something darker and more sensual. Golden eyes glittering with desire, Vale pulls me down a narrow path lined with flickering gas lamps. Tangled trees soar above us, the trunks far too thick and broad to be completely natural. No, this is an old-growth forest fueled by magic.

Out of nowhere, an ache bolts across my left wing. It's so unexpected, I suck in a breath.

Vale stops, his expression instantly alert. "You okay, baby?"

"I'm fine," I say, waving it off. Wherever he's taking me, I want to go. I squeeze his hand. "Too many croissants."

"Aww." Chuckling, he tucks me against him as we continue up the path. "It's true. We've pretty much eaten our way through the city over the past two weeks."

"Yeah, but we've burned off the calories." On the last word, another ache shoots across my wing. This time, I bite my tongue. For the love of Puck, what is wrong with me? I grit my teeth and ignore the pain.

But a few steps later, lightning strikes and I double over. Nausea roils my gut. The forest dims as a cold sweat covers my skin.

"Jasper!" Vale wraps an arm around my back. "What is it—" He inhales sharply, then he groans. "Gods, I am *such* a fool."

For a second, I think he means he's a fool for being with me. But then he sweeps me into his arms and strides down the path, rapidly retracing our steps.

"I'm sorry, baby," he says, his eyes contrite in his determined face. "I always forget how iron affects the young among us."

"Iron?" I rasp, the nausea receding.

"The Eiffel Tower. I wanted to show you the flowers that climb up the pillars." He hefts me higher in his arms and drops a quick kiss on my clammy forehead. "But we can still see it from across the river."

A moment later, he settles me on a park bench on the edge of the Seine. The twisted Eiffel Tower glitters across the water, its mangled arches contorted into loops and knots. Lights wind up the pillars, the bulbs fighting a losing battle against the riot of wildflowers and fat roses that crawl over the metal.

"Feeling better?" Vale asks, watching me closely. He takes my hand and rests our laced fingers on his thigh.

"Yeah." I tip my head toward the tower. "The iron really doesn't bother you?"

He shakes his head.

"Has it ever bothered you? When you were a young elf mixing it up during the Renaissance?"

He hesitates. "Not really."

Disquiet moves through me. But I shake it off and give him a saucy wink. "And now you're slumming it with me, Your Highness."

Vale stiffens. "Don't say that." Pain moves through his eyes, and his tone turns serious. "Don't belittle yourself like that. Please."

The disquiet makes another unsettling trip down my spine. "All right."

Silence stretches. Vale holds my gaze, a little frown forming between his brows. "Jasper…"

My heart stutters. *Oh no.* He's going to break it off. He's going to dump me right here on this park bench, and it's going to hurt so bad.

"There's something I need to tell you," he says.

Blood rushes in my ears. I brace myself for the inevitable. What was I thinking, hooking up with an elven prince? Bert warned me. He fucking warned me. And now Vale is going to crush my heart under his expensive boot.

He draws an uneven breath. "I don't know how to say this…"

"Just say it," I snap, tugging my hand from his. Gods, my palms are sweating. How embarrassing.

I stand, prepared to flee so I don't have to see his face when he attempts to let me down easy.

"No." In one movement, Vale jumps to his feet, seizes my hand, and yanks me into a kiss. And not just any kiss. He *devours* me, cupping my face in his hands and stroking his tongue boldly against mine. He growls, the possessive sound rumbling into my mouth and straight down to my cock, which throbs for him. Only him. His hot, perfect mouth and the pressure of his strong fingers on my jaw. His dick pressed hard against mine. I swim in his scent—sunshine and fresh-cut grass and *summer*. Vale Gentry smells like summer, and I want to bask in him forever.

When he breaks off the kiss, we lean our foreheads together, both of us panting. My vision fills with golden eyes and dark stubble and a pink, wet mouth that murmurs my name over and over. "Jasper… Jasper. I love you."

I jerk my head up, my heart pounding overtime. Triple time. "What did you say?" Because I couldn't have heard him correctly.

"I love you," he says, his voice hoarse. "I know we've only been together a short while, but I feel…" He swallows thickly. "I've never felt this way about anyone. Ever." Something fierce flashes in his eyes, and his glamour ripples, giving me a glimpse of the sun-god concealed under his more mundane wrapping. "I'll do whatever it takes to keep you. To keep us." The fierceness fades, replaced with uncharacteristic doubt. He searches my face, his mouth swollen from our kiss. "Is that what you want?"

"Yes," I breathe, disbelief and joy trembling inside me. "I've been afraid to say it. But yes, I want that. I love you, Vale."

He palms the back of my neck, the joy in his face mirroring the throb of emotion in my chest. "I love you."

I give a shaky laugh. "You said that already."

"I never want to stop saying it."

The joy inside me softens, melting into something sweeter. "Then don't," I say, twining my arms around his neck. "Keep saying it, my prince, because I love hearing it." I rise on tiptoe and nip his jaw. "And I'd *really* love it if you take me home and fuck me."

~

TWENTY MINUTES LATER, we stumble into Vale's bedroom, laughing and kissing and ripping at each other's clothes. Vale yanks my shirt off, sending buttons pinging across the hardwood as he backs me to the bed. When my hips hit the edge, he grabs me around the thighs and tosses me onto the mattress. My pants and underwear disappear in two quick yanks, then he stands back and groans.

"Fuck, baby, you're so fucking hot."

"And you're wearing too many clothes," I say, rolling my hips. Planting my feet flat on the mattress, I spread my legs wide.

He bites his lip, his breathing hitching as he strips. His warm, golden eyes rove my body, landing on my cock, which leaks all over my stomach. "Stroke yourself. Show me how you like to be touched. And drop the glamour."

I raise an eyebrow, but I wrap my hand around my shaft and start pumping. "So fucking bossy, Your Highness."

His lips curve in an arrogant smile as he grasps his own dick. "Drop the glamour, pixie. Show me those pretty wings and hot little hole."

"F-Fuck," I gasp, lust spiking. I obey, letting my glamour roll away so my wings spread under me. At the edge of my vision, the tips glow bright gold. I increase the pace of my strokes, jerking my dick under his watchful gaze.

Vale climbs onto the bed and settles between my spread thighs. He strokes a slow, reverent hand down the edge of my wing. "So beautiful. Do you control the color?"

"Sometimes." My strokes on my dick falter as raw, undiluted pleasure courses from my wing to my groin. "Oh fuck… I— Our wings mirror our emotions most of the time. We get better at controlling them with age. Among pixies, changing the color of the dust can be a form of honoring someone—or insulting them."

Vale rumbles a soft laugh. "I'll keep that in mind."

"Just keep fucking touching me, and we won't have a problem."

Another laugh, and he pushes my knees higher, opening me to his gaze. "Now who's bossy?" Batting my hand away, he takes over stroking my dick.

Pleasure lashes me, bowing my spine and pulling broken, desperate sounds from my throat. He drops his glamour, too, filling the room with light and heat as he pumps his big fist up and down my shaft. Precum beads at my slit, and he leans over and sucks it away, his honey-colored eyes locked with mine.

"Give me more," he orders softly, squeezing me. "Mmm, good boy." He sucks my cockhead into his mouth, pulsing his lips around my tip and hollowing his cheeks. He does this for several long moments, waiting patiently for precum to form at my slit before licking it away, his pink tongue wetting my tip until it glistens.

"Vale," I pant, rocking my hips up. Pleading for more with my body. I grab at the sheets, my whimpers growing more desperate in my ears. "Vale… Gods, I love you."

He pulls off my dick, the glow around him growing as bright as a halo. His ears taper to points as his glamour slides away completely. He lowers himself onto me, giving me his full weight as he strokes one golden hand over my cheek. "I love you, too, baby. *So* much." He drops kisses all over my face—tender, light touches on my forehead, my eyelid, the curve of my eyebrow. And he rocks his hips, grinding his erection into mine. We leak together, our bellies growing slick with desire.

"I could come like this," I groan, clinging to his shoulders and rolling my hips. The sounds we make are filthy—wet, fleshy friction. Hot, hard skin against hot, hard skin. My trimmed pubes grow damp from our mingled precum, and I rock harder, eager for more. Ready to be marked and claimed by my summer prince.

"I want you on top," Vale says suddenly. "I want you to ride me."

"Then flip the fuck over, cowboy."

Laughing, he gets us into position, his back propped against the pillows with me astride him. Eyes twinkling, he pulls a bottle of lube from under the pillow.

"Confident you were getting lucky tonight, huh?" I demand, swiping it from him.

He bucks his hips once, the twinkle in his eyes brighter than the stars over Paris. "I had a feeling."

I try to look exasperated, but I know I fail as I slather lube all over his dick. Then I settle over it, letting the thick length nestle between my cheeks. Palms on his golden chest, I roll my hips in a slow, sensual grind. As his cock drags up and down my hole, we both groan.

"You're so hard," he says, giving my straining dick a firm caress that makes me jump.

"I could say the same for—oh gods—you." My wings bat the air lazily as I work the furrow of my ass up and down and all over his length. His body is a work of art beneath me, every sculpted muscle and graceful, golden line more beautiful than anything he showed me in the city. His tattoo glows, sunlight gleaming along the delicate lines etched into his skin.

Bending, I kiss his chest before sucking a flat, pink nipple into my mouth. His delicious scent fills my lungs, and his summery taste explodes on my tongue. Groaning, I move to the other nipple, flicking and teasing while I rub my quivering hole up and down his dick. He trembles under me—a continent shivering and threatening to split apart.

"Baby," he gasps, squeezing my hips. "Baby... Fuck, yes. So good for me." He pumps his hips, thrusting against my ass. Then he reaches around me and slaps his dick against my cleft, the smack loud and obscene.

"Fuck," I whimper, biting at the round muscle of his pecs. I trail my tongue down the valley between them and sit up, rocking wantonly on his cock.

"Let's get you ready," he murmurs, slipping a hand under me and stroking my hole.

I squirm and moan, losing myself in the feel of his fingers playing around my rim. His skin is callused, the pads of his fingers rough and hard. Odd for someone of his station. Somewhere in my brain, curiosity forms and then flits away. Because his touch feels too good for questions. When he pushes a long finger inside me, I toss my head back and moan.

"There you go," he growls. "Open up for me, honey."

"Yeah," I gasp, rocking as he finger-fucks me. "So good."

"No, not good, baby. Amazing." He crooks his finger and hits my sweet spot, sending waves of pure pleasure through my body. My cock bobs wildly, slapping his stomach as I ride his finger, wanting more. Wanting to come all over him. Wanting him to fuck me so hard I feel it tomorrow.

He groans, pushing deeper and rubbing my gland. "Ready for more?"

"Please," I beg, squirming and writhing on his finger. He uses his other hand to torment me, playing with my balls, the base of my cock, my cockhead. He pinches my tip, swiping more precum from the slit and sucking it from his thumb. "Oh fuck," I whimper.

He carries my precum to my cleft, smearing it around my hole he's still fingering. Then he pulls my cheek wide and pushes two fingers inside. "You're so tight, baby. So fucking hot and tight. You think you can take my big dick? Because I want inside here so, so bad."

"Gods..." I thrash, back arching as my ass clenches around his finger. "Yes. I want it. I can take it."

He knows, of course, and he pushes another long finger inside. "You're so beautiful," he says as I moan. "So open for me. Fuck, Jasper. So damn good. That's it, baby. Squeeze me. Show me how much you want it."

Moaning, I oblige him, clamping hard around his fingers. The bedroom fills with our ragged moans and the wet squelch of his fingers pumping into me. Loosening me up. Getting me nice and juicy.

He sits up with me clinging to him, and he kisses me as we rock together. Neither of us are willing to break it off, so we bite at each other's lips as he lines his cock up with my entrance. When he pushes past the tight ring of muscle, I gasp against his mouth. And when he thrusts deep, I suck at his tongue and sink down until he fills me completely, his balls snug against my ass.

"You're so fucking amazing," he whispers, his dick throbbing inside me. He smooths his palms up my sides, his big hands bumping over my ribs. "You feel incredible."

"Fuck me," I whisper back. "Make me yours, my prince."

He lifts his head, his eyes gleaming with lust and love. "I love you so damn much, Jasper."

Tears burn my throat. "I love you, too."

"I love you," he murmurs, as if he can't stop himself from saying it. And he says it again as he begins to move, thrusting up and up. Pumping his dick into me—slow and easy at first and then harder and faster.

"Vale," I gasp, gripping his shoulders. Digging my fingers into the muscle. My wings flutter wildly, sending gusts of air around the bed. "It's so good."

"Yeah?" he demands, his eyes glittering. "You like this dick?"

"Yes. I love it."

"Want more?" He bounces me harder. "Your greedy hole can't get enough, can it?"

"No," I say, panting as I ride him like a jockey. "Give me everything. Fuck me hard."

"My baby gets what he wants." He picks up speed, thrusting hard and fast, driving his cock into me in a relentless rhythm. "So good," he rumbles, his thick shoulder muscles flexing under my hands.

Our gazes hold, and it's like looking into the sun. Golden, beautiful, all-consuming. I can't even blink as he thrusts into me, his cock hitting my spot every time. "I'm close," I whisper, my voice shaking. "I'm so close."

"Come for me, baby," he grunts, moving a hand to my dick. He strokes me as keeps up that maddening rhythm, fucking me hard and deep. Bouncing me on his lap, his balls slapping against my ass as his hand works my dick.

I'm lost. There's no part of me that doesn't belong to the sun prince. Heart and soul. Inside and out. My orgasm slams into me, and I spurt over his stomach and chest, cum spraying from my cock as I scream Vale's name.

He roars and thrusts a final time. Squeezes my hip hard and pumps his release deep inside my ass. Hot cum sears my passage, filling me up.

We cry out as we come together, and then I collapse on top of him with his pulsing dick still lodged inside me. He wraps his arms around me and presses his lips to my sweaty temple.

"Fuck, baby," he says, his heart pounding against mine. "You okay? Did I hurt you?"

I reach up and clumsily pat his jaw. "You could never hurt me," I murmur, my words slurring. Gods, he fucked me so hard I'm drunk.

His arms tighten around me. His breath shudders out, ruffling my hair. "You're mine. Tell me you're mine."

Something in his voice makes me push against his hold until he loosens his arms. I pull back so I can see his face, and I catch the worry he tries to blink away. "Hey," I say softly, stroking his stubble-covered jaw as I catch my breath. "I'm yours, Vale Gentry. Only yours. I don't give my love away lightly, my prince."

He cups my jaw, his roughened thumb brushing over my cheekbone. "I'm so glad I bumped into you in Mab's court."

Relief washes over me, and I laugh as I press a kiss to his lips. "You're lucky I didn't hex you."

"You can hex me anytime. Do whatever you want to me."

"I'll remember that." Smiling, I kiss the corner of his mouth before snuggling against him and stroking my fingers through his golden chest hair. "Pixies have long memories, Your Highness. We never forget a slight."

"Mmm." He returns my kisses, his arms tightening around me once more. "Then I'll have to work hard to stay in your good graces."

"Keep that dick in working order and you'll do just fine."

We cuddle in the ruined bed, sheets tangled around our legs. And we fall asleep wrapped in each other, smiles on our faces.

When I wake much later, predawn light streams through the windows. Vale is gone, a scribbled note in his place.

Went out for croissants (and maybe ice cream). Sleep in, mon amour, I'll return shortly.

Grinning like an idiot, I collapse onto my back with the note pressed to my heart. *Mon amour.* He called me his love in the language of love. Bert is going to puke when he hears it.

My grin spreads as I tune my senses to the sprawling house. The brownstone is silent. No doubt, Izig and Sulien went with Vale. But they'll come back soon, and I know exactly how to start the day with my summer prince.

Smile in place, I let myself doze, content to wait for Vale's return.

CHAPTER 4
VALE

I clutch a bouquet of golden-yellow roses in my hand as Izig and I cross the street. Normally yellow flowers are a sign of friendship, but I know Jasper will see this for what it is—the prince of the Summer Court is his. And he's mine. The last two weeks together have been utter bliss. Even old Izig is coming around. He's smiled more in the two weeks Jasper's been with me than he has in the two hundred years he's served as my butler.

I'm sharing an important secret with Jasper tonight. I suspect he'll be upset, but then he'll demand a kiss and a pastry and I'll lavish my love on him until he passes out. That's how we work—he brings the joy and I spoil him every chance I get.

Grinning, I step onto the sidewalk and look in the window of my favorite boulangerie. Jasper's obsessed with their chocolate-filled croissants. Dozens of other options sit in piles atop display stands. Izig stops next to me and crosses his arms as he peers in the window.

"*The dark chocolate,*" Sulien purrs in my mind, appearing from a dark alleyway and moving toward me. "*It's Jasper's favorite. But maybe add a spicy chocolate croissant for Izig. He doesn't want to ask you, but he grumbled when you came home without one last time.*"

"They were sold out," I return, glancing down as Sully sits by my side. "What about you? Do you want anything?"

He prowls forward and rears up, planting both front paws delicately against the glass window. Izig stares longingly at the pastries. Ogres are prickly about gifts. He won't outright ask me to buy him a pastry, but—

Movement draws my eyes up. I stiffen. Reflected in the window behind me stand three elven guards decked out in the red and gold of my father's court. The lead guard moves his hands to the hilt of a jagged dagger strapped to his thigh. The guards' glamours keep them hidden from the human world. To passersby, we'll simply look like a man, an ogre, and a cat surrounded by three ordinary frenchmen.

Sully yowls and steps in front of me, sitting protectively at my feet.

One of the three guards wears a captain's patch. I struggle not to sneer as I stare at it. The guard used to serve my father, but he gifted them to Zaphira when they married. They're on her payroll now, and they do her bidding above all else.

The captain gives me a snide look. "Your stepmother requires your presence, Prince. She'd like to discuss the wedding preparations."

I return the disdainful expression. "I don't think so."

He sucks at his teeth, lips splitting into an evil grin at odds with his noble features. "Queen Zaphira thought you might say that. Let me be clear. You return home, or the pretty pixie dies."

My mouth goes dry as a desert. How could she know about Jasper? How is she always one godsdamned step ahead of me? Will there never be a day she doesn't pull my strings as if I'm her personal puppet?

"You seem disinclined to obey," the guard snipes. "Let me make this more clear. Usually, there are four of us. Our companion is outside your brownstone as we speak, ready to do the queen's bidding if you don't come along nicely."

Sulien growls loudly. Izig steps to my side and lifts his chin defiantly.

Jasper. They can't get to him. I can't allow it. I'll never allow it.

And that's how I know I'll go to Zaphira. Because I can't risk the man I love. Not for anything.

A glittering golden carriage, glamoured to look like a decrepit old wagon, pulls up behind the elves. Horses from the Winter Court stop, the sleigh bells on their harnesses jingling. The beasts snort, and cold air puffs from their nostrils in little white clouds.

The captain goes to the carriage and opens the door. "After you, Prince." He says my title with a sneer, but I don't bother to correct his behavior. One day when I replace my father, I'll bury this male in a deep, dark hole. It's like I told Jasper the day we met—I'm a patient man. I play the long game.

I stop next to the guard, memorizing his dull brown eyes and scarred cheek.

"What're you doing?" he barks.

"Remembering who you are," I say quietly. "I don't forget a face. I'll remember yours."

He pales. Then he grips my arm and shoves me toward the open door. "Get in or I'll put you in."

I step into the carriage and sink into the plush leather seat. Sully darts through the door and sits rigidly beside me. The captain grabs Izig by the collar and tosses him in next to me. Izig's head strikes the back of the seat, knocking his bowler hat to the floor. As Izig rights himself, I scoop up the hat. One side is crushed, the felt misshapen.

The guard smiles. "That's a shame. You should have been more careful."

My butler snarls, baring his sharp fangs.

"Easy, old friend," I caution.

The captain of the guard smirks, then slams the door shut. A second later, the carriage starts to roll.

I pop the dent out of Izig's hat and hand it to him. There's still a slight wrinkle to the fabric.

"I'll replace it," I say softly.

"It's fine," he huffs.

"He's embarrassed," Sully says in my mind. *"He couldn't protect you."*

"I know." I couldn't protect Izig, either. I can only hope I protected Jasper.

The three of us fall silent as Paris passes outside the window.

An hour later, we pull through ornate steel gates and down a crushed gravel drive toward my father's manor outside of Paris. He owns houses and condos in most major cities, but the manor in Fourneclaire is Zaphira's favorite. I hate coming here. The sand-colored brick and pale blue shutters appear pleasant enough, but the reality couldn't be farther from the truth.

The manor at Fourneclaire is twenty-thousand feet of frigid, cruel cold.

The carriage stops in the half-circle drive. No one meets us, of course. Zaphira loves to remind me how little she cares for me when Father isn't around.

Izig, Sully, and I exit the carriage and follow broad stone steps to the lavish double doors. Icy tendrils of cold burrow under my collar and slide down my spine. Zaphira's Winter Court magic is strong here. It'll be freezing inside—a toxic, frozen wonderland she rules with a heavy fist.

"I hate this place," Izig mutters. Sully rumbles his agreement.

As we pause before the doors, I look down at my oldest friends. "I promise I'll find a way out of this for all of us. Do you trust me?"

Two sets of eyes peer up at me. Izig dips his head in a brusque nod, then returns his gaze to the doors. Sully caresses our bond softly, his way of showing support. I stroke it back, grateful for his partnership.

I grip an ornate carved snowflake door handle—something Zaphira added when she moved here from my father's townhouse in the city—and push the doors open. An icy blast blows my hair back, the freezing air pulling goosebumps to the surface of my skin.

"Seems like she's turned the cold up," Izig grunts.

"Always." I clamp my mouth shut. Zaphira has spies everywhere. The less we say in her house the better. I lead us through a short hall that opens into an enormous foyer. On the far side of the space, dual curved staircases lead to the second floor.

A hiss echoes across the marble floor, followed by the slither of rough scales. A snake-like head pokes through an open door to our right. Zaphira's basilisk familiar. Twin rows of spines rise from his forehead and point backward down his long body. They flare upright as he swishes the tip of his tail toward us. It's split into three dangerous spikes he can use to protect himself.

Or Zaphira.

"Hello, Ybris," I say.

Glacier-blue eyes narrow at me. The beast's black tongue darts out to taste the air. Dozens of conical teeth drip venom onto the checkerboard marble.

Beside me, Sully shudders.

"Easy," I reassure him through our bond. *"You're safe."*

"This time," he grunts back.

With a jerk of his long snout, Ybris demands we follow.

I keep my shoulders back as I cross the foyer. I refuse to huddle against the cold. That's exactly what Zaphira wants, for me to be uncomfortable and out-of-sorts. I stride through the open door as Ybris side-winds across the room.

The dining room is empty save for a glossy pale blue desk in front of a now-covered window. Sun used to beam through the glass, but it's hidden away by velvet drapes. A wingback chair sits in front of a fireplace crackling with blue flames—cold fire Zaphira brought from her court as a "reminder of home."

Ybris curls his long body around the chair's legs, his tongue flicking out as he hisses. I can't see Zaphira with the chair turned away, but her menacing presence reaches across the room, her icy wrath wrapping around me like invisible tentacles.

As I clench my teeth against the onslaught, her hand appears on the chair's arm. Long, navy-colored nails thump rhythmically against the blue velvet.

I clear my throat. "You summoned me, Stepmother?"

Her fingers stop moving. A loud sigh echoes across the freezing room before she stands and faces me.

Her beauty is as timeless as ever, her black waves pinned into an elegant updo and her icy blue eyes glittering in the room's freezing air. Blue diamonds drip from her pointed ears. My stepmother never hides behind glamour. Always, she shows exactly who she is—the frigid Princess of the Winter Court.

She wears a fitted ivory dress that accentuates her bust and flares over rounded hips. Even with the distance between us, the snowflake pattern embroidered on the fabric glitters like ice. The only sign that she's now part of King Nylian's court is a small metal sun pinned to her left breast. Not that he even knows. I haven't seen my father and Zaphira together in nearly fifty years.

She folds her hands at her waist. "Abelin. I hope you enjoyed your little dalliance in Paris." Her tone is light, but there's an unmistakable threat underneath it.

"It's not a dalliance," I say. "I'm in love, Zaphira. Jasper is my mate."

She laughs, and it's as brittle and harsh as the rest of her. As quickly as it comes, her laughter dies. Her wicked smile disappears as she walks toward me. "I don't care if he's the sun in elf form. You have responsibilities to this court."

I move forward, meeting her halfway across the room. "We don't have to continue doing things by the old ways. Mab invited us for a formal dinner in her court for the first time in elven history. I was successful in brokering that meeting. Things can change."

"Nothing ever changes," she hisses, her chest rising and falling with quick breaths. "You will marry your stepsister or so help me, I'll—"

"You'll what?" I interrupt. "I know you've never liked me, but you can't force me to marry a woman I dislike as much as she dislikes me. I can't marry Liriel. Not now. I won't live like that."

Zaphira puts her shoulders back. Her lips curve in a cruel smile. "You swore an elven vow. It's unbreakable. If you don't marry my daughter by midnight on the winter solstice, you'll die."

"I haven't forgotten." I lift my chin. "If anyone knows how to break an elven vow, it's my father. I'm going to ask him, because I refuse to marry a woman I don't love. Not now."

"Winter and Summer have always fought," Zaphira snaps, fisting her hands at her sides. "I put a stop to it. You speak of history? Consider what I've done, you spoiled child. *I* sacrificed to keep the peace between our courts. *I* remain here, alone, in this godsforsaken land, so that everyone else may sleep easy in their beds. *I* sacrificed, Abelin, and you will too."

I stand taller, Izig and Sully at my sides. "I won't," I say. "I can't. I will marry, but to the man I love. The Winter Court will have to accept it."

Zaphira sighs. She shakes her head slowly, the diamonds in her ears reflecting the pale firelight. "I thought you might say that. Guards!"

I freeze, muscles tightening. Sully yowls a warning.

A door to our left crashes open. A dozen of my father's guards storm through and pause, weapons in their hands.

I glare at my stepmother. "What's this? Whatever you're planning, my father won't stand for it."

She doesn't deign to answer, merely looks over at the guards. "You know what to do," she says softly.

They spring into motion, but I'm one step ahead. Grabbing Izig, I whirl and sprint for the door, only to be stopped by Ybris. The big basilisk's coils tumble over each other, his scales rattling against the marble.

Darting forward, I hit him with an uppercut, knocking his head back. Ybris snarls, body writhing in circles as he shakes his head and snaps his teeth. I leap over his round body with Sully at my side and Izig on my heels. I hit the door, flinging it open and stumbling into the foyer.

A spear tip lodges under my chin, the point grazing the hollow of my throat and forcing me to a halt. The guard who holds the spear glares. Behind him, a dozen more stand at the ready, javelins aimed at my chest.

Goddess help me, I pray. *Let me get back to Jasper. Let me bask in our love for a little while longer. I'll do anything.*

"We must fight," Izig growls. He widens his stance, raising both fists. He's a fair brawler. He should be—he learned from me.

The guards advance. I dip under the row of spears, punching the first guard between the legs. He doubles over, a grunt wheezing from his chest. The other guards pounce, javelins thrusting at me.

Izig throws a punch, sending a guard reeling. I spring into action, swinging as I dodge the guards' speartips. And then I'm a whirl of fists, desperation rising as I labor toward the doors. I've got to get to

Jasper—to protect him from whatever Zaphira might be planning. Grunting, I call on every fighting technique I've honed over the years.

Izig shouts. Sully screams in pain, and something clocks me on the back of the head. I fall to my knees but struggle back up, fury pushing me harder. I won't go down like this. I can't lose Jasper. I fucking refuse.

"Hold him!" Zaphira shouts behind me. Guards pile on top of me, flattening me to the marble. Sully screams in our bond. I struggle to press off the chilled surface, but I'm no match for a pile of elven guards. I call the sun, but I can't access Her here. I can't see Her or feel Her.

That's why Zaphira covered the windows. Why didn't I see it?

Hands grab at me, jerking me to my feet. I shove against them, head-butting the guard closest to me. He drops with a grunt, but another takes his place, and another and another. I'm fucking surrounded. There's no way out.

I roar. Zaphira appears in front of me, a vicious smile curving her lips.

"Tsk tsk, Abelin. I need your obedience, boy. Let me take your mind off that ridiculous pixie and any stupid ideas you have. Your betrothal to my daughter holds. You *will* marry Liriel at the winter solstice." She directs a sharp look at the guards. "Hold him still. If he jerks around too much, the geas won't hold."

A geas. Fuck no.

"You can't do this," I shout. "Nylian would never allow this."

She laughs, the haughty sound cutting through me like a knife. Guards pin me in place as she stalks closer. I push and shove as the others part, revealing two guards carrying Sully and Izig. Sully hisses and snaps his fangs, but the guards hold him by the scruff and tail. Blood drips to the floor from a slash above Izig's eye.

Zaphira's smile spreads as she moves to me and places a flat palm on my chest. I jerk away from her touch, but six guards hold me tight. I'm going nowhere.

"Your father will never know, Abelin. But don't worry." She scratches her nails down my cheek. "You won't remember, either. You won't remember we had this conversation. You won't remember that it was me who did this to you. And you sure as the gods of winter will never remember that bothersome pixie in your bed."

"No!" I bellow, jerking against the guards. I roar protests, but Zaphira's palm remains pressed to my chest. A chill starts at the top of my head and steals down my body. Sully screeches and hisses, but his fury is a dull thwomp around the muffled noise taking over my thoughts. I shake my head to dispel it.

No! Jasper!

I cling to a memory of him from last night. He threw his head back as he rode me. Held my hands as he screamed that he loved me.

Don't take him, I plead to the sun. *Please, don't let her take him from me.*

But the sun can't answer. Not here, in this cursed place where warmth is only a memory. Zaphira must have spelled the whole mansion somehow.

Murky fog descends on my consciousness as I scratch and kick and bite. Blood fills my mouth. I don't know if it's mine or someone else's.

I picture Jasper as I rage. But his face is a blur. The more I strain toward it, the foggier it gets. I scream in anguish as I tear myself from the guards' arms, only to be slammed to the floor by more bodies.

Time slows, and my mind grows hazy. Hands turn me onto my back. My vision narrows to the ceiling. It used to be painted with sunbursts and dappled glades filled with playful nymphs. Now, thousands of crystal-blue icicles point down like a wall of knives ready to impale me. Zaphira is ripping Jasper from my mind and I can't do anything to stop her.

I sob as I slog through muddy memories, trying to dredge up Jasper's face, or his hands, or...anything at all about the man I love. But there's nothing.

Nothing but icicles that seem to laugh at me from above. Or maybe that's Zaphira cackling with victory because she's won.

Ice is in my head, my heart, my soul. It's everywhere.

My mind goes blank, snowflakes falling somewhere inside me. I close my eyes, but the snowflakes pepper my face like tiny bullets. I hate the snow.

"Prince Abelin!"

A sharp voice cuts through my thoughts. I blink my eyes open to find snow falling inside the foyer of my father's house at Fourneclaire. Around me are two dozen of my father's—well, now my stepmother's—guard. They lie in various states of disarray, some passed out, most bloody. Izig and Sully stand by my side. The confusion on their faces matches my muddled thoughts. My body aches. I look down at my hand. My knuckles are split. Blood trickles down my fingers.

My stepmother moves in front of me, her hands braced on her rounded hips.

"I'll say this again," she snaps. "What in the frozen hells are you doing?"

I blink, desperately grasping at thoughts that seem to elude me. My head spins, confusion pummeling me. Did… Did I do this? Did I come here for some reason and attack my stepmother's guard? Why? Why would I do that?

Zaphira folds her arms and casts a piteous glance down my body. "I told you not to embarrass your father and me, Abelin." She gestures around the foyer. Blood smears the marble floor. It looks like a warzone. My stepmother glares at me. "Your father is expecting you at court for dinner. My carriage will take you there, and we won't mention what you did here. It would crush him to see you like this, Prince." She spits out my title like she can't stand to say it.

Everything hurts. What the fuck happened here? Was I drunk? I haven't partied since I was young. *Not a playboy anymore.*

The words rise in my mind. Inexplicably, tears prick my eyes.

Zaphira waits, anger huddling around her like a cloak.

I run both hands through my hair, still struggling to understand. But duty above all, that's what my father has always beat into me. So I drop my hands and nod. "Of course, Stepmother. I'm…sorry. I'm not sure I understand what's going on."

She glares at me. If icy daggers could shoot from her eyes, I know they would.

"You never do, Abelin. You never do."

CHAPTER 5
JASPER

By midmorning, I'm wide awake and growing more worried by the second.

"Where the fuck are you, Vale Gentry?" I murmur as I stand at the bedroom window wearing one of Vale's dressing gowns. Below, Paris is fully awake, too, the city's streets bustling with activity. Everyday noises drift up—music and chatter and dogs barking. But the brownstone is silent and still. If Izig and Sulien accompanied Vale, they haven't returned.

Movement on the streets catches my eye. Bert darts between the hooves of a bearded centaur pulling a cart.

"*Attention!*" the centaur cries. Watch out. His hooves clatter on the cobblestones as he scowls at Bert.

Bert pays him no mind, just streaks to the brownstone and disappears under the stoop. A few seconds later, he squeezes through a gap in the trim around the fireplace. His sides heave like a bellows. The tips of his ears are faintly green.

He takes one look at me and collapses on his side on the rug before the fireplace. His whiskers twitch, the skin around them the same sickly shade as his ears.

"Rough night?" I ask, folding my arms.

His voice in my head is laced with misery. *"Don't you dare lecture me about drinking. You're the king of overindulgence."*

"How much did you have? A thimbleful?"

"I hate you."

"No, you don't," I say, smiling as I stride from the room. "Don't move."

"Don't worry."

Any other time, I'd let my smile spread. Maybe tease him some more. But anxiety gnaws at me, threatening to bloom into full-blown panic. Where is Vale? How long does it take to buy croissants?

As I reach the brownstone's sprawling kitchen, I glance at the clock above the big bay window. It's been three hours. Vale could have hit up every boulangerie in the neighborhood by now.

On the other hand, he left a note. Maybe he's planning something special.

I stop on the threshold of a spacious butler's pantry, my heart thumping hard. Seven hells, is he going to *propose*?

No, of course not. Shaking my head, I search the cabinets, rummaging through spices and canned goods. I move to the drawers. The first is obviously a junk drawer with scissors and a jumble of pens. I open another—and stare into it with a frown tugging at my brows.

What the...?

Rolls of white tape are stacked in neat rows. Nothing else. Just tape —*a lot* of it. Does Vale have some sort of bondage fetish? Immediately, my head fills with images of me spread and bound on a chair, a gloriously nude Vale circling me with a wicked gleam in his eye.

"You've been holding out on me, you cocktease," I murmur, my dick tightening.

"Jasper?" Bert's voice in my head ends on a groan.

I shut the drawer and move to another set of cabinets. "Hold on, I'm coming."

"Speaking of..." A wet belch drifts across our bond. *"Did you jizz on this rug at any point over the past two weeks?"*

"Don't ask questions you don't want the answers to, Bertram."

"I knew it. Gross."

I rifle through yet another set of cabinets. At last, I spy my prize.

"Gotcha," I say, triumph filling me as I pluck a jar of honey from a shelf. Grabbing a bowl and a kitchen towel, I head for the stairs.

Bert's grumblings turn to groans as I reenter the bedroom. He keeps it up while I fill the bowl with warm water in the en suite bathroom that's larger than my apartment back in the Hallows.

"You did this to yourself," I remind him as I carry the honey water across the room and place it on the rug. I kneel next to Bert and tickle the fur between his ears. "Come on. You'll feel better."

"I can't move. I'm dead."

"That's what you said last time." I scoop him gently from the rug and guide his head to the edge of the bowl. "Small sips."

"Fine." He touches his tongue to the surface. After a moment, he drinks more quickly, lapping at the mix of honey and water. His greenish pallor fades, and the tips of his ears grow pink and healthy-looking once more. He flicks his tail once…twice. Finally, he springs to his feet. After a second of wobbling in my palm, he gives himself a vigorous shake.

"Better?" I ask mildly.

"Good as new." He cocks his head, his expression intent like he's listening for something. *"Where's the cat?"*

Worry roars back. Bert must see it in my face because he places one paw on my wrist, the soft pads between his toes resting over my pulse.

"Jasper? What's wrong?"

"Vale's gone," I blurt, my worry exploding into panic at last. Words gush from me in a breathless tumble. "He left to get croissants and he's picky about croissants so at first I didn't think anything of it because, you know, *the French*, but it's been three hours and now I'm fucking worried, except Izig and Sulien aren't here and I assume they're with him—"

"Jasper."

"—but I don't know that. It wasn't in the note. He's never been gone like this and—"

"Jasper!"

Bert's screech bounces between my ears, snapping my mouth shut. I swallow, and then I speak the fear I've been too terrified to acknowledge until now. "I'm worried something happened to him."

"Please," Bert scoffs, "he's an elf. Few among the Myth can take on a full-grown elf, let alone a prince." Bert's voice softens in my mind. "Besides, he's besotted with you. He might attempt to deny it, but the man is in love with you."

My stomach flutters, memories of the kiss in front of the Eiffel Tower playing in my head. I look toward the window, where the twisted tip of the tower peeks above the top of a nearby building. "He doesn't deny it," I say. "He told me he loves me last night."

Bert whistles in my head. *"And what did you say?"*

"That I love him, too." I look at my oldest friend. "And I do, Bert. I'm in love with him. I'm all in, and it's fucking terrifying." My throat burns. "But now he's gone."

"He's not," Bert says firmly. *"He left a note, right?"*

I nod.

"Well, there you—"

Loud knocking echoes through the brownstone. Sharp and insistent, it booms into the bedroom, making me jump to my feet with Bert in my hand. My heart lodges in my throat.

"Don't answer it," Bert says, his tone wary.

I look from him to the hallway outside the bedroom. "What if it's news about Vale?" I'm moving before I finish the sentence, my borrowed dressing gown flapping around my ankles as I head for the stairs. I descend them in a rush and hurry to the foyer. The knocking continues, each pound seeming to shake the whole building. Halfway to the front door, I bend and deposit Bert on the marble tile.

"Careful," he warns, and I nod as I go to the peephole and look out.

My breath catches.

A tall elven warrior stands on the stoop. There's no mistaking him for anything else. Long, pale hair cascades over his shoulders. Pointed ears peek from among the shimmering strands, which are braided away from his face. His features are flawless, but that's not what makes my stomach drop to my knees. No, it's not his looks. It's his clothing.

His golden armor and sunburst breastplate mark him as a warrior of the Summer Court. The silver greyhound badge pinned to his red cloak identifies him as a messenger of King Nylian.

Vale's father.

My hand trembles as I open the door.

"Jasper Lilygully?" the elf asks, his leaf-green eyes hard.

"Yes?"

The elf hands me a piece of paper. Then he turns and descends the steps.

"Wait!" I call. When the elf stops and gives me a cold look over his shoulder, it's all I can do to keep the tremor from my voice. "Vale… Is he okay?"

The elf's expression grows glacial. "I don't read the missives I deliver, pixie." He swings back around and leaves, his cloak flaring behind him.

Heart racing, I step back and fumble for the door, my movements clumsy. Bert appears, his dark eyes anxious as he looks from my face to the note in my hand.

"What does it say?"

"I don't…" My throat closes as I break the sunburst seal and see Vale's familiar, bold handwriting.

It's been fun.

My heart stops. Just seizes for a second before tripping over itself, the beats so hard and fast I stumble backward.

"Jasper?" Bert calls my name from somewhere. He paws at my legs, but I hardly feel it. My world shrinks to the words on the page. Three terse, black lines on paper the color of sunshine.

It's been fun. But I must return to my duties. You have my permission to remain in the brownstone through the end of the week.

Yours,
HRH Prince Abelin of the Summer Court.

The words blur. Dimly, I'm aware of Bert tapping our bond, of his voice flowing through my brain. But I can't make out things like speech and syntax. The only words that register are the ones on the paper.

It's been fun.

Duties.

You have my permission.

Over and over, the lines parade before my eyes—an inky marching band trampling my heart. Grinding that vulnerable organ to pulp.

My knees loosen. The foyer sways, the world threatening to slide from under my feet.

"No," I say aloud, and my voice in my ears brings me back. Gives me a solid foundation. I crush the paper in my fist, then fling it to the ground.

Bert chases it. Catching it between his front paws, he gives me a cautious look before unfolding the missive and reading it. *"Oh."*

"We're leaving," I snap, whirling and going to the stairs. "Right now!" I call over my shoulder. Bert is on my heels within seconds, his voice in my head labored as he runs up the treads.

"Where are we going?"

"Anywhere but here." Gods, he gave me permission to use his fucking house. I slam into the bedroom, flinging off Vale's dressing gown like it's poison.

No, *Abelin's* dressing gown. Vale isn't real.

He never was.

~

AN HOUR LATER, I stand in a queue on the outskirts of Paris. A castle looms above the line of Myth creatures and a few humans, its turrets scorched and blackened. Gazzag of House Florenti is a notorious pain in the ass, but he's the only dragon in France at the moment. Which means he's the fastest method of getting the fuck out of Paris.

"Are you sure about this?" Bert asks in my head, his voice cutting through the chatter around us. He perches on my shoulder, where he's

been casting me increasingly worried looks since we left the city. "Gazzag charges an arm and a leg for flights. Sometimes literally."

I fold my arms and ignore the pair of werewolves engaged in an animated conversation in front of me. "Gazzag owes me a favor," I tell Bert. "I helped him hook up with a banshee a few years ago."

Bert eyes the castle. "Will he charge extra for me?"

"If he tries it, I'll remind him I set him up with the banshee's twin sister, too."

"All right." Bert shifts his feet on my shoulder. If he harbors any reservations about conserving his limbs, he keeps them to himself. A heavy silence falls across our bond, which has been strained since I left Vale's place. It's like neither of us can bring ourselves to acknowledge what happened.

Vale dumped me. Like any other elf, he used me and then tossed me away.

Through a note. The arrogant asshole sent me a note.

It's been fun.

Anger burns my throat, the emotion so thick I could choke on it. One of the werewolves bursts into laughter. He slaps his companion on the back, then doubles over, the sound of his mirth like claws on slate.

Clenching my jaw, I face the stone curtain wall that stretches along the path leading to the castle. Flyers cover the surface, advertising weight loss potions and antidotes for curses. On one poster, a demoness with white teeth and glossy hair promises to "help you find your European dream home."

Yeah, right. Europe is where dreams come to die.

The werewolves begin bickering about which type of wolfsbane is more potent. A witch turns around and tells them they're both wrong. More creatures join the argument, quickly taking sides. The conversation becomes a lively debate. Ordinarily, it might be amusing. A distraction to pass the time. But right now, my fingers itch to hex the whole fucking queue.

Memories rise unbidden—Vale jerking me from the path of a bicycling Frenchman, then threatening to shove the man's bicycle up his ass.

You should have let me hex him.

No. Anyone who wants to fuck with you has to get through me first.

But that was a lie. My throat tightens as I return my gaze to the wall of flyers. Was *everything* a lie? Doubts prickle through me. I left the brownstone in a state of shock. But maybe I was too hasty?

Dammit, Vale owes me an explanation. He talked a big game about wanting harmony between pixies and elves. About leading his people into a new era. And then he acted like a fucking coward and broke up with me via note. It's not like him. And if it *is* like him, I deserve to hear it directly from his lying mouth.

Resolve pounds through me. Just as I prepare to leave the queue, a door opens in the wall. Two humans in white coveralls step through, a thick roll of paper balanced between them. The taller of the two has a metal pail looped over his forearm. Together, they carry the paper down the line, murmuring thanks when people step out of their path. Halfway down the wall, the men stop and begin unrolling their paper. One pulls a paintbrush from his back pocket. The other sets his pail on the grass. The scent of glue reaches my nostrils.

Conversation dies down as the men set about spreading glue over the mess of flyers and posters. The crowd watches, curiosity on people's faces, as the pair fixes the new poster onto the wall, revealing a brilliantly painted design. Two portraits: a man and a woman facing each other. Between them, elegant letters announce an upcoming wedding. The taller human pats the last corner of his side of the paper into place and steps back.

My stomach drops.

No.

No fucking way.

No *fucking* way.

The man on the poster isn't a man at all. He's an elf. Prince Abelin Vale of the Summer Court. His features are gorgeous in profile. A golden crown nestles among his honey-brown hair. He faces an equally gorgeous woman—another elf with pale hair and icy blue eyes.

Princess Liriel of the Winter Court.

Between their portraits, the scrolling words announce their

upcoming nuptials. Prince Abelin will wed Princess Liriel at midnight on the winter solstice.

"His stepsister," a gruff voice says beside me.

"What?" Bert says in my head, his voice ringing with shock.

I turn and meet the gaze of one of the werewolves. "Excuse me, what did you say?"

The wolf thrusts his chin toward the poster. "Princess Liriel is Prince Abelin's stepsister." The werewolf gives me a look. "The elves are into that freaky shit."

"You mean kinky shit," the other werewolf chimes in. The first wolf nods, and they chuckle as murmurs run through the crowd. Conversation starts back up, talk of the wedding spreading down the queue.

I hear none of it. Numbness settles over me, chasing away sorrow and anger. Chasing away every emotion until I'm hollowed out. Empty.

Bert is silent on my shoulder. But what can he say? Nothing will make this better. Royal weddings don't get planned in a couple of weeks. Vale was engaged when we met. He fucked me while he was engaged. He bought me ice cream and croissants while he was engaged to a woman. His fucking *stepsister*. He pulled me through cathedrals and museums. Bought me flowers and sucked my dick—and he didn't mean any of it. I was a diversion. One last gay fling before settling down to lead his straight, normal life as heir to the Summer Court.

Something inside me cracks. Cleaves in half. I'm moving before I know it, shoving Myth creatures out of the way as I storm up the path. Cries of "hey!" and "watch it!" follow in my wake, but they're nothing to me. Nothing matters except leaving this cursed place. This horrible city full of lying elves.

The castle gates appear. A lower house, non-shifter dragon in purple livery steps from the shadows and puts out a forestalling hand.

"You skipped the whole line, pixie."

I put my shoulders back. "Take me to your master. He knows who I am."

The dragon narrows his eyes, his gaze taking in Bert and my red-tipped wings. "You up to mischief?"

"No. Just done with men forever." To my horror, my voice cracks on the last word.

Abruptly, the dragon's expression softens. "Ah. So it's like that, then." He hesitates, then jerks his head toward the castle behind him. "Come on. I'll take you to Gazzag." As I fall into step beside him, he asks, "Where you headed?"

"Home. The Hallows."

And I'm never coming back.

PART TWO
WINTER

CHAPTER 6
VALE

I stare out the dining room window of my father's Paris estate. The Eiffel Tower sparkles in the distance, the twisted columns wrapped in lights.

It's beautiful. And it used to move me. A frown tugs at my brow.

Why doesn't it move me anymore?

"Vale!"

My father's deep voice breaks through my muddled thoughts.

I turn to my father. "Sorry, sir. I was lost there for a moment."

My king shifts backward in his chair and steeples his fingers in front of his broad chest. He's as regal and cold as ever, although I remember a time in my childhood when our home was filled with sunny warmth. But then Mother died. The Winter Court princess became my stepmother, and everything changed.

My father changed too. Streaks of pale blue glimmer in his once-golden hair. Navy flecks swim in his golden eyes. He and Zaphira live separate lives, but it doesn't matter. Her hold on him grows simply by virtue of their marriage. His griffin familiar, Olios, sits by his side. The beast shakes his lion's mane and lifts an eagle-like claw to scratch at the back of his ear.

"You're distracted, Abelin," Father murmurs. "It's been this way since Mab's court. Did something happen there?"

I look out the window again. Something about the Eiffel Tower draws me, like a memory I can't quite reach. Shrugging it off, I return my gaze to my sire. "You trusted me to visit Mab. She invited us to visit again. By all accounts, my mission was a success."

Father's golden eyes narrow. When I was a child, I swore the sun Herself shone from his eyes. Now I know it's simply a shrewd, assessing look. I've seen it hundreds of times in my four-hundred-and-some years.

I sigh. "I'm fine, Father, truly."

He lifts his chin. "The wedding is nearly here."

Something sour boils in my gut. The fucking wedding. I'd do anything to get out of it. I don't want Liriel. I want... Well, I don't know what I want. I suppose I want the freedom to love someone who loves me back.

"I'll do my duty," I say tightly.

"I have no doubt," Father replies with a brusque nod. Then his expression softens. "I know this feels like a sacrifice, Abelin, but in time you'll come to appreciate Liriel. The two of you have more in common than you think. You both lost a parent. Liriel doesn't speak of it often, but her father's death affected her deeply. The Winter Court was a sunnier place when King Filendor was alive." Father settles more deeply in his chair as he shifts from personal matters to the more comfortable subject of politics. "His brother, Elendor, has done a serviceable job since he took over, but I think there's room for improvement. That's why your marriage to Liriel is key. By forging yet another bond with the Winter Court, we can—"

"Will that be all, Father?"

My father's gaze sharpens. Olios stirs, obviously sensing the king's displeasure at being interrupted. Gaze on me, my father reaches over and strokes the griffin's shaggy head. He lets the silence hang for a moment before saying, "Zaphira tells me it's been difficult to get ahold of you for the final wedding preparations."

Anger sparks deep in my chest, and it's all I can do not to snap my fangs. "I've done everything she's asked."

"Clearly not if she's sending me messages to the contrary."

"She's always contrary," I say, hearing the bitterness in my voice. "Particularly where I'm concerned."

My father's tone turns frosty. "This attitude is unhelpful, Abelin. You could at least make an effort to get along with your stepmother."

"I agreed to marry her daughter. I'm doing my duty. Isn't that enough?" My anger spills into my voice as I lean forward in my chair. "Please, Father, do not ask me to choose between snowflakes or icicles on the godsdamned napkins!"

My father's golden eyebrows travel upward.

Olios lets out a warning growl, his amber eyes locked on me as he steps closer to the king. At my side, Sully hisses in return.

I sit back, and I drag deep breaths into my lungs as I wrestle with my runaway emotions. I've worked hard to prove my reckless playboy brawler days are over. "I'm sorry, Father." Inspiration strikes, and I force a smile. "Wedding jitters. I let my nerves get the best of me."

He rests his hands in his lap. I read nothing in his gaze—not anger or concern, not even irritation. How odd that someone who embodies the sun can be so cold.

"I'll speak with Zaphira," he says finally. "Why don't you take the next two weeks to travel and get your head on straight."

Surprise flits through me, followed by excitement at the thought of escaping court—and Zaphira's wedding preparations—for a bit. I let a wry smile touch my lips. "You're not worried I'll disappear to South America and become a recluse in the Amazon?"

My father smiles. "You've proven you can handle a king's responsibilities. I'm not worried about you, my son."

Pride blooms like a field of wildflowers in my chest. They warm me from within, almost as if the sun Herself shines inside me. This is what I've worked for—earning his trust, earning the right to lead.

"Thank you, Father," I murmur.

Silence stretches. When it grows uncomfortable, I clear my throat. But my father speaks first.

"I loved your mother. When she died, I longed to join her. Our marriage wasn't the typical royal business transaction. I was so lucky that we managed to find love." Bright eyes hold mine. "Perhaps you will, too, in time."

I clench my jaw. That'll never happen. But I can't tell him why—even if we both know the reasons. I'll never be physically attracted to Liriel. My father knows this, even if he chooses not to acknowledge it. Even if he understands full well that forcing me to wed a woman will doom me to a union as cold and loveless as his own.

But my father is the king. And we don't speak of the things he refuses to see. So I repeat the mantra he's beaten into me for hundreds of years.

"My duty to the Summer Court comes first."

"Glad you see it that way."

When a servant arrives to pour his tea, I look out the window again.

The Eiffel Tower rises high above Paris, a glittering black beacon of human civilization. Despite everything it's been through, it endures.

Just like I'll have to.

~

Two days later, I stand with Izig and Sully in the middle of what used to be Manhattan.

Glittering towers rise around us, the modern buildings filled with shops and thriving businesses. This is the only part of the Hallows that resembles New York before The War That Ripped the Veil.

Despite the chilly air, monsters and humans mingle on the streets. It bustles far more than Paris. Normally, I'd miss the slow pace of life in my home city, but I ache for something frenetic and chaotic.

I need to fight.

"This again?" Sully pokes at me through our bond.

"I just need to let off some energy," I say for the millionth time since arranging this trip to America. *"And we have plenty of friends here."*

Sully brushes against me, winding his long body through my legs while I stare up at the towers.

A gust of wind knocks Izig's bowler hat off. As I lunge for it, a dark figure drops out of the sky. Gasps go up as it streaks to the ground, landing with a thud. Wings flare wide, and the figure straightens, revealing a handsome male in an impeccably tailored suit. Golden eyes twinkle as he takes a pull from the cigar perched between claw-tipped fingers.

"Gothel," I murmur, greeting one of my father's oldest friends. "Good to see you again."

The Lord of the Air Syndicate stalks forward, his free hand outstretched. As I take it in greeting, his whiskey-colored eyes crinkle at the corners. His hair is longer, the ends brushing his white collar. Otherwise, he's unchanged from the last time I saw him.

Well, except that he looks happier. He's recently mated, word has it.

He casts a quick glance over me before nodding at Sully and Izig. "Glad you could visit." He looks at me and smiles. "Your father mentioned you need to let off a little steam, Vale. Something about upcoming nuptials?"

I hold back a growl at the mention of my marriage. Nothing about it feels right to me. In fact, I'd rather not even discuss it.

Instead, I focus on the first half of his comment. "Letting off steam sounds great. I haven't been to the Aerie in a hundred years. Tell me you've still got a brawling pit in the basement."

He laughs, the sound like rocks sliding down a slab of granite. "Of course there's still a pit in the basement." He jerks his head toward one of the towers. "Come have a cigar with me. I think I've got a better idea, actually."

He reaches for my suitcase, but Izig snatches it away.

"I've got it, thank you very much," my butler rumbles.

Gothel raises a brow. "Very well." Humor dances in his eyes as he takes another pull from his cigar. "Perhaps you could speak to my friend, Raoul. He never lifts a finger or dew claw to help me carry my bags."

Izig grunts as if such a thing is inconceivable. I can only grin. Gothel's grotesques are diminutive, stocky versions of him. They're a miniature army, but also accountants and builders and architects. They're adorable, although I'd never tell them that. I like my head attached to my shoulders.

Gothel leads us across the street. Humans and Myth creatures stop and stare as we pass. A few dip their heads, respect in their eyes as they acknowledge the powerful gargoyle.

What must that feel like? To be so obviously the master of your domain. For your people to speak in hushed tones when you go by? The elves of the Summer Court revere my father that way.

I want that for myself—the power and dominance. Or maybe I just long for freedom. Nobody tells my father no. He doesn't twist himself into knots to fit a mold that wasn't made for him. But I'm his heir, which means my options are limited. As in, I don't have any. If I want to be king, I've got to accept my responsibilities.

Ruling the Summer Court won't be easy. I know that, too. My future is full of sacrifice and hardship in the name of my Court.

That sacrifice starts with my wedding vows.

By the time we reach Gothel's office, the lightheartedness I felt on the street is long gone. Now, my gut churns as I contemplate my upcoming wedding. Visions parade through my mind—Liriel in her wedding gown, Liriel saying her vows at my side, Liriel naked and spread before me on our wedding night.

Nausea burns my throat. There's no love between us. She'll look at me with disdain and anger, and that'll be the way she looks at me for the rest of our lives. Duty is a noose around my neck. A weight across my shoulders. How long can I last before it presses me to my knees? A thousand years? Five thousand?

Gothel pulls a cigar from a box on his desk and hands it to me. He gives another to Izig, then produces a silver lighter and waits patiently as we touch the tips to the flame.

Sully sniffs at the air, his long whiskers twitching.

Gothel turns to me with a neutral expression. "I've got a proposal for you."

I suck at the tip of the cigar, relishing the rich spices and hints of something floral. As I let smoke curl from my mouth, something potent hits my system. My dick hardens, the need to fuck slamming into me like dual fists in the gut.

"Damn," I wheeze, just stopping myself from doubling over. I examine the tip of my cigar before meeting Gothel's amused gaze. "I don't remember your cigars packing this kind of punch."

The office door opens, and a slender male enters. In an instant, Gothel shifts his attention to the beautiful creature, who smiles as he heads for the gargoyle. Platinum hair is slicked back from his handsome face and knotted on the back of his head. When Gothel's horns straighten, the blond's smile widens, revealing a pair of sharp-looking fangs.

Ah. This must be Tower du Sang, Gothel's mate and leader of the du Sang crime family.

Confirmation comes a second later as Tower rises on tiptoe and kisses Gothel's jaw. The big gargoyle grips the blond's bun and bends him backward, deepening the kiss.

Izig casts me a disgruntled look.

"Well, this is indiscreet," Sully says in my head.

It's certainly unconventional—but I can't look away. Longing fills me, along with a melancholy that rises so sharp and swift it steals my breath.

I stare at Gothel and Tower, my heart pounding. The beat echoes in my head, my thoughts coalescing into one loud, thumping word.

Missing.

I'm missing this.

But…how? Confusion swaps me. I can't miss what I never had, and I've never had a passion like this. But the longing remains. As I watch the men, the longing sinks its claws deep.

Love.

Connection.

Desire.

I want these things I'll never have.

Panic grips me, and the sensation is as confusing as the longing.

Sully stares at me, his golden eyes sharpening. His voice fills my head. *"What's wrong? Are you sick?"*

I shake my head. *"I'm fine."*

Gothel and Tower part. The gargoyle turns whiskey-brown eyes back to me. The corners are still crinkled from his smile. He looks so godsdamned blissful. "Vale, this is my mate, Tower du Sang. Sweetheart, this is Prince Vale of the Summer Court."

Blue eyes flash as Tower smiles and offers his hand. "I've heard quite a lot about you, Your Highness."

I clear my throat as I shake his hand. "Call me Vale. And most of what you've heard isn't true. Or so far in the past that it doesn't bear mentioning any longer." I give my host a warning look. Gothel saw me during the very worst of my fiery playboy years. Gargoyles have long memories. Undoubtedly, he remembers my more outlandish exploits.

Gothel inclines his head. "You've arrived at the perfect time, Vale. The Hallows' annual Syndicate Ball is tonight." Gothel gives Tower a commiserating look. "I think the prince should serve as my champion. What do you think, my love?"

Tower smiles at Gothel like they're the only two men in the world.

Something inside me shatters into a million miserable pieces.

"Fuck, yes," Tower murmurs. "You said he can fight, right?" The vampire looks at me, his shrewd gaze sizing me up. "You ought to give Ursan a run for his money."

I cock my head. "Ursan?"

"A sea witch," Tower says. "And the new Lord of the Sea Syndicate. He's recently mated." Tower chuckles. "Well, doubly mated."

Gothel strokes a lock of platinum hair away from the vampire's face and coaxes it back into his bun.

My stomach churns at their happiness.

Two mates. I can't fathom it. I'd kill for one I actually wanted.

Gothel turns to me. "The Brawl is the highlight of the Syndicate Ball. I can't stray from my buildings, so Tower is going in my stead. Go with him, Vale. You can fight as my champion. Ursan will be a formidable competitor. Even without his magic, he's big and powerful. It'll be a lot more stimulating than the pit in the basement."

"And you look like you could stand to pound someone," Tower says, winking at me.

Gods, he's right. In every way. But there won't be any more pounding for me, at least not outside of a boxing ring. I grit my teeth so hard my jaw feels ready to crack.

Gothel takes another pull of his cigar, then smiles through a ring of smoke. "Well, Your Highness…you in?"

Izig shoots me a look of warning.

"This is a terrible idea," Sully says in my head.

He's right. They both are. But for the first time in months, some of the weight on my shoulders lifts. No one knows me here. And with a strong enough glamour, I can blow off some steam without anyone being the wiser.

I smile as I give Gothel a nod. "I'm in."

CHAPTER 7
JASPER

The Syndicate Ball used to be my favorite event of the year. Now, I'd rather be just about anywhere else.

I stand with my back against a wall in a shadowy corner, my arms folded over my chest. My wings are concealed under my jacket. A black silk half-mask imbued with a powerful glamour lends me additional anonymity. Before me, a wild party rages. Couples lean close, painted lips brushing. Hands roam silk-clad bodies. Laughter rings and champagne flows. It's every pixie's dream.

And I want nothing to do with it.

Music pumps through the old cathedral, the bass pulsing in sync with the bright colors that flash over the crowd. Creatures from every corner of the Myth fill the cavernous space. Tonight only, friends and enemies alike gather to celebrate another year of peace in the Hallows. Members of all four syndicates gather to fuck and feast anonymously.

Well, mostly anonymously. A few particularly boisterous revelers have knocked their masks askew, revealing their true identities. And not every mask can fool me.

Unbidden, memories rise.

I'm better than most at seeing under glamour.

In my head, in the places I've avoided venturing over the past six months, honey-colored eyes smile. *Is that so?*

"Damn you," I whisper as tears burn my eyes. I press my back harder against the wall on the edge of the crowd. In the center of the former sanctum, masked workers put the finishing touches on the elevated platform that will serve as the stage for the Ball's main entertainment: the Brawl.

Heads turn as the workers lift black fencing panels and secure them, slowly erecting a chain link cage. A masked man in a crisp tuxedo carries a pair of low stools through the crowd. When he reaches the platform, he ascends a set of stairs and places the stools in opposite corners. He pulls something from his pocket and places it on the center of one of the stools.

I lean forward as I struggle to make out the object. The man steps back, giving me a clear shot of a roll of gleaming white tape.

Memory tugs at me again. White tape. A whole drawer of it.

You've been holding out on me, you cocktease.

My throat tightens. On the dance floor, couples sway to the music. No one here is going home alone tonight.

Tears prick my eyes.

Fuck, I've got to get out of this place. I wipe at my eyes, but the damn mask gets in the way. Cursing under my breath, I lift it and wipe at my face as I lurch away from the wall. I get two steps when a heavy hand clamps down on my shoulder.

"Hold, Lilygully," a deep voice says, the tone more growl than speech.

I turn and meet the gaze of a towering, masked male dressed in a tuxedo working overtime to constrain his muscles. Blue eyes peer at me from behind a dark-brown mask. Shivers tremble down my spine, setting my senses tingling. For a moment, the man's eyes waver between blue and a deep, glittering amethyst. His hair flips from brown to black and back again.

Then it settles on black. His eyes shine that arresting purple.

"Wotan," I say, shrugging deliberately from his grip and letting my mask fall back into place. I flick an imaginary speck of dust from the spot on my jacket where Wotan rested his hand. "How wonderful to see you again. It's taboo to true-name someone at the Syndicate Ball. Then again, you hunt people for sport so I guess I shouldn't expect you to follow the rules."

He smiles, displaying white fangs. "You're one to talk, pixie. You never met a rule you didn't enjoy breaking."

I give him a mischievous look I can almost convince myself I feel. "Yes, but it's *cute* when I do it."

Wotan opens his mouth to reply just as a tall, broad-shouldered redhead appears at his side. The newcomer hands Wotan a drink before flashing a bright grin at me.

"Jasper! I thought it was you under there."

"Ryder Connelly," I say, "my favorite witch." As his grin spreads, I jerk my thumb toward the crowd. "Can you see under everyone's masks?"

"I'm better at it than I used to be," he says, his tone modest. "Probably not as good as you."

I smile. "Oh, honey, no one's as good as I am."

Wotan folds his arms over his thick chest and glowers at me.

I gesture from Ryder Connelly's shock of red hair to his brown silk mask. "Are you and Wotan wearing matching masks?" I look at Wotan. "You lost a bet, didn't you?"

"No comment," Wotan grumbles.

Ryder laughs and takes the Lord of the Earth Syndicate's hand. He gives the beast of a male a slow, easy smile as he laces their fingers together. "I made it worth his while."

"You did," Wotan rasps, his harsh features softening.

My gut clenches. I reach for my connection with Bert—and remember too late that I left him at home. The Syndicate Ball used to be one of his favorite events, too. But he declined to attend tonight. I should have followed his example. Although, our relationship has been strained since we returned from Paris. Before, we slipped in and out of each other's minds like a river. But lately, it's like every time I want to talk to Bert, that flow gets logged up. Dammed.

"Jasper?"

I jump as Ryder's voice yanks me from my thoughts. Worry shades his green eyes as he stares at me. Beside him, Wotan frowns.

I clear my throat. "I, uh…I should go."

Ryder's auburn brows pull together. "You're leaving before the Brawl?"

"Of course he's not," a voice rumbles behind me. Another hand clamps on my shoulder, and suddenly I'm surrounded by tall mermen.

And one smiling sea witch.

The new Lord of the Sea Syndicate sticks out his hand. "Ursan, Son of Crallek." He flashes a boyish, disarming grin. "I know we're not supposed to true-name, but Triton heard Ryder call you 'Jasper' and, well, I wanted to say hi."

"Did he, really?" I murmur, meeting Triton's gaze before looking at Ursan again. "Now that I think about it, I *do* remember something about the big guy having excellent hearing."

Triton grunts, adopting a pose similar to Wotan's.

"I'm not sure if you remember me," Ursan adds, pink dusting the bridge of his nose. A dimple appears in his cheek.

At his shoulder, Ari Razorfin stifles a moan, then coughs into his fist. Triton slides a satisfied look over both of his mates, a smile thawing some of the ice in his blue eyes.

"I remember, my lord," I tell Ursan, shaking his hand. Somehow, I muster enough energy to wink as I run my gaze over his thick pecs. "I never forget a chest."

Ursan's blush deepens. Ari rolls his eyes.

Triton chuckles.

I give him a pointed look. "I heard the same about you, Your Majesty."

The towering merman shakes his head. "All in the past now, pixie. I'm happily mated twice over."

Abruptly, the tears threaten to return. Clearing my throat, I look around the group. "No one brought flame zaddy tonight?"

"Fuoco is here," Wotan says, jerking his head toward the other side of the cathedral. "He's just busy snarling at anyone who dares to look at his mate too long."

I follow the direction Wotan indicated. Sure enough, Fuoco holds court in one corner, dragons from lesser houses standing guard around him and Beau. Fuoco is dressed to kill in one of his corsets and a tie glamoured to look like a waterfall. Beau's suit is just as extravagant, the amethyst shade a perfect complement to his dark good looks. As a man drifts toward the baker, green flames leap around Fuoco's head.

The man quickly spins and heads in the opposite direction. Beau shoots Fuoco an exasperated look. The giant dragon lord shrugs. After a second, Beau's shoulders shake with laughter.

Happy. They're happy. I helped bring them together. If only I could find that kind of love for myself.

Triton places a big palm on Ursan's shoulder. "We should get you ready."

"Ready?" I ask, looking between them.

Ursan's blush deepens. "I'm serving as the Sea's champion tonight."

I raise my brows. "You want to fight?"

"Well, it's not that I *want* to—"

"Yes, he does," Ari says, arrogance touching his handsome features. The sexy scar on his upper lip curls as he shoots his mate a look laced with pride. "I've been working with him. Taught him everything I know."

Ursan's blush spreads. But as he locks eyes with Ari, his bashfulness gives way to something undeniably heated.

A knife twists in my gut, the thrust so wrenching I suck in a breath.

All eyes turn to me. Triton's gaze sharpens, then sprints down my suit. "Black tonight, Jasper? That's an unusual choice for you."

More eyes travel down my suit. A few party-goers turn, curiosity gleaming in their eyes.

Unease settles over me. I force levity into my voice. "A gesture of goodwill. When you look as good as I do, you start to feel sorry for everyone else." I examine my manicure, which is the same glossy black as my outfit. "I didn't want to outshine you boys."

As soon as the words leave my mouth, I long to snatch them back. The towering males around me don't give a solitary shit about attracting notice. They're all happily mated—matched with companions handpicked by Fate.

And brought together with my assistance.

The knife in my gut sinks deeper.

Ursan steps toward me, his affable charm replaced with an unmistakable air of authority. "Is something wrong?"

"No," I say quickly, backing up. My shoulders bump the wall, and I shuffle sideways. As half a dozen worried eyes pin me, panic climbs up my throat.

I swallow it—and draw on ninety years of world-class snark. Still moving sideways, I fan my face. "Puck's ballsack, you're a thirsty lot. Sorry, fellas, but there's only so much Jasper Lilygully to go around." Stepping free of the scrum, I move a few paces away and toss an exasperated look over my shoulder. "Go suck each other's faces or something. I'm getting a drink."

Throat tight, I let the crowd swallow me—and I avoid eye contact as I make my way to the bar.

One drink.

One drink and I'll make my exit. If I leave any sooner, people might talk. The last thing I need is people gossiping about me. Irritation prickles over my nape. Damnit, *I* do the gossiping. Huffing, I signal the hydra behind the bar.

But she doesn't see me as she moves away, her heads swiveling in every direction but mine.

"Fuck," I mutter.

"Rough night?" a silky voice murmurs, and then Tower du Sang slides onto the barstool next to me. His true form is concealed under a mundane glamour, the nondescript brown hair and muddy brown eyes nothing like his staggering blond beauty.

The air crackles, and then a booming voice fills the air. "THE FIRST BRAWL BEGINS! EARTH VERSUS THE SEA."

The cathedral erupts in a chorus of cheers and catcalls. Revelers stream toward the platform, which is suddenly illuminated by a dozen spotlights. Ursan makes his way toward the platform, pulling off clothing as he goes. Triton and Ari flank him, both merman pushing away Myth creatures before they can get too close to the sea witch. When Ursan pauses to remove his trousers, Ari's gaze narrows on the brawny male's ass. The merman's green eyes glitter as he bites his bottom lip.

Sighing, I turn and rest my elbows on the bar. Wotan's champion mounts the platform, his ripped body encased in a pair of tight brown shorts. A second later, Ursan climbs the steps. The ass Ari admired is now covered in nothing but a thin layer of aquamarine-colored fabric.

A bell rings. The men advance toward each other with raised fists. Wotan's champion swings. Ursan ducks, then pops up and delivers a swift right hook to the other man's jaw.

The cathedral erupts with cheers.

Wotan's champion recovers, and the men bob and swing as they begin to brawl in earnest.

I watch for a moment before turning to Tower. "Are you wearing your Rune disguise just to fuck with Wotan?"

The vampire's lips curve. Slowly, he turns and matches my pose, his lanky body radiating elegance as he leans against the bar. "I thought that was your modus operandi, Lilygully." He looks at me. "Fucking with people."

I exhale noisily, and I don't throttle the irritation in my voice as I ask, "Is everyone in this place gifted with the ability to peer under glamour?" I wave a hand in front of my face. "Why wear a mask at all?"

Tower laughs softly. "Aw, but you look so good in it."

"Well, that's true," I mutter, turning my attention to the platform just as Ursan delivers a vicious uppercut to Wotan's fighter.

The crowd roars, the noise vibrating the marble floor under my feet.

Tower's regard is a weight against the side of my face.

I speak without taking my gaze off the fight. "Are you sizing up my jugular, du Sang? Because I should warn you, pixies taste terrible."

He laughs again. In my peripheral vision, he looks toward the platform. "Tempting, Lilygully, but I don't want to steal your magic."

"Making men lose their minds?"

"Matchmaking." Still gazing straight ahead, he leans into me and lowers his voice. "Rumor has it you're carrying on your grandfather's work." He pauses, and his voice dips a bit lower. "Your aunt must be proud."

On the platform, Ursan slams a fist into his opponent's face. Wotan's champion flies into the cage's chain link, which shudders under his weight. He staggers, then drops to the mat, knocked out cold.

Memories of a sun-dappled path flood my mind. Golden eyes twinkle as strong hands hold open a hedge for me to duck through.

But maybe I should call you Your Highness.

Only Mab uses a title.

But you're her nephew.

Yeah, well, I guess we've let that cat out of the bag.

The golden eyes smile. *Was it a secret?*

That smile. It glowed more brightly than the sun, warming me from the inside out.

I tried not to let it disarm me. But I was powerless from the moment its owner bumped into me. *You're the Prince of the Summer Court. You know damn well it was a secret.*

People are going to want to know more about you, Jasper. And I'm the first in line.

The roar of the crowd fills my ears, pulling me abruptly into the present. Tower straightens, his nonchalance replaced with razor-sharp alertness. His glamour flickers, giving me glimpses of the crime boss wrapped in a pretty package of bright blue eyes and long platinum hair.

"The Sky Syndicate is up next," he says, gaze on the platform as the next round of fighters replace Earth and Sea.

"You're not fighting in Gothel's stead?"

Tower looks at me. He flips up his mask, briefly dropping his glamour. "And risk *this* bone structure?"

I try for a smile but I'm not sure I achieve it, so I swing my gaze back to the platform. "Just admit you're scared, vampire." My throat burns. The phantom scent of French bread hits my nostrils. Fills my lungs. Climbs inside me and refuses to fucking leave.

I'm still calling this *French bread.*

Warm, teasing laughter fills my head. *Baguette, Jasper.*

The fighters representing Fire and Air face off in the center of the cage. One man wears burnt orange shorts. The other wears the light-blue shade of a cloudless sky. The flimsy fabric hugs an incredible ass. Desire thrums through me. As soon as it hits, I shove it away. Whoever the guy is, he's wearing a glamour. Those tight, round cheeks aren't real.

But, damn, they're sexy.

And…familiar.

Tower chuckles. "Fuoco's champion isn't going to know what hit him."

I lean forward, squinting at the platform. The blue-clad fighter's back is turned to me as he jogs in place. Something on his leg catches my eye. A tattoo?

The announcer strides to the center of the cage and raises his arms. His magic-amplified voice shakes the walls of the cathedral. "THE FIRE SYNDICATE VERSUS THE SKY SYNDICATE! WINNER FACES THE SEA IN THE FINAL ROUND!"

Fuoco's champion jogs in place, jabbing at the air. The fighter representing Gothel drops into a ready position, his muscled body taut. Some kind of markings trail down one thick thigh.

A bell rings. Fuoco's champion surges forward, big fists flying. Gothel's man dances back, bobs, and then throws a punch that connects swiftly with the other man's ribs.

Cheers split the air, but I hardly hear them. I lean forward, my gaze on the blue-clad fighter's thigh.

The markings flicker.

A glamour. No one is supposed to see that tattoo.

But I do. I'm the grandson of the old pixie king. Few can hide from my line.

Fuoco's champion swings.

Gothel's champion moves like water, sliding effortlessly out of the way.

I take a step forward, my heart thumping faster as I peer at his thigh.

With a roar, Fuoco's champion swings again.

The fighter in the blue shorts sidesteps, then brings up his hands.

Taped hands. I've been staring at his legs for so long, I didn't notice the tape.

My heart stutters.

White tape.

Rolls of it. A whole drawer of it.

You've been holding out on me, you cocktease.

Gothel's champion throws a punch—a vicious, precise right hook that crashes into the other man's jaw like a sledgehammer.

Fuoco's champion lurches sideways. Stumbles. Goes down.

The crowd cheers.

The man in the blue shorts turns all the way toward me. His glamour flickers. And, suddenly, I see right through it.

The sun's rays wind down his thigh. They wrap around his dick, too, even though no one in the cathedral but me knows it.

Because I know him. I wish I'd never met him. He broke my heart in Paris.

I swing toward Tower, and my voice emerges as a savage growl. "Gothel's champion is the Prince of the Summer Court?"

Tower shoves away from the bar. "Keep your voice down, Lilygully." He seems to realize what I just said, because confusion covers his features. "Wait. You know Vale?"

"Unfortunately. How the fuck do you know him?" The knife in my gut twists sharply. If Vale fucked Tower du Sang…

"His father is a friend of Gothel's," Tower says. The vampire glances at the platform, his air of arrogance replaced with unmistakable worry. "What's going on, Lilygully?"

"Nothing." *Just the man who dumped me showing up in my home unannounced.*

And unwelcome.

Abruptly, fury burns away every trace of heartache. It roars within me, obliterating the noise of the crowd until all that's left is the thud of my heartbeat in my ears.

I turn back to the platform, where the announcer raises Vale's arm in the air. "THE WINNER! GOTHEL'S CHAMPION ADVANCES TO THE FINAL ROUND: SEA VERSUS SKY."

Oh, fuck you. And fuck no.

I'm moving before I know it, shoving all manner of creatures from my path. I cross the cathedral, and then I'm gripping Ursan's bicep and tugging him around.

Startled brown eyes go wide. Ursan drips with sweat, the flush of his recent victory in his cheeks. "Jasper! Are you okay?"

"Let me be your champion."

Ursan's jaw drops open. Ari looms over his shoulder, his ruddy eyebrows pulling tightly together.

"You can't mean to fight, Lilygully," Ari says.

"I'm going to kick his ass." I rip my suit jacket off and look at Ursan. "Please. I need to get up there."

The Lord of the Sea Syndicate looks from me to the platform. When he returns his gaze to me, his eyes are wary but kind. "You know that man?"

"Yes. And I would very much like to kill him."

Ari makes a low sound. "Lilygully, I don't know the guy, but he's a pro. Only experienced fighters move like that. One punch and you'll be swallowing teeth."

I keep my gaze on Ursan. "Please. I need this."

"Why?" Ari demands. "You'll get—" He clamps his mouth shut as Ursan holds up a hand. The sea witch gives me an assessing look, his dark eyes so penetrating I fight the urge to squirm. After a minute, he nods.

"All right. You'll represent the Sea."

"Thank you." Triumph surges briefly, but it's quickly replaced with another spike of fiery anger. I turn to the platform, where Vale stands docile as two men towel him off and squirt water down his throat.

The announcer calls for the Sea Syndicate's champion to come forward.

Someone produces a strip of aquamarine cloth. Ursan ties it around my arm, and I make my way to the platform with Ursan and Ari flanking me. The crowd surges around us, the noise deafening. Magic shimmers in the air. Violence dogs my steps, but it's nothing compared to the rage searing my veins.

Ursan and the announcer engage in a brief shouting match as they struggle to hear each other over the crowd. After a tense moment, the announcer nods.

Ursan turns to me with a sober expression. "I hope you know what you're doing, Jasper." He puts a steady hand on my arm. "You're on."

I climb the steps. The crowd chants, the roar swelling as the spotlights hit me.

Across the platform, Vale stands near his stool. His golden eyes fill with confusion as he takes me in. Above his mask, his smooth brow furrows. He moves toward me, and my heart beats faster.

Now. Finally. I'm going to get some fucking answers. And then I'm going to tell him to go fuck himself.

His shadow falls over me. Sweat glistens on his skin.

The same as it did when he made love to me and said he'd do anything to keep me.

I clench my fists at my sides.

He stops. Hesitates. Offers his hand.

I squeeze my fists more tightly. "I'm not shaking your fucking hand, you asshole."

He frowns. His deep, French-accented voice is muffled by the crowd, but it reaches me all the same.

"I beg your pardon. Do I know you?"

CHAPTER 8
VALE

My hand remains outstretched between us, but my opponent doesn't take it.

He doesn't belong up here. The Sea Syndicate's champion looked like a fighter—brawny and quick on his feet in that first round. This male is...well, he's not that. I can't see his true form, but his glamour is lanky and lean. I run my gaze down his body. His fists are balled, his thumbs tucked inside his fingers—a surefire way to break bones when you punch.

I drop my hand and step back. Maybe this is a trick meant to throw me off guard. Undoubtedly, that's what Izig would say. Regret sluices through me. I probably hurt his feelings by asking him to stay behind at the hotel tonight. But I wanted to fight without my ogre butler shooting me reproachful looks from the crowd. Sully and Izig have never approved of my brawling habit.

Sully—who ignored my request to stay away—speaks softly in my head. *"Who is this new opponent? Why isn't the big guy fighting you?"*

"I don't know. He doesn't look like a fighter, and he's acting like he knows me."

Sully growls into our bond. *"We've seen this sort of thing before. He's probably trying to get into your head. Ignore it."*

I nod as I hold the handsome man's gaze. He's stunning. Beyond stunning. He's fucking gorgeous—or his glamour is, anyway.

He moves both fists to his hips, his stance not nearly wide enough to keep him on his feet during a fight. "Got nothing to say, Prince?" He spits my title with shocking venom.

I stiffen. Nobody should recognize me here. My face is well-glamoured. Yet the male before me not only knows who I am, but he seems to think I should know him as well. Growling, I shove into his space and snap my fangs.

He jerks and takes a step back, then flashes an acid smile. "Two can play this game, you fucking asshole." Reaching up, he undoes the string on his mask and rips it off. Glamour flows away from him, revealing the most beautifully sensual male I've ever seen.

A trick. It has to be. Narrowed blue eyes fringed with long, golden-brown lashes shoot daggers at me. Nostrils flare in apparent anger. Blond brows several shades darker than his short, platinum hair frame the man's delicate features. His ears taper to points. At his back, stiffly veined iridescent wings flutter.

A pixie. My confusion grows. Pixies aren't fighters. But this one looks like he wants to rip me limb from limb. Even so, he's not dressed to brawl.

His expensive-looking suit hugs a lithe body. I've stood across the ring from enough fighters to know when someone is out of their depth. There's a hint of muscle in the pixie's shoulders, but he's no match for someone my size. And if I had to wager, I'd bet he's never thrown a serious punch in his life.

Apprehension prickles down my spine. I spin in place and address the referee. "What are you playing at? This isn't right."

The ref shrugs, moving a toothpick around his mouth with his tongue. "The Sea says it's okay. Who am I to deny one of the four syndicate lords?"

The deep sense of *wrongness* swells. I'm an experienced fighter. Sometimes, the scrawniest opponents can be the scrappiest. But that's not the case here. I've fought enough to know it.

"Fight me, Vale," the pixie demands.

I whirl around and meet his angry blue eyes. He used my real fucking name.

As shock holds me immobile, he launches himself at me. Before I can react, he grips my throat and gives a savage hiss. Delicate wings flutter at his back. I could rip them right off his body. He's left himself totally open.

I pull out of his grip and shove him away. When he leaps for me again, I punch him swiftly in the gut. He doubles over and falls back against the cage's chain link, wheezing out a harsh breath.

He didn't block me. He's not getting up fast, either.

I swivel around to the ref, but he just crosses his arms and jerks his head toward the other male.

"You won't put a stop to this?" I ask the ref.

"If he's still on his feet, the fight's still on." The ref glances at the crowd, which surges around the platform. He lowers his voice. "Do *you* wanna tell them you're not interested in fighting?"

Frustration pounds through me as I face the pixie. Thankfully, he's back on his feet. He glares at me and raises his fists.

I drop mine and give him what I hope is an earnest look. "The boxing ring is no place for gentle beings, pixie. Let me fight the Sea Syn—"

"Gentle beings?" he snarls. "Are you fucking kidding me?"

"Stay vigilant," Sully says in my mind.

The pixie leaps forward. I seize his throat—a move any decent fighter would have sidestepped. Grunting, I walk the pixie swiftly backward and pin him against the side of the cage. He hits hard, and one of his delicate wings shoves through the chain link and bends at an odd angle. He cries out, his brow creasing with pain even as he shoots me a furious look.

The crowd is restless. Jeers and groans fill the cathedral, echoing off the high ceiling.

Confusion and concern war within me. I love a good fight. But there's nothing good about what's happening here. This would be a slaughter if I took it seriously.

Time slows. The pixie claws at my forearm, trying to pry my fingers from around his throat. His pulse pounds underneath my palm. Heat flashes through me as a sudden vision of me fucking him assaults my mind. His brows would be scrunched just as they are now, but in pleasure, not fury. And he wouldn't be trying to get away. No, he'd be writhing in ecstasy under my larger frame.

I shake my head in an attempt to dispel the vision, but others take their place. Vague, blurry images of bright blue eyes and fluttering wings. Like an old-fashioned film strip, the muddy, disjointed scenes dash through my consciousness. Does the pixie possess some magic to do this? Maybe he's not a physical fighter, but a mental one.

A quick knee to the groin snaps me back to the moment. Pain and nausea slam into me, but I shake them off as I tighten my grip on the pixie's neck. His eyes burn with hatred as he scratches and kicks. Suddenly, I don't feel the hits. They keep coming and I don't notice.

But every inch of me notices *him*.

The arena around us fades. The pixie's heart pounds under my fingers. I shake my head again, trying to clear the morass of confusion from my thoughts. Tower du Sang stands amid the crowd at the base of the platform. The vampire should be as outraged as I am about this imbalanced fight. Instead, his blue eyes brim with the same confusion that pummels me. It's clear he doesn't want me to fight this fight—not against *this* opponent.

Something is wrong here. Very, very wrong.

I drop the pixie's throat and step back. Turning toward the ref, I lift both hands in surrender. "I don't want this fight."

The pixie surges forward. "Fight, you coward! You're not getting away with this!"

I shake my head. "It's not a fair match. I won't do it."

He clenches his fists. Tears sparkle in his eyes as he screams—the sound so frustrated and grief-stricken, something inside me threatens to shatter apart.

"Don't," I say, stepping toward him. My head snaps to the side when he nails me with a quick right hook. My lip bursts and the coppery taste of blood fills my mouth. It was a weak hit despite its accuracy.

I spit blood on the ground and turn to the ref, shaking my head. "I'm finished."

He frowns as he moves between me and the pixie.

The pixie doesn't even look at him.

The ref gives me an impatient look. "You refuse to fight your opponent?"

The pixie stares blindly at the crowd, his chest heaving and his fists balled at his sides. The anguished look on his face makes me want to cradle him to my chest. I can't hit him again. I won't.

I look at the ref. "I won't fight this opponent. I forfeit."

The crowd erupts into thunderous jeers around us. The cage fills with overwhelming noise. The pixie glares at me, his blue eyes glittering with unshed tears.

The ref tosses me a disgruntled look, then grabs one of the pixie's fists and yanks it into the air. "The Sky Syndicate's champion will not fight. The Sea wins!"

A chorus of cheers from those who bet on the Sea fills the room, followed by the groans of those who just lost their bets.

The pixie uses his free hand to scrub the moisture from his eyes. His beautiful wings are stiff, the delicate edges sifting red dust.

The ref drops the pixie's arm and turns to him. "You're the champion. You know the terms. What boon do you claim for yourself as the winner?"

Brilliant blue eyes narrow. Slowly, the pixie looks at me, his expression shifting from despair to sinister glee. "Him," he rasps, pointing at me. "I claim him as my boon."

In my bond, Sully hisses. *"What the fuck is a boon?"*

◊

TEN MINUTES LATER, I trail the pixie down a darkened sidewalk leading away from the cathedral. Sully prowls in the shadows a short distance away. Chilly air coasts over my bare skin, cooling my sweat and making goosebumps race down my arms. The pixie didn't even allow me to change before he ordered me from the cathedral.

"Keep up," he barks, turning and snapping his fingers at me. His glossy black nails flash in the moonlight. "Not much of a boon if I have to fucking carry you."

"I'll ask you again," I say, my breath puffing in white, frosty clouds. "What the hells is a boon?"

The pixie whirls around. He stalks toward me, his fists balled once more. The bass thumping from the cathedral is a fitting accompaniment to the angry pulse throbbing in his neck.

"It means you're mine, Vale," he says. "Try not to run, although not following through on your commitments is par for the fucking course for you."

Confusion hits me, followed by equal doses of dread and anger.

I raise my hands in the same gesture of surrender I used in the cage. "You keep using my name. But I don't know you, and I can't be yours, regardless of what happened at the Brawl. I've got places to be."

My wedding, for instance. In two godsdamned weeks.

The pixie shoots me an incredulous look. "Oh gods, Vale, how inconvenient for you to have"—he makes air quotes with both hands—"places to be!" He shoots a disdainful look at my hands, which are still taped from the fight. "Kept that under your hat, didn't you? I guess when you're a liar, you lie about everything." He turns and stomps down the sidewalk, cursing under his breath.

Frustration joins the brew of confusion and anger. I raise my voice. "Wait! What is a boon?"

He stops and snarls at me over his shoulder. "It's a magical contract. Like it or not, and I don't give a single shit if you like it, you're at my mercy for the next two weeks. Come the fuck on." He turns and moves off again.

My gut clenches. Why the hell didn't Gothel and Tower mention this? I can't be locked into a magical contract for two weeks. My father will expect me home within the next few days. Zaphira is bound to notice my absence from court—or when I don't show up for a fucking cake tasting appointment.

Something pinches my skin—the sting like a rubber band snapping. "Ow!" I jump and examine my arm, expecting to see a welt. But there's nothing. When I look up, the pixie faces me across the length of the sidewalk between us.

"Did I mention the magical contract comes with an enforcement mechanism?" he says with a dark smile. "Move your ass or pay the consequences, Your Highness." He spins and strides away, his long legs eating up the sidewalk.

As I jog to catch up with him, the strangest sense of déjà vu hits me. He seems absolutely convinced that we know one another. But we can't. I'd remember a man like him.

I slow to a walk as I reach his side, and I curl my fingers into my palms to resist the urge to straighten his still-crooked wing. The delicate membrane is a mottled red, and the edges aren't dropping pixie dust like the other wing. The pixie ignores me as we walk, his gaze fastened on some point in the distance.

I've tried demands. Maybe charm will get me some answers.

"You seem to think we've met, pixie," I say, "but I'd remember a face as handsome as yours."

He stops so abruptly that I take another step before stumbling to a halt and facing him.

A disgusted look slips over his refined features. "Are you shitting me?" he asks in a low, dangerous voice.

Okay, so it's a no-go on the charm. "I'm not trying to," I say. "I'm sorry—"

"Shut up," he growls, his blue eyes glittering. Another phantom stinger pinches my skin. "This is what you need to know. You're mine for the next two weeks. When I say jump, the only thing I want to hear out of your mouth is *'How high, Jasper?'*"

I jerk like I just took a punch to the gut, my breath whooshing out of me in a great big wheeze. Dizziness assails me. And it's not because he snapped the rubber band.

Jasper.

The word swirls through me, joining the confusion that fogs my brain. *Jasper.* It circles my mind, and I reach for it but I can't quite catch it. I'm swimming for a shore that keeps getting farther away with every wave. Confusion fills my bond with Sully, who's still trailing us at a distance.

"Vale?" he asks, his mental voice concerned. *"Are you okay?"*

"Jasper?" I croak, my gaze locked with the pixie's as I shove the dizziness away. "That's your name?"

He huffs a disgusted, humorless laugh. Then he turns and heads up the darkened sidewalk once more. This time, he doesn't order me to follow.

But as I watch the stunning pixie move away, I know I *will* follow him. Every instinct I possess urges me to find out more about him. And that devastated look he shot me on the platform? I need to know why it was there. I start forward, my eyes on the pixie's delicate wings as he turns down a shadowy street lined with buildings draped in ivy.

Jasper.

I increase my pace. He shouldn't walk alone through the city. It's not safe. Any number of creatures could be hiding in that ivy. But I don't even *know* him. So why am I worried?

"We have to be back in Paris within two weeks," Sully reminds me. "We have *to, Vale.*"

"I know, old friend," I say, walking faster. "*That gives us two weeks to figure out what in the seven hells is going on here.*"

He purrs into our bond—his version of a quick hug. And then we turn the corner and follow the pixie.

No, *Jasper.*

His name is Jasper.

CHAPTER 9
JASPER

This is stupid. I'm an idiot. A stupid idiot.

Those thoughts pound through my head as I lead Vale up the two flights of stairs to my apartment. What the fuck was I thinking claiming him as a boon? And for two weeks? I could have done a million other things. Could have forced him to crawl around the cathedral shouting what a scheming, lying, cheating asshole he is.

But no, I decided to bring him home with me so I can be reminded what a scheming, lying, cheating asshole he is for *two weeks*. And now he's playing some cruel little game, pretending we've never met.

"Fuck," I mutter, stopping in the middle of the hallway. Vale crashes into me, sending me lurching forward. Just like in Mab's court.

Anger grips me all over again, and I whirl around, ready to punch him in the face. But my wing twinges, pain shooting from the middle of my back to the tip of the membrane. Nausea slams into me, and I suck in a breath.

Vale steps forward, his golden eyes both wary and concerned. "Are you all right?"

"No," I snap. "I'm not *all right*." Wincing, I curl my wing forward and examine the damage in the hallway's electric lights. Just a bruise. It'll be okay by morning.

"You should get someone to look at that," Vale rumbles. He drifts closer, his expression shifting. The wariness in his eyes fades, replaced with curiosity—and interest. Goosebumps cover his skin. His nipples are tight pebbles. December in the Hallows is no joke. He's got to be cold in nothing but those tight little shorts. The damn things are indecent, the fabric cupping his bulge like a second skin.

I flick my wing behind me, and he jerks a startled gaze to mine.

"Why the fuck do you care?" I demand. Then I raise a hand. "Wait, don't answer that. I thought I wanted to hear your excuses, but I've changed my mind." I turn and march to my door. My nape prickles as he moves behind me, drawing close. Gods, even now, my body responds to him. He's like a sickness I've caught and can't shake. A fucking virus.

As I fumble for my key, something thumps two apartments down. Two more thumps echo in rapid succession. A second later, a woman moans. A man's low laugh drifts from the apartment.

"What's that sound?" Vale asks, his breath coasting over my nape. "Intruders?"

I glare at him over my shoulder. "Would you back off? And no, they're not intruders. They're my neighbors."

His brow furrows. "Neighbors?"

"Yeah, not everyone can afford to buy a whole city block, Your Highness." I open the door and let it bounce off the doorstop. My apartment is nowhere near as luxurious as Vale's brownstone in Paris, but it's wired for old-fashioned human power. I flip on the lights as I toss my keys on the tiny table in my equally tiny foyer before stalking to the kitchen. Vale appears a second later, looking enormous and completely out of place in the modest space.

He gazes around, his golden eyes taking in the glossy cabinets, electric appliances, and exposed brick I was so proud of when I bought the place. In the adjoining living room, glass doors open onto a private terrace. It's the size of a postage stamp but it costs me a fortune. A fireplace with a roomy hearth softens the industrial look of the living room's brick walls.

Vale settles his gaze on me, his expression polite. Impersonal. "Your home is nice."

"It's not quite Villette," I say, my voice heavy with sarcasm.

His face goes from polite to intense. An air of danger rolls off him as he steps toward me. "You know my preferred name. And you know where I make my home."

"No shit." It's on the tip of my tongue to remind him that, for two weeks, his home was my home too. That in my heart of hearts, I dared to hope it might be my permanent home. But I can't bring myself to say it. The words already hurt badly enough living in my head. Sharing them with him will make everything worse. He doesn't deserve to know how I feel. I've already given him too much of myself. I won't give him anything else.

"How do you know these things?" he asks, his eyes darkening as he takes another step forward.

Anger boils up—the bubbling rage as hot as it was the moment I spotted him at the Ball. It tightens my chest and turns my voice into a growl. "I don't know what you're playing at, but you've got a lot of fucking nerve."

A deep groove appears between his brows. "I don't understand why you're so angry with me." He gestures to my injured wing. "I never meant to hurt you."

"Really?" I prop my fists on my hips. "You're really going there? Because from where I'm standing, you definitely meant to hurt me."

"I swear I didn't." His lips thin. "In my defense, you had no business being on that platform—"

"I'm not talking about the fucking platform!" I yell, my temper snapping. I rush him, and he takes a swift step backward, bumping into my refrigerator. "What is this act you're putting on?" I demand. "Is this some kind of trick?"

"No trick," he says, "just…" He trails off—and goes as green as Bert after a night of partying. Sweat beads on Vale's forehead as his breathing grows more labored. He leans against the fridge and lifts a shaking hand to his brow.

Alarm jumps through me. "Are you gonna pass out?"

"No," he rasps, looking like he's definitely going to pass out. "I'm fine." He lowers his hand and studies me like he's trying to see through me. "But it's like I've heard that"—he sways on his feet—"before," he finishes weakly.

"Okay, come on." I grab his arm and steer him toward the living room. Or try to. I take one step and come up short when Vale doesn't move. He just stares down at me with bewilderment in his eyes.

And touching him is the very last thing I should be doing. What I *should* do is end this conversation and go to bed. I'll figure out a way to dissolve the boon in the morning.

I drop his arm and tap the contract's bond as I point toward the living room. "Go sit on the sofa. I'm not scooping you off the floor if you keel over in my kitchen."

He grimaces as the magic hits him. Scowling, he reaches the sofa in half a dozen steps and sits down hard. Even in nothing but his ridiculous shorts, he's every inch a prince. With quick movements, he unwinds the tape from his hands and wads it into little balls.

I swallow hard and ignore the tendrils of desire that try to bloom inside me. He's an elf and an asshole. And now he's determined to gaslight me into thinking we're strangers. I need to keep my distance, both figuratively and literally.

He looks up at me. "I can't be part of this boon, Jasper. I have obligations to attend to. People are depending on me."

"Since when has that ever stopped you from being an utter disappointment?" My resolve of five seconds ago flies out the window as I round the end of the counter and cross the living room. I stop on the other side of the coffee table stacked with art books. A blown glass bowl holds a collection of seashells a siren queen gave me after I helped her patch things up with her girlfriend.

Bitterness washes through me. Is that the price of my gift? I can bring other people together, but I can't figure out relationships for myself? Somehow, that magic is beyond my grasp.

Vale watches me, his big hands braced on his knees. He looks so fucking good. I hoped to never see him again, but if I did, I thought maybe he'd look less stunning—that maybe my memories painted him in a better light than reality. But he's just as gorgeous now as he was in Paris. Just as ruggedly masculine. Just a little too rough around the edges to be a typical elf. Golden scruff covers his square jaw. The sun tattoo flares down his broad chest and over his rippling abs before disappearing beneath the waistband of his shorts. Honey-brown curls spread over his plump pecs. When we lay in bed, I used to trail my fingers through those curls.

My throat tightens.

Vale rises, worry in his gaze. "Jasper—"

"Don't." I scrub the heel of my hand over my eye. "I don't want to hear my name on your lips." In my peripheral vision, red dust sifts from my uninjured wing. "I don't want to hear anything you have to say. So sit down and shut up."

His nostrils flare as he obeys. "No one speaks to me this way."

"Maybe that's your problem. You've always gotten exactly what you want."

He gives a bitter-sounding laugh. "Is that so? Apparently, you don't know everything, pixie."

"Oh, I know plenty. You—" I clamp my mouth shut as the sound of light, rapid footsteps drifts from the terrace. A second later, Bert and Mert scurry through the mousehole at the base of the brick. They spot Vale and freeze.

"You brought a man home?" Mert asks in my head, mild surprise in his voice. Maybe because I haven't brought a man home since I returned from Paris.

Bert looks from Vale to me. His dark eyes are worried, but he stays silent in my mind. Our new normal. For the past eight months, it's like we've had an unspoken pact to never speak of Vale.

"Jasper?" Mert says, running to me and scratching at my foot. I bend and pick him up. He jumps from my palm to my shoulder and rubs his cheek against mine. *"What's wrong?"*

"Nothing," I rasp aloud, stroking his short whiskers. Plump and jolly, Mert has always been softer than his twin. Sweeter. But I can't handle sweet right now. If Mert is nice to me, I'll break down. I clear my throat. "Where is Luke?"

"Pub in the Earth Syndicate." Mert flicks his tail in Vale's direction. *"Who's the hunk? You pick him up at the Ball?"*

I look at Bert as confusion spreads through me. He and Mert are as close as any brothers. Closer, even. They share everything. But Mert doesn't have the slightest inkling who Vale might be. It's almost like he and Bert never discussed Paris.

"*You want some privacy?*" Mert asks. "*Bert and I can get lost.*"

"No," I answer through our bond, but I keep my gaze on Bert, who gives no reaction despite hearing every word of our conversation. A frown pulls at my brow as I stare him down. "*What gives?*"

Bert lifts a tiny shoulder. "*What?*"

I release an exasperated breath as I jerk my head toward Vale. "*You've got nothing to say?*"

"*I...*" His whiskers twitch as hesitation travels across our bond. After a second, he turns toward the mousehole. "*I'm going to my room.*"

Mert's bafflement is a cloud in my mind. "*Bert?*"

Vale stands. "Listen, Jasper. I don't know what happened back at the fight, but I can't stress enough how critical it is for me to return home immediately." His chest lifts as he draws a deep breath. "I'm betrothed, you see, and—"

"Are you?" I press my palm to my chest and widen my eyes dramatically. "Gods, I had no idea. If only someone thought to plaster you and your fiancée's faces on every billboard and building on two continents. Have you considered wedding announcements? Maybe some flyers with fancy gold lettering?" I fling my arms wide, jostling Mert. "I know! You and *Princess Liriel* could face each other so it looks like you're gazing into each other's eyes."

His scowl returns with lightning speed. "You're mocking me."

"Oh, I wouldn't dream of it, m'lord."

He opens his mouth—

Someone knocks on the door.

We both turn toward the foyer. My gut clenches as memories from that last morning in Paris flood my head. When the knock rings out again, I look at Vale and let every ounce of anger I've collected over the past eight months fill my expression.

"One of your people come to fetch you?"

His golden eyes, which were always so soft for me, go hard. "I have no idea. Maybe you should answer it."

I point at him. "Don't fucking move."

He clenches his fists at his sides but stays put as I head to the foyer.

"Jasper," Mert says carefully in my head, *"do you want to tell me what's going on?"*

"Not right now." I reach the door as a third knock vibrates the wood. The peephole reveals nothing but an empty hallway. But that doesn't mean anything. Several Myth creatures can cloak themselves for short periods of time.

"Fuck," I mutter.

"Maybe get the hunk to open it," Mert suggests.

The knock shakes the door again, followed by a low-pitched yowl. Mert and I look at each other.

"It's a cat," he whispers in my head. *"Don't open it."*

I pluck him from my shoulder and lower him to the ground. "Go find Bert."

"Jasper!"

The door rattles.

"Go," I say aloud.

Another yowl—more demanding this time.

"Fucking cat," I mutter. Straightening, I unlock the door and wrench it open. "You're as rude as your—"

Sully streaks past me in a blur of black fur and disappears into the apartment.

"—master," I finish darkly. I slam the door and stalk to the living room, where Sully weaves in and out of Vale's legs.

I fold my arms and thrust my chin toward Sully. "He can't stay. I'm allergic to cats."

Vale frowns. "No, you're not." He winces and clutches at his head. "Shit."

Sully rears up and plants his front paws on Vale's hip. The creature's golden eyes fill with concern as he buries his nose in Vale's ribs.

"I'm okay," Vale rasps, rubbing the top of the cat's head. *"Un petit mal de tête."*

The murmured French hits me squarely in the gut—a sucker punch that steals my breath more forcefully than any blow. *Just a little headache.* The words don't hurt. But hearing his voice curl around those romantic syllables is a fist to my solar plexus. Tears burn my throat.

Which makes everything worse. I reach for the anger, letting it burn away the regret and sorrow. Letting it sharpen my voice as I glare at Vale and Sully.

"The cat can't stay here. He'll scare my mice."

Vale rests a protective hand on Sully's head. "Sulien is my familiar. We're never parted."

"This will be a new experience for you, then." I look at Sully. "Get the fuck out."

"Don't speak to him that way," Vale says.

My anger flares higher. I jerk my thumb toward my chest. "This is *my* apartment, dick face. And your stupid cat isn't welcome."

Vale growls as he steps around the coffee table. "You have a filthy mouth, pixie."

I step backward. "You have no idea, *elf*."

In a blink, he pins me against the wall, his fingers tight on my throat. Brick digs into my back as six-and-a-half feet of furious elven prince stares down at me. His eyes are like chips of amber. His hot breath tickles my cheek as he bares his fangs.

"I've had enough of your insults," he growls.

My voice is a hiss as I let my gaze sear his. "No, you haven't. Not nearly enough, Vale Gentry. Not after what you—" I gag as my throat tightens.

Vale quickly moves his hand from my throat to the wall next to my head. But he doesn't move away. Slowly, the anger in his eyes fades. Bewilderment takes its place. "What I...?" He looks at my mouth, and his voice goes soft. "What did I do?"

A spell descends. My breath hitches. Sunshine and fresh-cut grass invade my lungs. Gods, his scent. *Summer.* It's cold outside, but the winter can't touch me. Not with Vale's body heat caressing my skin. Not with his golden stare locked on my mouth. Lust streaks to my dick.

"S-Stop," I whisper, unsure if I'm pleading with myself or Vale.

His dark lashes flutter as he drags his gaze up. Confusion and naked desire mingle in his eyes. "I can't," he whispers back. "You..." Beside my head, his hand curls into a fist. His lips part, and he frowns like he's concentrating hard. "Jasper," he rasps. "I feel like I know you from somewhere."

The spell breaks. With strength borne of fury, I shove him hard. He stumbles back, and surprise registers on his face for a fraction of a second before he recovers and comes at me again.

"No!" I shout, thrusting a hand out as I yank on the contract, snapping our bond and making him grunt. "Don't touch me!"

Vale stops. But he doesn't like it. His chest heaves, and a growl rumbles in his throat. Sully stands just behind him. The cat's black fur is lifted. His tail whips back and forth as he stares at me like he wants to take a bite. I can't speak to him. Elven familiar bonds are too personal. But it's clear from the look in Sully's eyes that there's no getting him out of the apartment.

I flick my wings, hiding a wince as the left one twinges. "You'll sleep on the sofa," I tell Vale. I let acid lace my tone as I tilt my head. "Or maybe you'd prefer the closet? I have a nice, big one you could hide in. Since that's where you're most comfortable."

Vale sucks in a breath.

"Did I strike a nerve?" I go to the hallway that leads to my bedroom. Vale is a silent, fuming presence as I pull blankets and a pillow from a linen closet. He watches with glittering eyes as I return to the living room and dump the bedding on the sofa next to him.

I yank hard on the contract, and Vale gasps before clenching his jaw.

"Don't leave the sofa tonight," I say. "If your cat bothers my mice, I'll hex him into the demon plane." I whirl and go to my bedroom, slamming the door hard enough to shake the pictures on the walls.

I give my bathroom door the same treatment. Then I crank the heat in the shower and strip without looking at myself in the mirror. I step into the shower and let the spray pound over my face.

When the tears come, the water washes them down the drain.

∽

I OPEN my eyes and immediately curse when sunlight blinds me.

"Go the fuck away," I mumble, squeezing my eyes shut. I fumble for the nearest pillow and press it over my face, blocking out the sun. It can't be morning already. I just shut my eyes.

Knocking drifts into the bedroom. Someone is at the front door.

A sigh builds in my chest. It's probably Horatio from two doors down. If he had a girl in his apartment last night, he almost certainly wants to talk about her. Satyrs have a reputation for playing fast and loose with romance, but they're actually—

I bolt upright, the pillow plopping into my lap as the events from the Syndicate Ball flood my head, clearing the fog of sleep. Morning sunlight pours through the window and splashes across my bed.

Vale.

My throat goes tight as I stare at my bedroom door.

Vale is out there. In my living room. On my fucking sofa.

More knocking—staccato raps guaranteed to piss off my neighbors. The witch down the hall once turned a delivery man into a toad and refused to change him back until he agreed to bring her free pizza for six months.

The knocking grows more insistent. Vale's deep voice rumbles through the door. His words are unintelligible but his tone is reassuring. Anger burns my chest. He's probably talking to Sully. He never speaks harshly to his precious cat.

The raps turn into heavy thuds. *Boom, boom, boom.*

Swearing, I fling the covers back and stride for the door. Halfway there, I scoop a pair of sweats from the floor and pull them on. My wing is better this morning, the pain faded to a barely-there ache.

The thuds continue as I leave the bedroom and make my way to the foyer, ignoring Vale and his rumpled, sexy bedhead. A pillow mark creases his cheek.

Fuck.

I yank the door open without looking through the peephole.

Izig freezes mid-knock. His dark, three-piece suit is impeccable as always. A matching bowler hat sits on his head, the sides supported by his rounded green ears.

He lowers his hand and gives me a curt nod. "I'm Izig. I serve Prince Vale of the Summer Court."

"I know who you are," I say tersely. Fucking tears burn my throat. I sniff. "What do you want?"

He blinks rapidly, confusion covering his squat, bulbous features. Then he gives his head a little shake as if he means to clear it. "I'm here to collect the prince."

I cross my arms over my chest. "Well, too fucking bad."

The ogre narrows his gaze, compressing the tiny warts around his eyes. To ogres, warts are a mark of great beauty. Izig is probably a Casanova among his people.

Right now, though, he looks like he wants to murder me. He glances at my wings, and his tone drops an octave. "Pixies are mischievous creatures."

A door down the hall opens, and a woman with frizzy black-and-purple hair pokes her head out. "Jasper? Are you causing this racket?"

"Sorry, Lydia!" I call, forcing a smile. "We'll keep it down."

She slants a look at Izig. "Did someone say prince?"

Another door opens, and a second woman sticks her head out. Snakes writhe among her pink curlers. "Prince?" She looks over her shoulder and shouts at someone inside her apartment. "Herman! We've got royalty visiting!"

"There's no royalty," I say through clenched teeth.

Lydia's eyes flash as purple as her hair. "The troll said prince. I heard it with my own ears."

Izig growls as he rounds on her. "I beg your pardon, madam. I am an *ogre*."

The witch looks him up and down. "Well, you look like a troll."

"Perhaps you should have your eyes checked."

She steps into the hall and cracks her knuckles. "Perhaps *you* should check your attitude."

"Izig?" Vale says behind me.

I whirl and bump into his chest. "What the fuck are you doing?" I hiss. "I told you not to leave the sofa."

Golden eyes gleam with triumph. "You told me not to leave the sofa *tonight*. As in, last night. Words matter, pixie."

I draw myself up. "How dare you—"

"Where's this prince?" a man's voice demands, followed by the clatter of hooves. "I wanna get a look at 'im."

Spinning, I grab Izig by the lapel and yank him into the apartment. Just as Horatio appears in the doorway, I slam the door and throw the deadbolt.

A chorus of disappointed groans drifts through the door.

"There's no prince!" I shout. Then I turn to a stunned-looking Izig and Vale and speak just above a whisper. "Unless the two of you want to get up close and personal with my neighbor's erect cock, you'll shut up and go to the living room!"

Izig and Vale exchange a look. As one, they turn and do my bidding. For a second, I sag in place, one ear cocked for noise from the hallway. When it stays quiet, I straighten and go to the living room.

Vale, Izig, and Sully stand in a clump by the sofa. Bert, Mert, and a confused-looking Luke perch on the edge of a glass-topped bureau. The two groups stare at each other like a bunch of ancient humans in the Wild Wild West.

I stop in the doorway. "Well, this is cheery. Should I fetch a tumbleweed?"

Luke turns to me. *"Did I miss something?"* he asks in my head.

"You have no idea."

He casts a wary look toward Sully. *"I don't like the cat."*

"Neither do I," I say out loud.

Izig glances toward the foyer. "Does your neighbor really walk about with his, uh, member exposed?"

I raise a brow. "You haven't spent much time around satyrs, have you?"

The ogre grunts, his cheeks growing pink under his green-hued skin. "Unseemly," he mutters to himself.

"Jasper," Vale says, stepping forward. The damn shorts look even tighter in the light of day. "You must release me from this contract. I know you feel that I've somehow wronged you, but—"

"I don't *feel* it," I say, frustration sharpening my voice. "I know it. I know what happened in Paris—" Pressure builds in my chest, choking off my words. More frustration follows, and I drag in a breath as I fling a hand toward Izig and Sully. "Ask your entourage, Your Highness." I wheeze, dizziness swamping me as I fight to spit the accusation from my mouth. The room spins, and I brace a hand against the brick wall. "They...were...there."

"Jasper!" Mert's voice echoes in my head. Suddenly, he and the others sit at my feet, their dark eyes worried.

"Allow me," a deep voice says, the sound coming from far away. Golden eyes swim in my vision, and then someone lifts me. The scent of grass fills my lungs.

Vale. I must say his name aloud, because his chest rumbles against my side.

"Easy, Jasper. You need to lie down."

"Don't," I croak. Gods, I can't let him carry me to bed. Of all the cruel things he's said and done over the past twelve or so hours, this is the worst. But I'm helpless as he shoulders his way into my bedroom and settles me on the mattress.

As he straightens, I drag air into my lungs. He stands above me, haloed in sunlight. So beautiful. A beautiful liar hellbent on convincing me we've never met.

"Why?" I gasp. "Why are you...?" My throat burns. More frustration punches through me, and I squeeze my eyes shut to block out the elven prince who refuses to stay out of my life even as he refuses to acknowledge being part of it.

The bed dips, and I open my eyes to find him frowning down at me.

"What are you doing?" I breathe.

"You're ill," he says softly.

"No, I'm not. I just hate you."

His lips twitch.

"I do," I insist. As the pressure in my chest fades, I put my forearm over my eyes and sigh. "Please go away."

"Not until I know you're well."

I pull my arm down. "Are you for real?"

"I..." An exasperated look flits through his eyes. "Yes?"

"Not literally. I meant..." I sigh. "Fuck it, I don't know what I meant." I flick a hand toward the door. "You can go. I don't like you in my room."

His lips twitch again. This time, the humor spreads to his eyes. "You're a very bossy pixie, Jasper." Abruptly, he drops his gaze to my chest. My *bare* chest. I didn't bother with a shirt, and my gray sweatpants don't offer much coverage. Right on cue, my dick decides it's perfectly fine with a half-naked Vale Gentry perched on the edge of my bed.

Vale's gaze travels down my body. The pulse in the hollow of his throat flutters faster.

My pulse picks up, too. "Stop looking at me," I say, my voice rough in my ears.

He lifts heated eyes to mine. "I can't."

Izig appears in the bedroom doorway. His dark eyes move from Vale to me and back again. "Sire, we can't linger in the Hallows. Your duties—"

"I'm aware of them," Vale says sharply. He rises and gazes down at me, his expression…bereft. "I…"

"Yes?" I ask cautiously, sitting up. Something like hope flutters at the edges of my mind. "What is it?"

He swallows. Then he shakes himself. "I have to go home. I can't miss this wedding. Liriel is waiting—" He sucks in a breath as I launch myself from the bed. Flapping my wings hard, I soar to the opposite side of the room and land as far away from him as I can get.

"Ah, yes," I snap, "your future *wife*." A bitter laugh spills from me. "How convenient for you to remember her just now."

Vale furrows his brow. And suddenly, I've had just about enough of that stupid, bewildered expression.

"Get out," I order, pointing toward the living room. Wicked inspiration strikes, and I tug on the bond I so recklessly set between us. "Go make yourself useful for once. The cleaning supplies are under the kitchen sink. Clean the whole apartment, Your Highness. Do a *merveilleux* job."

"*Un travail merveilleux*," he says quietly, correcting my Franglish.

"OUT!" I jab my finger toward the door.

Vale tosses me a scathing look as he goes. Anger flows off him. Abruptly, the sun blazes through the window, the rays so bright I throw up a hand and squint.

"And don't use your power!" I add.

Izig steps aside as Vale stalks past him.

The sun dims. The temperature in the bedroom plunges several degrees.

In the doorway, Izig holds my stare for a moment. Then he pulls the door shut, the hushed *snick* louder than a slam.

CHAPTER 10
VALE

I stand outside Jasper's room with confusion scrambling my thoughts. I wanted one last taste of freedom before the wedding. Instead, I find myself locked into a magical contract with a furious pixie who acts like he knows me.

He can't possibly know me. Can he?

A wave of vertigo crashes over me, and the hallway goes sideways.

Izig clamps a hand on my shoulder. "Sir? Is everything okay?"

"Fine," I rasp, swallowing the nausea that rises up my throat. "I'm fine." I turn toward the living room.

Izig keeps a hand on my shoulder as he guides me down the short hallway. By the time we reach the living room, the dizziness recedes enough for me to wave off his help.

"Thanks," I say. "I'm better."

His dark-green brows form a vee between equally dark eyes. "What's going on here, sir? We have to return home soon."

"I know." I rub at my forehead, where a headache lingers.

Sully prowls from the kitchen, his tail lashing from side to side.

I glance in the direction of Jasper's bedroom. *"You didn't eat any mice, did you?"*

Sully gives me a look as he jumps onto the coffee table and pushes books around to make a comfortable spot for himself. *"Please. I have higher standards than that."*

Izig crosses his arms over his broad chest. "What's this contract you spoke to the pixie about?"

Grimacing, I lower my voice and relay last night's events, starting with facing Jasper on the platform and ending with him ordering me to clean. "So I'm stuck," I finish. "Worse, I have to do everything Jasper says. I'm tethered to him somehow. I know it sounds crazy."

Izig grunts. "Sounds like the consequences of your actions. How many times have I told you brawling was going to get you into trouble?"

A growl rumbles from me. "You overstep, Izig." When he pales under his green-tinged skin, guilt rises. I've never been one to lord my authority over my household. I won't do it now just because I'm frustrated. "You've told me at least two thousand times, old friend," I tack on more gently. "And I should have listened."

Sully leans forward and runs his whiskers over my bare leg. I reach down and scratch absently between his ears.

Izig's brow furrows as he stares at the hallway leading to Jasper's bedroom. He turns his gaze back to me. "I don't understand. Who is this pixie?"

"You don't know?"

My butler frowns. "No. Should I?"

Exasperation swells in my chest as I shove a hand through my hair. "He acts like you should. Like *I* should. And he's furious."

"I noticed," Izig mutters. He looks at the rumpled sofa. "You spent the night here. Did you and he—"

"No," I say quickly. "Nothing like that." Even as I say it, an ache blossoms within me.

No, not an ache. Longing.

"You're certain you can't get out of this contract?" Izig asks.

"I was hoping you'd know of a way."

He grunts. "If I did, I would have already told you."

I rub a hand over my mouth. "Shit."

He hesitates.

I lower my hand. "What?"

"Nothing." He waits a beat. "It's just that the pixie mentioned Paris. And the more I think about it, maybe he *does* seem familiar. But I —" He doubles over and clutches at his stomach.

I grab his shoulder, worry replacing my anger. "What's wrong?"

Izig grunts and straightens, his face a mask of discomfort. "Just nauseated, sire. It hit me out of nowhere. Must be something I ate."

"Or maybe something in the contract," I mutter.

Sully jumps down from the table and rubs his flank along Izig's starched pant legs. I hide a smile at the thought of Izig taking a lint roller to them later. As they both look up at me, I school my features into a confident expression I'm not quite sure I feel.

"I'll think of a way out of this, don't worry. In the meantime, I'll clean like Jasper ordered. Maybe it'll put him in a better mood, and we can talk about the contract without it dissolving into an argument." My mind helpfully supplies me with a vision of Jasper on his bed, his dick tenting the front of his sweatpants.

I shove the image from my head and go to the kitchen, where I squat in front of the sink and open the cabinet. The scent of bleach fills my nose. A stack of sponges sits next to a variety of bottles filled with brightly colored liquid. "How much cleaning does he do?" I murmur, letting my gaze roam the options.

Blue.

Blue is a clean color, right?

Grabbing a sponge and the blue bottle, I stand and nudge the cabinet shut with my foot.

In the living room, Izig shakes his head. "That's oven cleaner, sir." He moves into the kitchen and extends his hand. "Allow me to help."

I hold the bottle of cleaner against my chest. "Jasper commanded me, Izig. And it wouldn't surprise me if he objected to your help. I don't want to give him any further reason to argue."

Izig nods, but reluctance is stamped all over his face. "At least let me ensure you don't harm yourself, sir." He casts a wary look at the hallway leading to Jasper's bedroom. "Or the pixie's upholstery."

I stand back so Izig can kneel before the cabinet. He rummages for a moment, then rises with a big bottle of purple liquid in his hand. "This should do the job."

I eye the bottle. "Are you sure? There's a skull and crossbones on the side."

Izig's expression turns mild. "Do you want to kill the germs or play with them, sir?"

Despite the circumstances, I manage a smile. "I bow to your expertise," I say, taking the bottle from him.

"There's a first time for everything," he murmurs.

The smile tugs harder at my mouth. I tip my head toward the refrigerator. "You and Sully haven't had breakfast. There's bound to be something edible in there. Go eat on the terrace. I'll take care of things in here."

"You haven't eaten, either," Izig says.

"I'm not hungry."

Doubt shades his eyes. "If you're certain…"

"*Oui. Je suis certain.*" Yes. I'm certain.

Izig's slight smile mirrors my own. "*D'accord,*" he says softly. All right. He finds a plate of scones in the fridge and carries them to the terrace. Sully looks at me like he wants to argue, but I nudge him through our bond, and he follows Izig.

Alone in Jasper's kitchen, I let my gaze stray to the hallway. Nothing but a few steps and a bedroom door separate us. I could walk into his room and demand answers. Insist that he break this silly contract. But he seems determined to punish me. Judging from the intensity of his anger, he believes I hurt him terribly. His fury is by turns absurd and heart-wrenching. It kindles my own anger, but it also draws me.

And it's no wonder. The pixie is captivating. Under other circumstances, I'd do whatever it takes to—

A fresh wave of nausea makes me grip the edge of the counter. Saliva fills my mouth as I take deep breaths and will the sickness to go away. Probably, I should have eaten with Izig and Sully. But I'm not sure I can keep anything down. Puking on Jasper's floor is unlikely to convince him to see reason.

Sighing, I spray lavender-scented cleaner on the countertop and wipe it down. A crashing sound comes from Jasper's room, followed by a curse. I stare into the hallway for a moment before misting the sink.

Another crash. Another muffled curse.

I go to Jasper's door and rap it with the back of my knuckles. "Everything alright?"

Jasper's loud, irritated-sounding sigh drifts through the door. "Everything's fine. Are you cleaning?"

I bite back the angry retort that springs to my tongue. "Yes." I put my ear to the door. "What's going on in there?"

Feet stomp toward me. I back up just as the swings open and Jasper appears, his wings fluttering rapidly at his back. One is still slightly bent and stained a dark color.

"I see you're busy cleaning," he says in a tone thick with sarcasm.

"What are you doing in here?" I lean to the side so I can look past him. A heavy wardrobe partially blocks the window.

"Nothing," he says, shifting to obscure my view of the bedroom. "What do you want?" He flicks his wings behind him in an irritated gesture—and doesn't quite hide his wince.

"Your wing," I murmur. I bend and set the cleaner on the floor. Jasper narrows his eyes when I straighten and reach for his wing.

He jerks it out of range. "Don't touch that."

"It's still bent."

"It's just bruised."

"Yes, but—"

"I'm not interested in your opinion on my wing, Vale." His voice is dismissive and cold—the same tone Zaphira regularly uses with me. *Your father will never know, Abelin.*

The memory of my stepmother's voice makes my headache pound harder, the pain blossoming into a migraine. What will my father never know?

Icicles on the ceiling.

Blood on marble.

Ybris slithering across the floor.

A window covered with drapes that block out the sun.

"Why are you staring?"

Jasper's question yanks me from my thoughts.

My heart thumps as I hold his gaze. "You reminded me of someone for a moment," I say after a second. "Someone back home."

"Ah, so you're a giant asshole there, too?" His mouth goes tight. "What a shock."

My head fills with visions of collaring his pretty throat and pressing him hard to the door. We're both soaked with rain, his clothing translucent from it. He teases me with a sultry pout, his eyes hooded with desire.

I swallow hard as my dick presses painfully against the front of my shorts.

Jasper tenses.

The air shifts, energy crackling in the scant space between us.

"Jasper." My voice is rough. He's so beautifully tempting—even if he hates me for some reason.

His blue gaze bores into mine. His scowl fades as his lashes flutter. When his plump lips part, I imagine feeding my cock between them. He's—

"Stop looking at me like that," he whispers.

"Like what?"

"Like you're interested."

His words are a punch to the gut.

"I find you entrancing," I say, bringing my hand to rest on the doorframe. "Enchanting. Fascinating. I don't want to fight with you, Jasper."

His scowl snaps back into place. He jerks his head toward the living room. "Floor needs mopping. Start there. I'll supervise." He shoves past me and goes to the living room. When I enter a second later, he's seated on the sofa.

Sully pokes his head inside from the terrace. He eyes Jasper before speaking through our bond. *"Looks like it's going well."*

I grit my teeth. *"I'm handling it."*

Jasper plucks a book from the coffee table and begins flipping through the pages. "Mop's in the closet next to the fridge."

Anger sparks in my veins. "I don't—" The bond snaps sharply in my chest, yanking me sideways. I stagger, then right myself and glare at Jasper.

A wicked smile spreads on his face as he continues flipping pages. "Get moving, Your Highness," he says without looking up.

Reining in my anger, I go to the closet.

Ten awkward minutes later, I wring the mop out under Jasper's watchful supervision. He examines his nails, reads his book, does anything to avoid my gaze. But the moment I don't clean something well enough, he's quick to point it out. Izig and Sully watch quietly from the terrace doorway.

"Missed a spot," Jasper says for the hundredth time, pointing to an invisible speck of dust on the floor.

Clenching my jaw, I go to it and swish the mop over the hardwood. Sully wanders in from the terrace and hops onto the coffee table. Out of the corner of my eye, I watch as he and Jasper engage in a lengthy staring contest. The moment Jasper lowers his gaze to his book, Sully slowly reaches out a paw and pushes one of the other books off the table.

Jasper jerks his head up and glares at my familiar. Sully blinks at him with a lazy expression.

"Sulien..." I warn through our bond.

"It was in my way," he replies.

"You're not helping."

He folds his paws under him atop the stack of books and purrs loudly, his eyes sliding shut. *"The pixie is mistreating you."*

Still glaring at Sully, Jasper licks his finger and turns a page.

"Let me deal with him," I say, returning to my mopping. I lose track of time as I perform the repetitive chore: mop, wring out dirty water, mop, wring out dirty water. On and on it goes, until my back aches and sweat prickles under my arms. But I have to admit the floor looks nice. The hardwood gleams, and the scent of lemon cleaner fills the air. I lean on the mop and take a second to admire it.

"Missed a spot," Jasper calls.

I stab the mop into the bucket and face him. "I'm done. This is ridiculous. I hoped you'd cool down and we could talk about this contract."

He quickly schools a surprised look into a now-familiar scowl. "There's nothing to talk about."

"Tell me why you think you know me." My head throbs, but I ignore it. "Tell me how you know where I live. What's going on?"

Frustration laces my tone as my voice rises.

Jasper jumps to his feet and stalks toward me. But he slips on the wet floor and loses his balance. I spring forward as he windmills his arms, and we crash into each other and start to fall. Instinct kicks in, and I spin us at the last second so I can take the brunt of the impact on my back. Jasper sprawls on top of me, his lithe body pressed to mine from shoulder to thigh. Our legs tangle together. The tip of his bruised wing flutters next to my head.

And his deep blue eyes blink an inch from mine. His breath flutters over my lips.

Time slows. For a moment, we gaze at each other, neither of us moving. His hips press into mine. And he's hard.

That makes two of us.

A groan rises in my throat. My hips lift of their own accord, my erection brushing his.

His nostrils flare. He shoves against my chest, trying to push away.

I tighten my arms, trapping him against me. When he groans and rocks his hips against mine, lust fires hot under my skin. Before I can think better of it, I run a hand down his side and up under his shirt.

Because I *need* to feel him. As my palm touches his smooth, warm skin, a moan rips from me.

Home. He's like coming *home*.

"What are you doing?" He's stiff in my arms, but he doesn't try to move off me.

"Keeping you from busting your ass," I murmur, staring at his mouth. He doesn't have fangs like mine, but his white teeth look sharp enough. He could inflict some damage with his bite…but it would be worth it if he followed it up with a kiss from those pouty, soft-looking lips.

"What do you taste like?" I whisper, blood pounding to my cock.

He jolts in my arms. "As if you don't already know, you ass—"

His insult cuts off as I grip his throat and roll us so he's pinned beneath me. As anger flashes in his eyes, I move my hand to the hardwood beside his head. I give him my full weight, and he makes a strangled, needy sound as our hips meet again.

He shoves against my chest, but I cover one of his hands with mine.

I guide it along my pec, dragging his warm palm over my sun tattoo. When he sucks in a breath, I rise to my knees between his spread legs and move his hand lower, trailing it down the dips and curves of my abs. As he traces the rays that fan across my stomach, fury fades from his expression.

Something darker replaces it. Something hungry and needy. Something that calls to my primal instinct to hunt, chase, and conquer.

I grab his other hand and place it beside the first, relishing the feel of his slim fingers exploring and touching me.

"You feel good," I grit out. "Perfect."

His eyes darken to sapphire.

"I want to kiss you," I say.

A pained look replaces the hunger. He nips at his lower lip. His eyes fill with tears.

Something shatters in my chest. It's like I'm a poisoned drink of water, and he's dying of thirst but knows better than to drink from me.

I bring his hands together and hold them over my heart. "How did I hurt you?" Pain lances my skull, and I suck in a sharp breath as I fight to ignore it. "Tell me, please. I can't stand the way you're looking at me."

"How am I looking at you?" he asks, his voice thick with tears.

"Like I'm the source of all that's wrong in your world."

Pain fills his eyes, the blue depths as bruised as his wing. The bluster and snark are gone, replaced with hurt so deep it reaches into my chest and squeezes my heart.

"Please tell me that's not true," I say.

"Vale, how can you ask that of me when you insist on pretending we—" His words end in a choked gurgle. He clamps his jaw shut, grief and a spark of fear in his eyes.

"What's wrong?" I demand, leaning over him and bringing the back of my hand to his forehead. "Are you hurt?"

He pushes my hand away. "You hurt me every second you're here."

My gut clenches. Unable to help myself, I stroke a lock of platinum hair away from his face. "Don't say that."

The pointed tip of his ear shivers. "I'm so stupid," he murmurs as if talking to himself.

The hint of sass in his voice makes it hard not to smile. For all his glares and hateful comments, something tells me he's not as prickly as he seems. The second the thought materializes, déjà vu slams into me, stealing my breath.

"No, you're not," I say, *knowing* it's true. "You're stunning, and I can't stop looking at you."

Jasper swats my hand away. "Stop, Vale. Just stop it. Don't fucking say that shit!" When I reach for him again, he shoves my chest hard. "Don't touch me!"

Confusion pummels me. I shift backward, pain lancing through me as he flits to his feet.

"Help me understand," I plead, standing and following as he moves toward his bedroom. "How did I hurt you, Jasper? Tell me!"

He rounds on me with wide eyes. "How *didn't* you hurt me? You —" He grits his teeth, and his face goes red like he's struggling to get the words out. Like he's too furious to speak. Then he drags in a big breath and speaks in a rush. "You broke me in Paris. And now you're rubbing salt in the wound." He strides to his room and slams the door.

Izig and Sully are frozen in the terrace doorway.

I stare at Jasper's door. Then I grab the mop, stalk to the kitchen, and dump the dirty water.

I don't know how to fix this. I don't know if I even can.

How did I break a man I've never met?

And why do I feel shattered into a million pieces, too?

CHAPTER 11
JASPER

I spend the rest of the day in my bedroom—and I *don't* listen for every little sound that comes from the living room. I don't think about elven princes or their mind games. I pay no attention to the murmur of masculine voices, and I don't strain for the deeper one —that soft, velvet rumble that streaks straight to my dick.

"Fuck," I whisper, my elbows on the balcony railing outside my bedroom. The terrace extends the full length of my apartment. Yet another reason I pay a small fortune for the privilege of living here.

I'm thankful for it now as I watch the sun sink behind the Old Manhattan skyline. *Good. Go away.* Snowflakes drift through the air. Gray clouds hover in the sky, the threat of a storm hanging like a weight over the city. The railing is icy through the sleeves of the thin shirt I put on after my cold shower—which I definitely did not take to cool the lust I felt after falling on top of a certain lying asshole.

Bert runs along the railing, his steps sure and quick. He leaps onto my shoulder and stares at the setting sun.

"Nice of you to show up," I say through our bond.

He stiffens. *"Did I go somewhere?"*

I put a hand to my shoulder so he can climb onto it. Turning from the railing, I lower him to a nearby table. *"You haven't said a word about*

Vale." Hurt rises, and it leaks into my mental voice. *"You've watched me flounder for eight months, and you've said nothing. Now he's here and acting like—"* The hurt swells, climbing into my throat and strangling my bond with Bert.

He winces.

"Sorry," I say aloud, rubbing a finger between his ears. He hangs his head and gives a mournful-sounding squeak.

"I'm the sorry one," he says quietly in my mind. *"You're right. I haven't been a good friend."*

"That's not true," I murmur.

"Yes, it is." He curls his tail around his furry hindquarters. *"I suck."*

"No, you don't." I flick his whiskers. *"I mean, you definitely suck when you chew through electrical cords. And the wood trim in the foyer."*

"And the table legs."

"Right," I say in his head. *"I forgot about those."*

He waves a paw in front of his face. *"It's a dental thing."*

"Totally get it."

"No one's perfect," he says, a smile in his eyes.

The tension drains from our bond, and I smile back. "Not even a little bit," I say out loud. "But I still love you."

"Gross. I love you, too."

We smile at each other for a long moment. Then he tips his head toward my bedroom. *"Did you push the wardrobe in front of the window?"*

"Yeah. I was trying to block the sun."

Bert's expression goes solemn. *"But it didn't work?"*

I sigh as I gaze over the city. "No," I say out loud. "It was too bright to be muffled."

He falls silent again. Then he looks toward the end of the terrace that borders the living room. *"So, what are you gonna do?"*

Another sigh lifts my chest. *"I don't know."* I give a humorless laugh and speak out loud. "I'm a prisoner in my own bedroom."

Bert's shoulders slump. Before either of us can say anything more, a pigeon swoops to the terrace and perches on the balcony.

"Hey, Lyle," I say. "How's it going?"

Lyle flutters his wings in the pigeon version of a shrug. *"Oh, you know, up and down."*

I look at Bert, who shakes his head. *"I'm not saying it."*

Lyle laughs, the sound emerging as a series of broken coos.

"Fine," I say on a sigh, "I'll say it." I give Lyle a pointed look, and he delivers the punchline with me: *"Like a bird."*

The carrier pigeon slaps one gray wing against his leg as he coos loudly.

Bert stares at Lyle like he'd love to push him off the balcony. "Yeah, that one never gets old."

"Lighten up, Bertram," Lyle says, his mental voice thick with an Old Brooklyn accent. He turns a sly look on me. *"Got a message for you, Jasper. Sloan is in town. He saw what went down at the Syndicate Ball and wants to meet for drinks."*

I snort. "You mean he wants to meet for gossip."

Lyle shrugs again. *"Is there a difference?"*

Good point. And Sloan is fun. Demons are always a good time. We dated a few years ago before we both realized we wanted different things. But we parted amicably.

Lyle coos, his orange eyes sweeping around the terrace. *"So you've got an elven prince locked in a magical contract, huh? Where is he?"*

"None of your business," Bert says, leaping from the table to the railing. He lands inches from Lyle's claws, forcing the pigeon to scramble backward.

"Hey!" Lyle flaps his wings and resettles. *"I'm standing here."*

"You mean squatting," Bert says.

Lyle draws himself up. *"It's called* alighting, *and it's very elegant."*

Bert takes a menacing step forward.

"All right, take it easy," I say, putting a hand between them. When Bert withdraws with a glower, I turn to Lyle. "Where does Sloan want to meet?"

"Al's Place in the East Village."

The last of the sun's rays disappear behind the towers of Old Manhattan. The temperature plunges, winter air swirling.

I meet Lyle's orange gaze. *"Tell him I'll see him there."*

Minutes later, I enter the living room with an armful of clothes. Vale rises from the sofa with a wary look. Sully jumps from the rolled arm and settles at Vale's feet. At first, I don't see Izig. Then I notice him in the hallway between the living room and the foyer, his bulky body as still as a statue.

I frown. "Have you been standing there all day?"

The ogre's expression is as inscrutable as ever. "I'm guarding the door. The prince's safety is paramount."

I go to the armchair angled near the sofa and dump the clothes on it. "Well, you can take a break and help His Royal Highness put some clothes on." I stride toward the foyer. "I'm going out," I toss over my shoulder.

"Where are you going?" Vale demands, a curious catch in his voice.

When I stop and face him, his golden gaze is locked on my hip, where the edge of a red thong—which I did *not* wear to show him what he can't have—peeks above my skinny jeans. I lift my brows. "I don't see how that's any of your concern."

His jaw tightens. He drags his eyes up to mine, and for a moment it looks like he'll challenge me. Then he gestures to the clothes. "These are too big for you."

"No kidding." I examine my nails. "They belonged to an ex. He left them behind after I threw him out."

Vale's voice goes soft. "You want me to wear your ex-boyfriend's castoffs?"

Goosebumps lift on my skin. His tone is soft, but the edge within it is as sharp as steel. He could flatten me. Pin me down again and stretch that muscled body over mine. I wouldn't hate it. Gods, even now—even knowing what an absolute asshole he is—I crave him.

And that won't do. Whatever it takes, I've got to get him out of my head. Then I can get him out of my home—and my life—for good.

Forcing a smile, I wave a hand around the room. "I think we can all agree we'd like you to wear *something*." I turn and move toward the foyer. Halfway down the hall, I pause and turn back. "Don't leave." I tap the bond, and Vale grunts. His eyes glitter.

"That's an order," I add, then I spin and walk away, his golden stare like a weight between my shoulder blades.

∼

Two hours later, I grimace as Sloan launches into yet another story about a wild party he attended at Wotan's club, Cauchemar.

"You would have loved it," he says, leaning over the table. A plate of onion rings sits untouched between us. Sloan's thick fingers curl around the base of his longneck bottle as he chatters on, his white fangs flashing in a handsome face I used to admire. The demon is undeniably hot. But every time my gaze lands on his dark curls, golden-brown waves take their place.

Around us, Al's Place hums with conversation punctuated by occasional bursts of laughter. Behind the bar, Al slings drinks, his tentacles writhing from under a blue velvet jacket. Bert would definitely have something to say about it, but I left him at home to make sure Mert and Luke steer clear of Sully.

Under the table, Sloan nudges my foot with his. "Hey, babe. You listening?"

I move my foot away. "Sorry." I pluck a string of seaweed from my Long Island Iced Tea and grimace as I set it aside. "I wish Al would find another garnish." I plaster a smile on my face as I meet Sloan's green gaze. "Krakens, am I right?"

Sloan's smile doesn't reach his eyes. He takes another pull of his beer before settling back in his chair. "You still haven't told me what's going on with this prince of yours."

"He's not mine." I force a shrug even as aggravation tightens my shoulders. "And there's not much to say."

"Really? People couldn't stop talking about it at the Ball last night." Sloan shifts forward again, his dark horns catching the light. "You and the prince looked…cozy up there."

"Well, we weren't." My voice rises without my permission, the last word lifting over the noise of the bar. Several people turn toward me, curiosity on their faces.

Sloan raises both hands as he laughs softly. "Sorry, man. I didn't mean to pry." He grins, and his green eyes make a leisurely trip down my body. "I guess I'm just jealous. You and I had a lot of fun together."

My nape heats, aggravation turning to discomfort. Coming out tonight was a mistake. It's been obvious from the start that Sloan doesn't want to reminisce. He wants to hook up. And maybe I thought I wanted that, too.

But now, my skin crawls at the thought of spending the night in his bed. At having his thick-fingered hands on me.

Unbidden, my mind fills with images of strong, tanned hands stroking over my skin. Wrapping around my cock and pulling just so—just enough force to drag me right to the edge without letting me fall over it.

"I have to go," I blurt, standing so abruptly my chair rocks onto its back legs. I grab it before it can fall.

In a blink, Sloan stands before me, his broad chest brushing my arm. "You didn't even finish your drink."

I dig into my pocket, then toss a pair of bills onto the table. "I know. Just not feeling it tonight." I step back just as Sloan grabs my arm.

His fingers tighten on my bicep as his green eyes flash neon bright. "I don't believe that for a second," he says, his beer-scented breath wafting over my face. He pulls me against him, letting me feel his erection as his lips quirk in a suggestive smile. "You're never not feeling it, babe."

I tug at his grip and promptly get nowhere. "Let me go, Sloan."

"Come home with me."

"Not tonight."

He dips his chin, his lips aimed at my mouth. When I turn my head at the last second, he plants a sloppy kiss on the side of my neck. "Damn, Jasper, you're as hot as ever," he rasps in my ear. "I like this little game."

Tugging harder, I let my outrage flow down my arm to my hand. I curl my fingers, ready to hex the shit out of him. "It's not a game. Let me go or you'll be itching for a week."

He lifts his head. His suggestive smile fades as his expression hardens. "You met me tonight. And now you're running off?"

"That's exactly right," I say, looking him straight in the eye. "The answer is no."

He bares his teeth. "I don't think so, you little dick tease."

Anger explodes in my chest.

At the same moment, light explodes inside the bar. It sears my eyes, and I stumble back as Sloan releases me and throws his arms up.

"What the fuck?" he cries, banging into the table and setting beer bottles trembling. Gasps and shouts fill the bar. Chairs clatter to the floor.

The light dims—and then concentrates on Sloan, who hunches over as the fat yellow beam forces him backward. He cries out again as he stumbles to the wall and falls against it.

Slowly, the source of the light comes into view. My breath seizes in my lungs.

Vale.

He stands a dozen feet away, his body lit up like the sun. Light flows from the center of his chest, the beam streaming from under the black T-shirt that fit my ex-boyfriend just fine but strains across Vale's thick, round pecs. Muscles bunch as he stalks forward, grips Sloan by the shoulder, and slams him into the wall.

"I believe the gentleman told you no," Vale growls, sounding more inhuman than I've ever heard him. His glamour drops like a curtain, revealing the shimmering elven prince with eyes like molten sunlight.

Sloan quakes under Vale's grip. "I-I'm sorry."

Without taking his eyes off Sloan, Vale jerks his head toward me. "Don't apologize to me. Apologize to him."

"Sorry!" Sloan turns frightened eyes to me. "I'm sorry, Jasper. It won't happen again."

Vale shoves the demon more forcefully against the wall. Sloan grunts as an ominous *crunch* splits the air. Vale leans in and flashes his fangs. "If you ever speak to Jasper again, if you even *think* about glancing in his direction, I will find you. No matter how long it takes or how many oceans I have to cross, I will hunt you down and end you. Do you understand?"

"Yes," Sloan says weakly. His lashes flutter as he draws a shaky breath. "I-I understand."

Vale steps back swiftly. Sloan darts around him and leaves the bar in a blur.

For a moment, no one moves. Vale rolls his head like a boxer stretching in the ring.

The sun winks out, and his glamour slams back into place.

"You!" Al lumbers around the bar and points a thick tentacle at Vale. Another tentacle pokes the air in my direction. "And you!"

Shock jolts me. I touch my chest. "Me?"

"Yeah, Lilygully," the kraken says, displeasure in his eyes. "Take your boyfriend and get out of here."

"He's not my boyfriend."

Al props his humanoid hands on his hips. "I don't give a fuck if he's your grandmother, he put a dent in my wall." The kraken jerks a thumb toward the door. "Both of you get out before I bounce you myself."

Laughter ripples through the bar. Suddenly, I realize everyone is staring, curious gazes moving from Vale to me. In one corner, a woman puts her lips to her companion's ear and whispers furiously.

Al starts toward me.

"I'm going!" Face flaming, I head for the door. Vale falls into step just behind me. I keep my head down and my wings folded close to my body as I shove the heavy door open.

Thunder greets me as I step onto the pavement. The scent of ozone hits my nose.

"Are you all right?" Vale asks at my back.

I whirl just as the door closes behind him, cutting off the noise from the bar.

"What the fuck?" I say on a near shout. "I told you to stay in the apartment."

Vale shakes his head. "You said *don't leave*. That could mean anything, including don't leave the Hallows."

"Well, I wish you would!"

Pain flits through his eyes. The electric bulb above the bar's painted sign flickers as it fights a losing battle with magic. Vale glances at it, and the light swells. In the distance, lightning forks across the sky. A second later, thunder booms.

Vale steps closer. "I don't think you mean that," he rumbles. "And anyway, you need me around."

I suck in a breath—and get a lungful of his scent. It makes me want to moan, so I cover my reaction by raising my voice. "I can take care of myself, you arrogant prick!"

"Of course," he growls, stepping so close we're practically nose to nose. "Because you were doing such a fine job of it in there."

"I was doing fine until you showed up!" I shove him. "I'm not an ancient, muscle-bound prince who beams sunshine out his ass, but I've managed to stay alive this long. And I've fucked about a thousand more guys than you, so back off."

Something savage flashes in his eyes. "If I had my way, you'd never fuck anyone else again."

Lightning flashes. The skies open, and rain falls in sheets.

I gasp as it soaks my hair and rolls down my neck. *Just like that first night in Paris.*

Vale stares at me, rain running down his face. His shoulders rise and fall as he pants like he just finished a sprint.

My heart pounds. I'm poised on the edge of a cliff. And I'm going to fall.

But I'm not sure I care. I step into him, bringing our faces a hair's breadth apart as I let venom soak my voice. "You don't need me, Your Highness. If you want to fuck so badly, you can run home and fuck your wife."

Lightning flashes, illuminating the barely leashed anger in Vale's eyes. "I don't have a wife. I don't want a wife." He drags in a breath. "Damn you, I want…" He blinks raindrops from his lashes as he drifts off.

"What?" I whisper. And I *know* better. I shouldn't ask what he wants. He's made it clear he doesn't want me. But I'm powerless where he's concerned. From the beginning, he has disarmed me.

Vale looks at me like someone just tore his heart from his chest. "Jasper," he rasps.

I swallow the tears that clog my throat. "Vale."

In one movement, he grabs me and pushes me against the side of the bar.

And then his lips are on mine. He cups my face in his big hands and plunders my mouth, kissing me and kissing me like he'll die if he doesn't. He plunges his tongue deep. Strokes it along mine before biting at my lips, my tongue, the side of my neck. He returns his mouth to mine and whimpers—the sound so broken and desperate it shakes something apart inside me. Cracks the veneer I painted over my heart. He kisses me, tasting of rain and summer and Paris under a canopy of stars.

"I don't want anyone else," he says hoarsely. "I only want you."

The veneer crumbles, leaving only my bruised and broken heart. I shove him away, and I sag against the side of the bar as rain soaks me to the skin.

Vale stands on the sidewalk, his mouth swollen from our kiss. He shivers as frigid rain plasters his shirt to his chest.

It's not summer anymore. It's winter. How could I forget?

I push away from the wall, tremors racking me. "You can't say shit like that to me," I croak.

"I'm sorry." He opens his mouth. Shuts it. Passes a shaking hand over his face and looks so lost and bewildered I can almost believe the act.

Almost.

Gothel owes me a favor. He's one of the oldest beings in the world. If it's possible to break the contract from the Brawl, he'll know how to do it.

"I'm going home," I tell Vale. I yank on the bond, and anger leaps into his eyes.

Good.

"Stay ten steps behind me and don't speak," I say. As the anger in Vale's gaze grows, I start toward home. When he falls into step behind me, I stop and look over my shoulder. "Tomorrow, I'm taking you to someone who can rid us of this contract. And then I never want to see you again."

CHAPTER 12
VALE

"Chilly out there today."

I look up from the corner of the elevator to see Gothel's right hand man, Raoul, staring at me. Izig is a solid presence at my side. Sully sits at my feet with his tail curled around my calf. Jasper stands in the opposite corner of the tiny space, his hard gaze on the silver doors as we speed toward the upper levels of Gothel's headquarters. The rapid ascent makes my migraine—which I haven't been able to shake—worse than ever.

Jasper hasn't looked at me once since we left his apartment. He hasn't spoken to me, either, unless filtering instructions through Izig counts. *"Please tell Prince Vale to walk faster. The sooner we get to the Sky Syndicate, the better."*

When Izig dutifully repeated the order, I cut him off. *"There's nothing wrong with my hearing, Jasper."*

I got no response.

Raoul clears his throat, yanking me back to the present.

"Uh, yes," I say, turning my gaze to the diminutive grotesque. "It's a cold one." But not as cold as a certain pixie who hates my guts.

A bell chimes, and the doors slide open. Raoul leads us from the elevator, the spade-shaped tip of his tail bobbing. My head throbs harder with every step, and I clench my jaw against the pain.

Moments later, we enter Gothel's office. The scent of cigars hits my nose as the big gargoyle rises from his desk. But he's not alone.

Another large male sits on the edge of the polished surface, a cigar between his fingers. Green eyes gleam in a handsome face. A green stud winks in the man's ear. More gemstones glitter on his fingers. A three-piece suit hugs his powerful body. But it's the green flames flickering among his dark, wavy hair that let me know exactly who he is.

This can only be Fuoco of House Drakoni, Lord of the Fire Syndicate. We've never met, but his reputation precedes him. So do whispers of immense power.

"Thank you, Raoul," Gothel says, rounding his desk. As the grotesque disappears in a cloud of smoke, the gargoyle looks between me and Jasper with a troubled expression. "The whole Hallows is buzzing with news of what happened at the Syndicate Ball." He looks at Jasper and lowers his voice. "King Nylian of the Summer Court is a formidable power, Jasper. He won't like hearing you've locked his heir in a magical contract."

Jasper lifts his chin. "That's why I'm here. I want to annul it."

Gothel frowns. "You mean rescind it."

"Whatever."

Fuoco stares at Jasper intently. Smoke curls from the cigar poised between his fingers, but he pays it no mind. His green eyes narrow as Jasper continues speaking, his voice growing thick with emotion.

"I was h-hasty when I claimed Vale as my boon."

Gothel glances at me with a startled look. "You know Prince Vale?"

Jasper opens his mouth. "I—" He seems to wrestle with himself as if he's searching for the right words. After a second, he makes a frustrated sound. "It doesn't matter. I don't *want* to know him."

Bert pokes his head from Jasper's breast pocket. Sniffing, Jasper strokes the mouse's whiskers.

Fuoco shifts his gaze to me. His nostrils flare. The flames in his hair dance higher.

My nape tingles. I look away, but the dragon lord's stare is a palpable weight. Beside me, Izig shuffles his feet.

"The dragon is staring at you," Sully says in my head.

"I know."

Jasper and Gothel continue their conversation. Their voices fade into the background as I endure the dragon's scrutiny. Jasper's tone is increasingly agitated. Gothel's voice stays at a low, gravelly rumble. But I can't follow the discussion with my heart pounding and knives stabbing into my skull. Nausea roils my gut. Despite the office's pleasant temperature, a cold sweat breaks out over my skin. I swipe at my clammy forehead.

"So, can you break the contract?" Jasper demands, his voice tight to the point of snapping.

"I don't know," Gothel says.

Jasper's wings beat the air, sending cigar smoke wafting around me. "That's not good enough! I need—"

"Wait," a deep voice says.

Jasper clamps his mouth shut. Bert ducks back into his pocket.

Fuoco eases off Gothel's desk. Power crackles around the room as he crosses to Jasper. The dragon lord's brilliant green eyes narrow as he tips Jasper's chin up with a glittering nail. Fuoco's expression goes soft, almost affectionate. "What happened in Paris, my friend? When I left you there, you were full of life. The male who returned home is not the same."

Jasper's lower lip trembles, and he looks away. Fuoco drops his hand and waits.

A tear slides down Jasper's cheek. "I— In Paris, we spent— We—" He makes a flustered sound as he pinches the bridge of his nose. "I'm sorry. It's difficult to talk about this."

Fuoco's gaze sharpens. "Difficult or impossible?"

Jasper lowers his hand. He opens his mouth. Shuts it. Bert reemerges, and he and Jasper stare at each other. "Yeah," Jasper says slowly, "we've both had a hard time discussing it. Ever since"—he inhales sharply as he looks at Fuoco—"I got back."

The room stills. A strange awareness fills the air as everyone stares at Jasper…then me.

Fuoco studies Jasper for a long moment. "Let's try this. When I ask you a question, don't try to answer. Just nod for *yes* and shake your head for *no*."

"Okay."

The dragon lord smiles. "No speech. Just gestures. You spent time in Paris this past spring?"

Jasper nods.

"Mmm," Fuoco says. "Did you meet someone new there?"

Jasper closes his eyes on a long blink. He nods.

"And you spent time with this person?"

Nod.

"You liked this person?"

Nod.

"And he liked you?"

A pained, breathless sound escapes Jasper's lips. He nods.

Fuoco's voice softens. "Was this person Prince Vale?"

Jasper nods.

The dragon lord looks at me, his green eyes gleaming more brightly than anything in the room. I fight the urge to squirm under his penetrating stare, which pins me like a butterfly on a mat.

Finally, he turns back to Jasper. "Something bad happened in Paris?"

Jasper nods, misery in his eyes.

"Prince Vale did something bad?"

Another nod.

My heart thumps faster. The pain in my head flares with every beat.

Fuoco touches Jasper's jaw, and his voice goes gentle. "You fell in love with Vale in Paris. And he fell in love with you."

Jasper nods once. Pale pink dust sifts slowly from his wings, which droop toward the floor.

"But something happened to that love," Fuoco says quietly.

Jasper nods.

"Because Prince Vale won't speak to you now?"

Jasper hesitates. Then he shakes his head.

"Because you don't want to be with him."

My heart skips a beat. I lean forward, poised on the edge of a cliff as I wait for Jasper's answer.

He shakes his head. *Wrong*. He *does* want to be with me.

Fuoco leans forward and sniffs at the air around Jasper.

Jasper stiffens. "What are you doing?" he asks hoarsely.

"Scenting you."

"Why?"

Fuoco gives him a patient look. "You know all about my power, Jasper. Allow me to use it."

Jasper's gaze lands briefly on mine. A frown appears between his eyes before he turns to Fuoco. "Go ahead."

The dragon lord walks a circle around him, staring him up and down before leaning in to sniff at his neck. I shove down a possessive snarl when his nose brushes the skin under Jasper's ear.

Several excruciatingly silent minutes later, Fuoco straightens. "Prince Vale doesn't remember you. And when you try to speak of it, you find that you can't."

Jasper's lips part. He nods.

Fuoco returns the nod, then lifts his voice as he addresses the room. "This is dark magic. A geas—and an incredibly powerful one."

Gothel sucks in a sharp breath, his whiskey-colored eyes going hard. "Who could have placed it? And why?"

Fuoco turns curious eyes to me. "I think the answer to that probably lies in Prince Vale." He advances toward me, his gaze taking in Izig and Sully standing like sentinels on either side of me. The dragon lord inclines his head. "May I examine you, Your Highness?"

"Of course," I say, my voice as hoarse as Jasper's. I can't help looking at him. He stands where Fuoco left him, a frown pulling his pale brows together.

Fuoco rests a big hand on my shoulder. "This might hurt a little."

"I can handle it." Nothing can hurt worse than the way Jasper has looked at me these past two days. Nothing could possibly drive a stake deeper through my heart.

The air around me heats, lifting the hair on my nape. I hold still as the other males watch. The heat intensifies, invisible flames crackling around me. My chest tightens until every breath is an effort. A wall of phantom fire blasts my face, ruffling my hair and searing my eyes like I'm standing before a roaring fireplace.

But there's no fire. Just Fuoco and his intense green eyes that seem to see straight through me.

I widen my stance as daggers of pain slice through my skull. At the edge of my vision, Gothel observes with a steady gaze. My father's old friend trusts Lord Fuoco. Right now, I can only hope his judgment is sound.

Sully whines across our bond as he leans hard against my leg.

Heat blasts me. Flames lick at my insides, filling my lungs with scorching air. My chest heaves as I try to draw oxygen into greedy, empty lungs.

Fuoco's brilliant green eyes fill my vision. The air grows hotter.

Unbearable. I was wrong. I can't withstand this.

The daggers stab more deeply, driving into my brain over and over. Someone cries out.

Me. I've lost control. Father will be so disappointed.

Your father will never know, Abelin.

The fire inside me soars.

Icicles on the ceiling.

Blood on marble.

Ybris slithering across the floor.

Jasper.

Pixies have long memories, Your Highness. We never forget a slight.

Stars reflected in the Seine.

Bright blue eyes smiling into mine.

The daggers in my brain twist sharply.

"I can't," I gasp, my voice coming from far away. "I can't bear it!"

Everything stops.

The fire disappears.

I stumble into Fuoco, who grips my shoulders and steadies me.

"Jasper," I say, lifting my head and searching for him.

"I'm here," he answers, and a hand slips into mine. When I straighten, he's beside me. We stare at each other, something tremulous and raw passing between us.

Fuoco steps back, his expression grim. "It's worse than I thought. The geas is the strongest I've ever encountered. It's a wonder you're not passed out on the floor simply by being in the same room with Jasper."

"Do you feel sick?" Gothel asks, moving forward.

"Yes," I rasp. "From the moment I saw Jasper at the Brawl. I feel dizzy, and my stomach churns. I've had a migraine since yesterday."

"Me too," Izig says gruffly. "And I've struggled with nausea."

Sully yowls.

I look down at him. *"You've felt sick, too? Why didn't you tell me?"*

My familiar rubs his whiskers over my calf. *"You had enough on your plate."* He gives my leg another smooth stroke. *"Although, it would have been fun to see the pixie's reaction if I puked up a hairball on his rug."*

I look at Fuoco. "We've all felt sick."

Fuoco's expression is thoughtful as he looks over Izig and Sully. "If members of your household were present when the geas was placed, it could hold sway over them, as well."

Cold fury replaces the sick feeling in my stomach. Tendrils of anger spread through my body. Someone tampered with my head. Izig and Sully like to say they protect me. But I protect them, too. And someone hurt them on my watch.

Jasper's quiet voice is like cool water on the rage sparking inside me. "I don't understand. If someone put this geas on Vale, why do *I* struggle to speak of him?"

"A geas can be transferred by touch or through an object," Gothel says. "A note, a book, something like that. Have you received anything like that recently?"

Jasper scrunches his brow. Then he gasps, his eyes going wide. "Your note, Vale. You left me a note in Paris when—" He stops. Shakes his head when the words won't come.

I squeeze his hand. "Don't worry about it."

Bert pops up from his pocket, and Jasper's eyes go wide again.

"Bert!" he gasps, looking from the mouse to Fuoco. "Bert chased after the note. He— Touched…"

"Bert touched the note, too," Fuoco guesses. "And he struggles to speak of Vale."

Jasper bobs his head up and down, his wings bobbing with him.

"Is there a way to lift this geas?" I ask Fuoco.

The dragon lord's expression grows sorrowful. "Only the being who placed it can remove it."

"Wait," Gothel says, meeting Fuoco's gaze. "There might be another way."

Understanding lights Fuoco's eyes. "Tower."

Gothel nods. "Give me a minute." He goes to the door and speaks to someone in the hall. Moments later, Tower du Sang enters the office. The vampire listens patiently as Gothel murmurs in his ear, no doubt giving him a quick summary of the last twenty minutes. When Gothel lifts his head, a look of determination fills Tower's eyes.

"I'll try."

Gothel caresses the vampire's smooth cheek. "Thank you, sweetheart."

Tower turns to Jasper. "Let's start with you first. If you simply touched an item tainted by a geas, that might be easier to remove."

"No," I say. "Start with me. I don't want to risk him being hurt. Try it on me."

Jasper makes a sound of protest as he swings toward me. "Vale. You don't have to do that."

I bring my thumb to his plump lower lip and stroke. "We'll figure this out, but I'd rather he try it on me first."

Blue eyes glimmer with moisture. Jasper threads his fingers through mine. "I'll be right here, okay?"

Tower holds out his hand. "Give me your wrist. I don't know if it'll work, but it's worth a try."

I let him take my arm. "Have you ever siphoned a geas?"

Arrogance flashes in his eyes. "No, but if anyone can do it, it's me." He bares his fangs and strikes hard, nailing the inside of my wrist. Blood spills from the wound as a warm, heavy sensation pools deep in my gut. I grunt as he drinks in great pulls that send pleasure tingling through me.

But after a second, the pleasure turns to discomfort. Then the discomfort becomes a fire under my skin.

I stiffen, memories of Fuoco's power threatening to drag a whimper from my throat.

Jasper squeezes my hand. It's an effort to turn my head toward him, but I do it. "Eyes on me," he whispers. "I've got you."

I return his squeeze, and I hold his stare as Tower continues to feed. An uncomfortable niggling sensation begins to worm its way through my mind. Doors lock and unlock somewhere inside me, fluttering open and shut. Pain explodes behind my eyes. My knees loosen, but Jasper holds me up. Keeps me steady. He grips my hand as the fire in my veins spirals into agony that steals my breath and makes my eyes water. Just when I can't stand it any longer, Tower releases his bite and staggers back.

Gothel catches him, his claw-tipped fingers curling protectively around the vampire's shoulders. The gargoyle dips his head and plants a soft kiss on Tower's neck. "You okay?"

"Yeah," Tower says, wiping blood from his lips. He gives me an apologetic look. "I'm sorry I couldn't remove all of it, but I think I blunted its side effects. You might be able to talk about Jasper without feeling ill. It's possible you'll regain a few memories, too."

Even before he finishes his sentence, I know he speaks the truth. My migraine is gone. As the pain of Tower's bite fades, glimpses of memories filter through my head.

Jasper on his hands and knees in front of my fireplace.

Jasper eating chocolate-filled croissants with Bert.

Sully rubbing his cheek along Jasper's when he thinks I'm not looking.

Love.

The memories shimmer with love. Blank spaces still dot them, but they're there.

They're mine.

Jasper is mine.

And someone took him from me.

"I know who did this," I say, certainty swelling as I look around the room. "My father's wife. I'm betrothed to her daughter, Princess Liriel. The wedding is in less than two weeks." I turn to Jasper. "Zaphira must have found out about us."

Hurt descends over Jasper's features. "You—" He clamps his lips together and makes a frustrated sound.

"Allow me," Tower says, stepping forward. Jasper's eyes flutter shut as the vampire strikes, and he groans as the feeding wears on. But he endures without complaint, and when Tower finally steps back, Jasper opens his eyes and speaks clearly for the first time since the Syndicate Ball.

"You could have told me about the betrothal, Vale."

The regret that clamps tightly around my heart is worse than anything I've endured since I entered the office. "I kept that from you?" I ask, but I already know the answer. Flashes of memory burst against the blank spaces in my mind.

Jasper tipping his head back to bask in the sun.

Barrels of bouquets wrapped in brightly colored paper.

Sully's voice in my head, warning of folly. Of duty.

Plans to speak to my father.

"I was never going to marry her," I tell Jasper now. "But you're right. I should have told you." I close my eyes and fight through the shadows, desperate to grab more glimpses of the past. "I wanted to tell you, and I would have," I say, opening my eyes. "I ask your forgiveness now, even though I don't deserve it."

Tears swim in his eyes. "We can talk about it later," he says thickly.

It's not a definitive answer. But it's a start.

Over the next few minutes, Tower removes as much of the geas as he can from Izig, Sully, and Bert. When he straightens from biting Sully, I stroke my familiar's whiskers away from his face.

"I need to ask a favor, Sulien."

He purrs into our bond. *"Anything."*

"Return to the Summer Court. Take Bert and Mert with you."

Sully startles. *"Mice?"*

"They can reach places you can't. People ignore things they don't want to see, and most people don't want to see mice. Use that to your advantage. Work together. Find out how Zaphira did this." I hesitate. *"And find out if my father had a hand in it."*

Surprise flares in Sully's eyes. Then my familiar dips his head. *"Consider it done."*

Gothel's office door swings open and a dark-haired man carries a platter of cookies inside. Fuoco springs forward, meeting the man halfway and taking the platter from him.

"Sorry to intrude," the man says, a dimple appearing in his cheek as he offers a shy smile. "I, uh, brought cookies."

"I see that, selsara," Fuoco murmurs, guiding the man to Gothel's desk. The dragon lord sets the platter down, then pulls the man into his arms and buries his face in the man's neck.

The human's cheeks go scarlet. "We have an audience."

Fuoco lifts his head and winks at his mate. "When has that ever stopped me?"

"Fair point."

Smiling, Fuoco turns to me. "Prince Vale, this is my selsara, Beau Bidbury. Beau, this is Prince Vale of the Summer Court."

"Pleased to meet you," I say, bowing.

Beau's smile transforms his face from handsome to dazzling. "The pleasure is mine, Your Highness." He gestures to the desk. "I don't have magic, but I brought sugar."

Fuoco wraps an arm around the smaller man's shoulders. "Sugar is its own kind of magic, my love."

My love. I'll do anything to regain what I've lost. What's been taken from me. When I turn to Jasper, I find him watching Fuoco and Beau. But as he feels my gaze on him, he turns his blue eyes to mine.

I hold out my hand. "Come home with me?" Memories whirl and spin through my head. I've said those words before. I have to hope his answer is the same as it was the first time.

He stares at my palm. Then he meets my gaze. "Okay."

My heart soars as I grab his hand. "Let's go home."

Because I'm keeping you. I don't say it aloud, but maybe he hears it anyway. Zaphira might have stolen him from me once, but I won't lose him a second time. She's always been one step ahead of me on our personal chessboard.

Not this time.

And never again.

CHAPTER 13
JASPER

Vale casts me anxious looks the whole way back to my apartment. He's right to be anxious. With every step, my temper flares. The sky matches my mood, dark clouds clustering around Gothel's skyscrapers and threatening another frigid winter storm.

Izig obviously senses the coming reckoning, because he murmurs something about buying lunch and peels off like a man with self-preservation on his mind. Sully slinks after him, his sleek form disappearing into the shadows.

Seconds later, Bert speaks in my head. *"I'll, uh, give you and Vale some time alone to chat."*

"Abandoning ship?" I say through our bond as I lower him to the ground.

"Never." He flicks his tail against my leg. *"But you and your man are gonna have it out, and I value my eardrums. Plus, Sully said he wanted to talk to me about something."*

"Hopefully not his favorite mouse-based cuisine."

As Bert runs off, Vale's apprehension becomes a palpable weight between us. "Jasper..." he begins.

"Not here," I say without looking at him. "You have no idea how nosy this neighborhood is." *Also, I will probably end up yelling at you in the street.*

I can't blame Vale for his memory loss anymore. His bitch of a stepmother has a lot to answer for.

But so does he.

As we enter the living room, I toss my keys on the coffee table and face him. "Well?"

He rubs his hand over his mouth, his golden eyes stark above his palm. "I...don't know what to say."

I direct a humorless laugh toward the ceiling. "Irony isn't dead, after all."

Vale frowns. "You're mocking me."

"Really?" I step toward him. "Your headache is gone. You finally have enough memories to know I'm not a total stranger, and you can't think of a single thing to say right now? How about, *'I'm sorry, Jasper, that I fucking lied to you about marrying my stepsister.'* Maybe start with that one."

"I'm sorry—"

"There you go," I say, sarcasm dripping from my voice. "Was that so hard?"

"Jasper—"

"And if you even dare to claim you didn't lie, I'm going to tell you right now that you're full of shit. A lie of omission is just as damaging—and intentional—as outright falsehood."

"I know—"

"You fucked me," I growl, stepping closer and stabbing a finger at him. "You were inside me, Vale, and the whole time you knew you were betrothed. Every walk in Paris. Every meal we shared." Tears burn my throat. "This betrothal should have been the first thing out of your mouth when we met. But you didn't want it that way, did you? No, you wanted to have one last gay fling before your big day."

"That is *not* true," he says, his eyes flashing. "You were never a fling for me."

"Says the man so deep in the closet I could throw a party in it."

"You're wrong." He thumps his chest. "I'm gay, Jasper. I've never denied it. Everyone knows it. You were never a secret."

"Then why—"

"Gods, will you let me finish?" When I shut my mouth and fold my arms, he releases a shaky breath. "I don't have any excuses. I had my reasons for not telling you about Liriel, and they were all the *wrong* reasons. They were wrong, baby."

I lift a hand as I close my eyes. "Don't," I say carefully, tears brimming under my lids. "Do not with that right now."

"Okay."

The air shifts, and I know he's moved closer. He knows better than to touch me, but his body heat caresses my skin, dispelling the last of the chill that clings to me after the long walk home.

"Everything changed when I met you," he says quietly. With my eyes closed, my senses are limited to his voice and his scent. I can't block them out, so I stand still as summer invades my lungs and his deep rumble fills my ears.

"*Everything* changed," he says again. "You're not going to believe me, but I knew it from the second I bumped into you in Mab's court. I didn't fall down, but I might as well have. That's what it felt like, anyway."

I open my eyes and find him inches away, his eyes bright with unshed tears.

He nods, his throat bobbing. "I remember it. I, uh"—he swipes a knuckle under his eyes—"I don't remember everything, but I remember that." He lowers his hand as his voice goes gruff. "I knew at that precise second that I would rather die than marry Liriel. And that's what I was facing—what I'm still facing. I took an elven vow to wed her."

"What?" I gasp, my heart speeding up.

He slashes a hand through the air. "It doesn't matter. Because I'm more determined than ever to get out of it. I won't marry her, Jasper. I can't. Not when you're in this world." Tears spill from his eyes, the tracks like trails of sunlight sparkling on water. "Life is worthless without you in it. Do you understand what I'm saying? If you kick me out right now, I'll go. I won't trouble you anymore. I'll do whatever you tell me to do. But I will go the rest of my miserable life holding you in my heart. If that's the only place I can hold you, that's what I'll do. Because there is *no one else* for me. No one. Even the glimpses of you I see in my memories are enough to convince me that you're meant to be mine. And standing before you now, I'm absolutely certain." He drags in a ragged breath. "I chose you once. I would choose you a thousand times. I'd choose you *every* time."

I put a trembling hand over my mouth. He goes blurry as the tears I've been fighting streak down my face.

"God, don't cry," he rasps, lifting tentative hands. When I don't stop him, he cups my face and rubs the tears away with his thumbs. "I love you. I'm an asshole."

A watery laugh bursts from behind my palm. I lower it and swallow against my burning throat. "If you ever hurt me like that again—"

"Never," he says fiercely. "I swear it on the sun."

I close my eyes again. This time, his light glows through my lids. When I open my eyes, his glamour is gone, all his glory revealed.

"I want to make love to you," he murmurs. "You're going to tell me to go fuck myself. You should. But I'll sit on this sofa and hope that one day you'll let me touch you again." He rests his forehead against mine. "That's what's going to sustain me, Jasper. The hope that, one day, I'll be a good enough man to deserve you again."

"Gods," I breathe.

"I'm so sorry," he whispers. "I can't tell you enough how much I—"

"Vale?"

He tenses. "Yes?"

"Shut up and take me to bed."

Slowly, he pulls back. Stares at me for one breathless moment. Then he grabs me around the thighs and lifts me, hiking me roughly into his arms. He seizes my mouth in a savage kiss as he strides toward my room. I throw my legs around his waist and grab his hair in both fists, climbing him like a tree. He bumps into the doorframe and grunts as he shoulders into the bedroom. Lust rides me hard, bowing my spine and putting a growl in my voice as I grind my cock into his stomach.

"Fucking need you," I say between kisses.

"You're getting me." He flings me onto the bed.

My back hits the mattress with enough force to knock the wind out of me and set the room spinning. It's still whirling when Vale rips my clothes off, feral sounds spilling from his mouth. He strips like a man possessed, then lands on top of me and slants his mouth across mine. His kiss is rough and insistent as he runs a hand down my body to cup my dick.

"Yes," I gasp, thrusting into his hand. He grips me hard and circles my tip with his thumb.

"So wet," he growls, rubbing precum around my cockhead. "Spread your legs."

The command yanks a whimper from me as I obey. I whimper again when he slides his wicked fingers under my sack and strokes firm circles around my hole.

Moaning into his mouth, I dig my hands into his hair and drag his head down my my neck. He goes willingly, biting along my jugular to my chest, where he swirls his tongue over the bar through one of my nipples. I hold my breath, then release it on a wanton cry as his teeth close over my nipple. As he suckles me, he continues tracing his finger round and round my rim, each circuit sending thick waves of heat rolling through me.

Lightning flashes outside, followed by a boom of thunder so loud it rattles the glass in the terrace doors.

Vale continues to tease my hole until a steady stream of whimpers fall from my lips.

"Hurry," I whisper, clutching his head to my chest. I buck against his finger, trying to coax it inside me.

"Not yet." Abandoning my nipple, he seizes my wrists and pins them beside my head. His eyes smolder as he looks me over, his gaze lingering on the juncture of my thighs. "Wider," he murmurs. "Show me where you want me."

Breathing heavily, I spread my legs until my tendons ache. "Please."

When he meets my stare again, he licks his lips. "I need to taste you."

My breath whooshes out of me. Cool air caresses my damp nipple. The thought of having his mouth on other parts of me makes me squirm. "I need you to."

"I know." He releases my wrists. "Arms above your head."

My heart pounds faster as I do what he says. Rain lashes the terrace doors, sending shadowy rivulets over the bed and our naked bodies.

"Stay like that," Vale says, trailing his fingertips down the valley between my pecs. He keeps going, traveling down my stomach and running his fingers through my pubes. As my stomach muscles tremble, he grips my cock and gives it a firm pump.

"Fuck," I groan, thrusting into his grip. Precum beads at my slit. "Faster."

Vale shakes his head. He works my shaft, his gaze locked with mine. "Not too much. Not just yet."

"Why?" I whine, thrusting harder. "I need to come."

He lets my dick slap against my stomach. "I told you." He grasps my ankles and holds my legs apart in a wide V. "I'm going to taste this pretty hole. And if it's as good as I remember, I'm going to eat your ass until you're out of your mind. And when you're begging, I am going to fuck you so hard and so good, baby." He gives my opening a light swat, making me jump and moan loudly. "I'm going to give you everything you want. And then I'll let you come." With that, he rolls me onto my shoulders, pushes my cheeks apart, and buries his face in my cleft.

At the first lash of his tongue, I shout loudly enough to rival the thunder. "Oh, gods!" I thrash my head back and forth as he laps at my rim. Folded in half, I dig my knees into the bed. My cock leaks onto my heaving stomach as Vale presses my cheeks wider and thrusts his tongue deep, fucking me with it.

"Seven hells," I groan, gripping the backs of my knees.

Vale lifts his head and meets my gaze between my spread legs. "You broke position."

"Can't help it," I say, my breaths ragged. "You're too fucking good at that."

His lips curve. "Look at you. So hot." He holds my gaze prisoner as he lowers his head enough to flick his tongue over my opening. "So pink and pretty for me." His eyes go heavy-lidded. "And I was wrong."

"About what?" I ask breathlessly, half out of my mind with need.

"You don't taste as good as I remember." He laps at my hole, and his eyes close briefly as a look of ecstasy spreads over his features. "You are, without question, the most delicious thing I've ever tasted, baby."

"I..." I shudder as he rubs his thumbs over my rim, holding me open. "I want you."

"I'm right here." Thumbs spreading me, he closes his mouth over my entrance and thrusts his tongue deep, nailing my gland.

Bliss. Raw and undiluted, it crackles through my veins as my mouth stretches on a soundless scream. I thrust my hips, shamelessly riding his face. Fucking myself against his mouth as he fucks me with his tongue. We meet somewhere in the middle, filling the bedroom with the heavy, slick noises of his intimate French kiss. He hums, sending vibrations into my opening as his stubble scrapes my sensitive cleft. Just when I think it can't get any better, he seals his mouth around my entrance and sucks, hollowing his cheeks with the effort.

"Fuck," I say, shuddering as my bones liquefy. "I'm going to—"

"No, you're not," he says, pulling back and then flattening his body atop mine. "Not without me." He kisses me, giving me my own wicked, forbidden taste as he rocks his hips so our erections slide against each other. He reaches down and lodges his dick against my opening, his cockhead prodding my damp entrance.

"Tell me," he rasps as he thrusts harder. "Tell me you want it. Tell me you want me."

"I want you." I gasp as he moves faster. "I want your cock."

"Lube?"

"Nightstand."

He fetches it and returns before the heat of his body leaves me.

Then he cranks everything up by a thousand.

He's everywhere, kissing me and stroking me. Kneeling between my legs and nuzzling my cockhead. Sucking my balls while he pumps a slick finger inside me, grazing my prostate over and over. He slides his hands up my thighs as he sucks my fingers into his mouth. Dips his tongue into my navel. Presses feverish kisses to my collarbone. I never know where he'll go next, and I'm too far gone to care. My mind blanks and sensation takes over, each brush of his skin against mine stoking the flames higher. Maybe they'll burn me up. Roar and climb and consume me.

"I want it," I tell him and everyone and no one at all. "I'm burning up and I want it." *I've always loved the sun.*

"Take it, then," he whispers, and he lines himself up and pushes inside me.

Lightning shears the sky outside. Thunder follows.

Vale braces himself above me, a lock of golden-brown hair hanging over his forehead as he works his cock deeper and deeper and then bottoms out. His balls press against my ass. His shaft throbs inside me. My dick lies trapped between us, the tip leaking all over my stomach.

Then Vale begins to move.

It's all heat and friction. Exquisite fullness. He pumps inside me, hitting my sweet spot and filling my vision with bursting stars. I wrap my legs around his waist and dig my heels into his back. Something this good can't last forever. It has to burn up on the way to the finish line. But I don't give a fuck. It feels too damn good to fight it.

So I don't. I let Vale take me to that place.

The place where pleasure overwhelms me.

The place where he's everything.

The place where it feels like this moment might last forever. A point in time I pinch between my fingers and stretch to infinity without the thread snapping.

Fires rage inside me. My whole body clenches as the flames become too strong to bear. I'm going to burn up, and I don't care. I've come this far. Or maybe I'm too lost to save anymore.

I'm lost.

I'm lost.

I'm lost.

But my elven prince found me. We can be lost together.

Vale's teeth graze my earlobe. His deep command rumbles in my ear as he works a hand between our bodies and pumps my dick. "Come for me, baby."

That's all it takes. My vision whites out as ecstasy floods my veins. I scream as I come, my release spreading over my stomach. The waves crash over me, each one higher and more powerful than the last.

Vale drives harder and faster inside me. He digs his fingers into my hips as he thrusts hard enough to shake the bed. Then he comes on a roar, spurting deep inside me. His big shoulders shake, and I reach up and drag him down. Pull him against me and hold him as he finishes with his face turned into my neck and his lips murmuring senseless things against my skin. And then his words are no longer senseless. They flutter against my ear, stirring my hair. Wrap around me and hold me as tightly as his arms. Pound as ceaselessly as his big heart beating against mine.

"I love you," he rasps. "I love you, I love you."

Rain spatters the glass doors and the terrace and all the rooftops of the Hallows. But the chilly drops can't reach us. Here, in the quiet room in the rumpled bed, there is only me and him.

"I love you, too," I whisper, and I close my eyes and hold the prince who found his way back to me.

∽

Hours later, I rest my head on Vale's shoulder and stroke my fingers through the light mat of hair that covers his chest. Dusk descended an hour ago, but we haven't left the bed. Outside, the rain has turned to snow. Fat flakes drift past the window.

"Do you think Izig is okay?" I ask, tracing the edges of Vale's tattoo.

He smiles as he captures my hand and brings it to his mouth. "He's an ogre." Vale kisses the tips of my fingers one by one. "Izig may look dapper, but he was brought up in a warrior culture. A little snow won't bother him."

I pull our joined hands away and study his knuckles for a moment before meeting his gaze. "Were you ever going to tell me about the brawling?"

Pink dusts Vale's cheekbones. "Of course." He turns his head on the pillow and gives me a tentative look. "But maybe you don't approve of it?"

"Did you worry I wouldn't?"

"Izig and Sully don't." He sighs as he plays with my fingers.

"When I was young, brawling was a way to release aggression—and I had plenty of it. I was trapped in this rigid role. Then my mother died, and all those expectations became...too much."

I squeeze Vale's fingers gently, stilling his agitated movements. "I don't disapprove. You can punch as many people as you want. If you ever punch me, though, I'll hex your jock strap. Your dick will never know another moment of peace."

Humor gleams in his eyes. Then he sobers. "Brawling was always the one thing I had that was solely my own. A secret that maybe hid my other secret."

"I thought you said being gay wasn't a secret."

His chest lifts in another sigh. "It's not, really. I've dated men openly in the past, although I never took them to my father's court."

I raise my eyebrows. "He wouldn't allow it?"

"It's more...nuanced than that."

I sit up and flick my wings out of the way. "How is it nuanced? Your father either accepts that you're gay or he doesn't."

"You can't possibly see it as that black and white," Vale says, his voice tinged with exasperation. "Not everyone can be as freewheeling as pixies."

"What's that supposed to mean?"

"Your species is literally known for throwing orgies. No one cares who you fuck."

"Right, because it's no one's business. Who gives a shit?"

"Not everyone thinks that way, Jasper."

"Well, they should."

Irritation moves through his eyes as he rises onto an elbow. "You don't understand. Elves are..." As my brows climb higher, he seems to grope for an explanation. "There is nothing relaxed or easy about the elven courts. The rules are rigid. Marriages are arranged for political gain, not love. My father adored my mother, but he didn't hesitate to wed Zaphira after Mother died. He sees no conflict between his personal desires, which he's content to keep private, and his public life. And his marriage to Zaphira is part of his public life."

Warning bells clang in my head. "What are you saying?"

"My father has spies everywhere. I don't doubt for a second that he's been aware of my love life from the start. But he doesn't speak of things that interfere with duty. I'm his heir. In his mind, there's no question I'll marry for political power and produce heirs to further our line. As long as I'm discreet, he won't bat an eye if I take lovers on the side."

My mouth goes dry. "I can't live like that, Vale."

"I know," he says quickly, sitting up and taking my hand. "I can't, either. That's the difference between my father and me." He flashes a wry smile. "One of several differences, but that's the biggest one." Vale rubs his thumb over my knuckles. "I would never ask that of you, baby. It's not an option. I don't love Liriel, and I refuse to live a lie."

My heart climbs into my throat. "But you took an elven vow. Those are unbreakable. If you don't walk down that aisle, you'll die."

"If I can't be with you, I'll die anyway."

It's my turn to be exasperated. "Those are pretty words, Your Highness, but this is real-life shit. I will *not* bury you." A tear sprints down my cheek, and I suck in a painful breath as my voice rises. "I look amazing in black, and I refuse to retire it as a color because you were a stupid fucking idiot and chose to die rather than live for us!"

Between one breath and the next, I'm in Vale's arms. He surrounds me, his broad chest pressed to mine and his hands moving through my hair. His lips graze my cheek before he speaks in my ear.

"I'm not going to die. I sent Sulien, Bert, and Mert to the Summer Court to figure out what's going on with Zaphira. Once I'm certain my father wasn't involved in the geas, I'm going to approach him. He's one of the oldest—maybe *the* oldest—beings among the Myth. All magic can be undone, baby. I'm confident there's a way to break this vow."

I squeeze my eyes shut as I breathe him in. "But it's unbreakable for a reason."

"It can be broken," he insists. "My father will know of a way."

"Because he's one of the oldest beings among the Myth, so he knows everything." Maybe if I say it enough, it'll be true.

Vale strokes my hair. "And he loves me. Even ancient, powerful creatures will bend the rules for the people they love."

I freeze in his arms.

"What is it?" He pulls back, instant worry in his eyes. "Jasper?"

"Your father loves you."

"Yeah," Vale says, confusion joining the worry.

"And he's old. He knows things."

"That's right. But—"

"He's not the only ancient power in the world," I say. "And he's not the only one who cares about his family." I untangle myself from Vale's embrace and jump from the bed.

"Jasper?" he calls, scrambling after me as I hurry to the living room. Nude, he watches with a baffled expression as I crouch before the hearth and build a fire. "Baby," he says carefully, "is everything okay?"

"It's gonna be," I mumble, going to a small desk in the corner and pulling a sheet of stationery from the drawer. I scribble a note, sign it, and fold it in half. Then I go to the fire and fling it into the flames. Vale gasps as they flare high and shoot red sparks. The flames change color in rapid succession, going from orange to yellow to green.

I hold my breath as the green darkens to emerald. When it stays the rich shade, I release my breath and smile. "There. She'll know what to do."

Vale moves to my side. "Should I ask what just happened?"

I let my smile turn smug as I look up at him. "Do you mean to tell me there's something the mighty Prince Abelin Vale of the Summer Court doesn't know?"

He pulls me into his arms, and his eyes glow like honey as he says, "I've told you more than once to call me Vale, pixie."

Desire streaks through me as I realize we're both still naked. "Why?" I ask, running the back of my hand over the scruff on his jaw. "Why do you use your middle name?"

A hint of pain moves through his eyes. "My mother called me Vale. It reminds me of her."

I press my palm to his heart, my fingertips resting on the rays of the sun. "Then I'll never call you anything else."

He kisses the curve of my eyebrow. "I hope you'll call me yours."

"I do, my prince." I nuzzle my cheek against his stubbled one. "I do."

He holds me for a moment, then eases back. "So, what's with the letter in the fire?"

I smile as I bat my wings lazily against the air. "It's a uniquely pixie form of communication. That message will go straight to Mab. I asked for her help. If there's a way to break your vow, she'll know."

"You're sure?"

"Pixies are experts in matters of the heart."

"Well," he murmurs, sliding his hands to my hips. "You've certainly captured mine." As he grows harder against me, he moves a hand to my ass and dips his fingers between my cheeks. One finger grazes my opening, dabbling in his cum that still seeps from me. "Are you sore?" he asks in a voice rough with desire.

I sling my arms around his neck and go on tiptoe so I can whisper in his ear. "Not even a little bit."

His shaky breath tickles my cheek. "So, we can…?"

"*Oui, mon prince.* Take me back to bed."

CHAPTER 14

VALE

Izig trundles from the foyer with an armful of groceries. After five days in Jasper's apartment, my butler doesn't bother knocking anymore. Of course, some of his stealth is due to a reluctance to alert Jasper's neighbors. Nearly a week has passed, and their nosiness shows no signs of abating.

As Izig enters the kitchen, his eyes flick to Jasper's bedroom door.

"He's in the shower," I say, rising from the sofa to join Izig in the kitchen. "Thanks for grabbing the groceries. Truly, I appreciate it."

He grunts and sets the bags on the counter. "You were right to send me, sir. Nobody pays me any mind. You're far more noticeable."

My heart aches at his assessment of himself. But he's right. Small things are often deemed inconsequential and overlooked. That's exactly why I sent Bert, Mert, and Sully to the Summer Court.

"Thank you," I say again, unpacking the groceries. "I don't know what I'd do without you, Izig."

The merest hint of pink tinges his wart-covered cheeks. "It was no trouble." He gestures to the groceries. "Olives. Fancy cheese. French bread." He glances at the bedroom door again. "Is there a romantic picnic in your future, sir?"

I know why he's asking. Jasper and I have been lying low ever since Tower du Sang weakened the geas. If Zaphira was bold enough to tamper with my memories, there's no telling what she'll do to ensure I go through with the wedding. If Izig suspects I'm going to leave the apartment, he'll undoubtedly have something to say about it.

I smile. "Yes, old friend, but the romance won't leave the living room."

The bedroom door swings open and Jasper saunters through, drying his hair with a towel. He's shirtless, the bars through his nipples gleaming in the afternoon light that streams through the terrace doors. Low-slung sweatpants accentuate the bulge between his thighs. He flings his towel over his shoulder as he enters the kitchen, then rises on tiptoe and presses a tender kiss to my lips.

As soon as his shower-warmed skin brushes mine, I grab his hips and yank him against me.

"*Oh*," he murmurs against my mouth. "Hello, Your Highness." His blue eyes sparkle with mischief as my erection grazes his dick. "*Both* of Your Highnesses."

Izig clears his throat.

Jasper turns to him with a bright smile. "Hey, Ziggy."

My butler's eyes widen slightly at the nickname. "Good afternoon, Master Jasper." Izig looks at me. "If you don't need anything further, sire, I thought I might take a walk by the Hudson."

"Enjoy yourself, Izig."

My butler inclines his head. As he turns and moves toward the foyer, Jasper leans on the counter. "We need to find you a girl, Izig."

Izig spins, a slightly horrified look on his wart-covered face.

Jasper tilts his head. "Or maybe a guy?"

Izig folds his brawny arms, stretching his suit jacket. "No, thank you. I don't want matchmaking from a pixie."

Jasper chuckles. "Oh, come on. I bet I can guess your type. I'm thinking tall and—"

"*No*, thank you," Izig says firmly. He mumbles something under his breath and disappears down the hallway. A moment later, the front door opens and closes.

Jasper straightens from the counter, a pleased look on his face. "He loves me. He won't say it, of course. Big, strong ogre, and all. But I can tell."

"Izig's affection runs deep," I say, "but it's under the surface. His family has served mine for generations. You'll never hear him utter the word *love* unless he's talking about chocolate-filled croissants. Spicy dark chocolate, to be exact."

Jasper grins. "A man after my own heart. Dark chocolate is the *only* chocolate."

I grab him around the waist and pull him into me so we're chest to chest. "No one else is allowed to have your heart. Only me. Because no one else will ever have mine. It's yours, Jasper. Every bit of me belongs to you."

His gaze turns thoughtful as he brings a hand to my chest and strokes the edges of my sun tattoo through my shirt. Behind him, his wings sift pale blue dust so fine it disappears before it touches the ground. Silence stretches until discomfort steals through me.

"Jasper," I say. "Look at me." When his blue eyes lift to mine, I tighten my arms around him. "There are still tender spaces between us. I know I can't fix all of them in a week, but I'm determined to try anyway. I'm a brawler by nature, baby, and there's never been a more important fight than this one. Right here, right now. You and me."

He tips his head toward the groceries. "Is that what this is all about? Fixing things?"

"I'm a Frenchman," I murmur, reaching around his hip and stroking the delicate edge of his wing. "Food is one of my love languages."

His eyes roll back in his head as a shiver passes through him.

"Feel good?" I ask quietly.

His response comes on a groan. "You have no idea."

I chuckle. "We need more wing play, my love."

He opens his eyes, his expression abruptly sober. "We need more of everything. Including time."

Fear dampens my growing arousal. The wedding is in six days. We haven't heard from Mab. There's been no word from Bert, Mert, or Sully, either. Jasper and I are in a holding pattern, hunkered down in his apartment like a couple of hunted animals. Zaphira is responsible for our helplessness and, right now, I don't see any way of outmaneuvering her. Not without risking Jasper's safety.

But I'm determined not to let my frustration interfere with this opportunity to make things right with Jasper. Gripping him around the waist, I lift him and set him on the counter amid the scattered groceries. Then I step between his legs and tip his chin up.

"We'll figure this out," I promise, brushing my lips over his. "In the meantime, we still have to eat, so I'm going to give you a picnic in front of the fire. I'd rather take you outside and watch you laugh under the sun, but it's December and cold as fuck in this city."

He laughs softly. "It's cold just about everywhere."

I take his hand and splay his fingers over my heart. "Not in here. Not for you."

His voice goes husky. "That's very romantic, Your Highness."

"It's the truth."

For a long moment, we just stare at each other, lust and other emotions sparkling in the air between us. My heart thumps faster, and he curls his fingers against my chest.

"Vale," he whispers.

"I know," I say, and I'm not quite sure what I mean. But my body seems to. More importantly, Jasper does, too, because he leans in just as I tangle my hand in his hair and tug his head back. A growl rumbles in my chest as I kiss my way up his throat before seizing his lips in a rough kiss. I grunt as I press my aching dick against his, which is rock-hard and so irresistible I slip a hand under his waistband. He's not wearing underwear, and I seize his dick and stroke the silky length. I swipe my thumb over his leaking slit and work moisture down his shaft.

"F-Fuck," he gasps against my lips. He squeezes my shoulder as he rolls his hips, thrusting hard into my hand. A groan rips from his throat. "You gotta stop. I'll come."

"Do you want to?"

"Yes," he gasps. "No." With a shaky laugh, he seizes my wrist. "You got all this food. I don't want to ruin your idea."

I pull my hand from his sweats and cup his jaw. "You won't. The food will keep, baby."

He shakes his head. "Let's wait. Call me greedy, but I really want you to fuck me later."

Lust bolts straight to my dick, and I groan as I ease my hips away from his. "If you keep saying stuff like that, we'll never eat again."

A mischievous smile plays around his mouth. "There's something to be said for anticipation, my prince."

"Just give me an appetizer," I murmur, and I kiss him while he's still smiling. A few breathless moments later, we part, both of us flushed and way too aroused for comfort.

"We should probably eat, right?" Jasper asks as I adjust my aching dick. He darts a look at the abandoned food. "Otherwise, I'm going to make a very big mess all over your camembert."

Laughing, I pull him from the counter and swat his ass. "*Ouais.*" Yeah. "Food first, fun later."

A wicked smile curves his lips as he holds up a thick length of pepperoni. "But not too much later."

Laughing and flirting, we work side by side as we prepare lunch. Jasper finds a charcuterie board, and I slice the cheese and meat while he arranges grapes, olives, and nuts into little islands. Our conversation is easy, and several times my shoulders shake so hard I have to pause my knife so I don't cut myself.

It's always this way with him. The thought materializes in my mind with clarity as clear and bright as a diamond. My memories are spotty. Bits and pieces of our stolen time come and go. But my instinct is still razor-sharp. I can trust that. And every bit of instinct points to Jasper. He's mine.

Jasper holds up a baguette, his eyes glinting with mischief. "Do you remember the last time we talked about French bread?"

I take it from him and plant a rough, quick kiss on his lips. With a wink, I smack the bread lightly against his ass. "It's called a baguette, pixie."

"*Oui oui, mon prince.*" Grinning, he heads for the living room. Halfway there, he tosses me a saucy look over his shoulder. "You're still contracted to serve as my boon, you know. So you carry the food."

Shaking my head, I obey, setting the charcuterie board on the coffee table while he spreads a blanket before the fireplace. He pops grapes in his mouth as I fetch wine and glasses. When we're settled before the fire with the food between us, I hand him a glass of wine.

"This is the kind of service I can get used to." He takes a healthy sip and gestures to me with his glass. "Would be better if you weren't wearing pants, though. Or a shirt."

I laugh as I pour a glass for myself. "You're incorrigible."

"Just a bowtie, then. And I don't mean around your neck."

We spend the next thirty minutes eating and teasing each other as the fire dances in the hearth. Eventually, I push the coffee table aside and lean my back against the edge of the sofa. Jasper lounges between my legs, his back to my chest and his fingers tracing lazy patterns on my forearm.

"So," he says, "have you remembered anything else?"

I stroke the curve of one gossamer wing, which he tucked close to his hip when he settled against me. "Nothing new." I gesture to the charcuterie board beside us. "I wanted to do this for you, but I was also hoping it might jog my memory. I hate that I can't trust it. That there are holes in our time together." Anger sparks in my chest, turning my voice into a growl. "I'm going to make sure Zaphira answers for that."

Jasper turns in my arms. Worry clouds his blue eyes, and I touch his cheek.

"What is it, baby?" I ask.

He hesitates. "We haven't heard from Sully or Bert. Do you think Zaphira would hurt them?"

I can't lie to him, not even to spare him pain. But I won't worry him unnecessarily, either. "Sulien isn't an ordinary cat. He was born in the Taranathen Forest when the magic beyond the Veil was at its zenith. If he doesn't want to be seen, no one will notice his presence." I smile as I rub a thumb over Jasper's high cheekbone. "And I have a feeling your Bert is just as magical."

Jasper smiles. "He is."

"How did you two meet?"

Humor dances in Jasper's eyes. "Nothing too dramatic or awe-inspiring, I'm afraid. I almost stepped on him in a bar. Then I took him home and helped him through a bad hangover." As I chuckle, Jasper resettles in my arms and resumes stroking my arm. "Tell me about when you first met Sully. How did you know he was the right familiar for you?" Jasper turns his head and looks up at me, blue eyes twinkling. "Fated mates, so to speak."

I laugh at his description until a sobering thought hits me. "Have we talked about this before?"

He shakes his head. "I'd like to hear about it now, though. Tell me some stories, my prince. Even if you can't remember telling me the first time, I'd like to hear them again."

My heart squeezes. I wrap my arms around him and let my cheek graze his. As the fire crackles and dances before us, I tell him of my life.

We talk for hours. About Sully and my mother. About my childhood growing up in the Summer Court. About my father's marriage to Zaphira and the bad behaviors I fell into as I struggled to adjust to the coldness she brought to my father's court. The only subject we don't discuss is Liriel. She's the one topic neither of us seems able to bring up. It's too harsh of a reminder that my wedding is mere days away.

Through the terrace doors, the sky deepens from blue to navy to black. Every moment Jasper and I reconnect drives home what I already know: I'll cast duty aside to keep him. I'll take on Zaphira publicly if I have to. But I've got to be smart. She's wily, and she's clearly determined to see the wedding through. It's only a matter of time before she finds me—or worse, Jasper.

As the fire burns low, he moves his hand to my thigh, his fingers kneading and stroking a slow path upward. Just as I allow my desire to flow unfettered, the fire roars back to life. The flames change color, flaring from orange to dark green.

Jasper sits up abruptly. The flames continue to dance, the color shifting to emerald. A second later, a letter flies from the blaze.

He plucks it from the air and turns to me with an excited expression. "It's from Mab! Gods, I hope she has some answers."

My heart pounds as he rips the letter open and scans it. His excitement dies, his jaw going tight. When he looks up, his blue eyes are stark. "She says the same thing as Fuoco. Only the being who set the geas can remove it."

"What about my vow?"

Jasper shakes his head. "Mab says she can't break it."

Bitter disappointment chokes me. Jasper reaches for me, and I pull him into my arms and bury my face in his hair. He smells of sandalwood and wine and the body cream he slathers on after he showers. As I hold him, the edges of his wings turn the gray color of cold rain. His shoulders shake, and a hiccuping sob breaks from his throat.

"No," I say, kissing his temple. "We're not giving up."

"But what are we gonna do?" He pushes away, his blue eyes as dark as a bruise. "We're out of options."

I take the crumpled note from his fingers and stuff it in my pocket. Then I maneuver us so my back is against the sofa and he's straddling me. I reach around him and stroke my hand down his spine, running a firm thumb over the strong muscles that support his wings.

He groans, his head falling forward. "Gods, that feels good."

"That's what I'm going to do," I say softly. When he lifts his head, I move my hand to the back of his neck and massage. "I'm going to make you feel good. First, I'm going to get the tension out of these muscles, baby. And then I'm going to make love to you. We can talk about everything else later."

His smile is sad. "Sex won't solve our problems."

"Not sex." I run my fingers over the delicate, iridescent membrane of one wing. "Love, Jasper. I love you. That's the only option I'm interested in."

"I'm afraid," he whispers, his wing shivering under my touch.

"Me too. But I'm also very fucking determined to keep you." Bringing my hands to his hips, I kiss him. He opens immediately, moaning as our tongues meet and stroke. The kiss quickly turns heated, and I pull his sweats down, freeing his dick. I cup his tight, swollen balls before sliding a finger back and teasing his hole.

With a soft, sexy cry, he grinds his hips, the damp tip of his cock slicking my stomach.

"Take these off," I whisper, tugging at his sweats. As he scrambles to obey, I pull my shirt over my head and wriggle out of my pants and boxer briefs. The latter tangle around one ankle, and Jasper rips them off and flings them across the room before straddling my thighs once more.

"There," he says with a satisfied sound. "My favorite mount."

Widening my thighs a little, I grasp my leaking, aching dick and slap it lightly against his stomach. "You forgot the most important part of your saddle."

A blond eyebrow sails upward. "Oh, is it important?"

With a playful growl, I dig my fingers into his ribs and tickle him. "*Very*, pixie." His laughter turns into squirming, which quickly turns into panting and thrusting. He takes both of our rigid cocks in hand, and my breathing goes ragged as he strokes us together.

"Yeah," I grunt, resting the back of my head against the sofa as I squeeze his hips hard. "So fucking good, baby."

"You think I'm good?" he rasps, his blue eyes locked with mine as he works our dicks.

"Mmm. The best."

Sensual satisfaction gleams in his gaze. "You're *so* right about that, my prince. But I can be even better." He slides down my body so he's on his hands and knees between my legs. Sinking to his elbows, he thrusts his ass high in the air and grasps the base of my shaft. With a look hot enough to melt glass, he wraps his pouty lips around my cock and takes me straight to the back of his throat.

"Gods," I wheeze, my hips lifting. I clutch his head as his hot, perfect mouth envelopes me and lightning zips down my spine. He bobs his head, sucking up and down my length. Getting me slick as he works his clever tongue all around my shaft and over my cockhead. He kneads my balls gently with my free hand before pressing two firm fingers to the sensitive skin behind my sack.

"Fuck!" I cry, thrusting hard. Fucking his mouth. I don't want to gag him, but I can't stop when he feels so good. When he looks so damn beautiful with the firelight dancing over his smooth skin and his shimmering wings and his insane ass. Panting, I sit up enough to run a hand over one round cheek before delving into his cleft.

He moans around my dick and bows his spine, thrusting his ass higher.

"Yeah," I rasp, sucking my fingers into my mouth before carrying them back to his crease. I tease his pucker as he continues sucking me. "Let me make you feel good, baby."

He nods as he sucks me, his hand working in tandem with his mouth. Pressure builds at the base of my spine, but I shove the orgasm away and continue fingering him. I don't want to come just yet. I need this to last a little longer. Our moments are slipping by so fast, and I need time to stop ticking.

The fire pops, bathing us in a soft glow. When Jasper sucks hard on the upstroke, I push him away as I cling to the edge of release by my fingertips. For one tense moment, I squeeze my eyes shut as I struggle not to come.

He rests his cheek against my thigh, his warm breath fluttering over my skin. "The first time we slept together, it was like this. In front of a fire. Do you remember?" His tone is curious but underscored by sadness.

I search my memory as I stroke both of his wings from base to tip. Silence stretches. "No," I admit. "There are flashes of you and me together in my bed in Villette. I don't remember a fire."

Jasper lifts his head. His blue eyes shine with unshed tears. "Let's make new memories, Vale. I hope we get the old ones back, but if we don't, I want new ones with you."

Assuming we get a chance to make them. That part hangs unspoken between us, but I hear it all the same.

"We will," I say, and I seal the promise with a kiss. It's tender at first, but soon the need to possess him completely takes over, and my mouth grows wild and hungry on his. I stretch him on his back on the blanket and kiss my way down his body, nipping at his throat, his collarbones, his pierced nipples. I run my tongue into the dips of his abs before kissing his twitching dick.

"Vale," he gasps, pulling at my hair as he lifts his hips. "You have to fuck me."

"I can't."

He rises to his elbows and glares at me. "Why the fuck not?"

Smiling, I seize his thighs and flip him onto his stomach. As he sputters, I press his cheeks apart. "Because I haven't had any dessert, and I'm craving something sweet." Holding him open, I bury my face in his ass.

Jasper goes limp. "Puck's knee socks, don't stop doing that."

My smile turns into a chuckle as I lick a circle around his hole. He spreads his legs wider, and I take it for the invitation it is and massage his balls as I rim his ass, opening him with my tongue. His moans and satisfied sighs fill the room, every sexy sound driving my lust higher.

As goosebumps lift on his thighs, I lick a stripe down his crack to his balls. I suckle them, tonguing each soft globe, before taking his swollen dick into my mouth and sucking him from behind.

"Vale!" he chokes out, lifting onto his knees as he claws at the blanket. "I'm gonna come," he pants, rocking back hard.

I pop off his dick and push a finger into his damp entrance. "No, you're not," I say firmly, using my finger in his ass to force him flat onto his stomach again. As he whimpers and clutches the blanket, I bite his ass cheek before climbing to my feet. "Turn over."

"Where are you going?" he demands as he rolls onto his back, his lips as pink and wet as his cock. "Oh," he says as I grab a bottle of lube from one of the side tables. "I forgot I put that there."

"*I* put it there," I say, kneeling between his thighs and dripping moisture onto my shaft. I slick myself before fingering lube into his opening.

He manages to give me a snarky look even as he shudders and clamps his hole around my questing finger. "You put a lot of planning into this picnic, huh?"

I sink another finger inside him and let a little cockiness leak into my smile. "Baby, *this* was the plan."

"Well—oh fuck, Vale—it's working." He pulls his knees to his chest, putting himself on display. "But if you don't get inside me right now, I'm going to throw you over the balcony."

"Noted, baby." I laugh as I grab my dick and brush it over his hole. As he shudders, I drag my cockhead up and down his cleft. Sparks shoot down the backs of my thighs. Pleasure coils like a snake at the base of my spine. Eyes locked with Jasper's, I call my power. Light bursts from the lines of my tattoo, sunlight spreading from my chest to the base of my dick. It vibrates against Jasper's ass as I press my hips forward, pushing my cockhead inside him.

He keens, his plump lips open on a desperate cry.

"Tell me how much you want this," I command, holding onto my control by a thread. "How much you need this. Only me. Only ever me."

"Only you," he pants. "I love you, Vale. Only you. Give it to me, please!" His cries rise higher as I press forward slowly, pleasure engulfing me as I watch my thick length disappear inside him. When I'm fully seated, I plant my forearms on either side of his head and seize his mouth in a sloppy kiss. He digs his fingers into my hair and bites at my lips. His ass clamps hard around my shaft, and I suck in a breath as desire crackles through me.

"You're going to make me come," I growl against his mouth as I start to move. I rock my hips and stare into his eyes, my thrusts jostling him on the blanket. "You feel so good with your tight, perfect ass gripping me. I can't last long, baby. You're going to steal my cum from me the same way you stole my heart."

"Fuck me," he breathes, his ankles on my shoulders and his breath puffing over my face. "Fuck me, Vale. *Gods*, it's so good. So deep. Don't stop."

"I'm not," I grunt, thrusting harder. Snapping my hips as sweat drips from my forehead and the sound of my dick squishing into his hole cranks my lust so high I think I might combust. "I'm not stopping. I'm giving you everything, and you're going to take it. Isn't that right?"

"Yes!" he cries, throwing his head back. His toes curl, and the tendons in his neck go taunt. His ass clenches rhythmically around me. My skin grows brighter, rays of sunlight spilling over Jasper's skin. The tattoo around my dick vibrates with every thrust.

We cry out together, lost in each other. He says my name over and over, the word spilling from him like a prayer as he threatens to fly apart beneath me. My power surges, painting ribbons of light over his sweat-slicked chest and delicate jaw. His flushed cheekbones and the long sweep of his lashes.

His wings glow golden at the edges. With a wild cry, he grabs his flailing dick and pumps it hard.

"Yeah," I grit out, thrusting so hard and fast the *slap, slap, slap* of my hips against his ass drowns out the fire in the hearth. "Come for me, baby. Every drop."

He gives his dick another quick stroke. Then he comes on a loud cry, creamy cum spurting in thick stripes that land as high as his chin.

That's what finishes me off. Pulling out, I jack my cock furiously, bliss rolling over me in fiery waves as I come all over his ass. Jasper groans and pulls his legs back, his splayed thighs and cum-covered chest so fucking gorgeous I cry out as more cum shoots from my dick.

"Yes," he gasps, his eyes glittering with something sexy and fierce. "Give it to me, Vale." He reaches down and strokes his fingers over his quivering entrance. "Fill me up."

Shuddering and gasping for breath, I drag my cockhead through a thick glob of cum and push it inside him. We moan, both of us shaking, as I repeat the motion, pushing the evidence of my possession so deep inside him I think I must eventually touch his heart.

I collapse on top of him with my dick lodged to the hilt and my heart racing so fast I can't catch my breath. We kiss again, and I'm burning alive. When this fades, there will be nothing left of me but fucking cinders. And somewhere deep in that pile of ash, Jasper will be the flickering ember that stokes me back to life. Our love is a phoenix. Zaphira might have killed us once, but we'll rise again. Over and over and over. Our love will never die.

It can't.

It won't.

Because I'll never let Jasper go.

~

Two hours later, Jasper lies on his back in bed, his soft snores filling the quiet room. One arm is flung over his head, the other draped across his stomach. The sheets are still tangled around his legs from our second round of lovemaking.

I sit on the edge of the mattress by his hip and stroke blond locks away from his forehead. Running my hand down his neck to his chest, I place my palm over his heart. The steady beat is as comforting as the sun's rays warming my skin. It's like Jasper found all the horrible, empty parts of me and filled them with love and light.

"I'll think of something," I promise even though he's not awake to hear me. "I will never let you go. Never." It's a promise to myself, too. I can't live with the lifeless chill of winter bearing down on me. I can't live without this pixie in my bed. In my mind.

In my heart.

Maybe I could have suffered through a loveless marriage before I found him. But now? There's no fucking way.

With a final, lingering look at Jasper, I rise and go to the main terrace off the living room. As I step outside, a wintry blast penetrates my clothes and steals my breath. Goosebumps cover my skin as I rub my arms to ward off the cold. The frigid air almost feels like a warning—a reminder that Zaphira's icy tentacles can reach me anywhere.

But that type of thinking won't help me. I've got to break my vow without dying, and I can't hide in the Hallows anymore. If Jasper and I are going to have a future together, I have to take some risks. Izig could stay with him while I return to Paris and confront Zaphira. Jasper won't like it, but I don't see any other options. I can't take him with me. If Zaphira got her hands on him…

Shoving down a growl, I study the city. It's still early in the night, but the Hallows is quiet. The whole world seems poised, its breath held as it awaits the next play in this deadly game of chess.

A tiny blue bird flits to the balcony railing, his delicate talons tight on the worn metal. He flaps his wings wildly, seemingly agitated. The hair on my nape lifts, and apprehension niggles in the back of my mind.

"What's wrong?" I ask. "Do you need help?" Maybe I should wake Jasper.

The bird darts forward and pecks me hard on the shoulder before zipping into the air and hovering out of reach.

"Hey!" I exclaim, rubbing at the spot. "What was that for?"

The bird hangs in the air, his wings beating so fast I can barely track their movements. Then he dives toward the street.

I lean over the railing. Below, the bird flies low to the ground and circles a dark shadow in the middle of the street.

I squint, struggling to make it out. Then I see it.

A black hat. A *bowler* hat.

Oh, fuck.

Heart pounding, I whirl and run for the bedroom. I'm halfway across the living room when the sound of the front door crashing open booms from the foyer. Seconds later, elven warriors with long, white hair fill the hallway. They're dressed in the colors of my father's court, but these are Winter Court elves. Each one wears a metal snowflake pinned to his chest.

"Hello, Prince Abelin," one of the men says. "We meet again."

A memory rushes back—the elf sneering before slamming a carriage door in my face. "You," I rasp, anger pounding through me.

Jasper stumbles from his bedroom wearing sweatpants and a T-shirt.

"Run!" I yell, stepping between him and the elves. "Go to the balcony and jump for the next one over!"

The warriors surge forward. "Go!" I scream at Jasper as a fist streaks toward me. I duck, then pop up and punch the first warrior in the jaw. As his head flies back, the others rush me.

"Vale!" Jasper cries.

"Run!" I shout as elves slam into me, trying to pull me to the ground. I break free and spin as two guards head toward Jasper. He raises his fists, but a guard backhands him. Jasper's head snaps back, blood spraying from his lip. He falls to his knees.

Red descends over my vision. Hands grab at me, but I roar and shake them off. I make it two steps when a guard seizes Jasper by the wing and yanks him to his feet. The wing crunches, and Jasper screams.

I bellow my rage and call on my power, tapping the battle magic reserved for the direst circumstances. The sun's heat boils me from the inside out as I summon every shred of light that dwells within me. With another roar, I thrust my hands out. Light streaks from my fingers in a glowing blade and strikes the elves holding Jasper. Terror flashes in their eyes just before they disappear in a puff of ash.

Movement behind me.

Jasper flings out a hand, his gaze on something over my shoulder. "No!"

I spin, but it's too late.

Pain blooms at the back of my head.

I fall, Jasper's screams in my ears as icicles drag down my spine. I must hit the floor, but I don't feel the impact as black snowflakes overtake my vision.

And then there's nothing.

CHAPTER 15
JASPER

The second I open my eyes, I know it's a mistake. For one thing, the world is blurry. Also, I'm as hungover as a demon getting his horns sharpened for the first time. I slam my eyes shut as needles stab my skull and nausea reenacts the ocean in my gut.

"Fuck," I mutter, taking shallow breaths. Wherever I partied last night, it must have been incredible. But damn if I'm not paying the price for it now. Bert is going to lecture me for days. He gets so sanctimonious whenever I indulge in—

I give a strangled gasp as my memories crash back.

Vale.

They took Vale.

"Vale!" I cry, struggling to sit up. Dimly, I realize I'm lying on some sort of bed. I fumble with the blankets as I swing my legs over the side. I get a glimpse of an elegant bedroom before pain lances my wing, making me suck in a sharp breath as a fresh wave of nausea hits me.

"Oh no," a soft voice says. "Take it easy." The scent of lilies surrounds me. A second later, gentle but firm fingers grip my shoulders and ease me back down. "You must rest," the voice says. "If you hurt your wing again, I'm not sure Ceri can mend it."

I go still. The world comes slowly into focus, revealing a woman frowning down at me.

No. Not a woman—an *elf*. And a familiar one. I've seen her before, when I stood in the queue to ask the dragon Gazzag for a flight back to the Hallows. On that occasion, she faced Vale with the details of her wedding printed between them in graceful calligraphy.

"You're Princess Liriel," I say.

Surprise registers in her eyes, which are wide and blue and fringed by curly black lashes. Her long, white-blond hair is caught back from her face, exposing the pointed tips of her ears. Her features are lovely, her skin as smooth as glass. Embroidered snowflakes march along the neckline of her light-blue gown, which hugs a slender, feminine figure. The bedroom behind her is decorated in the same pale blue as her dress.

"You know me?" she asks, her tone curious but kind.

I lever myself up, wincing as more pain zips across my wing. "I've seen the wedding announcements," I say, curving the injured wing inward so I can get a look at it. A fresh bruise covers the membrane.

But that's not the bad part. The edge is torn. If it doesn't heal—and tears sometimes don't—I'll never fly again. "Damn," I say, panic fluttering in my stomach. "Just my fucking luck."

"Here." Liriel leans a hip on the bed, sending more lily-scented air flowing around me. She reaches for my wing, then hesitates. "May I? I'm a decent healer." I must look skeptical, because she offers a soft smile. "If I wanted to harm you, I would have done it while you were unconscious. Besides, I already healed the bruise on your jaw."

I touch my face, memories of the Winter Court warriors swarming the apartment flashing through my head. Dread stabs through me. "Where's Vale?"

Liriel sobers. "He's uninjured, but my mother is holding him prisoner in one of the ice cells."

"Is an ice cell exactly what it sounds like?"

She nods. Then she glances over her shoulder and drops her voice just below a whisper. "I've long suspected my mother has spies who watch King Nylian. I think she found out he allowed Vale to travel to the Americas, and she had Vale followed. Once she discovered he was with you, she decided to kidnap him and hold him until the wedding." Liriel's eyes harden, and her beautiful features contort in a look of disgust. "My mother is obsessed with making this wedding happen."

A telltale tingling spreads down my spine.

Magic. The matchmaking gift I inherited from my grandfather. It's not limited to bringing people together. Sometimes, it lets me know when people prefer to remain apart.

"But you aren't?" I ask Liriel.

"Gods, no." She shakes her head vigorously, making a thick length of hair slide over her shoulder. "Vale is nice enough, but he's not my type." Her gaze softens. "And I think you know I'm not his."

Despite my shitty circumstances, I can't help but return her smile. "I have an inkling."

Without warning, a fuzzy head pokes from under the hem of Liriel's gown. Bright blue eyes blink at me, curiosity and intelligence burning in the sapphire depths.

"Oh!" Liriel exclaims. Smiling, she bends and lifts a fluffy white fox into her arms. "This is Neve, my familiar." Liriel smoothes a hand down the animal's luxurious-looking fur. "She's a little shy."

Before I can say anything, the door opens, and another beautiful elven woman walks in. A parrot perches on her shoulder. The woman stops short at the sight of Liriel seated on the edge of my bed. Then she frowns.

"He's not supposed to be sitting up!" She advances on the bed, her long yellow skirts swishing. Her hair is shorter than Liriel's and plaited in two braids the color of honey left in the sun. Freckles dust her nose, which turns up adorably at the end. The parrot's scarlet breast feathers are a dazzling contrast to her bright gown. The woman's leaf-green eyes narrow as she stops at the foot of the bed and gives me a stern look. "Do you want to spend the rest of your life on the ground, pixie?"

On her shoulder, the parrot tilts its head and mimics her expression as it stares me down. Its blue and yellow tail feathers trail over her shoulder.

Liriel angles her hand next to her lips and speaks to me out of the corner of her mouth. "In a good cop, bad cop scenario, I'm the good cop and Ceridwen is most definitely the bad cop." Her lips twitch. "She's also a much better healer than I am."

"It's not a competition, Your Highness," Ceridwen says.

"Murder!" the parrot screeches, one beady black eye pinned on me.

Ceridwen reaches up and taps its beak. "Sherlock! You can't just blurt that out every time you meet someone." She gives me an apologetic look. "I'm so sorry, Jasper."

"It's okay," I say. "A lot of people want to murder me when they first meet me."

"Oh no, he didn't mean it that way," Ceridwen says. "Sherlock loves detective novels." She looks at the parrot. "Don't you, Sherlock?"

"Whodunit!"

"Exactly," Ceridwen says. She gives the parrot a no-nonsense look. "But you could still greet our guest properly."

The parrot looks at me and bobs his head. "'Ello," he squawks in a Cockney accent.

Ceridwen gives him another pointed look as she moves around the bed. She sits opposite Liriel and runs a critical gaze over my wing. The sternness fades from her eyes as she offers me a reassuring smile. "It's not as bad as it looks."

"Oh," I say, relief coursing through me. "Thank the gods." I flutter my uninjured wing as I look from Ceridwen to Liriel. "My wings aren't good for much beyond short hops, but I'd definitely miss the hops."

Liriel grins. "Ceri will fix you up." She reaches over my legs and grasps the other woman's hand. "She's the finest healer in any court."

Ceri's cheeks go pink. "I don't know about that."

"I do," Liriel insists, her amusement fading to something more intimate as she gazes at Ceri. "You don't give yourself enough credit."

My magic sparks in a rush of effervescence like champagne bubbles tickling my veins. If I'm not mistaken, Princess Liriel has no problem with a wedding—as long as Ceri is waiting for her at the end of the aisle.

"How long have you two known each other?" I ask.

Liriel startles, her cheeks going as pink as Ceri's. She snatches her hand from the other woman's arm and casts a quick look around the room. "Um, forever, really. Ceri is my lady-in-waiting."

I look around the room, too, apprehension crawling through me. If Zaphira spies on her husband, she probably spies on her daughter, as well.

Especially if she suspects Liriel might not be keen on marrying Vale.

Puck's pierced taint, I can't escape matchmaking even in the middle of a kidnapping. On the other hand, if Liriel is in love with her lady-in-waiting, she could be exactly the sort of ally Vale and I need right now.

I lean toward Liriel and pitch my voice low. "Will your mother hurt Vale?"

She and Ceri exchange a nervous look. Then Liriel speaks in the same hushed tone. "Not where anyone could see. She knows the king would have her head."

"Where is the king?" As soon as the question leaves my lips, anger coils in my chest. Nylian isn't much of a monarch—or father—if he can't stop his wife from imprisoning his own son.

"King Nylian never comes here," Liriel says, worry in her eyes. "This is my mother's estate. Every guard in the manor answers solely to her, and she's spelled them so they can't speak against her. I doubt His Majesty is even aware that Vale is in Paris."

Ceri snorts softly. "And your mother probably fed him a line of bullshit to stop him from asking questions."

"Keep your voice down," Liriel says, looking around again. Neve must sense her distress, because the little fox places a fuzzy paw on Liriel's arm.

Ceri's expression goes contrite. She and Liriel exchange a meaningful look, and then Ceri gestures to my wing. "I believe I can heal it, but it'll probably take more than one session. Do you want me to try?"

"Fuck, yes." I glance at Liriel. "I mean, yes, please."

Liriel smiles. "The first one worked just fine."

Grinning, I fold my wing toward Ceri. "In that case, please fix my fucking wing."

Ceri laughs softly as she grips the edge. Her smile fades as she stares intently at the tear. On her shoulder, Sherlock once again adopts a similar expression as his mistress.

After a second, Ceri's hand begins to glow. The golden light spreads like the sun peeking above the horizon. Rays touch the tear, which slowly starts to knit back together. Heat suffuses my wing, and the sensation is so much like basking in Vale's power that tears prick my eyes.

Liriel grips my hand, her blue gaze full of understanding.

Sweat beads on Ceri's brow. Her skin pales, her freckles standing out boldly. Sherlock brushes his sleek head against her temple as if he means to comfort her. The golden light envelopes him, too, gilding his feathers and setting his round eyes shimmering.

Vibrations frazzle through my wing. The two edges of the tear press tightly together and shine like someone painted a golden stripe down the center. The heat flares higher, and then Ceri releases me with a gasp.

The light winks out.

I examine my wing. A combination of relief and awe spread through me as I study the faint scar. I look at Ceri, who watches me with a satisfied expression. "Thank you, Ceri. That was brilliant."

Pink touches her cheekbones again. "You're very welcome. We can do another round tomorrow. That should get rid of any scarring."

"Yes, please. I'm much too pretty to pull off a pirate look."

Ceri smiles as she rises. "I'll bring you something to eat. You're probably starving after that two-day flight."

My humor dies a swift death. "Two days?" But of course, she's right. Dragon back is the only reliable way to cross the ocean. If I've lost two days, that means the wedding is in—

"Three days," Liriel says, clearly discerning the source of my rising panic. "The winter solstice is in three days. If Vale and I don't say our vows by the time the clock strikes midnight on the solstice, we'll both die."

Ceri makes a muffled sound and presses slim fingers to her lips. Sherlock flutters his wings in an agitated movement.

My panic spirals higher, but I shove it down. "Is there any way I could speak to Vale?" I ask Liriel.

She shakes her head, regret in her eyes. "The dungeon is well-guarded. No one gets near it without my mother's permission."

My heart sinks, and I slump against the pillows as the reality of my situation sets in. How in the world am I going to get around an unbreakable elven vow? Mab couldn't help. I can't even see Vale, let alone talk to him. I have no way to contact Bert and Mert, assuming they're unharmed—and still alive.

No.

I refuse to acknowledge that as a possibility. I sit up as new resolve fills my chest. If I've learned anything over the six decades I've been matchmaking, it's that love is a potent form of magic. People like to underestimate it because it's not flashy or cool. But it's enduring. It fucking *persists*. Love thrives even in the bleakest, most inhospitable environments. Even in the coldest depths of winter.

Vow or not, Vale's evil stepmother isn't going to win. I have three days to save the man I love. If I fail, I won't just lose out on a life with Vale.

I'll lose him forever.

CHAPTER 16
VALE

I stare into an old-fashioned brazier in the bowels of Fourneclaire. Meager blue flames flicker among the coals—just another reminder from Zaphira that even the hottest of fires can be corrupted by winter.

My prison cell is six feet by eight feet and coated in a thin sheet of ice. The barred door never opens, although food appears whenever I nod off. A barred window high up on the wall reveals a dark sky. I woke here after the attack in the Hallows and haven't seen a single soul. I don't even know what day it is.

And I don't know if Jasper is okay. For the millionth time since I opened my eyes, the attack in the apartment plays through my head. *He's okay.* He has to be. I'd feel it if something happened to him. But even as I tell myself this, worry gnaws at me. Because the truth is, I don't know for sure.

All I know is that Zaphira is behind the attack—and my imprisonment. Undoubtedly, she plans on keeping me here until the moment I walk down the aisle.

I rub my arms for warmth as the stars outside wink playfully through the window. Grunting, I wander the cell for the hundredth time, yanking at the bars and checking for inconsistencies or weak points. After a frustrating half hour where nothing gives, I sit on the floor with my back to the wall. Drawing on my meager power reserves, I summon enough sunlight to melt the ice beneath me. The respite won't last long, and I'm not sure I'll have enough energy to do it again.

But I don't think Zaphira intends to starve me. She won't risk this wedding not happening.

That's the *only* thing I can count on.

A faint scratching sound draws my attention to the cell door. A second later, two small, furry bodies push through the spaces between the bars. *Mice.* My heart thumps faster as they scamper to me and sit on their haunches.

Hope soars in my chest. "Bert," I gasp, relief flooding me. I look at the other mouse. "Mert?"

The rodent nods, then releases a stream of high-pitched squeaks.

Frustration replaces my relief. I can't communicate with them. I glance at the cell door. "Is Sully with you?"

Bert squeaks. When I simply stare at him, the look in his dark eyes mirrors my frustration.

"I'm sorry," I say, "I don't understand." But the memory of Fuoco questioning Jasper gives me an idea. "Here," I tell the mice, holding out my palm. When they climb onto it, I bring them close to my face. "Let's do this. I'll ask questions, and you nod for *yes* and shake for *no*, okay?"

They dip their heads in unison, and I smile for the first time since I woke in my icy prison. But my next question wipes any humor from my heart.

"Is Jasper here?"

They nod.

My relief is so intense, it's a second before I can speak again. "Is he hurt?"

The mice look at each other. Bert nods as Mert shakes his head.

I frown. "What is that, a maybe?"

Bert and Mert look at each other again, and then Mert faces away, showing me his plump hindquarters. Bert waves a paw over Mert's back. Mert looks at me over his shoulder and bats his eyelashes.

"What...?" I shake my head. "I'm sorry, I don't— Wait, are you supposed to be Jasper?" As Mert nods enthusiastically, Bert waves his paw over Mert's back again. "Wings!" I exclaim. "Jasper hurt his wing!"

Both mice nod.

"But he'll be okay?"

The mice exchange a look I can't decipher.

"Have you talked to him?" I ask.

They shake their heads.

Confusion swamps me. "Have you seen him?"

Another shake, and my confusion grows.

"Have you seen Sulien?"

They nod.

My heart lifts. "What about Izig?"

Another nod. Bert jerks his head toward the cell door.

"He's outside?"

Bert gives me an exasperated look.

"He's in a cell," I amend.

Bert nods.

Fuck. Zaphira spells her ice cells so no sounds enter or exit. Izig could have been yelling for me since I arrived, and I'd have no idea. I can't do *anything* from where I sit. Once again, my stepmother pulls the strings, and everyone dances like her puppets.

"Do you have any information that can help me?" I ask the mice.

Bert places a paw on my wrist. Eyes solemn, he shakes his head.

A fresh wave of frustration fills me. Bert and Mert know Jasper hurt his wing, but they haven't seen him. And I can't unravel that mystery using our primitive form of communication. If only I could actually *talk* to them.

"Thanks, guys," I say softly, hearing the regret and fatigue in my voice as I lower the mice to the ground. They clamber off my palm, then watch as I pull Mab's note from my pocket. The paper looks a lot worse than it did when Jasper plucked it from the fire. It's my only link to him, and it's creased from all the times I've held it in the cell and run my fingers over the places where he touched it. As I unfold it now, Bert scratches at my arm hard enough to leave a mark.

Startled, I almost drop the note. "What is it?"

He tips his head toward the brazier.

"No way." I tighten my grip on the paper. "I'm not burning this."

Bert flicks his tail and releases an angry-sounding squeak. He points at the note, then runs to the brazier.

I look at Mert, who nods before copying Bert's actions. When he reaches Bert, he swivels around so he faces away from me. Bert waves a paw over his brother's back the same as he did when he tried to show me Jasper's wings.

A frown pulls at my brow as I watch the mice. Confusion growing, I lower my gaze to the paper. Bert and Mert are miming Jasper, but the note is from Mab...

I bring my head up sharply. "You want me to contact Mab."

Both mice let out pleased-sounding squeaks. Mert nudges his hip against Bert's, and they exchange a look like *finally, this dense elf gets it*.

I shake my head. "I can't contact Mab through the fire." Jasper's voice rings in my memory. *It's a uniquely pixie form of communication.* Before I saw Jasper throw the note into his fireplace, I had no idea pixies sent letters that way. Shame grips me as I realize I know far less about his culture than he does about mine. Even in the Summer Court, elves don't lower themselves to learn about pixies.

Except...pixies and elves share a common ancestor. My heart speeds up, and I stand and move toward the brazier.

Mert squeaks and beckons me closer.

"Our two species are distant cousins," I say, my breath puffing in the icy air. I reach the brazier and look down at the mice. "It could work."

They nod, twin expressions of approval in their dark eyes.

"Please let this work," I mutter, baring my fangs and biting the tip of my finger. Blood wells, and I touch my fingertip to the paper and scribble one word.

Help.

I fold the note and hold it over the flickering blue flames. "Um, please deliver this to Mab, Queen of the Pixies." Closing my eyes, I picture Jasper tipping his head back as the sun's rays slant over his face. Flames crackle, and I open my eyes and look down to see a regular fire burning among the coals. Holding my breath, I toss the paper into the flames.

Nothing happens.

"Damn," I murmur, defeat threatening to slump my shoulders. As I start to turn away, the flames shoot higher. Red sparks spill from the brazier like miniature fireworks. The flames change color, shifting from orange to yellow before settling on green.

I hold my breath.

The letter winks out of sight.

∽

AN HOUR LATER, I know Mab isn't going to show. I pace the cell, Bert and Mert tucked carefully inside my breast pocket. Uncertainty and fear war with my determination to get out of the elven bond.

Although, right now, I'd be happy just to get out of this fucking cell.

"Gods," I mutter, shoving a hand through my hair. My fingers are numb again, and I lower my hand and blow into my cupped palms.

A sudden twinkling in the sky outside the window makes me stop. Slowly, the twinkling becomes a glow and then an irritated-sounding voice chirps from the outside.

"Bars on the windows? Zaphira is really putting her whole heart into this bitchy villain thing."

Bert and Mert poke their heads above my pocket. My heart pounds as the twinkling light floats between the bars and moves to the center of the cell. It swells, and I throw up a hand as the glow blinds me. The air fills with pressure.

Pop!

The light disappears, and Queen Mab stands in the middle of the cell. Her hair is bubblegum pink and arranged in a messy bun on top of her head. She wears black combat boots, a black leather jacket, and a tutu the same shade as her hair.

She's also holding a wand with a little star on the end.

I blink to make sure I'm not dreaming. Or hallucinating. Probably, I'm hallucinating. I haven't eaten in a while.

Mab props a hand on her hip and gives me a cheeky look. "Well, Prince Vale, you're in a pickle."

"Uh…" I clear my throat as I look between Mab and the window. "I didn't know you could do…that."

"What?"

"Shrink."

"Oh, yeah, I'm a multitasker." She winks, her blue eyes the same brilliant shade as Jasper's. "You never know when you're gonna need to fit into a tight spot, am I right?" Before I can respond, she waves a manicured hand. "Plus, true love is like catnip for me. Oh! Speaking of catnip…" She puts her fingers to her mouth and whistles sharply.

In my pocket, Bert and Mert cover their ears.

Seconds later, Sulien slinks between the bars of the cell door and streaks toward me.

"Sully!" I go to one knee and then grunt when he plants his front paws on my shoulders, nearly knocking me over in the process. Joy bursts in my chest as he swipes his scratchy tongue over my cheek.

"Vale," he says through our bond, his mental voice strained. *"I'm sorry I couldn't come to you right away. Your stepmother has guards around every corner."*

"Don't worry about it," I say out loud as I stand and rub between his ears. "I'm just glad you're safe."

"Fourneclaire is a cesspool of dark magic," he growls.

Mab huffs. "Tell me about it."

I jerk my head toward her. "You can hear him?"

She lifts a shoulder, a pleased smile quirking her lips. "Cats love me."

The declaration is so reminiscent of Jasper that a fist squeezes my heart. Tears burn my throat, and I can almost hear my father's voice telling me to keep control. But I've already lost it. The proof is all around me in the form of four icy walls. I yielded the upper hand to Zaphira by hiding in the Hallows and doing nothing. Now she's got Jasper, and I'm powerless to help him.

Mab cocks her head to the side, her gaze on Bert and Mert. After a second, her eyes warm. "Well, of course they are, Bertram. Anyone with eyes could have told you that."

In my pocket, Bert sticks his chin in the air and releases a squeak that sounds suspiciously like *'hmph'*."

Mab chuckles. Then she looks at me, her expression abruptly razor-focused. "How serious are you about getting out of this vow?"

My heart skips a beat. "Very. But I thought you said you can't break it."

"True. *I* can't." She shoots me a mysterious little smile. "Words matter, elf." As I suck in a breath at having my line to Jasper parroted back to me, she claps her hands together, fumbles her wand, and sticks it into her bun. "Right," she says, rolling up her sleeves. "Let's get cracking. We've got twenty-four hours until the solstice—"

"What?" I gasp, panic rising.

Mab waves it off. "Don't worry, I'm excellent under pressure. Now, I have an idea for how to fix this, but it's just a theory." Her deep blue eyes bore into mine as her tone grows grave. "I need you to understand that it might not work. And if it doesn't, you could break your vow and die. Are you prepared to take that risk?"

At my feet, Sulien stiffens. When I look down, his golden eyes brim with worry.

Risk. It's what I've tried to avoid. From the moment I learned of the geas, I've sought to keep Jasper from harm.

But no, it started before that, when I kept my betrothal from him in Paris. I told myself I was waiting for the right moment to tell him—that I didn't want to risk ruining what we had—but, really, I was a coward. And I hurt him. Despite everything, he took me back. My mischievous, loving, wonderful pixie gave me another chance. Can I risk my life to give us a chance for a real future together?

I meet Mab's gaze. "Tell me what I need to do."

She grins. "How much do you know about glass slippers?"

CHAPTER 17
JASPER

The day of the wedding dawns cold as fuck. No surprise, considering Fourneclaire is a giant refrigerator.

As the hours tick by, servants come and go, curling and primping and preparing Liriel and her attendants for the ceremony. The mood is somber, and if I never see another snowflake again it'll be too soon.

"Is your mother aware that most people actively dislike winter?" I ask Liriel as I sprawl on the sofa in her bedroom. I lie on my back with my legs draped over the rolled arm. My newly healed wing droops toward the plush carpet I've grown tired of staring at over the past three days. I stare at the ceiling now as I bounce one leg up and down. A plaster medallion in the shape of a snowflake surrounds the crystal chandelier. *Ice* crystals. Zaphira's decor is woefully predictable. I bounce my leg harder and give the medallion the middle finger.

Liriel makes a low, pained sound. When I turn my head, I find her seated at her vanity with her elbows on the surface and her head in her hands. As she feels the weight of my regard, she lifts her head and meets my gaze in the mirror. Her pale hair is piled high in an intricate arrangement that defies gravity. Her silk robe is the same snowy shade as her hair. Servants did her makeup as we lunched. She looks beautiful—and utterly devastated.

"Hey," I say, swinging my legs off the sofa's arm and standing. I flick my wings as I move to her side and rest a hand on her silk-covered shoulder. Neve curls at her feet, the fox's posture defeated.

I open my mouth to ask what's wrong, but then I snap it shut. We both know what's wrong.

Liriel offers me a sad smile in the mirror. "I don't think my mother is interested in what other people like or dislike."

My gut clenches. For the past three days, I've done my best to put on a brave face. I've tapped every ounce of pixie charm I possess even as I've searched for a way to get to Vale. But I haven't been able to charm my way more than a dozen steps past Liriel's bedroom. In the beginning, the elven guards were posted at the end of the corridor. The second time I attempted to sneak past them, they moved to right outside the bedroom door—but not before they made me regret trying to evade their notice.

"Nice try with the glamour, pixie," the bigger one growled as he buried a fist in my gut. *"But your tricks won't work here."*

Gasping for air, I jerked out of the second guard's reach. *"Watch it, dickhead, this is cashmere."* As the first guard seized my elbow and hauled me toward the bedroom, I dragged my feet. *"You always sucker punch your prisoners, tough guy?"*

He thrust me away from him and delivered a brutal, open-handed slap that sent me reeling into the second guard. As I swallowed blood, the first guard shoved me toward the bedroom. *"Not always,"* he said with a cruel laugh. *"Sometimes, we slap them."*

Ceri scolded me afterward, but her hands shook as she healed the cut on my lip. *"You have to be careful, Jasper. They'll kill you if you push them too far."*

Movement in the mirror pulls me from my memories. Liriel reaches a hand up and wraps her slim fingers around mine. "We're out of time," she whispers, her blue eyes flicking to the window reflected behind us. Through the ice-coated bars, snowflakes swirl in the night sky.

My throat goes dry as I look at the small clock on Liriel's nightstand. One hour until midnight. And one hour until I watch Vale marry someone else. Or watch him die trying to break his vow.

"I'll think of something," I say, meeting Liriel's gaze.

"Will you, really?" a deep, feminine voice drawls through the door. It opens, and two Summer Court warriors with snowflake badges on their chests enter, followed by a tall, regal woman with black hair and skin like snow. She pauses just inside the threshold, a vicious smile curving her red lips as she pins me with a glacial look. "Typical pixie," she adds softly, "a lot of big talk and not much else. No wonder Abelin is infatuated with you." She rakes a dismissive gaze down my body, lingering on my wings. "He always did like useless, pretty things."

Anger flares, and I open my mouth with a demand to see Vale on my lips. My words die as Liriel gives my hand a warning squeeze that grinds my bones together.

Zaphira smiles and tilts her head to the side, setting the icy blue diamonds in her ears swinging. "Do you want to see him? Don't worry, you'll have a front-row view when he says his vows."

I clench my jaw as I hold her stare.

She raises her voice. "Ceridwen! We're all waiting!" A second later, Ceri rushes through the door with a billowing white gown in her arms. Sherlock swoops into the room behind her and settles on the back of a chair with snowflakes embroidered on the cushion.

"'Ello," he squawks, bobbing his head in Zaphira's direction.

She gives him an irritated look.

"Apologies for my tardiness, Your Majesty," Ceri says, her voice breathless as she dips a curtsy. She wobbles under the enormous dress before righting herself. "We were looking for the shoes."

Zaphira's eyes flash. "Did you find them?"

"Yes, ma'am." Ceri shifts the dress in her arms, revealing a pair of women's high heels pinched between her fingers. Dainty and transparent, the shoes gleam like glass.

"Take care with them."

"Yes, Your Majesty."

Zaphira motions Ceri toward Liriel. "Dress the princess quickly. We're running short on time." She turns to the guards. "And someone fetch the pixie's clothes." The temperature drops as Zaphira smiles at me. "We don't want our guest to miss the festivities."

Over the next half hour, servants move in and out of Liriel's bedroom like the tide coming and going. I change into a pair of white silk knee breeches and a heavy white jacket embroidered with silver snowflakes. Ceri and several other elven women help Liriel into her wedding finery under the icy supervision of Zaphira and the guards. When Liriel makes a sound of protest as the women begin to remove her robe, Zaphira rolls her eyes.

"Oh, don't be such a prude, Liriel."

Liriel glances at the guards. "I'm not a prude, Mother. I just—"

"Get on with it," Zaphira orders the women. Several cast Liriel apologetic looks as they pull the princess's robe from her shoulders, exposing her white lingerie.

"Bitch," I mutter, rage searing my chest as I glare at Zaphira.

She turns. As she lifts a hand, my heart speeds up. I brace for pain, but she flicks her wrist in Ceri's direction. A long, thin icicle streaks toward the lady-in-waiting, who gasps and jerks out of its path at the last second. The icicle embeds itself in the wall, its tapered length shivering.

I swallow hard as my heart thumps painfully.

"Did you have something to say, pixie?" Zaphira asks softly.

"No." As Liriel shoots me a pleading look, I dip my head and grind out, "Your Majesty."

After a few more minutes, Liriel is ready at last. Her white gown is adorned with silver snowflakes. Flurries dance around her billowing skirt. A crown of ice crystals glitters in her hair. Ceri stands to the side, her hands clasped in front of her and a look of such intense longing on her face that I have to bite back a sob.

Or maybe a scream. Because this is all *wrong*. My matchmaking magic pings in a thousand frazzled directions, my gift urging me to intervene as the guards move to the door. But I bite my tongue against the need to speak up. I have zero doubt Zaphira is unhinged enough to seriously hurt, if not outright kill, Ceri if I say anything else.

"Let's go," Zaphira says, impatience in her tone. When Neve starts toward the door, Zaphira makes a negative sound. "No. Familiars stay behind."

Ceri and Liriel exchange a tense look. After a moment's hesitation, Liriel bends and strokes the fox's head. "I'll be back later."

Neve rubs snowy whiskers along Liriel's hand before walking to Sherlock and sitting by his chair.

"Murder!" the parrot shrieks.

Zaphira turns to Ceridwen. "I told you to teach your bird some manners."

"I'm sorry, Your Majesty. I'll speak to him."

Liriel and her attendants move toward the door.

"After you, pixie," the guard who slapped me says at my shoulder. His eyes are a dull brown. A thick scar bisects his cheek.

My fingers itch, hexing dust flowing down my arm to my hand.

"Try it," he taunts softly. "Give me an excuse."

I hold his stare, and I let all the anger, fear, and frustration of the past three days coalesce into resolve. It must show in my eyes, because the guard's sneer falters.

"Soon," I promise, brushing past him and stepping into the wide corridor. Liriel and her attendants move toward a grand staircase. Ceri carries Liriel's train. I move to her side and lift a handful of gauzy material.

"Oh," I say, surprise flitting through me when the train melts against my skin only to immediately reform. "It's snow."

Tears brim in Ceri's green eyes before she blinks them away.

I move my hand along the edge of the train and grip her fingers.

"Someone will see," she whispers, fear in her voice.

"No, they won't." I reach over and flip more lacy snowflakes over our joined hands. "There's so much magical snow on this dress you could ski down it."

Ceri gives a watery laugh before quickly biting her lip.

"Steady," I tell her as we reach the stairs. "This isn't over until that clock chimes midnight. We're not giving up."

She nods, and as we descend the stairs I try to follow my own advice.

∽

TEN MINUTES LATER, anxiety and anticipation are a potent mix in my chest as we enter the ballroom where the ceremony will take place.

We pause just inside the huge double doors, guards flanking us. A string quartet sends classical music floating into the soaring space, which is dazzling but austere in silver and white with touches of pale blue. Icicles cling to the ceiling, their spiky points glittering like diamonds. Snowflakes drift through the air and disappear before they touch the floor. An ancient-looking clock hangs high on the wall, its long hands showing ten minutes until midnight. Elves from both the Summer and Winter Courts gather on either side of a long, silvery runner. Neither group looks pleased to see each other.

But the most displeased-looking elf in the room is Vale.

Vale.

My knees loosen, and I almost trip and fall headfirst into Liriel's train. Ceri tightens her grip on my hand, keeping me upright.

"Thanks," I say breathlessly, my heart threatening to pound from my chest and sprint to the dais where the love of my life stares at me with intense golden eyes. For a moment, the ballroom falls away, and it's just us. I drink him in greedily, letting my gaze roam from his mahogany hair and firm, stubbled jaw to his broad chest and strong legs planted on the snow-covered dais. Relief pounds through me at the sight of Sulien sitting at his side. Every few seconds, the cat rubs his whiskers along Vale's thigh.

I can hardly blame him. Vale has never been more radiant. His golden jacket hugs his muscular shoulders. Tight-fitting breeches make my mouth water. Black boots rise to his knees. A crown sprinkled with yellow gemstones nestles among his waves, which are tucked behind his pointed ears. As we stare at each other across the length of the ballroom, his hands twitch at his sides. He looks me over, his gaze returning again and again to my wing.

He worries I'm still hurt, I realize, tears burning my throat. Ahead of me, Liriel sinks into a low curtsy. As the other elves do the same, an ear-splitting roar rips through the ballroom. A second later, a griffin stalks from somewhere and climbs onto the dais. A tall, powerful-looking elf wearing an ornate crown follows in the beast's wake. As the elf steps beside Vale and faces the crowd, every knee in the room hits the floor. The musicians pause their music.

The temperature plunges.

Vale's jaw tightens.

Zaphira sweeps from behind me, moves past Liriel, and glides to the dais. She pauses before King Nylian and dips a shallow curtsy. "Husband."

The king inclines his head. "Wife." He sweeps a hand to the side, and Zaphira mounts the dais and settles on a small throne positioned next to a larger one.

King Nylian rests a hand on the griffin's head. Vale stands stiffly at his father's side. Seeing them together, it's impossible to mistake them for anything but father and son. Nylian's hair is longer, his build smaller, but his handsome features are so similar to Vale's it's almost like seeing double—or perhaps it would be if not for the king's cold expression.

My nape prickles as Nylian gazes at the crowd—because he doesn't appear to actually *see* anything. His stare is curiously blank, his expression almost...frozen.

"I bid you welcome!" he says suddenly, his voice booming through the ballroom. He lifts his hand from the griffin's head and motions to the crowd. "Please, rise."

Every elf in the ballroom straightens in one smooth, coordinated movement.

"Our people could never pull that off," Mab murmurs next to me.

I snort. "I know, right?" I jerk my head to the side so hard my neck twinges. "Ow! Fuck."

"Keep your voice down," my aunt says, her gaze on the dais. She furrows her brow. "I thought you weren't supposed to wear white to weddings." On the dais, King Nylian launches into a solemn-sounding speech about maintaining peace among the elven courts.

"Jasper?" Ceri murmurs on my other side. When I look at her, she's staring at Mab with a troubled expression. "Do you know him?"

Him? I swing back to my aunt, who winks at me as her glamour flickers, giving me a glimpse of a nondescript male with muddy brown eyes.

I lean into her and whisper in her ear. "Are you wearing Tower du Sang's glamour?"

"Oh, this old thing?" Mab looks down at herself with a distracted air. "I must have bought it off him."

"Wait, when did you meet Tower?"

"Who?"

I take a deep breath. *Tower du Sang.* The leader of the vamp— You know what, never mind. What are you doing here?"

Mab pulls a silver wand from behind her ear. "Fairy godmother shit." She flicks the wand over me. Nothing happens.

"Aunt Mab, that wand is plastic."

"Is it?" She peers at the star on the end. "Damn." She shoves it at me.

"What am I supposed to do with this?" I hiss, taking it.

"I don't know, put it in your pocket."

"In these breeches?" I mutter, stuffing the wand as deep as I can get it and flipping my coat over it.

Mab studies me, one manicured finger tapping against her lips. "Here, let's try this." She swipes a hand through the air and tosses a handful of hot pink pixie dust over me. Instantly, I stagger under the weight of an enormous wedding gown.

Liriel's wedding gown. I reach up and feel the ice-crystal crown on my head. I'm inches taller, my feet tucked into the glass slippers under my skirt of snowflakes. My glamour is seamless.

Ceri's jaw drops.

Mab flings another handful of dust at Liriel, whose back stiffens as she transforms into me.

For a moment, disorientation sweeps me as I stare at myself from behind, taking in my short, platinum hair and fluttering wings. Then Rufus steps beside me and runs his gaze down Me-But-Not-Me.

"Your ass looks halfway decent in those breeches."

"Fuck you," I murmur, "my ass looks stunning." I look at my aunt's steward and get a glimpse of his bushy red beard hidden under the glamour of an elven female. "How did you get past the guards?"

His teeth flash white against his bright red lipstick. "Trade secret." He nudges me in front of him. "Go marry your man before these elves figure us out."

As soon as he says it, King Nylian's voice soars through the ballroom. "...and we maintain this peace through the bond of marriage." No one has moved since Mab and Rufus showed up.

"Oy!" Rufus says, giving me another nudge. "Switch places with the princess."

Heart racing, I lift my gown and move forward as Liriel turns—and I experience the mind-fuck of seeing my own eyes go wide as Liriel realizes we've traded appearances.

Ceri beckons to Liriel, and I watch as understanding lights my eyes.

"It's always so sweet when they finally get it," Mab says beside me.

Hope and confusion swirl through me as I turn to my aunt. "I thought you said you couldn't break Vale's vow."

She reaches up and pats my cheek. "I'm not going to break it, honey. *You* are."

Liriel goes to Ceri as Rufus melts into the crowd.

Before I can take another step, a rattling sound fills my ears, followed by a hiss that makes me turn just as a basilisk slips between the ballroom's double doors. Fangs bared, it lunges for me.

I stumble backward, losing one of my slippers in the process.

Mab steps in front of me and flings a cloud of pixie dust into the basilisk's gaping mouth. The serpent snaps its jaws shut and recoils as red blisters spread down its body. Eyes rolling in obvious agony, it retreats through the doors.

Mab spins back around and waves me toward the dais with a frantic whisper. "It's five minutes to midnight. Go!"

Abruptly, music swells. Around me, the guards rouse as if waking from a daydream. In the crowd, a few elves sway on their feet. King Nylian goes to his throne and sits. His griffin tosses its head and follows the king. A tall, somber-looking elf dressed in bright yellow robes steps beside Vale and opens a book.

"Go *on*," Mab says, nudging me forward.

"My shoe," I protest, stumbling.

"Forget it. Your prince is waiting."

I lift my head and meet Vale's gaze as every set of eyes in the ballroom lands on me. But I barely notice. Memories swirl—warm, spring days in Paris and a summer prince smiling at me in the middle of a cobblestone street as I smooth my hair.

I'm better than most at seeing under glamour.

In my memory, honey-colored eyes smile, delight swimming in their depths. *Is that so?*

The same eyes smile at me now. I don't know if Vale can see under my glamour, but it doesn't matter.

He knows.

He knows it's me.

I'm coming, I tell him silently as I hold his gaze and move down the aisle. I walk the gauntlet of elves in my Liriel glamour, each step carrying me closer to Vale. *I'm coming, my prince.*

I'm not going to lose you.

CHAPTER 18
VALE

Hope and fear war within me as Jasper walks down the aisle. I don't need his gift to peer under his glamour. I'd know my pixie anywhere.

But I have to count on Mab knowing what she's doing. Because if this plan doesn't work, I'll die and leave Jasper at Zaphira's mercy.

Under my heavy court clothes, sweat trickles down my spine. Around me, no one seems to notice anything amiss. Elves from both courts follow Jasper's progress. From the looks on their faces, they see what they're supposed to see: Liriel in a stunning, winter-themed wedding gown that represents her court.

At the bottom of the dais, Liriel's uncle, King Elendor of the Winter Court, observes the bridal procession with a cool, detached expression. His warriors flank him, their faces just as dispassionate. Many of the higher-ranking elves have their familiars with them. At the edge of the crowd, Elendor's silvery reindeer noses the lower tiers of the towering wedding cake.

Sulien purrs softly through our bond as he sits at my side, a silent sentinel. Izig stands among the crowd. Thank fuck he's alright. Acrid bitterness underscores my relief at seeing him.

He'll suffer, too, if this doesn't work. Zaphira won't leave any stone unturned in her quest to punish me and the people I love.

The music swells. Heads turn slowly, all eyes on the bride.

Beside me, the officiant makes a pleased, humming sound. "Lovely gown." He sways toward me, his elbow brushing mine. "You're a lucky man, Your Highness."

"Thank you," I say under my breath. *Let's hope my luck doesn't run out.*

At the far end of the ballroom, Ceri stands next to Liriel glamoured to appear as Jasper. Their expressions are tense as Jasper lifts Ceri's hand and holds it close to his heart. His knuckles turn white as they stare into each other's eyes.

Stop it, I will silently. At the edge of my vision, Zaphira still sits on her throne. My father is a stoic presence beside her, his long fingers stroking absently through Olios's mane.

At last, Ceri and Jasper meet my gaze. When I give a subtle nod, they part and trail up the aisle behind Liriel, straightening her long, icy train.

Tension tightens my shoulders as Liriel nears the dais. She wobbles suddenly, and I catch a glimpse of bare toes peeking from under her gown's embroidered trim. She's missing a glass slipper. As she begins to unevenly ascend the stairs, I reach for her hand.

"Allow me, Princess," I offer.

She blushes and takes my outstretched fingers, letting me help her onto the dais. Her gown's snowy train bundles around our feet, sending a chill sweeping through me. Nerves trill alarms in my brain. My magic gathers, desperate to burst from me and blast my enemies to ash. Ceri flits around Liriel, smoothing wrinkles from the train. Jasper stands frozen at the bottom of the dais, watching us with a desperate look on his face.

The ancient clock that counts down the solstice begins to chime. Three minutes until midnight. Ceri curtsies and steps back. Jasper casts anxious looks at her, his fingers curling into fists at his sides. Ceri descends the dais and stands next to Jasper. After a second, she takes Jasper's hand.

My stomach churns as Liriel clutches my fingers more tightly.

Zaphira rises from her throne, her glittering eyes locked on Ceri and Jasper. She drops her gaze to their joined hands. "What are you doing?" she hisses, eyes narrowing.

Liriel stares into my eyes and gives me a slow, sly smile.

The clock chimes again. Two minutes until midnight.

"Stepmother," I call, drawing her attention back to me. Summoning the same swagger I use before every fight, I urge bass into my voice. "Let's carry on, shall we?"

Zaphira's eyes narrow further as she swings her head back to Ceri and Jasper. She rounds Liriel and begins to descend the dais toward the couple.

Shocked-sounding gasps rise from the contingent of Winter Court elves. King Elendor frowns as he watches Zaphira.

On his throne, my father continues stroking Olios's shaggy head.

The ballroom's double doors fly open and bang loudly against the walls. Icicles crack loose from the ceiling and rain down onto the floor, smashing into chunks that skid across the slick marble.

Bert and an army of mice rush in, scampering across the floor and climbing up the nearest chairs. Shocked screams echo off the chilly walls. Hundreds of hummingbirds follow the mice, diving toward the attendees as the room descends into chaos. Zaphira's guards rush in after them, stabbing and swiping at the tiny horde. Around the ballroom, elven familiars bark, roar, and screech as they join the fracas.

Zaphira screams and thrusts her hands out, shooting icicles across the room toward the oncoming army. Elves dive out of the way of her deadly attack.

"Mother!" Liriel shouts, her voice panicked. "It's almost midnight!"

Zaphira whirls around and stalks back up the dais, pointing a finger at the officiant. "Do your duty. Quickly!"

My father sits on his throne, his features emotionless as he gazes over the melee. If he's surprised or ruffled by the mayhem, he doesn't show it. A hummingbird flits past his face, but he pays it no mind.

Zaphira swats at two blackbirds as they dive out of the air and narrowly miss her head.

Liriel takes my hands and turns her wide blue eyes to the officiant. "Please," she urges, her voice tense. "We need to say our vows."

He clears his throat, his eyes flicking toward Zaphira as a dozen hummingbirds drop out of the sky to peck at her eyes. She roars and waves her hands around, ducking and diving to avoid their onslaught.

I smile, but my amusement vanishes as the clock chimes once more.

Sixty seconds.

At the foot of the dais, Jasper and Ceri clutch at each other. Tears stream down Ceri's face as she whispers in Jasper's ear. He squeezes his eyes shut and lets out a sob.

I turn to the officiant. "I order you to perform this ceremony. Now."

"Once upon a time," the officiant begins. "Winter was—"

"Get the fuck on with it!" Zaphira screams. "Just get to the vows!"

The hair on my nape lifts. *Tick, tock, tick, tock.* The clock's second hand rounds the bend toward midnight.

Thirty seconds.

The officiant snaps his book shut. "Prince Abelin Vale of the Summer Court, do you take Liriel Evanian of the Winter Court to be your most beloved of mates? Do you agree to cherish and hold her in winter's light?"

"I do," I reply, my gaze locked with Liriel's. A mischievous glint shines in her eyes. I resist the smile that tugs at my lips.

Liriel's face flickers, hints of a deeper, more brilliant blue shining through her irises. Spiky blond hair is visible and gone in a flash.

"Vail, wait!" Sully shouts in our bond.

Izig darts forward with a glass slipper in his hands. He sets it carefully at my feet, then moves back. With a shaking hand, he removes his bowler hat and holds it over his heart. "It has to be perfect," he whispers.

The glamour. Of course Mab briefed him on the plan. Leave it to Izig to always remember the details.

"Thank you," I murmur to my longtime friend. "For everything." If these are my last moments with my friends, I want them to know exactly what they mean to me.

Sulien is a dark shadow by my side as I drop to one knee, take the slipper, and lift the hem of Liriel's gown.

At the bottom of the dais, Jasper cups Ceri's face. "Marry me?" he asks under his breath.

Ceri's eyes brighten, and she nods, pressing both hands over his. "Of course," she whispers.

Zaphira slaps a hummingbird out of the air and rounds on me. "What the fuck is going on here?"

The clock chimes ten seconds until midnight.

I slide Liriel's foot easily into the slipper. Rising, I take her hands.

Chime. Five seconds.

Zaphira grabs the officiant by the collar of his robes and shakes him. "Faster, you fool!"

Chime. Four seconds.

The officiant turns wide eyes on Liriel. "And do you, Liriel Evanian, take Abelin Vale to be your most beloved of mates? Do you agree to cherish and hold him in the sun's rays? Say you will, please." He glances nervously at Zaphira as she grips his collar.

Chime. Two seconds.

At the foot of the dais, Jasper and Ceri gaze at each other, their lips moving as they mouth the same vows.

Chime. One second.

Liriel smiles, her eyes bright with love. "I do." Her voice rings out over the chaos.

Midnight.

Wrapping an arm around Liriel, I pull her close and slant my mouth over hers. As twelve resonant gongs announce the solstice, I palm Liriel's nape and deepen the kiss.

Magic. It shimmers in the air.

Around us, everyone stills.

Liriel's glamour slips away.

Now, it's Jasper's neck under my palm. Jasper's lips on mine. Jasper's love that wraps around me like the warmest ray of sunshine. It melts the ice at our feet, the last of the wedding gown's chilly train pooling on the stones beneath us. As the final clock chime fades, Jasper and I ease apart and smile at each other.

"What is the meaning of this?" King Elendor demands. Winter Court elves crowd around him, anger and confusion in their eyes. Behind them, Elendor's reindeer works its big jaws around a mouthful of wedding cake.

A desperate need to laugh and cry at the same time rises in my throat. I clutch Jasper's hand as we look at the clock.

The minute hand ticks to 12:01.

A choked sob bursts from Ceri's throat. Where she held Jasper, Liriel now stands, beaming at the woman she just married. The flapping of wings fills the air, and Sherlock soars through the ballroom and alights on Ceri's shoulder. Neve scampers after him, her white tail wagging as she runs circles around Ceri and Liriel.

"'Ello!" the parrot chirps, leaning his head toward Liriel and stroking his bright plumage over her cheek.

Relief floods me, followed by joy as Jasper leaps into my arms and buries his face in my neck.

"It worked!" a bubbly voice shouts from the back of the room.

My father sits on his throne, his eyes glassy as he continues petting Olios. A few elves dodge hummingbirds that still flit through the air. Mab strides up the long runner, her hands clasped together and a triumphant smile on her face.

I kiss Jasper's temple as I chuckle into his ear. "Part *deux* of the plan, *mon amour*."

Zaphira rounds on Mab, her face a mask of fury. "You! No one invited you, pixie." Zaphira looks around, something frantic in her eyes. "Guards! How did she get in?"

Mab stops at the bottom of the dais and examines her nails. "Bitch, please." She lifts her gaze and gives Zaphira a withering look. "You have your head so far up your ass, you never saw me coming."

"This will never work," Zaphira seethes. "This pixie trickery. Abelin swore an *unbreakable* vow to the Winter Court!"

Mab's eyes go uncharacteristically hard. "Your daughter took a vow, as well." She tips her head to the side. "How interesting that a mother would gamble with her child's life to gain political power. Or maybe it was just raw power you wanted."

Behind Mab, movement draws my attention.

Ybris sidewinds up the aisle, venom dripping from his fangs.

I jerk forward, but Jasper grabs my wrist.

"Patience, love," he says, his blue eyes trained on the basilisk. He reaches down and pulls a plastic wand from his pocket. Smiling, he looks at the star on the end. "I'm better than most at seeing under glamour."

Mab stands steady, a triumphant smile on her face. Her wings gleam golden in the frosty air.

Zaphira draws herself up. "What would you know of power, pixie?"

"More than you, apparently," Mab says. Her eyes glint like sapphires. "If you're going to wield it, sorceress, you should understand the consequences."

Ybris rears behind Mab and stretches his jaws wide.

Jasper leaps off the dais, his wings flapping. The wand shimmers and reforms into a glittering black sword. He darts through the air and swings it, slicing the basilisk's head off in a single slash.

Ybris's body whips around, spraying blood. Screams echo off the ice-encrusted ceiling. King Elendor's guards surround him, a dozen ice-blue daggers appearing in their fists.

"No!" Zaphira cries, rushing forward. Her features shift and shimmer then fall away, revealing a woman with long red hair wearing a tight-fitting black gown.

On his throne, my father makes a choking sound.

I rush to him and grip his shoulder. "Father!"

Golden eyes flicker as he looks up at me, recognition dawning. "Abelin? What—? What's…?" His voice trails off as he takes in the writhing basilisk, Queen Mab, and the ballroom full of shocked-looking elves. King Elendor shoves his guards aside, a furious look on his face.

The room stills. All eyes go to Zaphira.

She lets out a shaky laugh. "This is all a misunderstanding."

My relief at not dying swirls and builds into a raging tempest of fury at what she took from me. I could have lost everything tonight if the plan hadn't worked. I stride from the dais as Mab takes the sword from Jasper. When I reach her, she flips it and offers it to me hilt-first.

"Prince Vale," she murmurs, inclining her head.

"Queen Mab," I say, returning the gesture. Respect shimmers between us as I take the sword.

Jasper brushes my arm. "Your father looks a little confused. Let me help him." He rounds me and ascends the dais. My heart swells when he drops to one knee next to my father's throne and speaks to him in a low voice. I'd love nothing more than to watch them together.

But I have a sorceress to attend to.

Squaring my shoulders, I face Zaphira.

She backs up and throws both palms in the air. "Prince Abelin, this has all been a terrible mistake."

I put the sword's point under her chin, stilling her progress. "It's Vale," I say softly. "And I agree, Melusine, you made a terrible, deadly mistake when you killed the rightful princess of the Winter Court."

Around the ballroom, elves gasp. Indignant shouts rise from King Elendor and his guards. Elendor pushes through a wall of blue-clad warriors and draws a glittering dagger from his belt.

The sorceress Melusine's face contorts in obvious fury. "Zaphira was weak! My magic was always stronger!" She flicks her gaze to King Elendor. "Your brother was a fool. It should have been me on the throne!"

Liriel moves forward, Ceri's hand in hers as she stares at Melusine. "You killed my mother?" she rasps, her face pale.

"Yes," I say, holding the sword steady even as I long to plunge it into the sorceress's throat. "Melusine lusted for power. She knew your father would never choose a commoner as a mate, so she waited until your parents were wed. Then she infiltrated your mother's inner circle and took her place."

A fresh chorus of outraged shouts rises from the elves of the Winter Court.

I raise my voice as I glare at Melusine and relay the dark history Mab shared with me in the ice cell. "But that wasn't enough for you, was it? Because your magic feeds on sorrow. So you killed Liriel's father, and then you moved onto mine. You spelled him and his guards." A growl rumbles in my chest. "All these centuries, you took him from me. You would have taken my mate, too."

"A pixie?" Melusine mocks, hatred burning in her eyes. "A weak mate for a weak prince!"

"That's where you're wrong," I say, love for Jasper filling my chest. Bright joy spills into my magic, which flares from my fingertips and casts golden rays over the ballroom. The temperature rises, and ice begins to drip from the ceiling. Water pools on the marble as the man I love guides my father down the dais.

I hear the triumph in my voice as I smile at Melusine. "Jasper is a stronger prince than I'll ever be."

The sorceress's eyes flick to Jasper and my father. Her breathing grows uneven as fear replaces her anger.

I lower the sword and turn to King Elendor. "She killed your brother and sister-in-law, Your Majesty. I deliver her into your hands. Do with her as you see fit."

Elendor's pale blue eyes go hard. He gestures to his warriors, who spring forward and surround Melusine. "In the Winter Court, we have interesting ways of making examples of traitors." Elendor looks at me. "She won't live to see the morning."

Melusine pales. A whimper escapes her lips.

"One last thing," Jasper says, releasing my father and moving to my side. He pins Melusine with a look hard enough to cut diamonds. "Release Prince Vale from your geas or I'll kill you myself." He leans forward, the tips of his wings going black as night. "And I'll make it hurt."

Melusine draws a shuddering breath. She flicks a hand toward me. "It's done."

"Good," Jasper says. "Fuck you."

"Take her," King Elendor orders. Melusine cries out as the guards grip her arms. Frost spreads rapidly over her skin, coating her limbs and encasing her body in a block of ice. Her terror-filled eyes flick back and forth as the warriors lift her and carry her from the ballroom.

Pain shoots through my skull, the zing of agony doubling me over. The pixie sword in my hand vanishes, leaving me grasping at air.

"Vale!" Jasper's voice is strained as he grips my arm. When I straighten, his worried blue eyes fill my vision. Over his shoulder, his gossamer wings shimmer with a hundred different colors.

And, suddenly, I see him. All of him. Each minute with him. Every glittering, golden moment from Paris floods my head.

"Jasper," I whisper, grasping his shoulders.

His eyes shine with tears. "Vale."

I stare into my husband's brilliant blue eyes as I shake off the last of the geas's effects. Then I rest my forehead against his, sharing his breath as he holds me upright. The urge to sweep him into my arms and stride from the ballroom is so powerful I can almost taste it.

Except there's one last thing.

Drawing a deep breath, I set Jasper away from me and turn toward the ballroom's double doors. Zaphira's—*Melusine's*—personal guard stands there, their expressions shell-shocked as I run my gaze over them, searching for one particular face.

There.

That fucking face.

I eat up the distance between us in a dozen strides. As I stop before the head guard, he turns the color of fresh snow. Dull brown eyes fill with fear. The scar on his cheek is a livid pink against his wan complexion.

"I told you," I murmur, "I never forget a face."

"Prince Abelin..." he starts. But he never gets the chance to finish as I call the sun and let Her rays blast from my fingertips. I roar as white-hot sunlight slams into the guards, cracking their skin and lighting their skulls from the inside out. They fall to the ground, writhing in pain. With a last, violent shove of power, I explode their bodies into ash.

For a moment, no one in the ballroom moves. Dark embers eddy through the air, dancing on the warm breeze of my magic. When I turn, elves from both the Summer and Winter Courts bow their heads. At the foot of the dais, Jasper beams at me and holds out his hand.

I go to him, my boots splashing in the puddles formed by a thousand melted icicles. As I slip my hand into his, Mab comes to my side and gives my shoulder an affectionate pat.

"Well done, honey."

My father looks between me and the diminutive pixie queen. For the first time in hundreds of years, his eyes are clear of frost. As Melusine's spell lifts, anger brews in the golden depths. "Zaphira..." He squeezes his hand into a fist at his side.

Mab's expression is somber but kind as she nods. "Melusine was clever, King Nylian, and she grew bolder and more powerful as she fed off the misery she caused. She anchored her glamour in her familiar. You shouldn't blame yourself for not seeing it."

My father closes his eyes on a long blink. When he opens them and looks at me, they burn with pain. "I don't understand. How does Abelin live? I was there when he and Liriel swore an unbreakable vow."

"You stood witness," Mab says. "But so did Melusine. As you know, every elven vow requires witnesses to be enforceable. Melusine passed herself off as Zaphira for so long, she started to believe it. And beliefs can be powerful. But at the end of the day, she was an imposter." Mab shrugs. "I had a feeling the magic didn't take as well as it should have. There were weak spots. Your son and Liriel found them."

I meet Liriel's gaze. She stands hand in hand with Ceri, a tremulous smile on her beautiful face. I smile back, something raw and tender arcing between us.

Mab beams at the women, then bumps my shoulder with hers. "Love, *mon prince*. Everyone dismisses it."

Not me, I think. *Never again.*

Jasper looks at his aunt. "How did you know Zaphira was an imposter?"

Mab smiles as a hummingbird flits to her and perches on her finger. "I didn't until recently," she says, stroking the tiny creature's cheek. "But a little bird told me." She looks at me once more. "You'll be king one day. Never underestimate small, pretty things."

I swallow the lump in my throat as I slip an arm around Jasper's waist. "I won't," I promise.

My father looks at me with tears shimmering in his golden eyes. "I'm proud of you, son. You saw what I couldn't."

"And what you refused to see," Mab adds gently.

Father nods as he looks at the pixie queen with newfound respect in his gaze. "Yes. I've been wilfully blind."

Jasper takes her hand. "Thank you for everything, Aunt Mab."

Mab winks. "No worries. Nice job with the sword."

"Thanks. I liked it. Heavy, though."

"Right?"

"Your glamour on that wand was impeccable. I almost didn't catch it."

Mab grins. "Well, you and I are better than most at seeing through disguises. Family trait and all."

Jasper shoots me a smug look. "True."

Mab reaches up and tucks a lock of platinum hair behind his ear. "You'll be as good as me one day. Hopefully in time for you to take the reins."

Jasper stiffens. "The reins?"

She smooths her own hair back, poking pale strands into a sequined hair clip. "Yeah, you know, since you're my heir."

Jasper stares at his aunt, a look of shock on his gorgeous face.

Joy and amusement mingle in my chest as I wrap an arm around his shoulders. "You've finally rendered him speechless," I tell Mab.

"Aunt Mab," Jasper says carefully. "You didn't have me match all the syndicate lords just to maneuver me into meeting Vale, did you?"

Mab shoots him an exasperated look. "What? You didn't really think I was going to let my only nephew go without his fated mate, did you?" She mutters to herself. "Puck's jock strap, boys are so dense sometimes."

My father looks at Jasper, growing admiration in his eyes. "You're the grandson of King Cirro."

Jasper gives my father a wary look. "That's right."

"The finest matchmaker to ever live," Father says, something like awe in his voice.

"Until now," Mab says softly. When Jasper's breath hitches, she gives him a tender, affectionate smile. "Your magic has always been strong. But now you understand that true love is the most powerful magic. And it's worth fighting for."

Jasper nods, pink touching his cheekbones.

Mab turns to my father. "Perhaps, Your Majesty, the future pixie king is a fitting match for your son, after all?"

"Yes," my father rasps.

I cup Jasper's jaw as I run my other hand up his chest and rest it over his heart. "A perfect match," I agree, guiding his lips to mine. "Absolutely perfect."

EPILOGUE
JASPER

Summer

P aris in summer. Has there ever been anything better?

"Baby, will you hurry up?"

I dab gloss on my lips and smile at myself in the mirror as Vale's deep, exasperated voice drifts from his bedroom. *Our* bedroom. In the six months since we defeated Melusine, we've been busy traveling back and forth between our respective courts. The brownstone in Villette is a perfect base for both of us.

"I'm wrapping your wedding present!" I yell back, turning sideways and checking my reflection. "Don't you want your present?" I twist in the other direction and prop one French-manicured hand on my hip. *Damn, even better than I imagined.* Of course, the lighting is perfect. I wink at myself in the mirror. There's nothing like dusk in Paris for achieving peak hotness. It doesn't hurt that I'm completely, ridiculously, overwhelmingly in love.

Vale's tone grows more impatient. "We already gave each other presents." The bed squeaks.

"Don't you dare come in here!" I warn, glaring at the doorway.

Incoherent grumbling, followed by muffled footsteps that move away from me.

Smiling, I grab my favorite lotion—which is also Vale's favorite now—from the counter and rub it into my skin. In the mirror, my wings rise tall and proud over my shoulders, the edges sifting golden dust onto the bathroom floor. Izig will undoubtedly have something to say about it later, which is why I stashed a box of spicy dark chocolate croissants in the butler pantry this morning. It turns out the key to an ogre's heart is his stomach.

I set the lotion down and look at the door. As for the key to an *elf's* heart, well, I like to aim for something a bit lower.

When I enter the bedroom, Vale is slumped in his chair before the fire, his dressing gown gaping open and a disgruntled look on his face. That look vanishes, replaced with stupefaction, as I stroll toward him. I hide a smile as my husband slowly sits up, his jaw dropping.

"Do you like your present?" I ask, turning sideways and fluttering my wings. "It's me," I add. "I'm the present. Apologies in advance because I am *very* expensive."

"Worth it," Vale breathes, sitting forward and rubbing a hand over his mouth. His eyes glitter like chips of amber as he drags his gaze down my body. "Damn."

A thrill runs through me at the look of utter rapture on his face. I turn slowly, looking over my shoulder as I go, and he makes a choking sound. "Do you like it?" I ask, my tone all innocence.

He swallows hard. "Is that a…?" His chest rises and falls rapidly as he stares at my ass. "What do you call that, exactly?"

"It's a g-string." I flick one of the bows at my hip, and he groans. "I thought maybe the ribbons were too much, but I don't know." I face him and run a hand down my chest to my cock, which is barely covered by a patch of white lace. "What do you think? Should I go for a different color next time? Maybe—"

"I think you should get the fuck over here," he growls, gripping the arms of his chair so tightly his knuckles turn white. "Now."

"Bossy," I murmur, going to him and climbing into his lap. His dressing gown gapes wider, and I fling it open so I can spread my palms over his chest. His cock stands up proudly between us. "Happy to see me?" I ask, settling more firmly on his spread thighs.

"Overjoyed," he growls, turning savage as he grips my ass in both hands and buries his face in my neck. "Obsessed," he says roughly, sucking at my pulse before sliding his lips to the hollow of my throat. He speaks between kisses and nips of his fangs. "Enthralled…entranced…driven out of my mind…by you."

"Sounds serious," I say, squeezing his shoulders as I throw my head back and grind my leaking dick against his stomach.

"It is." He digs his fingers into my cheeks and pulls me closer, his erection rubbing against my mine through the lace. "You might say it's incurable."

"Guess you're stuck with me, then."

His growl rumbles against my throat as he kisses his way back up my neck. "Gods, you always smell so good." He skims his fingers down the tiny string between my cheeks. "Taste good, too. And I'm starving, baby."

A shiver rushes over my flushed skin. "Are you going to devour me, *mon mari*?" My husband.

"*Tout à fait.*" Absolutely. He bites my jaw gently before swiping his tongue up to the pointed tip of my ear. "The night you wore that little red thong to the bar, I wanted to throw you down and rip it off you with my teeth."

"Fuck," I whimper, thrusting my dick harder against his abs. "I wish you had."

"Yeah?" He yanks the g-string to one side and rubs a callused finger over my pucker. "You wanted that, baby? Wanted me to strip you bare and remind this pretty hole who owns it?"

"Uh-huh."

"Who owns it?" he demands, giving me the tip of his finger.

"You," I gasp, grabbing his face in both hands so I can slant my lips over his. Joy and lust fire through me as our tongues meet. Sex with Vale has always been incredible, but it takes on even more significance now that his memories are restored. We're not operating on glimpses and shadows anymore. Now, every bit of passion we shared when we first met is alive and real in his mind.

He takes control of our kiss, stroking his tongue boldly over mine. Still teasing my hole, he slips his other hand between us and frees my dick from the lace. Lust strikes like a hot iron as he wraps his hand around my cock and strokes.

"Oh, shit," I moan, bowing my spine and thrusting into his hand. He abandons my ass and smooths his other hand down my chest, toying with one of the bars through my nipples before continuing down to my abs. He leans back and watches me roll my hips.

"You are so beautiful," he whispers. Nostrils flared, he plays with the g-string, rubbing the ribbons at my hips and fingering the lace he pushed aside.

"Aren't you going to unwrap your present?" I ask, my breathing ragged.

A wicked expression gleams in his eyes as he continues pumping my dick. "I thought I might take it out and play with it a bit first. The packaging is so pretty, I don't want it to go to waste."

"It's probably a good thing you didn't open it at the wedding," I tease.

In one powerful move, he stands and lifts me into his arms. The wickedness in his eyes flares higher as he carries me to the bed. "I think I'd better open it now, though."

"Gods, yes," I moan as he settles me in the center of the bed. He flings his dressing gown away, grabs lube, and positions us so I'm on my side with him spooning me from behind with my wings folded tightly between us. He claims my lips again as he pulls my topmost thigh to my chest and presses slick fingers into my cleft.

My cock jerks, and I moan as he finds my opening and pushes a finger inside. He sucks at my tongue as he pumps his finger gently in and out, grazing the spot that makes stars burst behind my closed lids. The fullness and pressure are good but not nearly enough.

"Hurry," I gasp against his lips. I hook my forearm behind my knee and pull my leg higher. "I need you, Vale."

"I know, baby. Let me get you ready for me." He tugs me more tightly against him and kisses me again—a slow, searing possession just as intimate as his finger stroking inside me. It's so fucking good and I'm so fucking close that I reach my free hand down and squeeze the base of my dick so I don't come.

He's just as affected. As he adds another finger, he breaks off our kiss and trembles against me. "I've been thinking about this all day," he says hoarsely. "Fuck, baby, it's all I think about." He withdraws his fingers and pets the lacy fabric nestled next to my balls. "And then you go and wear something like this, and I'm so turned on I can't think at all."

Pleasure steals my breath as he pushes three fingers inside me and strokes my prostate again.

"Oh, *fuck*," I say, shivering. "I'm glad you like it."

"I love it." He sucks on my lower lip before moving his mouth to my ear. "But I like it even better when you wear something else."

"What?"

"My cum." As my moan echoes around the bed, he replaces his fingers with his dick and pushes inside me. I shake as he kisses the tingling skin under my ear and drops his voice lower than I've ever heard it. "I love seeing my cream on your skin. In your hole. I'm going to fuck you so hard you'll leak me for days. You'll be covered in me, baby."

"Yes!" I cry, looping an arm around his head and twisting my upper body so I can deepen our kiss. As he works past my body's resistance, a fire spreads under my skin. No matter how many times I take him, I'm always mildly surprised at just how big his dick is. But I want it. With every thick inch, my need climbs higher, and then it roars as he seats himself to the hilt. "Oh gods, Vale. Yes, just like that. Fuck, you're so deep."

He breathes against my lips as he holds still, giving me a chance to adjust. "I'm right where I want to be," he says huskily, rubbing his big hand up and down the back of my thigh. He takes my lips in a tender kiss as he slides his hand lower, cupping my balls before giving my dick a couple of lazy strokes. "You feel so good, Jasper."

"Fuck me," I say on a broken whimper, desire forking through me like lightning. "Please. I need it."

"*Avec plaisir, mon prince.*" With pleasure, my prince. The sweetest smile plays around his mouth as he uses the title I'm still not used to.

He strokes my dick faster as he begins to thrust. "Anything you want. Everything you want."

"I love you," I whisper.

"I love you, too," he whispers back. Then he loves me with his body, pumping into me with steady, thorough thrusts. He stares into my eyes and whispers in French, telling me how much I mean to him, how nothing on this plane or any other can separate us, how he'd rather die than live without me beside him.

Tears clog my throat as I realize he fucking means it. He stood on that dais and risked his life when we said our vows. Fate could have struck him down. Instead, it delivered him into my arms.

"I'm never letting you go," I tell him.

My summer prince smiles, my declaration reflected back at me in his eyes as he picks up the pace, giving me the deep, ruthless strokes I crave. Pumping into me so hard and fast that the bed shakes and we're both reduced to moans and ragged breaths that war with the sexy, filthy sound of his cock slamming into me over and over.

"Look," he rasps, his hand working my dick. "Look at us."

I look down at the place where our bodies join. Vale's cock pumps into me, every thrust driving us closer together. Suddenly, his tattoo comes alive, the fine lines of the sun's rays sending vibrations into the most intimate part of my body. At the same moment, the night outside the window turns to day. Dusk disappears and dazzling daylight takes its place as Vale calls up his power.

Light dances over my skin and the edges of my wings spread over the bed. I gasp and tip my head back, basking in the unexpected warmth.

"That's it, baby," Vale says, his hand flying up and down my dick as he thrusts up and up, his hips a blur. "So damn perfect. Come for me. Come on."

My orgasm slams into me, and I cry out as I spurt into his hand and over my heaving stomach. A split second later, Vale shudders against me. His hot cum floods my ass, and his labored breaths stir my hair. We tremble together, both of us sweating and gasping for oxygen. The sunlight recedes from the bed like the tide rolling back from the shore. Outside, the sky flips back to a twinkling, purple dusk.

I laugh weakly. "You're going to get in trouble for that one."

Even gasping like he just ran a marathon, my husband manages to look as arrogant as any monarch-in-waiting. "And why is that?"

"Humans don't like it when you turn on the sun without warning."

"Too bad." He strokes a lock of damp hair away from my forehead. "I wanted to see you as you were that first day outside Mab's court, when you took pity on a besotted man and let him take you to lunch."

"Mmm. It's a good thing you're so clumsy."

His smile is as bright as the sunlight that still warms my skin as he pulls out and rolls me under him. He reaches down and fingers my rim, stroking through his cum that seeps from me. "You know, now that you're officially Mab's heir, these kinds of insults can be considered a declaration of war."

"Oh yeah?" Aftershocks ripple through me as his wicked fingers continue their exploration. "You want to do battle with me, Prince Vale?"

"*Oui.*" He waggles his eyebrows. "I'm thinking a lot of skirmishes with swords."

I groan and shove him off me. As he falls to the bed laughing, I toss a handful of pixie dust at him. When he sneezes, I laugh and pull him up. "Come on, Your Highness. If you promise not to make any more bad puns, I'll let you wash my back in the shower."

~

ONE LUXURIOUSLY LONG AND frequently interrupted shower later, Vale and I sit before the fire in our matching chairs with wine glasses in our hands. A breeze from the open window tosses the flames.

"You know," I muse, turning my gaze to Vale, "I never told you how proud I am of you for not killing Melusine on the spot after Mab told you who she was."

Vale smiles, his golden eyes reflecting the fire. "Like I said, baby, I'm a patient man."

"Still, after what she did to your father, it took a lot of control to stand on that dais and let the wedding play out."

"I had to," he says. "I couldn't let anything interfere with my vow.

That was the trickiest part—making sure I kept my word and satisfied the magic. Thank the gods Liriel caught on and did her part, too."

"She's smart."

"She is," Vale says, affection in his tone.

We fall into comfortable silence, basking in each other's company and the wine warming our veins. Memories of the icy ballroom and the abrupt marriage ceremony run through my head.

After a moment, Vale looks at me. "What are you thinking about?"

"That I always envisioned my wedding as something far more ostentatious and colorful than what we had."

A smile dances in his eyes. "Nothing says we can't get married again."

"But...another wedding?"

"Baby," he chides softly, "you mean to tell me the future pixie king is thinking of turning down a chance to throw a party?"

"Never."

Vale extends his hand across the space between us. When I grasp his fingers, he rubs his thumb over my knuckles. "We'll renew our vows once a year. You can throw the biggest, most colorful wedding you want. Because my love for you is only going to get bigger."

My breath hitches. "You're a hopelessly romantic man, Vale Gentry."

"Hopelessly in love with you, baby."

"Of course you are." I gesture to myself. "I mean, look at me."

His eyes crinkle at the corners. "I'll take you on a honeymoon every year, too."

"Ooh, yes, and we'll take Liriel and Ceri."

Vale frowns. "On our honeymoon?"

"Just this first one. I promised them we'd take a gaycation together now that they're out. And our first stop is gonna be a clothing store because those two need to lose the floor-length gowns stat." As he grins, I squeeze his hand. "Plus, it'll give you and Liriel a chance to work on Summer Court stuff." My heart swells as I think of the surprising—and delightful—partnership that has sprung up between Vale and Liriel. Now that Vale is taking a more active role as his father's heir, Liriel has become something like a right-hand woman, serving as Vale's eyes and ears whenever he's away from court.

Vale's eyes soften. "I'd like that. Liriel is an excellent manager."

"Ceri and I have been calling it *manipulator*, but whatever."

"That's not too far off," Vale says, chuckling. "Despite my best efforts, the Summer Court remains a backstabbing, political place. But Liriel has navigated politics her whole life. She knows how to maneuver around petty disputes to achieve a goal. I'm grateful for her help."

"The two of you are going to change things, Vale. I see your vision for the future, and it's beautiful."

He lifts my hand to his lips. "Because you're in it."

"Do I look good in this future of yours?" I ask, my heart beating faster at the lust glittering in his golden gaze.

"Gorgeous," he murmurs, flicking his tongue over my knuckles.

"Do you two think you'll ever stop being gross together?" Bert asks in my head. A second later, he jumps from the windowsill into the bedroom. A yowl drifts from outside, and then Sully leaps through the opening and lands gracefully. Together, they move toward the fire—Bert's steps a whole lot less graceful than Sully's. The skin around his ears has a distinctive green tinge.

I set my wine glass on the table next to me. "Have you two been drinking?"

Sully goes to Vale and sits at my husband's knee. The cat blinks lazily at me, his expression as aloof as ever.

"Don't lie to me," I warn.

Sully licks a paw and swipes it behind his ear.

"You smell like gin," I say, glancing at Bert. "Both of you."

Vale laughs.

Bert staggers to the rug and collapses on his side. His tail thumps once against the floor. *"I'm dying. Don't let Mert give my eulogy. He's terrible at public speaking."*

Sighing, I stand and head for the bathroom, where I started keeping honey after the third time Sully and Bert hit the Parisian club scene. "I told you not to go drinking with Sulien," I say over my shoulder. "He's a bad influence."

"Please," Sully scoffs in my head. *"It's the other way around."*

"Yeah, right," I say aloud as I swing around. "Vale, tell your cat—" I clamp my mouth shut, shock rooting me to the floor.

Vale and Sully freeze, twin pairs of golden eyes going wide. On the rug, Bert lifts his head, his drunken stupor fading.

"Wait," he says through our bond. *"You heard him?"*

"Yeah," I croak, staring at Sully. "Clear as a fucking bell."

Sully tilts his head. *"You hear me."*

"Yes." I drag in a breath. "I hear you."

Vale rises slowly, his expression transforming from stunned to a mix of awe and curiosity. "Do you think it's because you've been working with Mab?"

"No idea." I swallow hard. "I mean, *she* obviously hears him. She mentioned something about me gaining new gifts now that she named me heir, but when I asked about it she said we'd cover it after we discussed the dental plan."

"The pixie court has a dental plan?"

"No."

Vale stares for a moment. Then he closes the distance between us and tips my chin up. Love and laughter glimmer in his eyes. "Never a dull moment."

I step into him and twine my arms around his neck. "If you wanted boring, Vale Gentry, you bumped into the wrong pixie."

"Oh, I don't want boring," he says. "I want you, baby, and every bit of your chaos." Resting his hands on my hips, he lowers his head and kisses me.

"Gross," Bert says in my head.

The fire crackles in the hearth as my summer prince deepens our kiss. And when he lifts his head at last, he tugs me to the window. In the distance, the Eiffel Tower twinkles under a sky full of stars.

"It's beautiful," I breathe, resting my head on Vale's shoulder. "I don't want this night to end."

"It's not ending." He runs a gentle hand down the curve of my wing, gathering pixie dust. He flings it into the night, setting all of Villette sparkling. Then he turns me toward him and cups his hands around my face. "This fairy tale is just beginning," he says softly.

And then he seals his promise with a true love's kiss.

~

BONUS CHAPTER
KISS THE SLIPPER

JASPER

Paris is wild tonight. But so am I.

Cinching the belt of my trench coat more tightly around my waist, I follow the sound of male grunting and flesh pounding flesh. Heads turn, and eyes follow me.

Lifting my chin, I let a smile touch my lips. Somewhere, a loud bell clangs.

Conversation buzzes, and magic sparkles in the air as I make my way through the sea of Myth creatures crowding the underground arena where immortals gather for boxing matches. Or, as my husband calls it, *la boxe*.

So fucking cute. A sigh eases out of me, and a fluttery sensation fills my stomach. I should be embarrassed. A year ago, the idea of marriage would have had me calling for a fainting couch and a glass of rosé. Now, I'm *fluttering* at the memory of my husband's accent.

In the ring just ahead of me, the husband in question staggers backward as his opponent—a minotaur with a pair of lethal-looking horns—lands a vicious right hook. Vale's head snaps back.

Murmurs ripple through the crowd.

I wince and keep moving even as worry grips me. *La boxe* is one of Vale's passions, but I could do without seeing the love of my life bloodied and bruised. In the ring, Vale recovers, then sinks into a ready stance, his broad shoulders sheened with sweat as he dances on the balls of his feet. The white tape around his knuckles gleams under lights bolted to the soaring stone ceiling that's probably older than most of the spectators. Black silk shorts cling to his thick thighs. His sunburst tattoo fans out from his shoulder, the rays spreading down his stomach. Sweat glistens in the deep V-shaped cuts on either side of his trim waist. Chocolate curls spread over round pecs before descending rippling abs and disappearing into his waistband. Black silk hugs an eye-popping bulge.

Sacre-fucking-bleu. Heart rate kicking up, I move faster.

A tall centaur wearing a bright green fedora steps into my path.

"You're late, Lilygully! And your man's taking a pounding." He snorts, the horsy exhalation ruffling my hair. "I got a nice chunk of change on this fight. He better not be trying to throw it!"

"Oy!" a familiar voice replies. Rufus, my aunt's steward, emerges from the crowd holding a fishbowl-size glass of hot-pink liquid with a tiny umbrella sticking out of it. The bold color matches his winged eyeliner. "That's *prince* to you, fuck-knuckle," he tells the centaur. "Insult the heir to the Pixie Court again, and I'll turn you into a glue stick."

The centaur scowls at Rufus. "Well, excuse the fuck out of me." Swinging back to me, he jerks a thumb at the ring over his shoulder. "I said what I said, Your Royal Highness. Legolas up there better not throw this fight."

Rufus surges forward, his wings sifting hexing dust the same bright red as his beard. "Okay, now you've done it—"

"No," I say sharply, thrusting a palm against Rufus's chest. As he clamps his lips together, I give the centaur the "royal glare." Well, Aunt Mab calls it RRBF (resting royal bitch face) but whatever. In my peripheral vision, the edges of my wings turn a glowing crimson. The centaur darts a look at it, his thick throat bobbing.

I let an acid smile curve my lips. "My husband doesn't throw fights, but if you slander him again, I'll throw you into the Seine."

Moving my hand from Rufus's chest, I take a moment to examine my fleur-de-lis manicure before meeting the centaur's stare. "Considering it's full of sirens right now, that would be an unfortunate turn of events for you."

The centaur pales, no doubt picturing Renna and her band of bad bitches arguing over which seasoning to use on his organs. He steps back in a clatter of hooves. "I was joking! No need to get your wings in a twist, Your Highness." Swinging around, he reenters the crowd, bumping Myth creatures out of the way as he breaks into a trot.

Rufus snorts. "That's a centaur for you. All balls and no bite." He leans forward, peering after the centaur. "Although, not gonna lie, he's got a nice enough set on him."

A gasp erupts from the audience, drawing our attention back to the ring where the minotaur delivers a series of lightning-fast punches to Vale's ribs, sending him stumbling against the ropes. The sound of flesh meeting flesh echoes in the arena, each strike accompanied by a collective groan. Pressing his advantage, the minotaur launches a volley of head blows. Vale lifts his hands, the white tape a sharp contrast against his flushed golden skin as he attempts to protect his face.

"Oof," Rufus murmurs, slanting me a worried look. "Hubby doesn't look good." He runs a suddenly perplexed look down my belted trench coat. "And you look…clothed."

"Just something I'm trying," I murmur, my gaze on the ring.

"Clearly." Rufus's tone grows more bewildered. "I would have sworn you didn't even own a coat."

In the ring, Vale ducks under the minotaur's fists and darts across the platform.

Anxiety replaces the flutters in my gut. "Excuse me," I say, slipping past Rufus. He calls some sort of encouragement after me, but I barely hear it as I push through wings, feathers, and horns. Friends and acquaintances offer greetings, but I don't hear those, either.

No, my sole focus is on getting ringside. On reaching Vale. The centaur's accusation thumps in sync with my quickening heartbeat. Is it possible that Vale would lose on purpose?

As soon as the thought forms, I quash it. Elves are proud. It's pretty much a factory setting. And my husband is *all* elf, from the tips of his pointed ears to the tip of his thick, veiny—

In the ring, Vale locks eyes with me, the force of his golden eyes stopping me in my tracks. The crowd and the arena fall away. Right now, it's just the two of us.

The minotaur charges him.

I suck in a breath, and my heart tries to beat from my chest. *Get out of the way!*

Everything slows. Vale's golden eyes travel down my body. On the return trip, he licks his lips.

Boom. Boom. Boom. The minotaur's hooves vibrate the floor under my feet. He swings one meaty, taped fist, the blow arcing toward Vale's jaw.

MOVE! I try to scream, but I'm frozen, panic rooting me to the spot.

Eyes still fixed on me, Vale *winks*. Then he moves.

Except that isn't quite right. *Move* is far too mild a word for what he does. No, my husband is a fucking blur as he comes off the ropes, his body a killing machine of muscle and menace. He batters the minotaur back, landing punches too quick to track. But they meet their targets, snapping the minotaur's head from side to side. Sweat flies from his snout and the curly hair around his horns. He windmills his arms as his feet threaten to fly out from under him.

Vale hauls back a fist.

Swings.

Connects with the minotaur's jaw.

The *crack* echoes through the arena. The minotaur's head snaps back, and for a second, time stands still as he teeters in mid-air.

My heart beats faster. Vale pauses, his chest heaving and his arms loose at his sides.

The minotaur's eyes roll back in his head. He crashes to the mat, landing sprawled on his back in an unconscious heap.

The crowd erupts, cheers and applause bouncing off the stone. A female pixie with spiky black hair and blue-tipped wings moves among the revelers collecting money as people settle bets. A pair of mermen with bare chests and iridescent trousers sway, their arms wrapped around each other's shoulders as they belt out an off-key version of "We Are the Champions." Several people vault into the ring and rush to the minotaur, who stirs on the ground.

I barely notice the commotion. Because, once again, all my attention is on Vale. He stares at me, sweat dampening the wavy hair at his temples. A mischievous smile plays around his lips, and unmistakable lust gleams in his eyes.

The last makes me catch my breath. Because lust isn't the only thing dancing in the golden depths. No, *promises* join the little flames of desire as he looks me over, taking in the coat that covers me from my throat to just below my knees. His eyes roam lower, then widen when he spots my black stilettos.

After a year of marriage, I don't need speech to know what Vale is thinking. I've got my husband's attention—and he wants to know what I'm wearing under the coat.

And that's where the *promise* in his eyes comes in. Vale Gentry wants a reveal, and he intends to get it *tout suite*.

Blood pumps to my dick. Gods, I'm going to tent the front of my coat like a teenager.

"Lilygully!" someone yells. "You gonna congratulate your man, or what?"

Vale and I are attracting attention. A spotlight swings over me. More heads swivel in my direction.

The female pixie stops a short distance away, a frown pulling her brows together as she looks at me. "I didn't know you owned a coat, Your Highness."

I swallow hard as the look in Vale's eyes turns primal. "Just something I'm trying."

An elf wearing a T-shirt with "Team Gentry" on the back climbs through the ropes with a medical kit tucked under his arm. Vale waves him off, then—in another blurry, mind-bending move—jumps over the ropes and lands on the balls of his feet. The crowd parts for him as he stalks toward me, muscles rippling under glistening golden skin. He's on me before I can blink, big arms scooping me off the ground and tucking me against his chest.

Cheers go up as he strides toward the arena's exit.

"Are you entering your caveman era?" I demand, doing my best to glower up at him. But my arms curl around his neck, and pink dust sifts from my wings, so the expression doesn't carry much bite.

Golden eyes crinkle at the corners. "I won the fight, *mon amour*. That means I get to claim the prize."

My dick tightens, and my voice goes breathless. "And I'm the prize?"

"*Ouais.*" Yeah. He lowers his voice. "You were late to my fight, Jasper love. Were you trying to make a dramatic entrance?"

I slide my fingers into the damp curls at his nape, a little thrill shooting through me when his nostrils flare. "*Peut-être.*" Maybe. "Were you toying with that minotaur, Vale Gentry?"

Vale's grin flashes white. "*Peut-être.*" He hefts me higher in his arms, his pecs bunching as he lowers his gaze to my mouth. "I wanted to show off a little more, sweetheart. Then I saw you in the crowd, and I had to cut it short."

"Why?"

His grin vanishes, replaced with a look hot enough to melt my clothes from my body. "Because you make me so hard I can't see straight. And the thought of another man seeing what's under this coat makes me want to do murder."

Violence shouldn't turn me on. But I can't suppress the groan that leaves me as I pull a hand from his nape and toy with the top button of my coat. "You think I have something you'll like under here, *mon mari?*" My husband.

"Fuck," he mutters, walking faster. His voice drops an octave as he darts a wild look around. "Where's Izig with the fucking car?"

Cool air washes over me, which is how I realize we've left the arena and are headed toward the magic-powered sedan with a hood-mounted engine that sends bubbles ascending lazily into the Parisian sky. Stars twinkle overhead as Izig holds the rear door open for us.

"Hey, Ziggy!" I call, waggling my fingers.

"Prince Jasper," the ogre manservant acknowledges in a polite rumble. In the past twelve months, Izig has grown accustomed to ignoring all sorts of questionable activities of a decidedly *sexual* nature. I might feel embarrassed if I hadn't caught him smiling a time or two. And a few weeks after Vale and I tied the knot, Izig pulled me aside and swore in the ogre tongue to keep me safe from all harm. *"You're my family now,"* he said in his gruff voice. *"The same as Prince Vale."*

Vale bundles me into the car, then slides in next to me. The scent of clean sweat and masculine aggression washes through the car's interior as Izig shuts the door behind us. Seconds later, a smooth glass partition rises from the seats in front of us. The second it locks into place, Vale tugs at my belt.

"Show me, baby," he orders in a rough voice. "Show me what's mine."

The sexy striptease I'd planned flies out the window. My fingers tremble as I work the buttons through their loops, and I hold my breath as I open the coat.

Vale freezes.

Well, not completely. His throat bobs as he stares, running his eyes over me like he's cataloging every detail. And I have to admit there's a lot of detail. Custom Parisian lingerie doesn't come cheap, but the *couturier* earned his eyebrow-raising price tag.

A skimpy bra covers my chest, my pierced nipples visible through the delicate black lace. My dick thrusts against a matching thong that barely manages to cup my balls. Silk bows ride high on my hips. A silk garter belt secures black stockings that shimmer in the moonlight pouring through the sedan's darkened windows. My skin shimmers, too, my chest and arms sparkling as I drop my glamour. The glow spreads down my abs to my groin, where I have another surprise waiting for my husband.

"I waxed," I murmur, easing my thighs apart. Moving a hand to my cock, I stroke it through the peekaboo lace before curling my fingers around my sack. As the edges of Vale's tattoo begin to glow, I draw one foot up and prop the tip of my stiletto against the leather seat. "I waxed everywhere, *mon mari*." Sliding a finger under my balls, I stroke the place where I desperately want Vale to be. "Do you like it?"

Eyes riveted to my finger, Vale bangs his fist on the glass partition. It slides down half an inch.

"Yes, Your Highness?" Izig's mild-sounding voice drifts back.

Vale closes his eyes briefly before responding in a voice so deep it rumbles the leather under my ass. "Drive fast."

∼

VALE

I MAKE MYSELF WAIT.

Every part of me wants to rip the lingerie from Jasper's body and fuck him senseless. But my pixie deserves better than the backseat of a car. And I need space for the things I plan on doing to him.

A *lot* of space.

"You're a fucking tease," I say under my breath, the glow from my tattoo casting prisms on the length of the seat between us.

Outside, Paris zips past in a mix of magic and electricity. I busy myself unwinding the tape from my hands. It's the only way to keep from reaching for Jasper. If I get even half an inch closer to him, I'm going to fuck him. So I keep my distance.

He shrugs out of the coat, then toys with the tiny black bow between the cups of his bra. He crosses one long leg over the other, his spiky stiletto bouncing and the curve of his bare ass drawing my gaze like a beacon. "Will you spank me for teasing you?" he murmurs.

The remaining blood in my head pumps to my dick, so it's a miracle I'm able to form enough coherent thought to growl, "Jasper..."

His glossy lips curve as he offers a coy look from under his thick lashes, his blue irises almost purple against the dark paint smeared over his lids and dusted along his lower lashes. The *waterline*, he informed me recently. In the year since our midnight wedding at Fourneclaire, he's turned my townhouse's master bedroom into a "Jasper bedroom." His presence is everywhere, from the makeup that litters our dresser to the clothes and jewelry that seem to find their way onto every available surface, hook, and stretch of carpet. Perfumes and lotions cover our bathroom counter. I opened the medicine cabinet the other day and nearly perished under an avalanche of nail polish.

Do I mind? Fuck no. Jasper can take over my house. He's already taken over my heart. I'd thought that organ was permanently frozen after a lifetime of duty and disappointment. Then my pixie came along and saved me, the Summer Court, and everyone I care about. Jasper saved my life in more ways than one. For a moment, gratitude wells, the sweet, quiet edge of love just as sharp and powerful as my lust. It thrusts deep, stealing my breath.

"What is it?" Jasper asks, immediately sobering. "What's wrong?" Panic leaps into his eyes as he runs a searching look over my face and chest. "Are you hurt?"

"No," I say quickly. "I'm totally fine. Just thinking of how lucky I am." Throwing caution to the wind, I reach over and snag his hand. Lifting it to my lips, I brush my mouth over his knuckles. "You're the best thing that's ever happened to me."

The worry leaves his eyes, and he slides closer, then squawks when I grab him around the waist and settle him over my thighs. His hair is its natural platinum tonight, the tips of his ears as spiky as the short strands. His wings gently bat the air, sending a sweet-scented breeze dancing around us.

"You're all sweaty," he breathes, smoothing his hands over my chest. He drags manicured nails filed to saucy points through the tight curls that cover my pecs. "You need a shower, *mon mari.*" His accent is terrible. I'll never tell him. He sounds too damn adorable with his slightly nasally New York spin on my native tongue.

Sliding my hands up his stocking-clad thighs, I groan at the sight of his nipples in their triangles of lace and his cock straining against more flimsy lace. "Are you going to wash me when we get home?" I ask, my voice gruff in the quiet space.

He sinks white, even teeth into his plump lower lip, and a flush spreads under his rouged cheekbones. "Mmm, I might. If you ask me nicely." He tilts his head. *"S'il vous plaît, n'est-pas?"* Please, right?

"S'il te plaît," I correct, running a finger under the edge of the lace that covers his sack. He's smooth as silk, and my voice goes lower as I give him a light stroke. "Use the informal."

Jasper huffs, batting his eyes as he grinds his erection against mine. "You Frenchmen and your rules. So complicated."

"I don't know," I murmur, moving a hand to his cleft. Another groan slips from me as I move the flimsy strip of silk aside and run a fingertip around his hole. "I'm a pretty simple man, sweetheart." I press slightly, holding his gaze as I penetrate him. "Simple to please."

His swift intake of air is loud in the car's cabin as he spreads his thighs wider, rolling his hips. Precum swells at his slit, the bead of moisture dampening the lace. "Is that so?" he gasps, his wings fluttering as he flexes around the tip of my finger.

Fuck. Can't wait.

"Yep," I grunt, flipping him around and yanking the thong aside.

"Vale!" he protests, clutching the back of the seat in front of us. As the car moves faster, one of his stilettos slips from his foot and tumbles to the floor of the car. He releases another series of gasps as I haul his hips up. "Izig will hear!"

"That glass is soundproof," I say, sliding down so my face is level with his cleft. "You can yell as loudly as you want. And you will, baby, because I'm going to make a meal out of this pretty little hole."

"Fuck," he whimpers, squirming on my hands.

"Hang onto that seat," I order. Then I push his cheeks wide and plunge my mouth to his opening.

His moan is loud enough to reach the Bastille. But I don't fucking care. I hardly remember my own name as I hold him up, licking and sucking at the tight whorl of muscle. Jasper bucks against my mouth, his pleasured moans accompanied by gusts of his wings. Pixie dust sparkles in the air as I dabble my tongue around his hole, lapping at the twitching entrance to his body before trailing kisses to his tight, swollen sack.

"Vale…" he gasps, grinding his ass on my face. "Oh…my gods."

"You like that?" I whisper, sucking at the tender, swaying globes.

"Uh-huh," he whines.

"You want more?" It's a rhetorical question, of course. Pausing to nip at one round cheek, I free his cock from the lace and pull it backward between his thighs.

"Yes!" he cries, shamelessly pumping his hips. His cockhead bats my mouth, dotting my lips with precum as his wings rain more pixie dust over my thighs.

"Oh, gods, Vale, please."

"So pretty," I murmur, eyeing the shimmering dust. Like Jasper, it's sparkly but powerful, the glittery powder capable of deep, ancient magic. "You're a prince," I tell him, stroking his rigid cock. "But you're *my* princess."

He shudders, his hips rolling as he clings to the seat. The bra strap wrapped around his lean, muscular back is insanely hot. I suspect he knows it. Jasper knows the location of all my buttons, and my pixie never fails to punch every single one.

"Isn't that right?" I demand, abandoning his leaking dick to run my palm over the silky black bow on his hip. "My pretty princess. So sexy for me, aren't you, baby?"

"Yes," he sobs, dick swinging. He cranes his head, his big blue eyes meeting mine. "I'm yours. All yours."

My own cock strains the fabric of my shorts as I resume stroking him. "What does my princess want? Name it, and I'll give it to you."

"Suck me," he says, the entreaty more breath than speech. "Please, Vale, I need it so bad."

I do as he asks, drawing his cock backward again and closing my lips around his tip. Sugar and salt explode on my tongue, and I moan as I suck him, his sweet essence more intoxicating than any wine I've tasted over the hundreds of years I've lived. I suck gently at first, but soon I'm devouring him, swallowing his shaft to the root over and over. The slick sounds of my mouth war with his moans and breathless pleas as he urges me to go faster. His cockhead nudges the back of my throat. His wings blur at the edges of my vision as he bats the air to keep his balance.

Come for me, I think, squeezing his hip. I can't say it, but it doesn't matter. Jasper and I don't need words. *Come on, baby. Give me everything.*

His moans fill the car, the pitch increasing as his cock leaks more precum onto my tongue and down my throat. He bucks his hips, his wings scattering dust in all directions. I suck harder, stroking his shaft with a tight fist as I swallow his dick.

Jasper comes on a final, high-pitched cry, his cum spurting down my throat. I drink him eagerly, my mouth stretched wide as he shudders against my lips. When he goes soft on my tongue, I ease him off my face. For a moment, we're an awkward tangle of limbs and elbows as I straighten against the seat and help him maneuver so he's facing me again, his sated cock still hanging from his panties. The thick length glistens with my saliva, the tip drooling seed against his taut thigh.

"Your turn," he murmurs, sliding off my lap and kneeling between my legs. The sedan is as luxurious as they come, but it's still a tight fit for him as he drags my shorts down.

"No," I say, catching the waistband as my dick pops free, the tip dark red with arousal. "I'm a sweaty mess, baby. I can wait."

Jasper gives me a look that lets me know that's one of the dumbest things I've ever said. Batting his lashes, he tosses his head as he yanks my shorts from my grip. "I never said I was going to use my mouth, Your Royal Highness." He grips my shaft in one hand and uses the other to cup my sack. "Now, sit back, shut up, and let me give you the best hand job you've ever had in your life."

My head hits the back of the seat as bliss streaks from my cock to the rest of my body in a thick wave. "Yes, sir," I say weakly.

Jasper delivers, his skilled fingers bringing me to a roaring orgasm in seconds. Cum lands on my thighs and stomach in milky white stripes. I sprawl against the seat, my breathing ragged as my senses return.

"Now, you *really* need a shower," Jasper says, swiping a finger through the cum on my chest and sucking it into his mouth.

The familiar shape of the townhouse appears outside the window. Fresh arousal pumps to my dick as I tug Jasper to his feet.

"Get that coat on. If I'm not inside you within the next fifteen minutes, I'm going to explode."

～

JASPER

Fifteen minutes later, I moan to the bed's canopy as Vale thrusts his tongue in and out of my hole. Flat on my back, I hold my legs wide, wanton sounds spilling from my throat as Vale preps me.

He's still damp from the world's fastest shower, his golden-brown waves dripping water onto my balls and inner thighs. Soft smacking sounds lift around the bed as he sprawls on his stomach between my legs and fucks me with his tongue, every wet, slippery thrust spurring my arousal to new heights. My dick leaks onto my stomach, the blow job in the car a distant memory.

"Enough," I pant, the canopy going blurry as I squeeze the backs of my thighs, my knees pressed to my chest. "I'm ready. Fuck me. Please. Vale. Gods. Fuck."

My husband lifts his head, amusement dancing in his eyes as he licks his lips. Rising to his knees, he pushes a lubed finger into my ass, grazing my prostate. "I love it when I reduce you to monosyllables."

Summoning another RRBF, I lift my head. "If you don't get your stupid dick inside me, I'm going to hex you into the next century."

Seconds later, six-and-a-half feet of chuckling elf prince stretch on top of me, and heated golden eyes gaze into mine as Vale notches his cockhead against my damp entrance. "You looked so fucking sexy tonight. Like a dream come true." He watches my face carefully as he eases his hips forward, filling me inch by glorious inch. I'm loose and open, and the burn fades almost immediately, leaving me full, my ass throbbing around his dick. Fucking perfect.

Moaning, I skim my nails down his back as I hitch my thighs over his hips, my cock pressed between our bellies. "I'm glad you liked your surprise." I lift a hand from his back and point toward the lingerie strewn over the rug in front of the crackling hearth. "But you owe me new stockings since you ripped mine."

"I'll buy you a hundred pairs," Vale murmurs, dipping his head to drop gentle kisses on my eyelids and the tip of my nose. "And you'll model each one for me, won't you, princess?"

A shiver courses through me as he slides deeper. "I suppose that's only fair."

Smiling, he rolls his hips, his balls pressing hard against my cleft as he seats himself to the hilt. When I tighten around him, his eyes go heavy-lidded. "You feel so good, baby." He lowers his head again.

"You feel like home," he whispers before he takes my mouth in a deep, possessive kiss.

Our tongues stroke and slide, both of us giving and taking as he begins to move inside me. He's slow at first, taking his time as the fire crackles and the bed squeaks softly. Then he picks up speed.

And it's everything. I clutch at his shoulders before spearing my fingers into his hair. Our glamours are down, our magic turning the bed into a shining, sparkling platform. The soft, golden glow is the same—a testament to our people's shared heritage. The family tree split a long time ago, but the roots between elves and pixies run deep. Except my elven prince comes from a long line of predators. Beyond the Veil, the elves hunted their prey.

I can't help but feel a little like prey now, my body pinned under Vale's larger, heavier form—his cock thrusting inside me and the tips of his fangs trailing my jugular as his sun tattoo warms my chest. The heat spreads down my stomach, the temperature rising.

It reaches my groin…then my ass.

Then it's *inside* me.

"Fuck!" I gasp, rocking with Vale's thrusts as the vibrations ripple across my balls and up to my throbbing, leaking dick. "Fuck, Vale! Oh gods, fuck me!"

"Yeah?" he growls, pulling back. Propping himself on his forearms, he stares down at me with a possessive glint in his eyes as he snaps his hips, his balls smacking my ass. "You like this, baby?"

"Yes," I gasp. "I love it. I love you."

"I love you, too. I want you on top of me."

"Okay."

He flips us in a smooth movement, his cock lodged deep in my ass. Straddling him, I ride it, my wings flared wide at my back.

"That's it, baby," he says, his eyes on my bouncing dick. "Fuck, you're pretty. Ride me, sweetheart. Gods, yes, Jasper, just like that."

Our panting, gasping breaths mingle as he seizes my hips, holding me steady as he pumps his own up and up and up, topping me from the bottom. My dick slaps his stomach. Iridescent dust sifts from my wings and shimmers in the air. Sparkles of it cling to the tips of Vale's eyelashes and the playful curls that spill over his forehead.

Our eyes lock, lust and love arcing between us. Vibrations course through my passage, each wave spreading wider. Filling me and overflowing me. Vale's cockhead nails my prostate every time he slams me down.

"I'm gonna come," I gasp, reaching for my flailing dick.

"All over me," Vale orders. "I want to see it."

"Ahhh!" I cry, my head going back as my ass tightens. Then I'm coming, color exploding in my head as I spurt over Vale's stomach and chest. He follows on a roar, and I sob as heat scalds my ass, and all rational thought leaves my head.

Bliss.

Euphoria.

Ecstasy.

I run out of words. And, at some point, I collapse on top of Vale, my lips against his neck and my heart thundering against his. He murmurs silky French in my ear, the words far too quick and complicated for me to unravel.

But I don't need translation to know what he's saying.

I love you. I love you. I love you.

With you, I'm finally home.

Tears burn my eyes as I flop into his arms, our mingled sweat cooling on my body. After a minute, he pulls back enough to meet my gaze.

"You okay?" he murmurs, something infinitely soft in his golden eyes.

"*Parfait,*" I say, running my nails over his stubble. "I'm perfect with you."

ABOUT AMY PENNZA

Amy Pennza is a USA Today Bestselling Author of steamy paranormal and contemporary romance. After stints as a lawyer and a soldier, she discovered her dream job is writing about stubborn alphas and smart heroines. She lives in the Great Lakes region with her husband and five children.

Keep up with new releases by visiting amypennza.com

Sign up for Amy's newsletter and get a FREE scorching-hot paranormal romance!
www.amypennza.com/subscribe

Also by Amy Pennza

Check out all my books by visiting my Amazon author page or my website.

The Bitten and Bound Series. Dark Fantasy MMF Menage:

Given

Stolen

Kept

The Dragon Lairds Series. Paranormal Romance MMF Menage:

Kiss of Smoke

Dark Fire Kiss

Kiss of a Dragon King

Kiss of Frost

Kiss of Embers

The Royal Lycans Series:

The Lycan King's Captive

Prisoner of the Lycan Prince

Lux Catena Wolf Shifters Series:

What a Wolf Desires

What a Wolf Dares

What a Wolf Demands

What a Wolf's Heart Decides

Printed in Great Britain
by Amazon

BOOKS BY ANNA FURY

DARK FANTASY SHIFTER OMEGAVERSE

Temple Maze Series

NOIRE | JET | TENEBRIS

DYSTOPIAN OMEGAVERSE

Alpha Compound Series

THE ALPHA AWAKENS | WAKE UP, ALPHA | WIDE AWAKE | SLEEPWALK | AWAKE AT LAST

Northern Rejects Series

ROCK HARD REJECT | HEARTLESS HEATHEN | PRETTY LITTLE SINNER | SALVAGED PSYCHO | BEAUTIFUL BEAST

Scan the QR code or visit www.annafury.com to access all my books, socials, current deals and more!

@annafuryauthor
liinks.co/annafuryauthor

About Anna Fury

Anna Fury is a North Carolina native, fluent in snark and sarcasm, tiki decor, and an aficionado of phallic plants. Visit her on Instagram for a glimpse of the sexiest wiener wallpaper you've ever seen. She currently lives in North Carolina with her Mr. Right, a tiny tornado, and a lovely old dog.

Keep up with new releases by visiting annafury.com

Sign up for her newsletter to get access to most of her books spicy epilogues, including hours of free audio!